UNION'S DAUGHTER

Sabra Waldfogel

Table of Contents

PART 1

Divided Loyalties

1862

Chapter 1: Bittersweet Homecoming

EMILY JARVIE LEANED AGAINST the railing of the steamer *Columbia*, bound for the Union army's stronghold at Port Royal, South Carolina. As the ship passed Fort Sumter, she gazed at the unfamiliar sight of the Confederate flag flapping in the breeze. She had seen the fort from the Battery many times before the war. On her trip north, she had been too frightened to see it from the sea. She had fled just before South Carolina seceded from the Union, her cousin Caro, her father's slave, in her care. Now Emily watched Charleston disappear from view. She thought she had left South Carolina forever. She had never expected to return.

Since the war broke out, she had been the editor of the women's magazine *Hearth and Home* in Cincinnati. Asa Reed was her assistant. It was an unusual arrangement, but the previous editor—her fiancé, Joshua Aiken, once a South Carolina man, now a lieutenant in the Union army—had been adamant about it. Caro had teased her. Laughing, she said, "You order a man about!"

It had begun when Asa Reed asked her, "Miss Jarvie, did you see the latest from South Carolina?"

Emily reminded Mr. Reed, saying, "I follow all the news of the war." She read the newspaper accounts alongside Joshua's letters, not only the Cincinnati *Gazette*, but the *Liberator* as well, which she could now peruse in undisturbed freedom.

"The latest from Port Royal?" he prodded.

"I know of the battle," she said, hoping he could hear the reluctance in her voice.

"And the rest?"

She never sought news of South Carolina or Charleston, and she never received letters. When she left, she had cut her ties with her family. She sighed. "You won't rest until you tell me."

"Miss Jarvie, how could you ignore it? The planters fled and left the slaves to fend for themselves! How the contrabands suffered! The government stepped in to manage the cotton plantations, and missionary societies in New York and Boston recruited teachers for the children." With envy in his voice, Reed said, "The first group of teachers left a week ago." Emotion made him wheeze a little. Asa Reed was so pale that his veins showed blue in his temples. His eyes were also blue and pale. He was no taller than Emily, and he had the manner of the youngest boy in a family of sisters.

"Do you want to go?"

He wheezed again. "As though I could," he said. He had been turned away when he tried to muster in. He was an ardent abolitionist, but he had, as he called it, "this blasted asthma." He looked at her with bright eyes. "But you might."

"Back to South Carolina?" She was so discomfited that she laughed and tossed her head, the belle's reaction that she thought she had left behind. "You recall how I left."

She had told him a partial truth—that she had gone north in defiance of her family because she disagreed with them about slavery. She kept the rest a secret, for Caro's sake. Now Caro was safe in Oberlin, Ohio, but back in South Carolina, she was still considered a fugitive slave.

And Emily, who had helped her escape, had abetted a fugitive, a crime punishable by hanging.

He said, "There's a war to fight. It seems wrong to watch it from afar." He extended his arm to take in the office, with its neat shelves full of back issues and manuscripts. Emily, raised with high standards of house-keeping, had the windows washed every week, and the March sun streamed into the room. "To stay here," he said, "when you could be *there* instead."

Emily felt discomfort and anger rise in her, and with it, the admonition that a lady does not raise her voice. It was odd to feel the Charleston constraint after more than a year of freedom in Ohio. "Mr. Reed, are you referring to me?"

"To anyone of good conscience."

"Mr. Reed," she said, in a tone too sharp for a South-ern lady. "My conscience is my own business."

But Reed had disturbed Emily's conscience. He had troubled the water, in the words of the slaves' song she had learned from a friend of the Reed family, who maintained a stop on the Underground Railroad. Cincinnati, just over the Kentucky border, had long been the conduit to safer places in northern Ohio and farther north in Canada.

That night, her boardinghouse room was too cold without a fire, and she pulled her shawl tightly around her as she sat.

Emily thought of the grand house in Charleston that she left behind. It had been in her family for generations. Inside, the elegant furniture of the past century had been preserved, as had the iron barbs, the cheval-de-frise, on the front fence, erected after the Vesey plot was discovered. Her father inherited the house when her uncle died. He had also inherited a slave that his brother, James Jarvie, had considered his wife and a slave girl he had cherished as a daughter. His will had beseeched her father to treat the slaves, Kitty and Caro, as "members of the family."

Emily closed her eyes as she recalled her first gesture of Christian charity for the widow and her daughter. She had brought them each a shawl. She was shocked—and forever transformed—when the slave girl Caro had asked her for a book instead.

It was a slippery slope, Christian charity. It led to friendship. And affection. And something more dangerous: the beguiling whisper of freedom. Because of

Caro, Emily began to write for *Hearth and Home*; she began to correspond with the editor, a South Carolina man, Joshua Aiken; and she fell in love with Joshua, who had been disowned by his family for his feelings against slavery.

When she went north, she abandoned everything that made her Charleston's daughter. All that remained of South Carolina was her accent, which made Yankees wonder about her and abolitionists doubt her.

As she sat, shivering in the spring dusk, she realized that it was one thing to condemn slavery from the safety and comfort of Cincinnati. It was another to go south, to go back to the place she fled, the place that cast her out, the place that represented everything she loathed, to fight slavery on its home soil, which was no longer her own home.

She closed her eyes and clasped her hands in her lap. She prayed, asking God to help her. To guide her. She quieted herself until she felt her heart beating.

But God was silent. Instead, she could hear the voice of her cousin Caro. An amused voice. "Now you know what it's like to be godless," she imagined Caro saying, as she laughed. "You're on your own!"

☙❧

A WEEK LATER, WHEN Emily knocked on the door of Mrs. Williamson's boardinghouse in Oberlin, Ohio, Caro answered. "You're here," Caro said, and pressed her cheek to Emily's even before Emily could come inside. Emily hugged Caro. "It's been too long since I've seen you," she said.

Mrs. Williamson, who stood behind Caro, chided her. "Let Emily come in. She looks chilled to the bone."

Emily sighed with relief as she removed her cloak and let Mrs. Williamson seat her in the guest's chair close to the hearth. It had been a long day on the train in uncertain March weather, Cincinnati to Cleveland, Cleveland to Oberlin. The last leg of the journey had been a hired carriage that had seen better days. The cold evening air had seeped through the windows, and the worn seat offered no comfort. She was grateful for the heat of the fire and the cup of coffee that Mrs. Williamson pressed into her hands.

She sipped it and sniffed the air. "Is that a roasting chicken in the oven?"

Mrs. Williamson smiled. "Yes, it is." She touched Emily's cheek.

Emily's breath caught in her throat. When she had fled Charleston on the eve of the war, she had renounced her slave-owning family. Since the war began, there had been no word, not even the briefest of letters. Caro and the Williamsons were the closest that she had to family now.

"It's from the farm," said Frankie, the eldest Williamson daughter. Since the elder Mr. Williamson's death, his sons had taken over the farm in rural Lorain County, where they grew corn and raised hogs, selling whatever they didn't eat. They had been raised in North Carolina, and Emily wondered what the sons of a black cotton farmer made of life in Ohio.

Widowed, Mrs. Williamson had brought both her daughters to Oberlin to be educated at the College. If the rest of the world thought that it was odd for a woman of color to insist that her girls get a college education, Emily didn't. Caro, once a slave in Charleston, now attended Oberlin herself and boarded with the Williamsons.

Later, at the table, with the roasting chicken savory on its plate, the candles flickering and casting a soft light, there was a further pause for grace. They joined hands. Emily clasped Caro's hand, glad to feel that it had lost the roughness from slavery in Charleston and had softened in months of reading and writing at Oberlin. Mrs. Williamson softly thanked God for the bounty of this meal and for the good fortune of freedom in Ohio. Emily joined the Williamson daughters to murmur "Amen."

As they ate, Emily thought of her childhood, when she sat at her ease in the kitchen on her father's plantation in Colleton County, surrounded by black women who fed her and showered her with affection. They had all been slaves. But it seemed perfectly ordinary to her to eat dinner in the company of women of color, even though they were born to freedom and the younger generation studied at Oberlin College.

"How is your Lieutenant Aiken?" Mrs. Williamson asked Emily.

Emily tried to sound light of heart, but every thought of Joshua struck terror for her. He had already been in battle, and even though armies didn't fight in the winter, he would soon be back in the fray. "He's well. Unhurt. Unhappy to be in camp." She sighed. "Eager for battle again, as they all are."

Frankie asked, "Emily, have you heard about the latest news from Port Royal?"

In the privacy of the Williamson home, she and Frankie called each other by their Christian names, as she and Caro did. It was an unusual intimacy for a white woman to allow a woman of color. "Oh yes, I have," she said. "I hear the missionary teachers are bound for Port Royal."

Frankie said passionately, "Such an opportunity! To educate the former slaves. To uplift them. To aid Christ's poor!" She used the phrase common among the missionaries. Her eyes shone. "I wish I could go."

Mollie, who wished to follow her older sister in everything, said, "So do I."

Frankie said, "Emily, you could go. You should!"

Emily didn't reply.

Caro looked shocked. "Don't even think of it. Back to South Carolina!"

Emily was silent, and Mrs. Williamson's reaction was swift and stern. "No one is going anywhere, except for Emily, who is going back to Cincinnati on the Sunday train. The rest of you will stay here in Oberlin and finish your education."

೧೨೦೧೩

THE WILLIAMSONS RETIRED EARLY, and Emily and Caro
went upstairs to Caro's room, where they would share a
bed. Both regarded the narrow mattress. Caro said, "I
doubt that both of us will fit."

"How do Frankie and Mollie manage?" Emily asked.

"They curl up together like kittens." Caro began to
pull away the blanket. "I'll make up a pallet on the floor,"
she said.

"Oh no," Emily replied. "I shouldn't displace you."

"You're my guest tonight."

"No, no. It's your room. Make me a nest."

Caro said, "I guarantee you won't sleep well."

"I'll manage," Emily said.

Caro was right. Emily slept fitfully on the floor. As
she woke, she shifted, trying to make herself comfortable,
and she heard Caro cry out in her sleep. Caro woke with a
start and sat up. It was too dark to see her face, but Emily
heard a sob.

Emily rose, groping her way in the dark, and sat on
the bed. She whispered, "Caro, what's the matter?"

"A dream," Caro whispered back, not wanting to wake
the sisters sleeping in the next room. "Just a bad dream."
But she began to shake as though she had the ague.

Emily put her hand on Caro's arm. "What did you
dream?" she asked softly.

Caro pulled away and wrapped her arms around herself. She was still shaking. "I dream it over and over," she
said.

Emily peered into the darkness, trying to see Caro's face. "Tell me."

Caro raised her head. Her voice was so low that Emily had to strain to hear it. "I dream that I'm on the steamship again. The boat we took north, when we left Charleston."

Emily felt a chill.

"I'm in a dark corridor. I have a heavy tray in my hands, full of china and cutlery and covered dishes. And I hear footsteps behind me."

Emily began to shiver.

"They come closer. I can't run. And I can't put the tray down. And the steps come still closer. And closer."

Emily closed her eyes.

"And then I turn my head to see who it is." She bent and shook, as with fever. "It's the slave catcher."

They sat side by side on the bed, both of them shivering, chilled by more than the cold air of a room without a fire.

Caro's voice was low and hoarse. "Do you dream about it?"

Emily couldn't reply. She had her memories, even worse than Caro's nightmare, and at this moment, it was too hard to push them away.

But she had her answer. When she returned to Cincinnati, she wrote to arrange for a teaching position in the Sea Islands.

₧₧

Now, EN ROUTE TO St. Helena Island, Emily remained at the railing to watch as the coastline came into view, the sandy expanse that the construction of Charleston concealed so well. The shore was absolutely flat; a line of pine trees stood back from the beach. As the steamer approached the mouth of the harbor at Port Royal, the water became thick with boats, Union gunboats as well as steamships, and schooners that traveled by sail as well as steam, a reminder that Port Royal was the Union army's stronghold for the defense of the coast between Charleston and Florida.

But this boat, a commercial steamship, wouldn't stop at Port Royal. It would continue upriver to the town of Beaufort.

It didn't look familiar. When her family traveled to the Sea Islands from Colleton County, they had always taken a packet down the Combahee River to St. Helena Island.

When the steamship docked at Beaufort, Emily joined the other passengers who descended to the lower deck. "We're to wait," the man ahead of her said. "We can't disembark until the provost marshal visées our passports."

The provost marshal was the military man in charge of all those who came and went. Emily had a passport in her pocket, as every traveler to the Union outpost of Port Royal must, stamped by the customs official at New York, where she had sworn an oath of loyalty to the United States of America. Her hand had shaken as she signed it. Despite her practiced handwriting as a journalist and editor for a year, she had left a blot on the paper.

She thought of Caro, now safe at Oberlin. The provost

marshal checked soldiers on leave, passengers, and contrabands. Would she have been counted a contraband if she came south?

They waited until the steward had found the provost marshal a table to set his stamp on and a chair to sit in as he stamped. The passengers formed themselves into an orderly line, chattering in their excitement to have arrived in the Sea Islands at last. The process of viséeing proceeded without incident. Emily presented her passport. "Miss Emily Jarvie, sir," she said.

Hearing her accent, he asked, "You're a Southerner?"

"Born in South Carolina, sir, but I moved to Ohio before the war."

He frowned.

"Is there a problem with the passport, sir?" she inquired politely.

"We don't see many Southerners with passports," he said.

"The American Missionary Association has approved me as a teacher here," she said. "I'll be teaching at the school at Ocean Point. Would you like to see the letter?"

The provost marshal gave her a doubting look. He scanned her passport again. "It looks to be in order," he said, and he viséed it with some force.

Free to go, she walked down the gangplank and onto the dock, which bustled with the passengers who had preceded her. Soldiers in every kind of blue uniform, from the plain coats of privates to the gold braid of officers, intermingled with the Northern missionaries, the men in dark suits and the ladies in gray or brown traveling dresses. Emily breathed the warm air that was filled with the dockside odor of tar and salt and sweat. Nearby, a group of men, dressed in the worn trousers and flimsy cotton shirts of their former slavery, descended on the steamship to unload the trunks and boxes the passengers had stowed. As they emerged, carrying the trunks on their shoulders as they'd carry sheaves of rice at harvest time, they sang. Emily recognized the song. It was "Poor Rosy," which she had heard sung in Charleston in heartbreaking melancholy; these men sang it with a snap that accompanied their labor and made it into a cheerful tune.

She scanned the crowd for Mr. Harry Phelps, the teacher she would replace, and his sister, Miss Phelps, who both lived at the plantation at Ocean Point.

The man who approached her must be Mr. Phelps. She had not expected him to look so young or so merry. His tousled curls were boyish, and his neckcloth was carelessly tied for a Boston man serious enough about abolition to decide to become a missionary for freedom in the Sea Islands. Joshua Aiken, who had attended Harvard College before the war, had written to his Boston friends to put in a good word for Emily as missionary and teacher.

The young man said, "Might you be Miss Jarvie?" He put out his hand. "It's a pleasure to meet you."

"Likewise," Emily said.

He said, "This is my sister, Miss Eliza Phelps, who manages everything that isn't in the cotton field."

Miss Phelps was Mr. Phelps's elder by a decade. She had no sunniness. Her face was arranged in practical lines, and her hair had been captured in a tight bun as though she brooked no nonsense from it. She looked like a woman who could write an abolitionist lecture with one hand and make jam with the other. She clasped Emily's hand and made an appraisal. Emily had seen that look in Ohio, too. As though she were not good enough to be there, in the company of those who hated slavery.

Harry said, "The ferry leaves in an hour. Would you like to rest for a bit, Miss Jarvie?"

"No, I'm not the least bit tired. Could we walk through the town? I haven't seen Beaufort since I came here as a girl."

A shadow fell across Harry's amiable face. "There isn't much to see these days."

"Why? I recall it as a lovely place."

"No longer," Eliza said.

Emily replied, "Show me."

The once-neat sidewalks were filthy, and in the gutters was a debris of whiskey bottles, as though the Union army had drunk itself into a stupor and cast every empty vessel into the street. Pigs, usually confined to backyards, roamed the streets, sharing them with horse-drawn carriages and carts, and chickens had overrun the sidewalks, as bad a barrier as the mud on the cobblestones.

Emily paused before a graceful, two-story house, the steps choked with mud and debris, the fragrant shrubbery of camellia and magnolia untrimmed and overgrown.

She recalled this house well. Her family knew the Rhetts, who owned it, and she had played with the Rhett children when her mother came to call. Even to her child's eyes it had been a graceful house.

On the front lawn reposed a broken chair and the top of a marble washstand and bits of white and black debris. She nearly asked, "What is strewn all over the lawn?" when she realized that it was piano keys. Someone—the Union army, she realized with a pang—had torn a piano to shreds and left its keys on the grass.

She said, "I thought the capture of Port Royal was easily accomplished, without destruction."

"The sea battle was swift," Harry said.

"Who did this?"

Harry said, "After the planters left, the army streamed in. They took what they fancied—there are other pianos in storage; I could get you one if you wanted—and they smashed up the rest."

Eliza said, "The former slaves were no better. They stole and they destroyed. And worse. When we moved into our place, we found human waste on the floor of the parlor."

"I had no idea it was so despoiled," Emily said.

Eliza said, "We vanquished slavery here. They got what they deserved." Her face was set in disapproval.

Emily turned her face away, unable to look at the wreckage that her allies, the enemies of slavery, Joshua's army, had wrought.

Harry chided his sister. "Eliza, how would you feel

if a hostile army invaded Boston and burned it to the ground?"

"Don't sermonize me, Harry," she told her brother. To Emily, still stricken, she said, "He studied Divinity at Harvard College, and he hasn't lost the minister's habit."

"I hope I won't," he said, and despite his tone of gravity, he looked younger than ever.

ⁿⁿⁿ

THEY TOOK THE FERRY from Beaufort to Lands End on St. Helena Island, and at the pier, Emily had a vivid memory of her last visit here for her uncle's funeral. It had been August—feverishly hot. Her uncle's house had smelled of lavender water. The two women laying him out, dressed in the black silk of mourning, had been his housekeeper Kitty and her daughter Caro.

Her cousin Caro.

She missed Caro keenly. It was selfish to wish her here. Caro should stay in Ohio, where she was safe.

They disembarked to find a sleepy street—a widening of sand and dust—where dogs curled in the middle of the road, too enervated to wake or bark. By the side of the road a cart waited.

Mr. Phelps waved as they approached the cart, and the driver smiled at the sight of Emily. He was as tall as Mr. Phelps and toughened by a lifetime of work in the cotton fields. The muscles of his arms and shoulders swelled under his cotton shirt. There were deep crow's-feet at the corners of his eyes. He was well used to observation, close up and afar.

Mr. Phelps said, "This is Rufus Green."

Emily extended her hand. Rufus Green glanced at Mr. Phelps. "Shake a white lady's hand?" he asked. "Is it seemly?"

Eliza looked askance.

"I think so," Emily said. She had extended this courtesy to people of color in Ohio. "Don't you, Mr. Phelps?"

With great politeness, Rufus Green said, "Miss, I ain't quite there yet. But I welcome you."

Mr. Phelps said, "This is Miss Emily Jarvie, the new teacher."

Rufus Green smiled. "We sorry that Marse Harry won't teach anymore," he said. "He teach my girl Phoebe to read and cipher. But we glad you come to take his place."

Mr. Phelps said, "The newly free are very eager to learn."

Emily thought, *And the formerly enslaved are still good at foxing white people.* She heard an internal voice she thought had gone quiet forever in Ohio. It was the collective tone of her mother, dead these ten years, and the stepmother who had raised her, still alive and well behind the Confederate lines in Charleston. It said, *A lady is gracious to everyone.*

She said to Rufus Green, "I'm very glad to be here and take up the task that Mr. Phelps began."

He inquired after her trunk. Mr. Phelps offered to help him, but Green said, "No, don't trouble yourself, Marse Harry." He returned with the trunk, carrying it on his shoulder as though it were no burden at all. He smiled at Emily. "Weigh less than a bale of cotton," he said.

Emily, a planter's daughter, knew that a bale of long-staple Sea Island cotton weighed two hundred and fifty pounds. She watched as Green set the trunk effortlessly into the cart and wondered what else he did to ease the work of the men he had always labored for.

஁௰

ONCE THE CART LEFT the ferry and made its way onto the road, Eliza settled onto the rough seat. Her back was very straight. She was silent, and Emily rushed to fill the silence. She asked, "How many scholars do you have, Mr. Phelps?"

"About fifty."

"Fifty! How do you manage?"

"They teach each other. As soon as they learn their letters and numbers, I let the most promising children help those who are just behind them. I teach the beginners because they need the most instruction."

"Where does the school meet?"

He grinned. "We're fortunate that the plantation house is so big," he said. "The former owners would be scandalized to see that we hold the school in their former ballroom."

She laughed. "I never danced at Ocean Point," she said. "What brought you to the Sea Islands, Mr. Phelps?"

"Didn't Joshua tell you?"

"Only a little." She was glad of it because he had been discreet in not telling Mr. Phelps, or the Boston missionaries who had approved her teaching position, too much about her.

"We knew each other a little at Harvard College," he said. "But our paths diverged there. He studied literature, and I studied divinity."

"Did you intend to be a minister?"

"It runs in the family," he said.

Eliza said, "Our uncle is well-renowned as an abolitionist minister."

Emily smiled at Eliza. "Even I've heard of your uncle."

"Quite a lot to live up to," Harry said. "I do my best, don't I, Eliza?"

"Don't tease, Harry."

Emily asked, "What brought you to South Carolina?"

"When the war intervened, many of my friends mustered in, but I couldn't bring myself to take up arms. I was glad to learn that I could come to Sea Islands to fight with a slate in one hand and a speller in another."

"And you flourished as a teacher. Why did you decide to become a superintendent?"

He met her eyes, his blue gaze abruptly serious. "I admire what Mr. Chapman has been doing," he said. William Chapman was the head superintendent at Ocean

Point, charged with managing the cotton crop and the people who worked it. "I saw that there was much to accomplish in uplifting the newly free through labor."

Rufus, who had been pretending not to listen, suddenly chortled. He called, "Marse Harry, after you try your hand at labor, you find out how much it uplift you." Rufus Green, who wasn't ready to shake a white lady's hand, was evidently on joking terms with Harry Phelps, even though he still used the old address of slavery.

Harry laughed. "Oh, I'm sure I will."

They drove into the countryside, where the road was shaded by sycamore and gum trees, and the cotton fields stretched beyond. Many fields were full of cotton plants choked with weeds; no one had chopped the rows for weeks. Other fields had never been planted, and last year's dead stalks and cotton trash stood like a ghost of a cotton crop.

Memory wafted toward her, stronger than the scent of magnolia or trumpet honeysuckle. It belonged to Colleton County, but it supplied a vision of cotton cultivation stronger than the scene before her. She recalled fields thick and lush with the long-staple bolls that were the finest cotton in the world chopped and tended by bent figures: the men in straw hats, the women in the ornate kerchiefs of the islands, bending to use their hoes. She could remember the Low Country slaves singing slow and lugubrious tones to match the even rhythm of the hoe meeting the earth.

She observed, "The cotton crop looks poor to my eye."

"You're still a planter's daughter," he said.

She could give him—and Eliza—this much of her past. "My father never had a place on St. Helena," she said. "But he had two big plantations in Colleton County up the Combahee River. I lived there when I was a girl." It caused her pain, as remembering her father always did.

"Is he there now?"

"He took a commission in the First South Carolina Infantry, Confederate States of America," she said. "They fight in Virginia." Where Joshua's regiment also fought. Her father and her fiancé had very likely faced each other on the battlefield. She reminded herself that she was protected by all the power of the Union army in the Sea Islands. The Confederacy—and her father—could not touch her.

Harry said gently, "Joshua told me that when you left South Carolina, you became estranged from your family. As he was."

She stared at her hands, which she knotted in her lap. She forced herself to look up. Eliza looked disconcerted. Harry's expression was sympathetic. "It must have been difficult for you to return home," he said.

Eliza said, "Miss Jarvie, if you would rather not speak of this…"

Emily spoke to Harry, and let the main point go to argue with the lesser one. "Oh, this was never home," she said. "Charleston was home." And at that admission, tears rose to her eyes and she bent her head to hide her face inside her bonnet. She fought against them. She would not weep before this well-meaning missionary from Boston. And certainly not before his stern sister.

Eliza looked away, to give her privacy, and Harry gave her time to compose herself. He said, "It was brave of you to come back to the South."

She gave them both the answer she'd given everyone in Ohio. She let herself sound arch. She let her prewar tone, her belle's tone, creep into her voice. "I hardly think I'm in danger here. Surrounded by the Union army."

"I understand," he said. "But I meant brave in your spirit."

She forgot that both Eliza Phelps and Rufus Green were listening. She let her voice shake a little. "You're very kind, Mr. Phelps." Try as she might, she couldn't offer the same to Eliza.

∞○∞

As THEY APPROACHED OCEAN Point, Emily thought of the plantation houses set back from the road, lovely white houses with their shaded piazzas on both stories to catch the breeze from the sea. She recalled the summer parties on the lawns, the tables groaning with food, the air filled with the sound of fiddle music, the slave musicians released from labor for the day. She didn't have to close her eyes to remember her mother in a white dress that floated like an angel's breath around her. Her mother had worn orange blossom in her hair with that dress, and the fragrance of orange blossom was as vivid as anything that grew in the gardens beyond the fields.

Emily blinked, trying to unsee the past and to focus her eyes on the vista before her. She reminded herself that leisure and her pleasure had lain in the hands of sweating, silent slaves, who worked from sunup to sundown so their masters and mistresses could amuse themselves.

They turned into the driveway of the place the Phelpses had appropriated and passed the stately avenue of live oak trees. As they approached the house, Emily was overwhelmed with the smell of orange blossom.

On the steps of the big house, two women waited, starched white aprons over their dresses and white kerchiefs wrapped around their heads. Emily thought with a pang, *The servants, waiting to welcome young miss.*

Rufus Green helped her down from the cart. Emily straightened despite the cramp in her back. She knew how her mother would have spoken to these people. She wondered how an abolitionist should greet people who were no longer slaves.

Eliza said, "Juno, Phoebe, this is Miss Jarvie." She added, "Juno is Rufus's wife, and Phoebe is their daughter."

Juno was full-figured and serene, her eyes large and almond-shaped, her fingers long and elegant, even though her hands bore the evidence of a lifetime in the kitchen.

Emily extended her hand to Juno, as she had for Rufus Green. Juno was as startled by Emily's courtesy as her husband had been. She inclined her head and murmured, "How do." Phoebe echoed her.

Rufus Green, husband and father, let his eyes rest on

his family. Emily saw his pride in them, and his worry for them.

Eliza said, "Miss Jarvie has come here to teach." She took Emily's hand between both of her own. Her hands were surprisingly rough, as though she worked alongside her servants. She said, "There'll be no dearth of work for you here."

Harry said good-naturedly, "My sister has a New England spine, even in the indolent climate of South Carolina."

The dour face softened. "Harry, I despair of you. You'll become one of those slothful Southerners, in a white suit in all seasons, making excuses for how lazy your workers are."

Emily wondered if she had seen a glint of humor in Eliza Phelps's eyes. Did she love her younger brother? She must.

Harry laughed. "Eliza, Miss Jarvie has just come all the way from New York. Let her rest from her travels. We'll set her to work tomorrow."

Eliza said, "Phoebe, will you help Miss Jarvie get settled?"

Emily was startled to hear a tone of command that reminded her of life before the war. Neither Juno nor Phoebe looked ill-used, but Eliza must make sure they had no dearth of work, either.

Eliza led them inside. The interior was much changed from the place where Emily and her mother had so often called, her mother sipping tea in the parlor while she had sat quietly, a miniature lady, polite and bored, itching to be released to romp with the children of the house.

The front parlor had lost most of its furniture—the modest settee and several mismatched armchairs did not fill the empty space—and the lovely silver and china that Emily remembered was gone. There had been a crystal vase that caught the sunlight and cast a rainbow on the opposite wall. The portraits of the family had not been removed. Someone had slashed them with a knife, and they remained on the wall.

"The portraits," Emily asked. "Why do you keep them?"

"I would burn them," Eliza said.

Harry said, "Of all the things we've set to fire, I can't see that. I let them stay as a reminder. That we have vanquished them, and they are only ghosts here." He gestured toward the portraits. "They fled when the Union army approached. Most of them left before the conquest of Port Royal, when they could still get a boat out."

Emily shivered. Her family's portraits adorned the walls of her father's place on the Combahee River. Would her father's slaves destroy her father's likeness as a token of their freedom?

"It was such disorder here," said Eliza, who had been charged with the task of creating and maintaining order in the house. "We were lucky to salvage what we could, and the army found a few whole things to furnish the rest. Your room is sparse, but we have a bed and a press and a chair for you."

"We can ask for anything else, if you want it," Harry said. He smiled at Emily. "Your room used to be the music room. We can get you a whole piano, in working order, if it would please you."

Emily shook her head. The ghostly sound of piano music—a little daughter of the house, tinkling out a Chopin etude before the war—filled her ears, and she had to wait for the music to subside before she could hear again.

∽∂◯ଔ

EMILY FELT DISCONCERTED FROM the moment she sat down in the dining room. It was familiar and it was not. The white walls, with their ornate moldings, had been simplified, not to fit Yankee taste, but because of the war. The paint was darker where the paintings and mirrors had been removed. Had they been taken away, or had they been destroyed?

The table had been set with good china, but it was mismatched. China was an easy target for the conquerors, army and slave. She picked up her spoon. It was silver plate. Had the family secreted the silver in their trunks when they left, or had it passed into other, more vengeful hands? She sighed. It should not be so difficult—so philosophical—to sit at a table in the South. She said politely to Eliza, "It looks very comfortable here."

Eliza said, "You should have seen this place when we first came."

"The mahogany furniture was in splinters," Harry said. Emily thought of the grand mahogany table at

Colleton County, waxed to a gleam by slave hands, and the dozen mahogany chairs upholstered in red velvet. "It hurt me to do it, but we used it for kindling. There was nothing else to do with it."

Eliza said, "Remember, Harry, how you used that marble top as a writing desk?"

The marble-topped chest that had stood in the parlor. The crystal vase had sat upon it.

"I still do," he said. "It's a fine, firm surface for writing. At least it still has a purpose."

Phoebe appeared in the doorway, a tureen in her hands, and hesitated.

Harry asked, "What is it, Phoebe?"

"You don't wait for Marse Chapman?"

Eliza asked, "Where is he, Harry? Do you know?"

"Detained again, no doubt," Harry said.

"No, we won't wait." A little sharply, Eliza said, "Set it in the middle of the table, Phoebe, and we'll let him catch up when he gets here. Harry, will you serve?"

Emily had expected Yankee food, or something derived from army rations, and the smell from the tureen that Phoebe brought was a welcome surprise. "Ah, turtle soup," Harry said. "I can't bear to watch Juno prepare it. I feel too sorry for the turtle."

Eliza said, "It doesn't stop you from eating it."

"Miss Jarvie, pass me your plate."

Odd again, to see these Yankee manners at a plantation dining table.

When they were halfway through the soup, Mr.

Chapman hurried into the room. He had cotton debris stuck to his sleeve. He removed it and stowed it in his pocket. "Excuse me," he said. "My business was pressing and couldn't wait." He sat in the empty chair at the head of the table and sighed as he handed his soup plate to Harry.

Mr. Chapman was a man in good order, even though he wore a rough coat and nankeen trousers. His collar was tightly buttoned to his throat, despite the day's heat. A full beard covered his face, and above it, his eyes were gray and keen. His crow's feet gave him dignity. He tasted the soup and said, "Juno has outdone herself," and began to spoon it up with a hunger encouraged by effort.

"What kept you, sir?" Harry asked.

"A superintendent's work is never done," he said. "As you'll find out."

"Any trouble?"

"No disputes or broken heads," he said. "But it's an endless effort to encourage them, as you know."

Emily asked, "What does a superintendent do, Mr. Chapman?"

"You must be Miss Jarvie, our new teacher," he said.

"I am, sir," she said, echoing Harry's address.

"We welcome you," he said, and at his words, her eyes stung a little. He put down his spoon and wiped his mouth. "A superintendent is charged with the cotton crop," he said. "Its planting, its care, and its harvest. But also with the people who work it. Their effort, their welfare, and their condition, spiritual as well as worldly."

In her best demure tone, she said, "Not so different from a master." What possessed her?

"We are nothing like the former masters," he said.

"How so?"

He sat straight, a Yankee attitude. "We don't compel them with the lash," he said. "We impel them instead, by paying them wages."

"I see," she murmured.

He said, "We educate them in our effort to civilize them and accommodate them to freedom. Your effort in the classroom is as necessary as ours in the field. It's an important task you undertake, Miss Jarvie."

He would impel me, too. She inclined her head a little. "I hope I can realize your faith in me, Mr. Chapman."

⁂

AFTER DINNER, HARRY ASKED her if she would like to see the schoolroom. She wondered what she would see there, but she dutifully followed him up the stairs to the ballroom, now put to its new use. On the threshold, she remembered the last ball she had attended in Charleston in a room just like this one, in a dress with a great bell of a skirt, smiling as she waltzed with a young fop, her mind frantic with worry for Caro and herself. She took a deep breath. Now she wore a traveling dress as sober as any missionary's, she was in the company of a Boston Yankee who was nearly a reverend, and the ballroom was filled with rough wooden benches for the scholars.

He strode to the table, which was neatly piled with

books and slates. The slate pencils were side by side, evenly sharpened, in a wooden box. "We use the McGuffey Primer," he said. "I find that the illustrations help the children." At her polite, noncommittal look, he asked, "Miss Jarvie, have you any experience in teaching?"

She hesitated. What had Joshua told him? Had he fibbed to the nearly reverend Harry Phelps?

Harry Phelps said, "Miss Jarvie, I'm curious. What did you tell the head of the educational committee in Boston?"

She said, "My task was easy. Evidently Lieutenant Aiken was very persuasive."

He gave her a quizzical look. "You've no experience of teaching," he said.

She drew herself up. "Mr. Phelps, I believe that I'm as conversant with teaching as you are with growing cotton," she said.

He gave her a searching look. It reminded her of Eliza's gaze, fraught with judgment. He set the book back on the table. "I'll be glad to teach you how to teach," he said, "if you'll be willing to school me, as the former slaves say, in the cultivation of cotton."

She laughed. "A fair bargain, Mr. Phelps," she said. She held out her arm. "Now show me your new domain as a superintendent."

❧❦

THAT EVENING, ADMITTING TO how tired she felt, Emily sat in her room. She wore her dressing gown—she had refused Phoebe's help, glad of a corset that unhooked in front and a dress with buttons she could undo herself. Harry hadn't exaggerated. The room was big enough for a piano and an audience to listen to it. Her mother had sat before that piano, playing a Schubert lied so that the older daughter of the house could show off her lessons in singing. On that long-ago afternoon, as on this evening, the air was warm and scented. In the fading light of late evening, as the fragrant breeze billowed her curtains, Emily let herself feel overwhelmed by melancholy and memory again. She thought of the despoiled houses of Beaufort, the slashed portraits in the parlor, and interleaved with it, she thought of the ghosts—the beauty of St. Helena before the war, gone forever, and of her mother, dead so many years.

She was too tired for tears. She needed the voice of the present.

Joshua had mailed her a letter that had reached her in New York, and she had read it in distraction on the steamship, too excited to take it in. Now she opened her reticule and pulled it from the envelope to read it with care.

Joshua's letters always terrified her. How bad was the peril of the last fight? Was he whole, or was he writing to tell her that he had been wounded, that he was near death, or worse still, that he was writing to say goodbye forever? Even though he didn't give her the worst details of battle—he knew better than to frighten her that way—she could read between the lines, and she had the accounts of every battle and every major skirmish because she had easy access to the Northern papers, which had correspondents salted all over Virginia.

But this was a letter written in camp, in a dull moment after drill and bad coffee and bad meat—even lieutenants ate salt beef and hardtack—and he was reminding himself, as much as telling her, of the reason he put up with hardtack and boredom and when it happened, the valley of the shadow of death on the battlefield.

My dearest Emily, he wrote, *at times like these, I remind myself why I am fighting. Many men talk of the Union, but for me it is always slavery, the evil of slavery, the moral wrong of slavery, which corrupts everything it touches, and rots the souls of master and slave alike. Every shot, every battle, every advance, every victory brings us closer to the end of slavery, and in the thick of it, I never lose sight of that wonderful vision, of that day of jubilee.*

Emily laid the letter on her lap. She rubbed her eyes. Eliza Phelps's zeal was hot under her skin. *I have a war to fight, too,* she thought, wishing she could tell the absent Joshua. Whether it was a war against slavery, or a war within herself, she wasn't yet sure. She could hardly blame Joshua for his fervor. But she was weary of zeal today, and wary of it.

She let the breeze stir the ghosts of the antebellum world again. And with the ghosts came the memories, of Colleton County, too close by; the too-recent memory of Charleston; and the worst memories of all, of her father.

Chapter 2: Border to a Border State

WHEN CARO GOT OFF the train in Cincinnati, she let the crowd on the platform surge around her. She smelled coal smoke, horse manure, brick dust, and sweat. After the isolation and quiet of Oberlin College, she was starved for city life. Despite the way she had left Charleston, she missed the excitement of a city.

The man who pushed through the crowd toward her was stocky, well-dressed, and light brown in complexion. It was Mr. Ezra Baker, who had been barber to Joshua Aiken, Emily's fiancé, the former editor of the ladies' magazine *Hearth and Home*. Both Emily and Joshua had persuaded the new editor to take Caro on. The Bakers had offered to put her up over the summer.

After greetings were exchanged, Mr. Baker said, "I've hired a hansom. We'll ask the driver to help with your trunk."

Before she could thank him, someone elbowed her. She called out, "Excuse me!"

The stranger, a white man, turned to glower at her. "Watch yourself," he said unkindly, as he hurried away.

Shaken, she addressed Mr. Baker. "I heard that Cincinnati was in a hurry. I didn't hear that it was so impolite."

Mr. Baker sighed and offered her his arm. "I'm sorry," he said.

As they made their way to the cab stand, Caro took in the crowd. Half of the people in this crowd were black. Caro breathed a sigh of relief to know that she would live in a city full of people of color again. She was glad to see that the women of Cincinnati were fashionably dressed, a welcome change after earnest, sober, dowdy Oberlin College. When she got her pay, she would buy something new, something pretty.

The hansom driver was black, too, and at the sight of Caro, he jumped down from his seat and smiled as he doffed his cap.

When they settled into the cab, Caro leaned forward to look out the windows. Cincinnati was newer than Charleston, but it was uglier and full of the wooden buildings of quick construction. Their journey was short.

The cab turned down a street that was crowded with older houses, densely built, wood and brick construction jumbled together. A smell of sewage wafted through the air. White and black mingled on the street, some of the people of color well-off, others not. The white people had the look of working men and women who had seen better times. They were thin and their clothes were shabby. It reminded Caro of Charleston Neck, the neighborhood on the outskirts of Charleston, where black and white jostled together. "Where are we?" she asked Mr. Baker.

"It's called Bucktown. People of color live here."

"Only here?"

Mr. Baker sighed. "We're very close to Kentucky," he said. Kentucky, a border state and a slave state, had struggled to remain neutral in the war. In abolitionist Oberlin, she had not realized how nearby slavery was in Cincinnati.

As they alit from the cab, two white men in worn coats watched them with a sullen look that reminded Caro of the Guard, the police force of Charleston.

"Why do they stare so?" Caro whispered to Mr. Baker.

"They're Irishmen. The neighborhood is full of them. They don't like us, and they say we take their livelihood away."

Caro remembered her friend in Charleston, fatherly Sunday Desmond, idled by the resentment of the white carpenters and masons who believed the same thing of him. The Charleston fears stirred. "Are we in danger?" she asked, upset.

"No," Mr. Baker said, turning away from the bad-tempered stare. "Not as long as we keep to ourselves."

Amidst the crowded buildings of Bucktown, the Baker house was unremarkable, a plain two-story structure. But it had been recently painted, the porch was in good repair, and the steps were swept clean. Like Mr. Baker himself, the house looked well-ordered and respectable.

A passel of Bakers clustered inside: Mrs. Baker, Ezra's wife, tall and spare, with a smile of welcome on her face; a grown son, a little darker and stockier than his father, next to his wife, who smoothed her skirt in a way that told Caro she was expecting a baby; and four younger Bakers, all dressed as for church, two boys and two girls, ranging in age from fourteen to six. There was a friendly flurry of greeting. The boys grabbed Caro's trunk. The eldest girl received her shawl, and the daughter-in-law led her to the parlor settee. Mrs. Baker offered refreshment.

As they fussed over her, Caro gazed around the parlor. Like the face the house presented to the street, everything spoke of success in life and the comfort it could bring.

The settee was slippery with fresh upholstery, and the furniture—the chairs before the hearth, the little tables, the china cabinet—were new, in the dark Victorian style that Caro had never become accustomed to, having grown up with the graceful mahogany furniture of the previous century. In the corner reposed a whatnot, its shelves adorned with china figurines. With a pang, she thought of enslaved Sophy, who had befriended her in Charleston after her father died, who had owned a china shepherdess just like the one in this parlor. In the corner stood a shelf full of books, and on the sofa table lay a newspaper she had never read before, the *Christian Recorder*. Curious, she picked it up. It was a newspaper for people of color, published in Philadelphia.

Mrs. Baker emerged from the kitchen with a coffee-pot. The littlest girl followed with a plate of cookies. Smiling, she said, "Mama made these specially for you!"

"Thank you," Caro said, suddenly overwhelmed by the kindness of these strangers.

Mr. Baker said to his wife, "This is an occasion! We should bring out the claret!" He glanced at Caro. "Do you drink claret, Miss Jarvie?"

How she had missed a glass of wine in temperance-mad Oberlin! She would get on well with the Bakers. She smiled at her host. "I would, thank you," she said.

ഇോരു

CARO SLEPT LATE ENOUGH on Sunday morning that the smell of coffee and bacon woke her. Lucy, already dressed, pulled her quilt away. "Get up, you lazybones!" she teased. "You'll be late for church!"

Caro sat up and stifled a groan. The elder girl, Amanda, said, "Didn't you go to church at Oberlin?"

Caro groaned outright. "All the time. Chapel every day, and a long service on Sundays."

Lucy asked, "How can you not like church?"

Caro's father had raised her to read the sages of classical literature, not the Bible, and he had taught her to appreciate the pleasure of a silk dress and a glass of hock with dinner. Oberlin's piety had been hard for her to take. Only her gratitude to the Williamsons, who had taken her in and championed her education at Oberlin, kept her from making her opinions known.

Lucy grabbed her hands. "It's such fun! You'll meet our friends and show off your new dress!" She glanced at her sister, who was busy braiding her hair into a circlet around her head. "And flirt with the boys!"

Caro asked, "Flirting? In church?"

Amanda pinned her hair into place. "Before and after. In church, we listen to the sermon." She directed her remarks to Lucy. "If we don't fall asleep and start to snore."

"I never did!" Lucy protested.

Amanda laughed. "Just last week," she said. She threw a last look at her sister. "She drooled while she was asleep."

"I did not!" Lucy said.

Laughing, Caro rose to splash cold water on her face. She said, "Amanda, when you're done, I'll need the mirror."

∾∽

After breakfast, the Baker family took her to the Allen African Methodist Episcopal Church. Caro was curious. She had attended churches with a preponderance of black congregants, but she had never seen a church founded by black ministers for black people.

The Bakers, who were prominent members of the congregation, seemed to know everyone, and they made much of her, praising her as a scholar at Oberlin College and boasting about her employment at *Hearth and Home*. Her hand was shaken and pressed so often that her wrist began to hurt.

Once the adults had their fill of her, Amanda pulled her aside. Amanda said, "You must like being fussed over. You're glowing."

Caro thought, *Your mother and father fuss over you every day. Don't begrudge me a little attention.*

Lucy cried, "Meet our friends, too!"

After Oberlin, where she was always the only young lady of color at any gathering, it was odd—and pleasurable—to be amid a crowd of young ladies of color. They had the confident carriage and the educated tones of people born in freedom, and they were dressed as fashionably as the illustrations in the pages of *Hearth and Home*. They asked after her origins. She said only, "South Carolina." They asked after her family. "Gone, my mother and my father both, before the war." And they asked about Oberlin College. "Do you study hard? Are you lonely there? How do they treat you?" That was easy. She gave her polite, public speech. "I'm very grateful to be at the College," she said. "I'm not the only student of color, but I do my best to represent our race. And the other students are very fierce in their feelings against slavery."

She thought, *How well I fox them! Emily would be proud of me.* Surrounded by members of her own race, she suddenly missed Emily so keenly that she felt a physical pang.

The young men hung back, letting the young ladies have their turn. But when they encroached, the girls turned from Caro to greet them and to smile. They, too, were fascinated by Caro. One of them, tall and fair of skin and wearing a well-tailored suit, welcomed her to the church and said, "I hope that we'll see you here often, Miss Jarvie."

She felt another pang. She thought of her Charleston beau Danny, who had also been elegant in dress and fair of skin. Before the war, he had fled Charleston without her, leaving her behind, and since she had come north, she had no idea where he had gone or what he did now.

She smiled at the stranger. "I'm sure you will," she said.

Amanda said to her, her tone sharp, "The service starts soon. Mama will want us in church." She tugged on Caro's sleeve.

"Excuse me," Caro said to the young man, and she turned to follow Amanda, whose skirt twitched with her emotion as she walked toward the church door.

Caro whispered to Lucy, "What is it? Did I do wrong?"

Lucy leaned close and her breath was warm in Caro's ear. "The boys like you too much," she said, laughing softly.

∞≪

IN OBERLIN, SERMONS WERE the occasion for diatribes against slavery. She had listened to earnest white ministers talk of the evils of bondage and the hope that the war would free those held in chains. Caro had watched the white abolitionists of Oberlin lean forward, their eyes bright, their cheeks flushed, as they sympathized with slaves and contrabands and prayed that the Union army would fulfill its role in emancipation as well as in combat.

It was different to hear the same sentiments preached by a black minister to a black audience.

On the way home, after the sermon, Mr. Baker said to Caro, "That was a fine sermon."

"Yes, it was," she agreed.

"Our church is a bastion of the struggle against slavery," he said.

Caro now knew Ohio was full of runaways from nearby Kentucky. She also knew that he meant that Allen AME was a stop on the Underground Railroad.

❦

THAT NIGHT, CARO DREAMED. She was on the steamship again, the boat she had taken north, when she left Charleston. She was in a dark corridor. She held a heavy tray in her hands, full of china and cutlery and covered dishes, a slave's burden. And she heard footsteps behind her.

She didn't want this dream. She struggled to wake, and could not.

The steps came closer. Her feet wouldn't move; they felt like they were trapped in mud. She couldn't run. She couldn't put the tray down. The steps got closer. Louder. And closer.

Why couldn't she wake to know that this was a dream?

She turned her head to see who it was. A man with dark curling whiskers in a checked suit.

She woke in a sweat of fear. She must have cried out because she woke Lucy, who sat up to ask, "What's wrong?"

Her sister said sleepily, "A bad dream, Caro?"

Caro didn't reply. Lucy's voice took on an edge of fear. "What kind of dream?"

Still sleepy, her sister said, "Lots of people who come here have bad dreams. Go back to sleep."

Caro pulled the comforter to her chin, as though it could comfort her, and in the summer heat, she shook as though she had caught a chill.

§)C₃

On Monday morning, Caro paused before the *Hearth and Home* office. She glimpsed her reflection in the plate glass window, and the sight of the new dress, made up before she left Oberlin, gave her courage. She had chosen a heavy cotton in a navy color, and she had added brass buttons and striped ribbon to the jacket. Her thought was to hide ink stains, but at the breakfast table, Mrs. Baker had admired it. "It looks just like a Union army coat!" she said.

She needed the courage. Mr. Asa Reed, current editor of *Hearth and Home*, had agreed to hire her on the recommendation of Emily and Joshua alone. They had never spoken. They had never met. What had seemed like an adventure from the safety of Oberlin College now seemed foolhardy.

Now she smoothed her skirt and grasped the doorknob.

Her first impression was of light. *Hearth and Home* occupied the first floor of a storefront with huge plate glass windows. The windows sparkled. She had expected disorder inside, but she was wrong. On the opposite wall stood a bookshelf, where past issues of the magazine had been neatly shelved. On the unoccupied desk, manuscripts sat in a tidy pile. In a corner of the room were reams of paper, carefully stacked.

And at the occupied desk sat Mr. Asa Reed. He was a man dwarfed by his furniture. When he looked up, he wheezed a little.

At the sight of Caro, he extricated himself from the chair and stood. He extended his hand as though she were any business associate. Smiling, he said, "Your cousin has spoken so often of you that I feel I've already been introduced to you. I hope that isn't forward of me." He was a head shorter than herself, and soft-spoken.

Relieved, she shook the proffered hand. "I'm glad to hear it, Mr. Reed. I'm very grateful to you."

He said, "It was the least I could do for a fellow Oberlin scholar."

Emily hadn't told her. "When did you study there, Mr. Reed?"

"I finished my education just before the war," he said. "I had a fondness for literature, like my predecessor Mr. Aiken. How do you find Oberlin, Miss Jarvie?"

Miss Sass stirred in her, but she bit her tongue. "I'm very grateful to be there, too."

He met her eyes and said in his soft voice, "I understand that it wasn't an easy journey."

She hadn't expected sympathy. "Did my cousin tell you?"

"She was discreet about you, as she was about herself. But my late father was a minister, and he was a friend to anyone who opposed slavery."

Lowering her voice to match his, she said, "Not all are, in Cincinnati."

"I hope to live up to my father's example."

He had lost a father, as she had. She felt her worry dissolve. Miss Sass raised her head again, and this time, she let her speak. "And I hope to live up to your hope of me."

"I believe we'll both find out," he said. He gestured toward the empty desk, which had been cleared and readied for her. There was a green paper blotter, an inkwell, a set of pens with steel nibs, and a ream of plain paper. He said, "Your cousin told me that you write a fair hand."

"I do, sir."

"I can put your talent to use right away." He pointed to the manuscripts on the unoccupied desk. "So many of our writers send us a scrawl, and I've made further changes. It can't go to the printer that way. Can you make fair copies?"

"I'll do my best, Mr. Reed."

He picked up several sheets of paper, heavily scored with inky writing. "No blots. No misspellings. Nothing illegible. From your hand to the typesetter's eye."

"I'll do that."

He opened a new ream of paper for her and set it down on the desk. As she sat and took up one of the pens, he said, "If you can't read their scrawl, either, consult with me."

"I won't be interrupting you?"

He smiled, and she saw the adult's charm that overlaid the biddable boy he must have been. "Miss Jarvie, an editor's life is one interruption after another," he said.

She took the story from him and settled herself at the desk. She picked up the pen. Holding it, she was assailed by the memory of her father, who had taught her to write so carefully, and a pang of loss shot through her. She controlled herself and reached for a clean sheet of paper, then dipped the nib in the ink. She read the lines, and as she copied them, she was beset by a very different feeling. Her father would be filled with pride to see her make a living by wielding a pen.

∞⌀℘

As CARO SHOOK HER wrist, which had begun to ache, the bell on the door jangled, and a young white man rushed in. He wore a plaid suit and a rumpled cravat, and his hair descended in a Bohemian tangle over his collar. He stared at Caro. "Reed, what in hell is that?"

Reed flushed. He rose. "This is Miss Caroline Jarvie," he said. "My new assistant."

"It wasn't enough to work for a girl," the man said. The stare was disconcerting, meant to be rude. "And now you have a—"

"A young lady of color," Reed said. "A scholar from Oberlin College."

"Oberlin! That nest of vipers."

"Miss Jarvie is well educated and well qualified to be

an editor's assistant." Reed's pale cheeks were fiery with emotion.

"Jarvie?" the man asked. "Any connection to the other one?"

Caro said quietly, "Miss Emily Jarvie is my cousin."

The stranger stared at Caro again, then at Reed. "Good God, Reed, being antislavery has addled you."

"And the *Gazette* hasn't improved you, either." Reed said to Caro, "This is my friend Mr. Perry, who should know better than to be so rude to a young lady."

Her Charleston self, Miss Sass, rose up in her. She held out her hand and said firmly, "I'm very pleased to meet you, Mr. Perry. How do you find the *Gazette*?"

He didn't shake her hand, and he didn't reply. She didn't move her hand and let him feel the awkwardness.

He turned away. He said to Reed, "I came to tell you that my editor's looking for stringers. If you ever want to try your hand at being a reporter."

"I'm doing well here."

"My editor talks of sending me to the western front." Perry laughed, not pleasantly. "You won't write about the war at *Hearth and Home*."

Reed wheezed. "That's cruel, Perry. I'd be in Virginia if I could."

"If your mama would let you!" Perry laughed as he left, letting the door slam after him.

Reed wheezed so badly that Caro felt alarmed. She asked, "Are you all right, sir? Can I bring you a cup of water?"

"Yes, please."

He could not drink and wheeze at the same time. When he recovered a little, he said, "He knows how much I want to be at the front myself. Not as a reporter, but a soldier."

So this gentle little man thirsted to fight. "And you can't," Caro said.

"Blasted asthma!" he said, with a final wheeze. "They won't have me."

∞⃝⃝

As CARO WORKED FOR Asa Reed, she came to know him better. He missed his departed father, whose abolitionist views he shared. As the only son, he had become the man of the family, even though he was the youngest. He had taken the position at *Hearth and Home* to support his mother. "I grew up with four older sisters," he told Caro. "They talked of dresses and bonnets and ribbons all the time. The arrival of *Godey's Lady's Book* was the occasion for great excitement and endless squabbling over who could use the patterns to make an old dress into a new one."

"Four older sisters!" Caro said, laughing at the thought. "Did they pet you or torment you?"

"Both," he said.

He was easily teased, and as she lost her fear of him, she let him hear the voice that had gone quiet in her flight from Charleston and her life in staid Oberlin. She let him hear Miss Sass again. She didn't tell him about her life

49

before the war, but when he asked her about Oberlin, she said, "I feel like a raisin that fell into a bowl of rice pudding."

He laughed until he began to wheeze. "Oberlin is like that," he said. "Wholesome but very bland. Rice pudding, indeed!"

At the end of her first week, when she held her pay envelope in her hand, she thought of her promise to herself.

Reed saw her smile. "You're thinking of buying some-thing," he said, daring to smile too. "Ribbons? A bonnet? A length?"

"You don't think it's frivolous?"

"Of course you should be a fashion plate. How else should the editor's assistant of *Hearth and Home* dress?"

She thought, *He must talk to his sisters like this.* She wished she had a brother like that. It was odd to think of this asthmatic abolitionist, white as a pan of skimmed milk, in such a familiar way. "Then the pleasure will be in deciding," she said.

⚬⚬

SHE PROLONGED THE PLEASURE. She visited the dry goods shops, discovering that white shopkeepers could be rude with impunity to anyone of color, even someone well-dressed and well-spoken like herself. She stopped in a few tailoring establishments, remembering her uncle Thomas's lovely shop on Queen Street in Charleston, with its marble countertop and mahogany chairs for guests. She had not thought of Thomas, or her mother's sister Maria, since she left Charleston. The memory of the Bennett family gave her no pleasure.

After her third dismissal by a dressmaker, she thought that she should ask Mrs. Baker, who very likely patronized a woman of color. She sighed. Cincinnati was full of the promise of freedom, but in practice, it was even harsher to a person of color than Charleston had been. She had been treated with more politeness as a slave in Charleston than as a free woman in Cincinnati.

When she finally asked, Mrs. Baker said, "I know just the dressmaker."

"Where can I find her?"

"She's at Bennett's Tailoring, near Canal Street."

Her heart seemed to constrict in her chest. She recalled those words in gold paint on a shop window in Charleston. "Is the owner a man of color?"

"Of course! That's why I'm sending you there."

She shook her head. Certainly there was more than one tailor named Bennett in the world.

She would find out.

The shop was just off Canal Street, near the market. She hesitated, but she thought of the new dress she wanted and the money in her reticule to pay for it.

She pushed open the door, jangling the bell, and the young woman behind the counter looked up. She was neatly dressed and quickly arranged her face into an expression of welcome for a customer.

The look of welcome swiftly changed into one of confusion. She put her hand to her mouth to stifle a cry and fled into the back room.

Charlotte Bennet had recognized Caro and had fled before Caro could cry out in surprise.

Charlotte returned with a very familiar figure: Thomas Bennett, tailor, once of Charleston, in a beautifully cut suit that looked, to Caro's now-practiced eye, to be several seasons old. He looked tired and worn. His hair was now shot with gray.

Her uncle leaned against the counter and splayed his hands on it. She saw the toll that a lifetime of tailoring had taken. His fingers were swollen and a little bent. This counter was wood, decent oak, but nothing like the marble in the shop in Charleston. He asked, "What are you doing here?"

She approached the counter. "I'm in need of a dressmaker, Uncle Thomas," she said. "This shop was recommended to me."

"No, no. How did you come to Cincinnati?"

"I'm here for the summer to work for *Hearth and Home*. The magazine that Miss Jarvie wrote for." When he didn't reply, she added, "I study at the college at Oberlin. I'll return there in the fall."

He struggled to shape the words. "I never expected to see you in Cincinnati."

She said, "I might ask the same of you, Uncle Thomas. I thought you were in Philadelphia."

"We were." His voice was slightly hoarse, as though he

had developed a catarrh in Ohio. "We came here because we heard that business would be better."

She let her eyes travel around the shop, seeing the wooden counter and the sawdust on the floor. He understood what her appraisal meant. He didn't contradict it.

"I've brought you some custom," she said.

He straightened with the deliberation of a man whose back hurt. "We choose our custom," he said.

"I thought you'd welcome it," she said.

He stood, unmoving.

She leaned against the counter, and he took his hands away. She asked, "Where is Danny?"

His expression faltered. His memories must be as painful as her own. But he swiftly righted himself. "He's well. He's safe."

"Where is he, Uncle Thomas?"

He shook his head. He turned to his daughter. "Charlotte, will you show Miss Jarvie out?"

As though she needed an escort to take the few steps to the door! He meant to throw her out. She fumed at his refusal to answer her.

She swept her gaze around the shop again and let it rest on both the diminished Bennetts. "I can see myself out, thank you," she said, and had the satisfaction of turning her back on them as she left.

∞∞

AFTER CARO HAD MADE fair copies of this month's articles, Reed said, "Now we can paste it up." He explained what he meant, and they spent several days arranging the pages and a pleasant afternoon pasting them together, like the pages in a scrapbook. Reed asked her to take the pages, which he called proofs, to the printer. "Make sure he checks them before he accepts them," he said. "They've made errors before."

She took the sheaf of pages, which had been carefully wrapped in brown paper like a gift, and felt a surge of loyalty toward the magazine. "We can't have that!"

At the printer's, she pushed open the door and was overwhelmed by the clatter of the press and the smell of hot metal and ink. Near the press, a black man, his apron ink-smeared, swept away bits of metal and crumpled paper. Caro hesitated, the magazine's proofs in her hand. The black man looked up. "Miss?" he called, above the machine's noise. "Can I help you?" He had the slur of Kentucky in his speech: "He'p you."

She knew him from Allen AME, where he was called Mr. Benjamin Holloway, and he was a dignified deacon with a fine singing voice. He didn't admit that he recognized her. She thought, *He lives a different life here*, and she didn't betray him. She said, "I'm looking for the printer."

He pointed to a disheveled white man in a black suit, his tie askew, who stood beside the press. Caro approached him, saying politely, "Sir?"

He looked up. "What are you doing here?" He also had the slur of the South in his speech.

Caro said, "I'm from *Hearth and Home*."

"Where's Reed?"

"I'm Mr. Reed's assistant." She raised the packet. "I've brought the proofs for you to set."

He stared at her. He called, "Benny!"

He replied, "Yes, suh?"

"Take care of this, will you?" He said to Caro, "Leave them with Benny."

Caro addressed him. "No offense, sir," she said. She raised her voice to talk to the printer. "Mr. Reed directed me to give these to you, and for you to examine them, to be sure they're in order to print," she said, as firmly as she could.

The printer turned away. "Give them to Benny," he repeated.

Caro trembled, but her voice remained firm. Reed's words bolstered her. "Sir, yours is not the only printing firm in Cincinnati," she said. She forced her voice to remain steady. "If you don't want to deal with us, we can take our custom elsewhere."

A younger white man in shirtsleeves and inkstained apron touched the older printer's arm. "Take the proofs. What does it matter who brings them?"

"I don't care to deal with...her," the older printer said. A worse word hung in the air like a bad smell.

"Then I will," the younger man said. He stepped forward and stretched out his hand.

Caro knew not to shake his hand. She extended the packet so that he could take it from her without touching her. He asked, "Who am I addressing?"

"Miss Jarvie."

"The assistant." He nodded. "I'm the assistant here. One assistant to another."

The older printer looked at Caro with distaste. "When you come back, you can leave the proofs with my son," he said.

As she turned to leave, Caro found that she was shaking. She caught the eye of the man who was Mr. Benjamin Holloway when he was not Benny. He looked at her with the faintest smile of satisfaction on his face.

ഓൾ

As SOON AS THE current issue went to press, Reed began to put together the next. She came into the office to find him looking worried. "What is it, sir?" she asked.

"Writers," he said, wheezing a little.

She had learned that writers were a variable lot— some prompt, their copies clean and easy to read, and others slow and scrawling. "Did someone disappoint us?"

"Yes," he said. "Now we're short a piece for the next issue."

"What was it?"

"A squib." He meant something short and humorous. "About the war and how it's affected fashion."

Caro's eyes gleamed. "War? Fashion? I believe I could turn my hand to it."

He smiled. "Your fine hand," he said.

"How many words, sir? When do you need it?" A writer's questions.

"Five hundred words, a week hence," he said.

She remembered Emily's effort in writing her first piece for *Hearth and Home*, when they both lived in Charleston. Emily had been so worried that she had asked for her slave cousin's opinion. For Caro, the writer's task was easy, and she felt smug.

Reed liked her piece. "Only a few changes," he said. "Can you make a fair copy, Miss Jarvie?"

After her initial success, he assigned her another piece, then another, and then said, "An assistant editor is different from an editor's assistant. Two dollars a week different." At her startled look, he said, "That's a dress length's worth, is it not?"

She laughed. She had not felt so encouraged since her father died. She thought of Reed's rude friend Mr. Perry, and asked a question sideways. "Mr. Reed, you're a man of talent. Do you have any ambitions to write elsewhere? At the *Gazette*?"

"Oh, I'm sure they'd have me, if I wanted to."

"Which you don't."

He looked at her a little too keenly. With friendship had come an acute understanding. Emily had seen her and seen through her like that. He exclaimed, "Don't tell me that you do!"

"Why shouldn't I? You think I'm a good writer."

He didn't reply.

She pressed him. "Might I inquire of them? To learn if the *Gazette* might see to hire me someday?" She tried to tease. "We know they need stringers!"

He flushed. "I would hate to see you refused." He flushed a deeper red. "Or humiliated."

"As though I've never heard an insult before."

"Why go looking for one?"

"Could I speak to someone at the *Gazette*?"

He said, "Even if anyone would speak to you, it won't be pleasant for you."

She knew what he meant. He had created an abolitionist haven for her at the *Hearth and Home* office. Outside these walls, she was not a talented writer or a valued assistant editor. To polite people, she was a girl of color, and to those not-so-polite, she was a nigger gal. He couldn't protect her, as much as he wanted to. "Nonetheless, I'd like to try."

He flushed. "I could ask Mr. Perry. But you've met him, and you know what he's like."

"I'll be ready for it."

෨෬

ON THE DAY OF her interview, she hesitated before the door of the *Gazette*. She thought of Reed's trust in her. *I have every reason to be here*, she thought, as she pushed open the door.

The *Gazette* offices, unlike *Hearth and Home*'s, were a jumble of messy desks piled with papers at which men in shirtsleeves scribbled on sheets of foolscap. The room was thick with smoke, and every desk had a spittoon. A rushing, rumbling noise underlay the loud conversation.

They had their own press, and it was running as she stood there.

No one greeted her. She approached the nearest desk. "Sir?" she asked.

He looked up briefly and went back to his article. When she didn't move, he said, "What?"

It's just rudeness, she thought. *As Mr. Reed warned me.* "I have an appointment with Mr. Perry. My employer, Mr. Reed, made it for me."

The reporter looked up. He scratched his chin through his beard. "Reed? The one at that ladies' magazine?"

"*Hearth and Home,* sir." Caro kept her voice polite.

He stared at her. "And what in God's name do you do there? Sweep the floor?"

Caro flushed. "I'm the assistant editor."

The man sniggered. He gestured with his thumb. "Perry's desk is over there," he said. "He isn't here. You can wait." As she made her way, he called, "Don't you sit down!" She felt ungentlemanly eyes on her and heard ugly laughter.

She stood. She waited. The reporters stared. They sniggered. They commented. One of them said, "Who's the nigger gal? What does she want with Perry?" Her face flamed. Her back began to ache. She waited.

When she had been waiting for twenty minutes by the big clock on the wall, Perry breezed into the office. When he saw her, he said, "What are you doing here?"

"Mr. Reed said that you would speak to me about writing for the *Gazette.*"

"You took that seriously?"

She said nothing and hoped that he would hear his own rudeness.

He sat down, taking his time, and said, "Do you really think the *Gazette* would hire a colored girl who's written about dresses and bonnets for two months to be a reporter? Are you mad?"

No, he would never hear his own rudeness.

He said, "I'll have a word with Reed about wasting my time. Dresses and bonnets!" He returned his attention to his desk, dismissing her.

She walked the gauntlet of stares and laughter again, ignoring all of it.

∞∞

As Caro walked home from the office—she was in Bucktown, not far from the Baker house—she heard the steps behind her. How could she discern them in a crowd? But they were right behind her. Closer and closer. A man came alongside her and reached for her. He wore a checked suit.

As in the nightmare.

He said roughly, "How much?"

Not a slave catcher. Relief flooded through her. She said sharply, "Sir, you have mistaken me."

"Do you charge extra because you dress like a lady?"

"Sir, you want the bawdy house. The Shakespeare House. Two streets over."

He tightened his grip on her arm.

A familiar voice said, "Suh." It was Mr. Holloway, dressed in the workmen's clothes that made him "Benny" to the white eye. He said, "The bawdy house. Like she say, the Shakespeare House."

The man stared at Mr. Holloway. Very softly, Mr. Holloway said, "Don't want no trouble, suh."

"It ain't worth the trouble," the man said. He shook off Caro's arm with distaste. He spat, turned, and walked away.

Mr. Holloway patted Caro's arm gently. "Are you all right, Miss Jarvie?"

She was so shaken that she blurted it out. "I thought he was a slave catcher."

He looked at her with pity and understanding. "You watch out for that too, Miss Jarvie," he said.

∞∞

THAT NIGHT CARO SLEPT lightly, and the sound of voices in the house in the middle of the night woke her. The room was stuffy and dark. No moonlight tonight.

The Baker girls in the other bed also stirred and woke. Caro whispered, "What's that downstairs?"

"Nothing," the elder girl murmured sleepily. "Pay it no mind." She rolled over, needing no effort to fall asleep again.

Was that sobbing Caro heard? She rose and fumbled for her dressing gown in the dark. She turned the knob and pulled open the bedroom door. "Quiet," came the sleepy, annoyed voice from the bed.

Light spilled up the stairs and onto the landing. The flickering light of candles, not the kerosene lamps that burned during the family's waking hours. The sobbing grew louder. Mrs. Baker's voice, pitched low, floated up the stairs. "It's all right," she said. "It's all right now."

What had gone wrong?

Caro crept down the stairs, trying to see who stood in the foyer. Halfway down the stairs, she saw Mrs. Baker embracing a sobbing woman in a rough calico dress. Two children clung to her skirt, their eyes wide. At the sight of Caro, they burst into tears.

Caro froze. "What's the matter?" she asked Mrs. Baker. "Who are they?"

At the sound of Caro's voice, the woman turned. Under her kerchief, her face was ashy with fear and dirt.

Mrs. Baker said, "Go back to bed, Caro."

But she could not. She knew that look and that fear. They had fled, just as she had. She stretched out her arms, wanting to gather those crying children close. "Can I help?"

Mrs. Baker's face went grim. "The less you know, the better."

Despite the war, the Underground Railroad was still in operation in Ohio, border to a border state. They were fugitives. Fugitive slaves. As she was.

Chapter 3: The Cat Sat on the Mat

As she waited in the schoolroom with Harry, Emily smoothed her skirt. "Don't worry," Harry said. He touched her arm, the lightest touch. "I have faith in you."

The front door opened. Emily heard Phoebe greet the children. Their bare feet pounded on the steps, and they burst into the room, smelling of that odd metallic odor of sweat in children, with a whiff of unwashed clothes. They ranged in age from toddlers to nearly grown up, the boys pushing each other, the girls holding the littler ones by the hand. They stared at Emily and ran to Harry, encircling him, jostling to get closest. The eldest girl cried, "Marse Harry, is it true that you won't teach us no more?"

Harry said, "Any more. Yes, it's true that I'm going to be a superintendent."

At this news, the littlest children clung to his pants legs. The worried girl said, "Don't go, Marse Harry! Don't go!" The clingers began to cry, and all of them took up the refrain: "Don't go!"

He embraced as many of them as he could reach, patting heads and shoulders. "I'm not going away, children.

I'll still be here. And Miss Jarvie is here to take over my duties in the classroom. You'll come to love her, too."

They stared at Emily, their faces tear-stained, and Emily wondered if that would ever be true.

Harry said, "Now you settle down, all of you." They jostled and elbowed each other as they sat.

Harry smiled at his charges. "Good morning, dear scholars!" he said.

There was the sound of snuffling. One of the snufflers wiped his face with his sleeve. Several thin voices spoke, and in the Sea Island greeting said, "Huddy, Marse Harry."

"I want you to welcome our new teacher, Miss Emily Jarvie, who has come to us all the way from Ohio."

A little girl asked, "Where that?"

"Do you mean Ohio, Bina?" Harry said gently.

Emily said, "Ohio is up north."

Bina said, "You talk just like young miss on my place."

An older girl said sharply, "Bina!"

Emily thought, *They are only children. They used to be slaves, and no one has raised them gently.* She laughed a little. "That's no surprise," she said, looking from one saddened, puzzled face to another. "I was born in Colleton County, just up the river, and I lived in Charleston before the war."

"Why you go up north?" Bina asked.

Emily hesitated. What could she tell them?

Bina asked, "Did you run away?"

"Bina!" the older girl chastened.

Yes, Emily thought. But she said brightly, "Of course not! I traveled on a steamship."

"My daddy a pilot on a steamship," a little boy said. "On a river boat."

Bless you, Emily thought. "And now I've come back to teach you. I hope that I can be as good a teacher and a friend to you as Mr. Phelps has been."

Bina put her thumb in her mouth.

Harry asked, "Who is new today?"

Several children chorused, "Me! I am!" in tones loud enough to be heard across a cotton field.

"Quiet, quiet," Harry said, soothingly. "In this room, there's no need to shout. Raise your hands to show me."

Several hands rose into the air.

Harry said, "Those of you who have advanced to the First Reader—I know who you are—sit on the back benches, and I'll set you to your lesson. Beginners, sit in front, and Miss Jarvie and I will start you on the Primer. Miss Jarvie, will you help me?"

It was clear that some of the children had never held a book before. They hefted it as though it were a basket of rice and turned it around in their hands. A few of them held it upside down.

Harry raised his copy. "Like this, children," he said, and they righted their books to show the ship on the cover sailing properly on its sea.

"Now we open it," he said, showing them the first page, where two children reclined in a hammock. "See how happy they look? How much at ease? Reading will be a joy to you, and it will become as easy as resting in a hammock."

He turned the page. "This is the alphabet," he said. "The letters that make up words."

They squinted. "Them little black marks?" a boy asked.

"What's your name, young sir?"

"Called Will, Marse Harry."

"Yes, Will, that's what we'll learn. The alphabet."

Will turned the page ahead of the rest. He laughed and held up the book. "A cat!" he said. "Look like Maum Juno's cat that live in the kitchen."

The pages rustled, and the rest of the children began to exclaim over the cat. Will turned another page and laughed again. "That a rat," he said. "We learn to read about a rat, Marse Harry?"

Harry's eyes twinkled. "The cat and the rat," he said.

"What happen with the cat and the rat?" Will asked.

Harry laughed. "We'll find out!"

They worked their way through the first lesson. They struggled mightily with the letters *a*, *c*, *r*, and *t*. And suddenly Will let out a shout. "I see it!" he cried. "Them marks *c*, *a*, *t*. Mean a cat, like the picture!" He looked up, beaming. "Is that how to read, Marse Harry?"

Harry's face shone with delight. "Yes," he said.

Emily thought, *His spirit is here, in the classroom. What a loss for him to be a superintendent.*

෨෬

AFTER DINNER, WHEN ELIZA went back to the kitchen, Harry lingered in the dining room. He asked Emily, "I'm going to face my new duties. Will you come with me?" He looked tentative, as she had felt that morning.

"Of course I will." She put on her bonnet against the midday sun, and they took the dirt path that led to the fields. In June, summer had arrived in full force and she was glad of the trees that shaded the way.

As they walked toward the cotton fields, she said, "Now I can see that you worry."

He tried to smile. "It is my worry now," he said.

She halted to look him in the face. "What did you tell me this morning? To have faith? Do you recall?"

"Yes," he said, a smile creeping onto his face.

They walked past the fields. "Where are they?" she asked, teasing a little. "Your new charges?"

"They break at midday for their meal and a little rest."

But as they walked farther, they could see a lone figure, hoe in his hands, chopping at the weeds. Harry sighed. "It's Rufus."

"He doesn't take his meal? Or his rest?"

"Rufus!" Harry called, and Rufus straightened, rubbing his back.

"Marse Harry," he said respectfully. "Miss Emily."

"Rufus, we don't begrudge you a few minutes at midday," Harry said.

"Oh, I stop for a bit," he said. "But we so far behind. It bother me."

"What about the others?" Emily asked. "Don't you work together?"

"Oh, they do, Miss Emily. But we don't have gangs no more," Rufus said.

Harry explained, "The people refused it. It was the first vestige of slavery to be abolished here. They insisted on working their own plots, at their own pace."

Rufus gestured toward the cotton field. Emily, cotton planter's daughter still, could see how far behind they were. "A slow pace, with respect, Marse Harry."

"Rufus was Mr. Dalton's driver in the days of slavery," Harry said.

Emily asked Rufus, "Didn't Mr. Dalton have an overseer?"

"No, Miss Emily. He make me the driver over all the place. Get the work done, hand out the meat and meal every week, punish if I have to."

Emily looked from Rufus to Harry. "That's a great responsibility."

"I know, Miss Emily. But Marse Dalton trust me with it. And I bring in the crop for him many a year."

Emily thought, *He ran the place.*

Harry said, "Rufus has been a great help to Mr. Chapman. I hope that he'll be a help to me, too."

"Of course, Marse Harry."

"What about the others?" Emily asked.

Rufus hesitated. Emily had seen that before. He had a decided opinion, but he was loath to express it without knowing where Harry stood.

Harry said, "I wish that everyone understood it as well as you, Rufus. About getting paid now and about getting a share once the crop is ginned and baled."

"Bigger the crop, bigger the share," Rufus said. "And harder you work, the bigger the crop."

"You see it," Harry said. "Will you help me with the others? Help them to see it, too?"

Rufus hesitated again. He leaned on his hoe. "Do my best, Marse Harry."

They turned to go, and they heard the sound of the hoe cutting into the earth, Rufus at his labor again.

They continued their walk. The cotton fields gave way to bare earth, and beyond it, a plot where a woman and three children knelt in the dirt. Emily recognized one of the boys. It was Will, who liked reading so much.

At the sight of Emily and Harry, all four of them clambered to their feet. "Marse Harry," the woman said.

Harry kept his voice polite, as though he were in the parlor. "Maum Cindy, I believe the cotton field needs attention," he said.

"Oh, it all right," Cindy said. "I finish my task already, and now I attend to my garden."

"Rufus is worried about the crop," Harry said.

She considered this. "Marse Harry, his thoughts still back in slavery days, when he drive us. But now he don't."

Emily asked, "Maum Cindy, what do you grow?"

Cindy gestured toward the garden. "Greens," she said. "All kinds of vegetable. And berries. Berries come ripe soon."

"For yourself?"

Cindy looked past Emily to Harry. She said, "Marse Harry, Mr. Chapman know all about this. He say he don't mind it. What we grow, we take to the market in Beaufort to sell."

Harry hesitated, seeming to search for the words that would sweeten the command. "I don't mind, either. As long as the cotton fields get their proper attention."

Cindy didn't drop her head or murmur, "Yes, Marse." Instead she regarded Harry with a thoughtful gaze. "They will," she said. "We all promise that."

As they walked away, Harry said ruefully, "I have my work cut out for me."

"As every planter does."

He met her eyes. The look on his face was not at all businesslike. "I have the advantage of wages. And suasion."

She thought of the schoolroom, where he had reaped what he had sown. She put her hand on his arm. "And faith," she said.

He touched her hand, as though he were safely a reverend and she were safely his parishioner. "Both of us," he said, smiling and suddenly not like a reverend at all. He started and took his hand away.

To her regret.

He said, "We'll have faith in leading them to enterprise as well as to freedom."

She couldn't resist the impulse to tease. "They are enterprising! Just not in the direction that you want."

He gestured toward the fields where the produce destined for the Beaufort Market ripened. "I see that," he said.

❧

On Sunday, the Phelpses took her to the service at the White Church. Once it had been a chapel reserved for the planters on the island; the slaves had worshiped at the Brick Church, big enough for slaves as well as masters, or at their own little churches, called praise houses. Now the White Church was open to the faithful from Boston and New York, and any freed people who cared to join them.

In the churchyard, Emily met a new crop of missionaries: superintendents on the neighboring places, friends of Mr. Chapman's, Bostonians like himself; several teachers, all men; the Reverend Dysart, a New Yorker passionate against slavery, and his wife, equally strong in her antislavery feeling. Mrs. Dysart had curls too young for her middle years, big eyes moist with emotion, and damp hands. "You're a Southerner!" she exclaimed, hearing Emily's accent.

"Yes, South Carolina born," Emily said.

"From a family of slave owners?"

Emily sighed. "My father is the slave owner," she said, trying to impress that she kept her distance.

Mrs. Dysart pressed Emily's hand between her palms. "And have you truly renounced slavery in your heart?"

Emily drew her hand away. She said tartly, "My reasons were good enough for the Boston Education Commission. They should be good enough for anyone."

She adjusted her bonnet. "Miss Jarvie, you surprise me," she said. "A Southern lady with a sharp tongue!"

Eliza was at her elbow. She said to Mrs. Dysart, "Haven't you heard a Southern lady bless you in tones that clearly wished she could stab you?"

For Mrs. Dysart, who had no subtlety, Emily smiled and said in her best belle's inflection, "Oh, bless your heart, Miss Eliza! Was it like that?"

Eliza said, "Miss Jarvie, you have more humor than we do."

"Miss Phelps!" said a woman with a low, pleasant voice. "As though humor were a bad thing. Is this your new teacher?"

"Miss Easton," Eliza said. "Yes, this is Miss Jarvie, who has taken Harry's place in the classroom. Miss Jarvie, this is Miss Easton, our doctress, who looks after the women and children."

Miss Easton was a tall, broad-shouldered woman with hands big enough to examine a baby and gentle enough to cradle one. She had large gray eyes; her lips were full and gave her a permanent, serene smile, even in repose. Her features were plain, but her face was made beautiful by an expression of interest in the world, and kindness toward it.

She laughed at Eliza's introduction. "Doctress! It makes me sound like something in a menagerie. Welcome, Miss Jarvie. My friend Miss Sterling is the teacher on our place. You must come to visit. She would be glad to show you her classroom."

Emily was still smarting a little from Mrs. Dysart's interrogation. She said tartly, "Don't you want to ask me how I get on? A Southerner at Port Royal?"

Miss Easton threw a disparaging glance at Mrs. Dysart's overdressed back. "Some of these people are nothing but busybodies," she said. "You're here, are you not? Doing what you think is right."

ഊൠ

ON MONDAY, THE DAY that Harry left her alone for good, the children trooped into the classroom. Will was the first to say it. "Where Marse Harry?"

"Mr. Phelps is starting his new duties as a superintendent today." Emily stood as tall as she could. "As he told you."

Bina said, "I want Marse Harry."

Emily thought, *They are just children*, and she curbed her irritation. She said sweetly, "Well, you'll have to make do with me."

"Don't want you," Bina said. "Want Marse Harry, who love us."

"Bina!" said her sister, sharply.

Emily gestured toward the benches. "Sit down, all of you, and we'll get settled for the day," she said.

Among the newcomers was a girl who held her baby brother in her arms. The baby wore no swaddling, only a shirt. He was a mess waiting to happen. Emily said, "Will he be quiet?"

The girl said, "Mama have to work, and I have to watch him. If I come to school, he come with me."

The readers, experienced in the classroom, clustered on the back benches. Among them were several older boys who had been especially attached to Harry. As soon as they sat down, they began to pinch each other, then to cuff each other on the arm. "Boys, boys, stop that," Emily said.

The boys ignored her. The scuffling was accompanied by laughter.

"Now you stop that!" Emily said, trying to raise her voice enough to carry to the back of the room. She sounded thin and shrill to her own ears.

More scuffling, and more laughter.

She strode to the back of the room and called again, "Now you stop that!" She reached for the collar of the nearest boy. His face flashed resentment. He said, "Marse Harry say that it wrong to put hands on us!"

Emily said, "He did not."

The boy glared at her. "Will you whup us?"

Emily flushed. Every teacher reserved the right to birch a misbehaving student. But she could not risk the reminder of slavery. She said, "I think it's wrong, too. But you must settle down for your lessons today." She appealed to him. "Will you?"

From the front of the room came another cry. It was Bina, her voice piercing. "Biscuit!" she called out. "When we have biscuit?"

Flustered, Emily ran to the beginners at the front.

"First we learn," she proclaimed. "Then Phoebe will bring us refreshment."

"Hungry now!"

Emily threw a glance at Bina's older sister, hoping for help in reining Bina in. But the older girl rolled her eyes and said nothing.

"Later," Emily said.

Emily picked up the books and handed them out. The readers fidgeted and whispered. The beginners let the books sit on their laps. The littlest among them began to sniffle. "Marse Harry!" one of them said. "I want Marse Harry!"

Emily appealed to Will, the boy who had deciphered the word c-a-t. She said, "Will? Can you start us today? We can learn of the cat and the rat, and two children named Ann and Nat." McGuffey's was fond of rhymes, which the children had liked when Harry taught them.

Will stared at her, tearless but clearly upset. "I want Marse Harry, too," he said.

The fidgeting in the back room returned to scuffling, and in the front, all the little ones began to sob in earnest. "Marse Harry!" rose as a ragged cry. "We want Marse Harry!"

Emily regarded the disorder with a sinking heart. It was a juvenile insurrection, and she had no authority to quell it.

Light footsteps sounded on the stairs, and Phoebe poked her head into the room. With a surprised expression, Phoebe asked, "Miss Emily? Do you need me?" over the sobs and cries of "Marse Harry!"

"I come to tell them about the refreshment," Phoebe said.

"Biscuit!" Bina called.

Phoebe faced the class. "Hey!" she called over the noise, in a voice like her father's, strong enough to carry over a cotton field. She whistled for good measure, and added, "Quiet!"

They quieted.

Phoebe said, "This a schoolroom! Not a rumpus!"

"We want Marse Harry," Will said.

"Quiet! Miss Emily your teacher now."

"Biscuit?" Bina asked.

Phoebe glared at Bina. "You stay quiet and learn your letters, you get biscuit," she said.

It was quiet. And in the silence, the girl with the baby on her lap held him up to make an announcement. "He wet. And now I all wet, too."

Phoebe sighed, loudly enough to carry to the back of the room. She pointed at the girl. "You come with me. I clean you up, both of you." Then she said to the rest: "When I come back, I bring you biscuit."

In the doorway, she turned. "And you stay quiet until I come back!"

While she was gone, they fidgeted. They shuffled their feet. They whispered. But there were no fights and no cries of "Marse Harry!" Emily watched in pleased surprise. She had seen them behave worse in church.

But when Phoebe returned with the tray, laden with a plate of cornbread and a pitcher of buttermilk, the cry of "Biscuit!" broke out. They rose from the benches, rushed toward the table, and jostled each other in their eagerness to eat and drink.

Phoebe whistled again. She said, "What do you learn from Marse Harry?"

Abashed, Will said, "We wash our hands before we eat."

Bina wailed, "I hungry now! Want to eat now!"

Phoebe stood protectively by the tray of food and said fiercely, "In this room, you do what your teacher say. Used to be Marse Harry, but now it Miss Emily." Phoebe nodded toward the washbasin. "Wash your hands!"

The jostlers, snifflers, scoffers, and whiners bowed to the authority of Phoebe, who had inherited her mother's dignity and her father's voice of command. They washed their hands, and to Emily's astonishment and delight, they waited to eat until Phoebe said grace.

ଛଠଔଓ

AFTER THE CHILDREN FINISHED for the day, Emily remained in the empty room. She had dreaded this day, knowing that she was unprepared, and now she was ashamed of herself. She had no experience as a teacher, and she had none of Harry's gift for teaching. They were only children, but they were dirty, impudent, and little enough to be incontinent. She heard Eliza's disapproving voice—Eliza, who struggled with slavery's legacy and called it ignorance and laziness.

I know better, she thought. As a planter's daughter, she understood slaves and slavery as Eliza Phelps did not. And as an abolitionist, converted in the most painful way possible, she had a well of Christian charity that Eliza seemed to lack.

She would not resent these children, so recently freed, for her own failing. She thought of Phoebe's air of command, inherited from her mother the house servant and her father the driver, both of them subtle in slavery. She might be able to enlist Phoebe to support her where she faltered—in gaining the trust of the newly free.

She would find Phoebe to thank her.

Emily made her way to the kitchen. She had spent little time here, but she thought of the kitchens of her youth, fragrant with the smell of the next meal, where she had eased into the comfort of a sturdy pine chair at the scarred pine table and stroked the soft fur of the kitchen cat that wound around her ankles. She had been welcome in the kitchen of every house she had ever lived in.

She opened the door and felt the heat of the oven billow out. Juno stood at the stove, stirring a pot with a wooden spoon. She turned at the sound of Emily's entrance.

"Yes, Miss Emily?" she asked. Her forehead was slick with sweat, and fatigue shadowed her eyes.

"Excuse me, Maum Juno. I was looking for Phoebe. Is she here?"

"No, Miss Emily. Do you need her?"

"I just wanted to talk to her."

Juno was too well used to slavery to frown, but a cloud passed over her face. "Did she do wrong?"

Emily could hear a long history of Juno's relationship with Missus in the question, and she suspected that Eliza hadn't improved things. "Oh no, Maum Juno," Emily said. "She helped me in the classroom today."

"I hope she don't overstep," Juno said.

"Not at all. I wanted to thank her. Do you know where she is?"

"She in the ice house," Juno said. The ice house was a leftover from the prewar days, to keep food cold and make sherbets even in the heat of summer. Mr. Chapman, who hated spoilage, bought ice from the army.

Emily lingered. She wanted to ask Juno if there was coffee, and she hoped that Juno would ask her to sit while she drank it. But Juno didn't offer either one. Instead she said, "Miss Emily, I need to finish up dinner for Miss Eliza." Her tone was cool.

Emily thought, *Eliza is too much like a missus for Juno's comfort.* She wished she could tell Juno how well she understood. But Juno was not like the cooks of her childhood, bound by slavery to fuss over young miss and treat her with kindness. She thought of the children to whom she was doubly suspect as a guest of the Yankees and a native-born South Carolinian. She was sorry that Juno shared their distrust.

The door opened with no preliminary knock, and

Eliza put her head into the kitchen. She asked, "Juno, is dinner close to ready?"

"It all ready, Miss Eliza. Just keeping hot."

"Did you knead the loaf like I showed you? To give it a fine grain?"

Juno's face tightened. Emily had seen that tiny expression of rebellion on a slave's face many times. When the mistress left, the slave would roll her eyes and say, "Do she think I can't knead a loaf of bread?" Juno said, "The loaf have a fine grain, Miss Eliza."

Emily felt for Juno. She addressed Eliza. "Everyone remarks on how fine Juno's baking is," she said.

Eliza was unmoved. "Emily, come with me."

Emily followed Eliza outside. Eliza walked into the side yard, out of earshot of anyone who might want to listen through the door. She pitched her voice low. "Why were you in the kitchen?"

"I was looking for Phoebe, and it seemed only polite to have some conversation with Juno."

"It causes difficulty if you're familiar with the servants," Eliza said.

Emily was so surprised she nearly laughed. Reprimanded for being familiar with a servant who disliked her! Perversely, she said, "A little kindness goes a long way with these people."

"They are no longer slaves," Eliza said. "They are free, and they need to learn how to act as servants do." She gestured toward the kitchen. "You undermine my authority to teach them when you encourage them like that."

Emily couldn't help it. "That's what my stepmother used to say, too."

Eliza flushed. "Don't try to bait me," she said. "I know who I am and why I'm here." As she turned to go back to the main house, she said, "You'd do well to remember your task, too. You have your work cut out for you."

⁎⁎⁎

BUT IT WAS WELL after dinner, after the dishes had been cleared and washed in the kitchen, when Emily found Phoebe in the back parlor, the feather duster leaning against the leg of the settee on which she sat. *Harper's Weekly* was spread open on her lap. At the sight of Emily, she thrust the paper aside and rose. "Miss Emily."

Emily glanced at the newspaper. Phoebe said, "Just looking at the pictures, Miss Emily."

"You can read," Emily said softly. She had wondered why Phoebe had never attended the school.

Phoebe ducked her head in a way that made Emily recall Juno's words: *Did she do wrong?*

"Phoebe, don't worry. Everyone here would be glad that you can read."

"Miss Eliza might not," Phoebe said. She reached for the duster. "If she expect me to be working."

"How did you learn? Who taught you?"

Phoebe ducked her head again and didn't reply.

⁎⁎⁎

AFTER THAT, WHEN PHOEBE brought the refreshment, she lingered in the classroom. Emily thought of Caro, who had been bold enough to ask her for a book when she was still a slave. That book had begun their friendship and everything that sprang from it. She debated with herself about offering Phoebe such a gift.

Caro had read *Aesop's Fables* as a girl. The Dalton family library had been left untouched after the family fled. Emily would look for a copy.

She hoped that the room would be empty, but she found Mr. Chapman seated at the desk, the ledger open before him. It gave her a twinge. Her father had stared at his ledger with the same expression of concentration and worry.

He looked up. "Miss Jarvie? Is there some way I can help you?"

"Oh, I don't mean to disturb you. I wanted to look for a book." At his expression—a little annoyed—she said quickly, "Not for myself. But for Phoebe. Did you know that she can read?"

"I didn't, but it doesn't surprise me, since her father can."

"Do you know who taught him?"

Mr. Chapman looked thoughtful. "I've never inquired," he said, in a way that meant he would now. "What do you want for Phoebe?"

"I thought that Aesop would suit her."

He turned to study the books. "Do you think you'll find a copy here?"

"If this is like my father's study"—she felt the familiar pain, even speaking of him in passing—"there will be a shelf of the Greek ancients, and Aesop will be among them."

He smiled. "Is Phoebe talented enough to read in Greek?"

"Someday, perhaps," she said, thinking of Caro. "But we'll start with the translation."

She went to the shelves and soon found she was right. She lifted the slim volume from the shelf and opened it. "Oh, she'll like the illustrations," she said.

Mr. Chapman regarded her with an odd expression. A pensive look. He said, "Let Phoebe know that she's welcome to any book she pleases."

∞∞

EMILY SOUGHT PHOEBE IN the parlor and interrupted her dusting. She asked Phoebe to sit and offered her the book.

Phoebe took it tentatively. "For me?" she asked.

"Yes, for you, with Mr. Chapman's blessing."

Phoebe opened with book with care and turned the pages with equal care. "Pictures, Miss Emily!"

"It's a book of tales about animals. Every tale has a moral."

Phoebe laughed. "Like Br'er Rabbit and Br'er Fox!" she said. "But writ down."

Emily knew those tales, too. Every white child with a slave nurse knew them.

A few days later, when Emily had reason to be in the kitchen, Juno looked up from kneading bread to wipe her hands, and to say stiffly, "You give my girl a book."

"Yes," Emily said, thinking again of Caro.

As though it cost her, Juno said, "Wanted to thank you."

"You're welcome," Emily said.

"She read them stories to me. To Rufus, too. He like the story about the ant and the grasshopper."

Of course he would.

"Maum Juno, do you think Phoebe would like to continue her education?"

Juno raised her eyes to Emily's, and Emily saw how she struggled, her hopes for Phoebe warring with her wariness about Emily. "She already read and write and cipher. Do she need more?"

Emily thought again of Caro. "She might have it, if she wanted to."

Juno pursed her lips. "Don't want her so educate that no one marry her!" she said, and Emily saw how hope and fear still contended in her.

☙❧

PHOEBE'S CLEVERNESS—AND THE FUTURE it might summon for her—troubled the water of Emily's conscience, as Asa Reed's rebukes had back in Cincinnati.

On a hot summer day after class, they made their way to the kitchen together. Phoebe carried the tray, and Emily, not wanting to burden her further, carried the slop jar.

"Miss Emily, they do good today," Phoebe said.

"With your help."

"Oh, such a little thing, Miss Emily."

Emily halted to look Phoebe in the face. "God sees everything we do, even the littlest things," she said. Her heart pounded, but she tried to keep her voice light. "Phoebe, might you consider helping me in the classroom?"

"More than I do now?"

"Instead of working in the house."

Phoebe drew in her breath. "Like my mama say, don't want to overstep."

"Oh, Phoebe. It's not overstepping to use the intelligence God gave you."

As a fervent congregant at the Brick Church, Phoebe considered this, her brows slightly furrowed. She said, "My mama and daddy have to say yes. And so do Miss Eliza."

"Not asking?" Emily said, laughing. "I wouldn't dream of it. Now that would be overstepping!"

In the kitchen, they found Phoebe's father at the table with her mother. Rufus put down his coffee cup and rose at the sight of Emily.

Emily said, "Please, don't get up for me."

He hesitated, but he obeyed her.

Emily took a deep breath and glanced from Rufus to Juno. "I want to talk to you about Phoebe." Hastily, she said, "No, nothing wrong. Something right, in fact." She gestured toward the chair. "May I sit?"

Both Rufus and Juno suddenly realized the anomaly of making a white person ask for a courtesy. "Of course, Miss Emily," Juno said, a little flustered, as Rufus pulled out the chair for her.

As Emily outlined her plan, Juno's face brightened. Emily had never seen her look so pleased. But she tamped down her own hopes, clearly not wanting to dash Phoebe's. After she composed herself, she said, "It ain't up to either of us. It up to Miss Eliza."

Eliza, whom Juno saw as a missus in Yankee guise. Eliza, who bristled at anything Emily suggested. Eliza, who felt that servants belonged in their proper place.

In the silence, Juno leaned forward, her eyes bright. "Won't do me any good to talk to Miss Eliza. But you, Miss Emily, you get on with Marse Harry, and Miss Eliza think the world of her brother. Do anything he ask."

Rufus smiled and Phoebe smothered her laughter behind her hand. They had all read Aesop together, but they knew Br'er Rabbit better.

∞⌀

AFTER MIDDAY DINNER, EMILY followed Harry into the foyer, where he put on his hat before returning to the fields. She asked him, "Mr. Phelps, may I walk with you?"

"Of course, Miss Jarvie," he said, offering her his arm.

They saw Eliza, who had lingered in the dining room and now hesitated in the hall. Her eyes rested on the two of them, taking in Harry's gesture. Harry flushed and took his arm away. "What is it, Eliza?"

"I wanted to make sure you were wearing your hat," she said, as though he were a little boy who needed chiding.

He adjusted the hat on his head. "Of course I am."

Eliza cast her gaze on Emily. "Remember your bonnet," she said, making it sound like a moral failing to go without one.

Emily felt an unladylike irritation, but she said sweetly, "Yes, ma'am," as her mother and stepmother and Madame Deveraux at her finishing school had taught her. Ladies, like former slaves, knew how to fox those in command.

Careful to keep a polite distance, Emily descended the front steps with Harry, and she waited until they were out of sight of the house to make her request. In the shadow of the trees that separated the house from the path to the fields, she halted and turned to him. "I have something to ask of you," she said. When his face brightened, she swiftly added, "It's about the school."

"What is it, Miss Jarvie?"

"It's about Phoebe. She's been a great help to me in the classroom." She told him how, and she told him about her hope for Phoebe.

"I wish I had seen that," he said.

"Now we both know."

"What shall we do about it, Miss Jarvie?"

She warmed to hear the echoed "we." Common cause. "I would like—I would hope—to make her my assistant."

"To pay her for it?"

"I hadn't got that far, but it would be right, wouldn't it? There's something else I'm worried about."

"What worries you?" he asked.

It gladdened her to hear his concern for her. "I don't mean to speak ill," she said.

He smiled. "You foresee a difficulty with my sister."

"She's been clear that Phoebe has duties in the house."

"And you'd like to release Phoebe from them. To dedicate her to the classroom."

"Yes." She lowered her head and raised her eyes at the same time. Why did she always act the belle when she felt nervous? "Could you speak to her? She takes everything from you in the best possible light."

He said, "My sister doesn't always spare me, Miss Jarvie."

Emily said, "She's kinder with you than with anyone else, Mr. Phelps. Everyone sees that."

He rubbed his face. "Oh, Eliza," he said ruefully. "My poor Eliza."

She was surprised by the rueful look on his face. "Is she kinder than I know? Tell me."

He said, "She hasn't had an easy life. When my mother died, she was old enough to raise me. And once I was old enough, Father wasn't well, and she looked after him. She never married because of it. When I decided to come South, she insisted on coming with me. She never liked it, and she was longing to go home when the Education Commission sent you to take over for me. She chose to stay to chaperone you. She never acts to please herself. She never has."

"It doesn't seem to make her happy."

"She lives for her duty, but her soul is kind. But she has a great deal of difficulty letting anyone see it."

She said, "Would you ask her? Tap that kindness?" She nearly said, "For Phoebe's sake," when she recognized the expression on Harry Phelps's face.

That expression said, *I will do it for you.* He looked away and spoke in a low voice. "I'll do my best."

☙CR

IF ELIZA WERE A different kind of woman, they would buttonhole her before the dinner hour and give her a glass of wine to ease their way. But Eliza was as fierce for temperance as she was against slavery. They had to bring her into the parlor with only a glass of water to aid them as Harry made an entreaty for Phoebe.

Eliza looked from Harry to Emily. "Of course I won't stand in the way of the girl's education."

"Thank you, Miss Phelps," Emily said, weak with relief.

"Did you really think I would?" At Emily's embarrassed silence, she said, "What you must think of me."

Trying to tease, Harry said, "You are very firm in your convictions, Eliza. Very firm!"

She fixed Emily with a sharp look. "I don't like being got round, as the people here say. Did her mother put you up to this, Miss Jarvie? Did her father?"

"They were pleased with the idea," Emily said, which was the truth.

"Did you put my brother up to this? To get round me?"

When Emily didn't reply, Eliza asked, "Did she, Harry?"

Harry tried to make light of it. "Miss Jarvie can be very persuasive."

"Yes," Eliza said, looking at her brother as though she'd found him with his fingers in the jam jar. "She certainly can. Especially with you."

ഓര

THE NEXT DAY, WHEN Emily came into the kitchen, Juno said, "Will you set? I have fresh coffee, and there's biscuit, too."

She sat in the pine chair and rested her hands on the scarred pine table. Juno's cat, which usually slept under the table, woke to twine around her ankles. She reached down to rub the soft fur and scratch the fragile ears.

A cup of coffee, freely offered. She smiled as she accepted it from Juno's hands.

As Emily drank, Juno said, "Miss Emily, can't tell you how glad I am for what you do for Phoebe."

Emily set the cup down. "It delights me too, Maum Juno. I can't think of anyone who deserves it more."

As Emily sipped, Juno asked, "Been meaning to ask, Miss Emily. Is you connected with the Jarvie who used to live on the island?"

"Mr. James Jarvie? Yes, he was my uncle."

"And the Jarvies who own a big place on the main? Is they any kin to you?"

Emily said stiffly, "That's Lawrence Jarvie, my father."

Juno regarded her with surprise. "Then why you come here to Port Royal, to be with the Yankees?"

Oh, to tell the whole of it. She said, "I came because I hated slavery too much to stay in South Carolina."

"A slave owner's daughter? Marse Jarvie's daughter?"

"I came to disagree with my family about slavery—so much that I left for the North before the war."

Juno gave her a long, appraising look. "And you don't go with their blessing."

"No. Not at all. After I left, they never wrote to me. Not even before the war, when they were still able to."

"They cast you out?" Juno asked.

The flight. The steamship. The slave catcher. The price on her head. It was too easy to remember. "Yes. And I cast them out, too."

ഔൽ

SEVERAL DAYS LATER, WHEN Harry had left the room after midday dinner, Eliza turned to Emily, her face inscrutable and her tone cold. "Come with me. I'd like to speak to you in private."

"Of course, Miss Phelps," she said pleasantly, wondering what Eliza could possibly chastise her for after being so agreeable about Phoebe.

Eliza led her into the back parlor, a place for ladies

to speak in confidence. How much gossip had this room seen? How much whispered anger and sadness?

Eliza took the chair. As she sat, she didn't arrange her skirt, but she straightened her back so that it would not touch the chair. Emily had never seen her sit in a relaxed posture.

Emily took the settee. If she was going to hear a lecture, she might as well be comfortable. "What is it, Miss Phelps?"

Eliza knotted her hands in her lap. By the standards of a Southern lady, those hands were red and coarse. Her hands saw rough soap and hot water, and Eliza was proud that she shared the tasks she ordered of her servants. She raised her head. "You understand that when you came here, I was charged with supervising your conduct and your morals, since you are very young to be a missionary and a teacher."

"Of course." Why did she feel guilty? She had no reason to.

"I'm very disappointed in you."

"What's the matter, Miss Phelps?" As always when she felt her nerves, the belle's tone rushed back. She knew how much Eliza disliked it, but it was like a cough, something she couldn't prevent.

Two bright spots of color appeared on Eliza's cheeks. She said, "It's very wrong of you to encourage my brother."

Why would she think so? Why would she say so? Emily felt herself flush. "But I haven't encouraged him."

"I've seen you."

Emily now sat up straight. She would have no comfort, even on the settee. "What have you seen?"

"You walk together. Laugh together."

"As friends do. I'm honored that he considers me a friend."

"I saw you put your hand on his arm. And I saw him put his arm through yours."

"Courtesies that ladies and gentlemen offer one another. Nothing more."

Eliza leaned forward. "You must stop it."

"Friendship? Kindness?"

"Encouragement," Eliza said, her posture even more rigid than before. "Nothing could be more unsuitable."

Emily leaned forward and allowed herself a spark of anger. "You're absolutely right. Since I'm an engaged woman, promised to the man I love, who loves me. Encouragement! I encourage him in his duties as a superintendent, and if I tease him, the way a sister or a cousin might, there's no harm in it! Should I stop that, Miss Phelps?"

Eliza sat unmoving. "I'm well acquainted with the Reverend Channing in Boston," she said. "I could easily persuade him that you're no longer suited to be a teacher."

"Would you? Insist that a dedicated teacher, a missionary loyal to the task of uplifting the enslaved, be removed from her position because she has been pleasant to one of the superintendents?"

The red spots on Eliza's cheeks faded to a frosty paleness. "I wonder about your loyalties."

Emily was so angry that she felt dizzy. She longed to tell Eliza Phelps the truth about herself and Caro. Only her fear for Caro stayed her tongue. Trembling, she said, "I believe I have shown my loyalties, Miss Phelps. Every day since I've come here."

Eliza rose. "Leave Harry alone. And do your duty." In a swish of narrow skirt, she was gone.

Chapter 4: The War Comes to Ohio

When Caro returned from her visit to the *Gazette*, Asa Reed said nothing, even though he couldn't hide the worry on his face. But he was kind enough not to pry by asking right away. Not at that moment. He waited several days.

When he did, she said, "Mr. Perry was very rude to me."

Crestfallen, he said, "I warned you."

"Well, you were right," she said. Her eyes stung, but she blinked back the tears. "I could write for the *Gazette*. Certainly I'm good enough. I know that you think so."

"Oh, Miss Jarvie," he said, and the sympathy in his voice made her eyes sting even worse. "I do. But you should seek out a newspaper that will welcome you. Like the *Liberator*."

She recalled the words on the masthead of the paper in the Bakers' living room: *For the dissemination of religion, morality, literature, and science.* She said, "Or the *Christian Recorder*." At his puzzled look, she added, "The newspaper published by the African Methodist Episcopal Church."

His face lit up. "Even better."

"Mr. Reed, will you help me?"

He reached for her hands. She looked down, and he blushed, taking his hands away. "You know that I will."

"Will you write to the editor of the *Christian Recorder* on my behalf?"

He was brisk and businesslike again. "Miss Jarvie, I can do better than that," he said. "I can recommend you highly."

She brushed her eyes with her hand. She blinked hard. "Mr. Reed, was your father a kind man?"

"By all reports, and by my own recollection, he was."

"You do his memory justice," she said.

⊱⊰

THE *Christian Recorder* COVERED the war from the antislavery point of view, and many of the pieces were written by correspondents on the battlefronts in Virginia and Tennessee. The Bakers read the paper from cover to cover. Mr. Baker had just finished the new issue before dinner.

At dinner, just after Asa Reed had made his promise, Caro asked Mr. Baker, "What is the latest news in the *Recorder*?"

He ignored his wife's stern look. Mrs. Baker encouraged polite conversation at the table, and war was hardly genteel. He said, "News of the plight of the contrabands, which grows greater every day," he said. "And agitation for making them into free men."

"Is there any news of South Carolina?"

"No, since the war is lukewarm there."

"Nothing about Port Royal?"

Mrs. Baker said, "I thought you heard all the news of Port Royal from your cousin."

"Oh, I hear from her," Caro said. "I wondered if the *Recorder* had sent a correspondent to the Sea Islands." She gave Mr. Baker a sidelong glance, the kind that had once beguiled and persuaded her father. "Because of the condition of the contrabands there."

He sighed. "There's so little news of the fate of people of color," he said. "Your cousin's letters are better than any correspondent's." He brightened a little. "Perhaps she would send them to the *Recorder*."

Caro gave Mrs. Baker a sidelong glance, too, even though it had never worked on her mother. She said, "Or perhaps I might go there to write for them."

Mrs. Baker drew in her breath. "Caro, how could you think of going south?"

Inside, she wavered, but she lifted her chin, feeling defiant. "At Port Royal, I wouldn't be a fugitive," she said. "I'd be a contraband."

Mrs. Baker shuddered. "I couldn't tolerate it," she said. "Ezra," she entreated her husband, "talk her out of it so that we don't have to forbid her."

Mr. Baker said, "Caro, you know—better than I can

tell you—that it's not safe for a young lady of color to go to the South."

"Port Royal is protected by the might of the Union army," Caro said. "I can't imagine anywhere that I'd be safer."

"No," Mrs. Baker said. "Ohio is safer. You aren't going anywhere, until you go back to the college at Oberlin."

In the kindest way possible, they had forbidden her. Even though she feared going south as much as she longed to, she hated to be forbidden.

℘℧

THE HOSTILITY OF THE white men who lived adjacent to Bucktown, the Irishmen, had never abated, and every day, as Caro walked home from the magazine's office, she braved the gauntlet of their gazes and their insulting remarks. Often, Mr. Holloway caught up with her, taking her arm in his fatherly way. It didn't help that he was at her side. As much as she fought her fear, she was still afraid, and wished more than ever that it would ease her mind to pray.

On a day in July, when the heat of the South seemed to seep across the Kentucky border to make Ohio a Southern state, too, Mr. Holloway appeared at the office of *Hearth and Home* at closing time. Reed asked who he was, in the politest of tones, and Caro explained, "Mr. Holloway is a deacon at the AME Church," she said. "He's well acquainted with the Baker family."

To her surprise, Mr. Holloway said, "Let me escort you all the way home today, Miss Jarvie."

Asa Reed asked, "Is there some trouble? Should I send Miss Jarvie home in a hansom?"

"No, suh. Just a little scuffle down at the docks. No love lost between white stevedore and black. I feel better if I take care of Miss Jarvie."

Asa frowned. "I don't like it."

"None of us do," Mr. Holloway said, as Caro put on her bonnet.

As they walked, Mr. Holloway kept a tight grip on her arm. Caro said, "I know you're worried. It's more than a little dustup at the docks."

Mr. Holloway's mouth tightened. "Mr. Baker will tell you all about it when you get home safe," he said. "I don't want to alarm you."

Of course she was alarmed. As with everyone who had lived in Charleston, black as well as white, the thought of insurrection was never far from her mind. "Now you have," she said, swallowing hard.

"Hush," Mr. Holloway said.

But they walked through the streets and into Bucktown without incident, only the usual sullen stares and mutterings about "jumped-up niggers." On the Bakers' doorstep, Mr. Holloway let go her arm, but he remained to watch as she knocked on the door, and Mrs. Baker opened it to let her inside.

When she tried to untie her bonnet, her fingers were

trembling. She asked Mrs. Baker, "Did you hear about the trouble today?"

Mrs. Baker sighed and smoothed her skirt with her palms. "It won't get any worse while you take off your bonnet and wash your face and sit down to dinner," she said.

As agitated as she felt, Caro waited to speak. She murmured the words of grace with impatience and fidgeted as Mr. Baker passed the dishes around. It seemed rude to upset everyone while they were eating. The smell of Mrs. Baker's good meal, pork roast with mashed potatoes and greens, aggravated the knot in Caro's stomach, and she toyed with her food rather than eating it. Amanda noticed and spoke to Caro as though she were younger than little Lucy. "Caro, don't play with your food. Eat it."

Caro put down her fork. She said, "Mr. Baker, may I ask you about the news of the day?"

"Surely," he said. "What news, Miss Caro?"

"The trouble down at the docks."

"Oh, the scuffle between the stevedores?"

Hiram, the married son, said, "It was more than a scuffle, Papa. There was a fight. A black man struck a white man, and the white men attacked all the black stevedores. The police called it a riot."

"It's unfortunate, but it has nothing to do with us," Mr. Baker said.

Hiram curled his hand into a fist. "It should," he said. "If only we could join the militia."

"No," his father said.

"If we could prove ourselves as soldiers!"

Mr. Baker shook his head. He spoke to Caro, whose worry still roiled her stomach and pounded at her temples. "We went to the police, we men of color. We offered to join the militia, to keep order in the city or to defend it, if the Confederates made good on their threat to cross our border. And do you know what the chief of police told us?"

"Nothing good," Caro said, curling her own hands into fists.

"He said, 'This is a white man's fight. You damned niggers stay out of it.'" He admonished Hiram, "That's why we'll keep our heads down. It's not of concern to us."

Caro thought of the runaways who had hidden in this house a few weeks ago, and her fear worsened.

∽◯◎

THE NEXT TWO DAYS passed without incident, but rumors of trouble flew through the city, especially in Bucktown, where people were jumpy. The city council, also nervous about the Confederate threat to the South, decided to send more than a hundred militia men to join the troops. Caro watched this development with alarm. She said to Mr. Baker, "What if there's trouble? Who will stop it?"

By Sunday, worry threaded through every conversation. Even though Mrs. Baker struggled to maintain the usual Sunday ritual over dinner, and Mr. Baker silenced all conversation about trouble, violence, and the militia, the atmosphere in the Baker house was quiet and strained. Caro pressed her fist to the knot in her stomach as though she could knead it away. She still felt too sick to eat.

Amanda and Lucy tried to entice Caro with the newest issue of *Godey's Lady's Book*. Caro waved it away. Amanda said to Lucy, "I never saw her refuse to look at a dress pattern before!" But her laugh was brittle. Under her effort to stay calm, she was rattled, too.

Caro tried not to snap. "On occasion, I think about something more important than a dress pattern," she said.

"Girls, girls," Mrs. Baker said. "Don't fuss. It doesn't help."

Caro cried out, "Does it help to pretend that nothing is wrong?"

Then they heard it. The shouting. A crowd large enough to drown out any one man's words. A roaring sound, like an oncoming train.

Caro rose and ran to the window. "What is that?"

Mr. Baker pulled her from the window. "Don't stand there," he said.

Before she could move, she saw the crowd surge down their street. White men. Irishmen. Angry men. Shouting. Roaring.

Something hit the house. The sound was irregular, dull and thudding, and she thought wildly that it had begun to hail. But it was accompanied by shouts.

Mr. Baker dragged her into the middle of the room. His face grim, he said, "All of you, go upstairs. Stay in the hall. Lie on the floor. Don't get up, and don't make a sound."

"What's happening?" Caro cried.

"There's a crowd throwing stones at the house! Get upstairs, and hurry!"

Amanda grabbed Caro's wrist hard enough to hurt and hauled her up the stairs. Now that Caro knew what the sound was—stones hurled by white men, propelled by hatred—she thought she would faint. Amanda fell to the floor, taking Caro with her.

Lucy whimpered. Mrs. Baker reached out to stroke her hair. "Hush," she whispered.

Caro pressed her fist to her mouth, struggling not to cry out. The hail of stones continued, dull and thudding. She could hear laughter and jeering voices: "Niggers, are you afraid now?"

What if they broke in?

A sob escaped her lips. Mrs. Baker's whisper was fierce: "Hush! The runaways keep quiet, and so will you."

I am a runaway.

Over the shouting and the laughter, a new shout emerged, a bellow. "Police! Police! Break it up, boys! Break it up!"

More shouting: "Scare them niggers..."

And an even louder bellow: "Break it up!"

The hail of stones diminished. The shouting subsided. And then both stopped. The crowd's noise dropped to an angry mumble, and footsteps shuffled on the street as a group of disgruntled men were herded away by the police.

Someone was shouting, but it was far away. Outside their windows, it was quiet again.

Mr. Baker and Hiram ran up the stairs, their feet thunderous in their worry. Mrs. Baker rose, and Amanda, who had not let go of Caro's wrist, hauled her up. Mr. Baker threw his arms around all of them without discrimination. "They're gone," he said, a sob catching in his throat. "It's all right."

Caro leaned into Mr. Baker's expansive hug. Her wrist throbbed from Amanda's grip, and her eyes ached with tears.

≈⁂≈

THE HOUSE HAD SUSTAINED little damage—only a few nicks and dents to its siding—but Mrs. Baker was upset enough to forbid Caro to leave for work the next day. "It isn't safe for you to go out."

"But Mr. Reed expects me," she said, wanting very badly to leave Bucktown and to think of something besides being in danger.

"Send him a note."

Evidently it was safe for a ragged little boy to take a note to the office of *Hearth and Home*. Caro spent the day in a wretched state of agitation. It was quite familiar. When she had run away from her master's house in Charleston, she had been confined to her refuge in Charleston Neck, forbidden to leave the house, afraid to look out the windows, too worried to settle her mind to a chore or a book.

She felt like that now.

That afternoon, when the knock sounded on the door, even Mrs. Baker started. She said, "I'll get it," and Caro sat on the edge of her chair, catching the fear in the room as though it were a fever.

But it was Asa Reed.

Mrs. Baker did her best to behave as though he were an ordinary visitor, offering him Mr. Baker's wing chair and refreshment. He perched on the edge of the chair—much too big for his frame—and said quietly, "Don't trouble yourself, Mrs. Baker. I came to see if Miss Jarvie was all right."

Caro pressed her hands into her skirt to control the way they trembled. "We're all right, Mr. Reed."

"I heard about the trouble last night."

Mrs. Baker said firmly, "The police came in time."

"Miss Jarvie, I came to offer you the safety of my mother's house. We would be glad to aid you."

Mrs. Baker's expression hardened. She struggled to be polite. "Mr. Reed, that's thoughtful of you, but Miss Jarvie should remain here."

Caro said, "Why doesn't anyone ask me what I think?"

Mrs. Baker ignored her. She said to Reed, "Sir, thank you, but this is trouble, and you don't want to be part of it."

"My father, the antislavery man, felt differently."

Mrs. Baker shook her head. "She stays here. And she'll be back in the office when it's safe again."

Reed sighed. He rose and extended his hand to Mrs.

Baker. Mrs. Baker hesitated before she took it. Reed said, "I'm very sorry for all of this."

Caro heard a voice from Charleston that had been quiet for mouths. It was Sophy. Sophy's voice echoed in her head: *Sorry ain't good enough.*

∞⟩⟨∞

THE NEXT DAY, THE rumors flew and the newspaper confirmed them. Groups of white men gathered to assure each other that "the niggers would be cleaned out." Up and down the streets of Bucktown, their neighbors packed a few things and left, in too much of a hurry to explain where they'd gone. At midday dinner, which no one was hungry for, Mrs. Baker asked her husband, "Should we leave too?"

"Of course not."

Mrs. Baker glanced around the room as though the parlor held danger. "Should we stay here to be 'cleaned out'?"

"No. We'll stay here to defend ourselves."

"Against a mob of white men who hate us?"

Mr. Baker had gone as grim as a Union army officer. "We have rifles, Hiram and I. We'll barricade the door and board up the windows. And if there's trouble, all of you will go upstairs and lay low on the floor and be as quiet as mice in a church."

Caro felt a wave of panic. She asked, "Will you give me a rifle, too?"

"Do you know how to shoot?" Mr. Baker asked.

"I could learn." It would ease her panic to heft a gun and feel that she might be able to defend herself.

"Not today," Mr. Baker said.

After dinner, Caro watched as Mr. Baker lashed a broom handle across the door and piled the heaviest chairs against it, as he nailed boards across the first-story windows. It was like preparing for a hurricane and an insurrection at the same time, and she was so much on edge that she wished she could drink enough to be insensible.

Hardly wise, if she might need to defend herself.

They sat in the darkened parlor, their eyes traveling to the barricaded door, and waited. Mr. Baker and Hiram sat with their rifles over their laps. Hiram's eyes gleamed. "Not a nigger's fight, is it?"

At six in the evening, it began.

They could hear a crowd surging, tromping, and shouting. Then the sound of glass breaking. And a great yell from the crowd.

The crowd roamed through Bucktown, shouting, "Clear out them niggers" as they smashed windows where they could. The noise seemed to come from every direction.

When the glass broke on a house down the street, Mr. Baker ordered them upstairs. Amanda reached for Lucy's hand and for Caro's. Caro said, "Don't grab my wrist." She was hoarse with anxiety. "It still hurts from yesterday."

Amanda's face had gone gray. She whispered, "I'm so afraid."

Caro swallowed hard. "Then take my hand, but be careful."

It was agony to lie facedown on the hallway carpet and to hear the shouting and the breaking glass. Lucy whispered, "Mama, will they kill us?"

Mrs. Baker broke the silence. "No!" she said sharply.

Then the gunshots began. Fire and returning fire, a deadly popcorn. How far away were they? The shouting got louder, and so did the sound of gunshots. They all heard the thud from downstairs. Someone had fired a bullet at the house.

And the returning crackle of fire echoed soon after.

Caro closed her eyes. They would storm the house. They would find her. She would go back to South Carolina in manacles. She would become Lawrence Jarvie's property. Once again, she would be a slave.

Gunfire. Call and response. A sharp pop when the bullet went wide. A dull thud when it struck the house.

Someone yelled, "Niggers, are you afraid now?"

Mr. Baker and Hiram were too prudent to reply. They didn't speak. They shot.

More gunfire.

Then a disgusted cry. "They ain't scared. Why waste a bullet?"

And miraculously, the sound of the crowd moving, yelling as it went, hotheads still shooting at something, and then the sound of glass breaking next door, where the house was empty.

೮೦೮೩

BY THE TIME ORDER was restored, Bucktown was deserted, since so many people of color had fled to the countryside. Houses up and down the Bakers' street had been vandalized. The AME Church and the Shakespeare House had lost most of their windows. Upset as she was, Caro found some humor in learning that the house of God and the house of ill repute had suffered the same fate.

Caro and Mrs. Baker watched as Mr. Baker removed the boards from their windows. Most of the houses along the block had been vandalized. Where the residents had fled, the broken glass had remained on the front yards and the sidewalks.

Mrs. Baker bent close to put her finger in a depression in the wood. "Bullet hole," she said, and her composure crumbled. She wiped a tear from her cheek. "Could have hit any of us." She glanced at Caro. "You don't have to go south to be at war. The war has come to you."

৯৩৫

THAT NIGHT, CARO BLEW out the candle and settled down to try to sleep. For a moment she longed for the luxurious bed in her room on her father's plantation, a mahogany four-poster with silk curtains, swathed in netting to keep the mosquitoes away. She could still remember the feel of sheets made of Sea Island cotton against her skin. She sighed, pulling the quilt up to her chin as though it would really comfort her. She sighed again and closed her eyes in the summer darkness.

And tonight it came to her, the memory she pushed away in daylight.

The steamship. She walked down the corridor in the darkness, a heavy tray in her hands. She moved slowly, so slowly. She tried to hurry, but the tray was too heavy and at every step, the cups rattled. Footsteps echoed behind her. She turned her head to stare down the dim corridor.

He was behind her, and he was coming closer.

Closer.

And closer.

She woke to hear herself screaming. Ashamed through her terror, she thought: "I'll wake the whole house." She forced herself to stop and began to quietly sob instead.

෨෬

CARO RETURNED TO WORK the next day. As she walked through the streets of white Cincinnati, she was astonished to see that it had suffered no damage. For white Cincinnati, the riot was far away, an ugly tale in the newspapers, a difficulty that people of color had brought on themselves. A random shout in the street made her flinch, and she tried not to bolt.

When she opened the door, Asa Reed rose from his desk, his face full of concern. "Are you all right, Miss Jarvie?"

"I wasn't hurt," she said, going to her desk, taking off her gloves, then her bonnet, as she always did, trying to find respite in the ordinary.

He observed her keenly, and she was sure he saw her tremble. His normally amicable expression changed as he struggled to find some words of apology or consolation, but he couldn't.

She said, "There's nothing to say, is there?"

He nodded.

She rested her hands on her desk to steady herself. She met his eyes. That pale gaze was saddened and troubled.

She said, "I'm a fugitive slave."

"I always thought so," he said.

She took a deep breath. "I'm not safe here. I'm not safe anywhere." It was a relief to admit to it. "Don't argue with me."

"I won't."

She took a deep breath. "I've decided that I might as well go south to fight."

"What about your education?" he asked softly.

"This is important, too."

"Get the degree if you can," he said, the staunch Oberlin man. "That's another way to fight."

She knew he meant to be kind. But her resolve made her short with him. "You don't have to tell me." She would go back to Oberlin for another term while she made her arrangements. But not because he entreated her.

"You'll go to Port Royal?" Where the Union Army held sway.

"To the Sea Islands. Back home."

Chapter 5: Soldiers and Traitors

AFTER SHE DISMISSED HER scholars, Emily slipped from the classroom and made her way down the stairs. Now that Phoebe kept them in order, they behaved better, but they still pined for Marse Harry. Emily sighed. Harry had been wrong. These children had not come to love her.

At the foot of the stairs, she found Mattie Easton. Mattie visited Ocean Point every week since someone always needed medical attention. She was wiping her hands on her skirt. She said to Emily, "It's all right. I washed my hands well at the pump."

"Is anyone ill?"

"Cuts and scrapes. Nothing serious." She observed Emily carefully. "Now you look peaked, my dear."

To Emily's surprise, Mattie had become her friend—as Phoebe could not and as Harry should not. Mattie had guessed early on that Eliza rubbed her the wrong way. "You don't get on with her," Mattie had said.

"It's unchristian of me."

"Nonsense," Mattie had said cheerfully. She was matter-of-fact about religion, as she was about the human body and its ailments. "Miss Phelps makes herself disagreeable. Has she said something mean to you?"

"Mattie, she isn't mean. She's just thoughtless."

Mattie had squeezed Emily around the shoulders in a sisterly embrace. "As though that's better," she said, her eyes agleam.

Since Eliza had chastised her, Emily kept her distance, not wanting to feel the edge of her tongue again. More painfully, that also meant keeping her distance from Harry. She was so hungry for warmth that hearing Mattie call her "my dear" made her eyes sting a little. She tried to joke. "No castor oil, please. Miss Phelps already offered me some."

"Castor oil is nasty stuff. I prefer a lighter touch. A little happiness, perhaps, to bring the color back to your cheeks."

Happiness seemed far away. Every day, she wondered why she had come to the Sea Islands and why she remained there. The thought of returning to Ohio gave her no pleasure, either. Joshua's letters from Virginia would follow her, and she would anticipate each one with the dread of learning that he had been shot or that he was dead.

She said, "Happiness in the midst of war? It seems wrong."

It was early fall, cotton harvest time, when the heat of summer had waned enough for the breeze to feel pleasant against the skin. The fragrant trees of the islands continued to bloom, and the air still smelled of magnolia and heshaberry. The crickets, more active in fall than in summer, buzzed and rasped outside. On St. Helena Island, the war seemed far away.

Mattie put a light hand on Emily's arm. "Especially in the midst of war," she said.

Emily stared at Mattie's hand, the skin freckled, the veins prominent, the nails scrubbed clean. She forced herself to sound light. "Doctor's orders?"

"No. Only a friend's hope for you."

Suddenly Emily longed to tell Mattie the real trouble that took the bloom from her cheeks. Her secrets pressed against her chest like a flood against a levee. Her worry for Joshua and her regret over Harry were nothing to the burden that she carried to protect Caro.

෨෬

A FEW DAYS LATER, on Saturday evening, Captain Charles Trowbridge joined the Phelpses at dinner. Emily knew him slightly, as she knew most of the Union army officers. Like Chapman, Trowbridge had been an engineer before the war. His military task was to build bridges and fortifications, and he led a brigade of contrabands, ex-slaves who carried shovels. For the few months that General Hunter headed a black regiment, Trowbridge had drilled the contrabands as soldiers, but when the regiment had disbanded in August—there was no money to pay black soldiers—Trowbridge returned to his earthworks.

He was surprised by her accent. She was polite as she explained. "I grew up in Charleston," she said.

"But you've joined us now."

Emily tried to sound light. "My crisis of conscience is so well-known here that I'm surprised you hadn't heard of it," she said.

"I hadn't, and I beg your pardon, Miss Jarvie," he said.

She liked him better for that.

Harry asked Trowbridge, "Captain, how goes the war?"

Trowbridge laughed. "As usual," he said. "We build earthworks. We welcome the contrabands who risk their lives to come to us. And we skirmish with the secesh pickets. Someday we may take the railroad behind the lines at Pocotaligo. But anyone who wants a pitched battle won't get one in the Low Country."

Harry said, "I heard you captured some Confederate prisoners."

"Did you?" Trowbridge asked. "The soldiers are worse gossips than schoolgirls. Yes, we did. Officers of the Charleston Light Dragoons." He shook his head. "The Charleston Light Dragoons are the worst soldiers I ever saw. None of them carried a rifle, just pistols and swords. I don't know what war they think they're fighting." He glanced at Eliza. "And when we captured them, they were so drunk, I'm surprised they could seat a horse."

"Shameful," Eliza said.

"Once they were our prisoners, they showed nothing but contempt," Trowbridge said. "For us. For the Union. And for the cause we hold dear." Now he looked at Emily. "They boasted to us that they had shot a former slave who was running to us. Chased him through the woods and shot him, as though they were hunting for sport. They laughed to think they had killed him."

Runaways. Fugitives. Emily thought of Caro, not safe enough in Ohio, and a wave of fear passed through her. "Your prisoners, who are they? Where are they from?"

"Might you know them?"

Emily flushed. "Very likely."

"Local men. The family name is Hayward. Stephen and John Hayward."

The Haywards owned the place just up the river from her father's in Colleton County. The Hayward brothers had never been her friends, and when she got old enough, they had never been among her beaus, either. They liked horses, drink, and cards, in that order, and their only advantage for a Low Country planter's daughter was that their father was a richer planter than hers: a thousand acres in rice and cotton and six hundred hands to work it. In addition to the place in Colleton County, they had a mansion in Charleston and a pleasant summer house in the pines.

Before the war, the eldest son had been sent to Germany to study, a kind of finishing for young men. He read literature and philosophy and bought so many pictures that they had come back in two dozen crates. The younger boys were a different matter altogether, gentlemen only by rank. Like most younger sons in the Low Country, their main occupation was to wait for their father to grant them something useful to do. While they waited, they fell into dissipation. Before the war, they joined the Charleston Light Dragoons for their drinking parties. Being initiated into the Dragoons, Emily heard, was a matter of providing enough drink for the existing troop to drink itself into a stupor.

"Yes, I knew them before the war," Emily said. "I played with them when I was a little girl. The family used to visit my father's place in Colleton County. And I danced with them, all of them, in Charleston the year I came out."

"Were they gallant before the war?" Trowbridge said.

"Oh, they never were," she said. "It seems the war hasn't improved them." She was trembling. She lowered her hands into her lap to hide her agitation.

Eliza asked, "What are you going to do with them, Captain?"

"We don't like them, but they're prisoners of war, like any other. We won't mistreat them, but we expect them to behave themselves decently, and if they want to be released anytime soon, they'll tell us what they know about their commander's plans, especially for the defense of the railroad."

"And they haven't been forthcoming," Harry said.

Trowbridge glanced at Emily. "No. Nothing but contempt."

Emily knotted her hands in her lap. Loyalty and disloyalty roiled inside her as though she had been drinking. "Perhaps I could help you."

"How, Miss Jarvie?" Trowbridge asked.

"They know me. They might talk to me, even though they refuse to speak to you and your men."

"Miss Jarvie, the army wouldn't ask you for such a thing."

"I'm offering it."

Trowbridge frowned. "I doubt that it's a good idea, Miss Jarvie."

She felt hot with anger and cold with fear. "That I would help you in your war effort?"

Harry said, "Miss Jarvie, why would you suggest such a thing?"

"Harry, Miss Jarvie is perfectly capable of making her own decision, even if the entire Union army advises against it." Emily felt Eliza's sarcasm.

"I would hope to spare her pain, Eliza."

"That isn't up to you."

ഇരുജ

ON THE FERRY TO Hilton Head, Emily watched as the September breeze wrinkled the surface of the Harbor River. The air smelled of the salt of the open sea just down the river. She was bound for the Union army camp at Hilton Head to visit the Hayward brothers.

She wondered again why she had come. The Hayward boys were less Christian in their feelings than the little ex-slaves she taught every day. And they were much too proud of their status as South Carolinians and Dragoons to betray their war secrets to her. If they knew any.

The warships grew thick as the ferry neared Hilton Head. The Union navy had won the battle at Bay Point for Port Royal in 1861, and its warships enforced the blockade that kept rice and cotton in the South, and all of life's goods—necessities and luxuries both—out.

When the ferry docked, Emily asked the way to General Hunter's headquarters. As in Beaufort, where General Saxton had taken over the house of an absconded planter, General Hunter had established himself in a townhouse once owned by someone with many acres of cotton and many hands to work it. The house had suffered some damage—the columns in front had been slashed and scorched—but it was otherwise in good repair. Emily climbed the steps, and the soldiers who stood at the door inquired after her business. When she told them, one of them said, "General Hunter isn't here, but you can speak to his aide-de-camp."

The aide-de-camp was a young white man with thick curly dark hair whose weary face topped an immaculate Union coat bright with buttons and crisp with a lieutenant's insignia. He led her inside, settled her at a desk—it had been a planter's once; it was scarred mahogany—and asked why she had come.

"I want to visit two of your prisoners. They're from the Charleston Light Dragoons, and the name is Hayward."

"Miss…"

"Jarvie. My name is Emily Jarvie."

"Miss Jarvie, how in the Lord's name did you get behind our lines?"

She said, "I'm a missionary attached to General Saxton's command. I teach in the school on a plantation on St. Helena Island. It's superintended by Mr. William Chapman."

"But you're a Southerner."

She sighed and gave him her catechism. "I was born in Colleton County and raised in Charleston. But I decided I hated slavery, and I came here to defeat it."

"Can you prove that to us?"

She thanked the Lord that Captain Trowbridge had given her a pass from General Saxton himself. She handed it to the aide-de-camp.

He read it. "It looks in order," he said. "I know General Saxton's hand. I don't think you forged it."

Emily folded her hands in her lap. "Why would I?"

"Miss Jarvie, if you sat where I sit, nothing would surprise you. Our enemies spare no effort to infiltrate our ranks, to spy upon us, to take advantage and bring the intelligence back to the Confederacy."

"I swear I have no such intention."

"I can't take your word, but I'm content with General Saxton's that you are who you say you are. Confederate prisoners, then. Why do you want to see them?"

"Christian charity, sir. I knew them when I was a girl. I hoped to speak to them kindly of the recollections we have in common."

The aide-de-camp laughed. "That beats all," he said. "Charity!"

Emily flushed. "And if I can speak kindly, perhaps

they might be more inclined to talk to your men," she said. "To give up what they know, so they can be paroled. Isn't that a form of charity in wartime?"

The aide-de-camp shook his head. "Rules of war," he said. "Not charity, Miss Jarvie."

"May I see them?"

"What could it hurt?" the aide-de-camp said. "You have to see them in the presence of a military guard, who will keep you from doing anything untoward and will protect you, if they take offense at your *kindness*."

"You think I'm a fool," Emily said.

"Oh no, Miss Jarvie. I would never call a lady a fool. But I think your errand here is very foolish."

She waited until he called for a guard to take her to the prison. He was a sergeant, short, compact, and ruddy in the face, and carried a rifle with the ease of someone well used to shooting. "These men ain't very pleasant," he said to Emily.

"I know. I've known them since they were boys. They never were."

The sergeant laughed. "And you want to soften them up for us?"

"I don't know," Emily said.

She had never seen the encampment at Hilton Head, and she was surprised at how orderly it was. The army had built two rows of barracks along either side of a greensward, which was large enough to accommodate a cluster of cooking tents and rows of tables shaded by awnings. The smell of coffee and beans lingered in the air. Men in uniform, all of them white, sat at the tables, drinking coffee, cleaning their rifles, mending their shirts.

"How many men are here?" Emily asked.

"Thousands, miss. It's the biggest Union encampment in this part of the South."

In the greensward, black women stood over washtubs as children played alongside. Emily heard them singing in a rhythm that matched the way they stirred the clothes. Black men came through the greensward, too, carrying shovels over their shoulders as the soldiers carried their rifles. The sergeant said, "The first contraband came here, after we took Bay Point. Hundreds of them. They work for us now."

The jail was set aside from the barracks. "We keep a better eye on it over here," the sergeant said.

"Do they try to escape?"

The sergeant grinned. "Of course they do."

"Do they succeed?"

"They don't."

It was a stouter building than the barracks, with a heavy door and iron bars over the windows. She thought, *It looks like a slave jail*, and wondered how the Haywards felt to be locked in it.

The sergeant greeted the men who stood at the door. "I have a visitor for the Hayward brothers," he said. "A lady who says she knew them before the war."

"Visitor? We can't accommodate a visitor here."

"Figure something out. Find a table they can all sit at.

I'll be there to make sure nothing goes awry." He touched the rifle slung over his shoulder.

"Visitor!" said one of the guards. "This ain't a parlor."

The other, disgruntled, said, "Do she have a calling card?"

"She has a pass from General Saxton. Fetch the prisoners and find a place to sit."

Emily felt her spirits sink as she followed the sergeant into a small room a few minutes later. The bars over the windows darkened the building inside. The room was crowded with a battered card table and three fragile chairs. At the table sat the Hayward brothers.

They had always been bony and milky-pale, despite their love of horse riding, and imprisonment had made them look bored and sulky as well, like boys whose entertainment had been taken away. Stephen, the elder, was also the taller; John was a little broader in the shoulders.

"You have a visitor," the sergeant said.

They stared at her. "Did you bring us a bottle of hock?" John asked.

"I'm afraid not," Emily said.

Stephen said, "Did you come here to get us out?"

"Perhaps," Emily said. She realized they didn't remember her.

"You can sit, miss," the sergeant said. He glared at the Haywards. "No foolishness from either of you," he said. "Or I take you right back."

"Who are you?" Stephen asked her.

Emily smoothed her skirt. "Don't you remember me, Stephen?"

Stephen shook his head.

John snickered. "It's Emily Jarvie," he said. "Miss Emily Jarvie. Lawrence Jarvie's girl. The one who run off with the slave she called her cousin."

"I recall the slave. Name of Caroline. Now that was a juicy piece," Stephen said.

"Don't speak of her like that," Emily said hotly.

John said, "We'll speak of her however we like. Ran north, did you? And where is she? I'm sure it's someplace the slave catcher can find her."

"As though I would tell you," she said.

"There's a price on your head in Charleston," Stephen said.

That startled the sergeant, a phlegmatic man. He had been listening, but Emily now saw his interest was keener. Emily said, "I know. That's why I'm behind Union lines, where the Confederacy can't touch me."

"Why are you here at all?" John jeered.

They have contempt for everything we hold dear, Trowbridge had said. She let her dislike for them sound in her voice. "I teach on St. Helena Island."

"Teach!" Stephen said contemptuously. "Who do you teach?"

"I teach the children who used to be slaves," Emily said.

"Used to be! Damned runaways. They're still slaves, and if I catch any of them, acting like they think they're free, I'll give them a good whipping and return them to their masters."

John said, "You teach the little niggers?"

"The children of the freedmen," Emily said stubbornly.

Stephen laughed, an ugly sound. "A nigger teacher," he said. "Your father would be proud of you!"

John said, "You and Joshua Aiken, that traitor to the South. Whatever happened to him? Did he join up with the blue-bellies? I bet your father's shot at him in Virginia."

"I don't doubt it," Emily said.

"Didn't he go off to Ohio?" Stephen asked.

"Yes," John said.

"Now that we've met you," Stephen said, "we can write to your papa and let him know where you are and what you're up to. And tell him about that runaway slave of yours. Where is she?"

John said, "I bet she ran to Ohio, too."

It was an empty threat, but the mere mention of it made her sick to her stomach. They held her in contempt, and they had exposed the secret of Caro to a Union soldier who had no reason to keep his mouth shut. In a few hours—certainly in a few days—the story would be on the lips of every gossip on the Sea Islands, Union soldier and Gideonite alike.

Emily rose. "You have nothing to say to me, and I have nothing to say to you," she said. She leaned against the table to steady herself. "There's no reason to remain here," she said to the sergeant. "Would you escort me away?"

"With pleasure, miss."

As they left, she was shaking so much that the sergeant offered his arm to support her, as he would help a wounded comrade. He asked her, "Miss, are you all right?"

"Just take me to the ferry," she said.

ഇൽ

ON THE FERRY BACK to St. Helena Island, Emily tried to steady herself, her emotions sloshing within her like the waters in the boat's wake. She clenched her handkerchief in her hand until her knuckles showed white.

Someone joined her—familiar, though not as cheerful as he had once been. Harry Phelps, who stood at a careful distance, as though Eliza had warned him, too. "I thought you might want to see a friendly face," he said.

She wanted to lean against him and sob as he embraced her.

He said, "I take it that they weren't kind to you."

"They were hateful," she said. "As everyone warned me."

He shook his head. He asked, "We haven't spoken much lately. Did I offend you, Miss Jarvie?"

"No, not at all."

He gripped the railing. "Did my sister offend you?"

"That's not my tale to tell," she said.

He said, "You look so distraught. Is there any way that I can help?"

She turned toward him. His blue eyes held no merriment today. The air smelled so strongly of salt that she could taste it. "By tomorrow, everyone will know," she said. "But I'll tell you first." And for the first time since she had come south, she revealed the truth of her flight from South Carolina, and she exposed Caro.

∞☾☽∞

HARRY BETRAYED HER CONFIDENCE right away, and later that afternoon, when she passed Eliza in the parlor, Eliza called to her. When Emily entered the room, Eliza rose and reached for Emily's hands. She clasped them in her roughened ones. Her voice full of sympathy, she asked, "Emily, why didn't you tell us?"

"Would you have liked me better if I had told you?"

Eliza's mouth tightened. "We would have understood you better."

"For a story that eased your conscience? The anti-slavery heroine who risked her life to rescue a slave?"

"For the truth," Eliza said quietly, her expression rueful.

Emily pulled her hands away. "Did it ever occur to you that I might have a good reason to keep Caro a secret?" she said, letting the anger bubble inside her. "By law, she's a fugitive slave, as much in Ohio as in South Carolina. I wanted to protect her."

Eliza flared. "Do you think we're fools, we Boston abolitionists? Do you think we don't understand the Fugitive Slave Law?"

"Oh, I'm sure you've read it, as you've read *Uncle Tom's*

Cabin and the autobiography of Mr. Frederick Douglass. But you've never fled from a place that would put your cousin in chains and capture you to try you and hang you for breaking the law. I'm not sure you understand that, Miss Phelps."

Emily fled upstairs. In her room, she felt so faint that she fell on the bed fully dressed, not caring if her shoes dirtied the coverlet. The levee broke and the memories flooded in. She remembered the first time she had seen the slave catcher in her father's study. The second time, he sat beside her in the dining room of the steamship that she had booked for her flight north with Caro. His voice was polite as he pretended he had never seen her before. The third time, he stood in the door of her cabin on the boat, still polite, much too quiet for a man charged with seizing a runaway slave and returning her to captivity.

He had come to capture the fugitive, but he had come for the planter's rebellious daughter who had stolen her, too.

ဆာ၅

LATER, AS EMILY LAY on her bed in full daylight, feeling too ill to move, Mattie came into her room. Eliza must have sent for her. Mattie dragged a chair to the bedside and sat down. "What is the matter, Emily?" she asked gently.

Emily didn't move. "Can you doctor away memories?" she murmured.

Mattie touched Emily's arm, a light touch, sisterly

and doctorly at once. "There's no medicine for that," she said. "What is it?"

She had hoped to prove her loyalty and all she had done was to put Caro in further danger. If she carried the burden of her betrayal all the way to hell, she deserved it.

Emily said, "My father hired a slave catcher."

Mattie tightened her grip on Emily's arm. Emily sat up. She said, "I thought we'd be safe once we boarded the steamship."

"And you were not."

"The slave catcher was on the boat. He came to our cabin. He didn't push his way in to grab Caro and take her. He wanted me, too."

"You!" Mattie exclaimed.

Emily met Mattie's eyes. "I'd broken the law. I'd stolen a slave to help her escape. In South Carolina, you'll hang for that. So my father sent a slave catcher to capture us both. To bring us back to the fate he thought we deserved."

"That's monstrous!" Mattie whispered.

Bitterness had dried Emily's tears. "He thought he did his duty, as a father and a master."

"Your own father!"

Emily extended her arms and crossed her hands at the wrist, as though she were in manacles. She said, "He wanted Caro enslaved. But he wanted me dead."

PART 2

Lines of Battle

1863

Chapter 6: The Press Pass

CARO ARRIVED IN BEAUFORT two weeks after President
Lincoln's proclamation of emancipation. She had been
right: it had taken months, a full term at Oberlin College,
to arrange to go south, time enough to earn her degree.
Her journey south could not have been a greater contrast
to her flight north. Her fellow passengers included several earnest teachers from Boston and New York and a man
of letters who wrote for *Harper's New Monthly Magazine*.
Learning of her connection with Emily, the Gideonites
insisted that she dine with them. They were zealous in
a way that was all too familiar after Oberlin. They had
been shocked that she asked for a glass of claret with her
dinner.

The Gideonites had spoken with excitement about
the Proclamation. For Caro, the president's words were
more than a blow against slavery. They were her safe pas-
sage. She read and reread the words, taking comfort in
the president's reassurance that "the Executive government of the United States, including the military and

naval authorities thereof, will recognize and maintain the freedom" of those who had been slaves. She knew that Port Royal, home to so many contrabands since its capture, was a haven for fugitives. But she held onto the Proclamation's promise like a talisman—that the Union army and navy were now charged to defend her freedom.

At night, alone in her cabin, she lay awake, hearing the rumble of the steam engine but listening for the sound of footsteps. She knew there was no slave catcher aboard this ship; she had met all twenty passengers. But her mind refused the evidence of her eyes and ears. She had been afraid to sleep. She didn't know what was worse: to hear the slave catcher's knock on the door or to dream it.

Now, as she stood on the dock in Beaufort, she shivered despite her new cloak. The Sea Islands had been unseasonably cold this winter, and Emily had advised her to bring something warm. It was odd to be cold in the Low Country.

She recognized Emily from afar: a slim figure with a resolute walk. Emily embraced her tightly, pressing her cheek to Caro's. "You're here," Emily murmured. "You're safe."

Caro returned the embrace. "As safe as anywhere," she murmured back.

Emily released her. Caro said, "You look better than you did when you left Ohio. Happier."

"Oh, I am," Emily said, twining her fingers with Caro's. "Teaching at the Oaks suits me."

"Miss Phelps didn't mind that you abandoned the school at Ocean Point?" Caro asked.

"Miss Phelps was overjoyed that I left. It allowed her to go back to Boston."

Caro said slyly, "And having Joshua here suits you, too."

Emily's fiancé, Joshua Aiken, had arrived at Port Royal just before Christmas. He had been offered—and had taken—a lieutenant's command with the First South Carolina Volunteer Infantry Regiment, Colonel Higginson's black regiment.

Emily blushed. "That's hardly a secret."

A man called out, "Miss Jarvie!" and both of them turned. He was short and slender, his milk-pale face engulfed by great sideburns and a bristling mustache, and he wore a coat with the insignia of a senior Union officer.

Emily broke into a smile. "General Saxton, this is my cousin, Miss Caroline Jarvie."

He reached for Caro's hand. He looked weary and saddened, but his eyes were kind. "Have you come to teach, too?" he asked.

"No, sir. I'm here as a correspondent for the *Christian Recorder*," she said.

"Ah, a reporter," he said, looking her up and down, taking in her dual anomaly as a reporter and a woman of color. He said, "Your cousin has told us quite a story. You were a fugitive?"

Caro's hand stole to the viséed passport in her pocket. She had traveled from Ohio to take the oath at the

Customs House in New York. In Ohio, she had been a fugitive slave; once sworn, she would go south as a citizen of the United States, loyal to the Union. Tears had fogged her eyes when she signed her name. Once in Beaufort, the provost marshal had stamped the passport without fuss or comment, just as he had for the rest of the passengers. She had choked at that, too. She said to General Saxton, "No longer, sir."

He took her hand softly, a gentleman extending a courtesy to a lady. "Welcome to Port Royal, Miss Caroline Jarvie. Come to see me about a press pass."

✌✍

EMILY HAD INSISTED THAT she stay at the Oaks. When she lived on the island, Caro was familiar with the Oaks, the plantation that used to belong to the Dalton family. As a slave, she had never walked through the front door or sat in the parlor. Now, she was free to notice the absence of the portraits and the silver, and took in the mismatched chairs and the room's lack of decoration. What the Daltons hadn't spirited away, the army and the former slaves had ruined.

She met Mattie and Anna, both familiar from Emily's letters. They greeted her with a matter-of-fact warmth, as though she were only another guest, not a novelty. They were intrigued by her work as a reporter, and they asked her about *Hearth and Home* and the *Christian Recorder*.

Emily was part of the family here, as though a Southern abolitionist were ordinary, too.

At the rap on the door, Emily smiled. "I'll answer it," she said, nodding to Daisy, their maidservant.

She soon led Joshua into the parlor. Caro, who remembered him as a man with an easy smile, was surprised at how haggard he had become. The war in Virginia had given him a military bearing, and it looked as though it had given him ugly memories. She would not be surprised if he had nightmares.

But now he smiled. He clasped Caro's hands and greeted her by her Christian name, allowed since they were about to become cousins through Emily. He said, "I hope you don't tire of hearing this, but I'm relieved that you're here."

"With the army's eye upon me."

He said, "I heard about the riots in Cincinnati."

She held herself rigid. "We came out unscathed."

"That's what soldiers say when the battle is over," he said.

Emily took Joshua's hand, and he squeezed hers in return. "Tell us about the First South," she said. "No battles yet, and a happier tale."

That cheered him. "The 'Fust Souf,' as the men call it," he said. "Let's have dinner."

Over dinner he told them about the Sea Islands' success in raising a black regiment, commanded by Thomas Higginson, Boston minister and abolitionist, good friend to Rufus Saxton and William Garrison. These men had freely mustered in and were eager to see battle. They drilled with enthusiasm, and in their free time, they learned how to read and write. "They're good, good men," Joshua said. "There's only one thing they dislike. The army has sent us red trousers for their uniforms. They tell me they feel like turkey cocks in those pants."

Caro said, "How do they feel about you? A Southerner?"

"I've heard them tell me that I sound just like ole massa," he said.

Emily said, "He tells them what I tell my scholars— that it's not surprising, since he's South Carolina born and bred."

"And if I get any resistance, I remind them that I left the South before the war and mustered into the army in Ohio. I say that I doubt that ole massa fought for the Union all over Virginia."

"Do they obey you?" Caro asked.

"Most of them do," Joshua said. "A few can't get past the way I talk. One of them told me, 'I didn't join the army for you to order me like I was back in slavery.' I told him that if he felt that way, he'd made a bad bargain to muster in. A private obeys the order of his commander, and I told him further that I didn't order soldiers of color any differently from the white men who used to be under my command."

"Did that satisfy him?" Caro asked.

"So far. If it doesn't, I'll let him transfer to Captain Trowbridge's command. Trowbridge sounds so much like a Yankee that the Low Country men have trouble understanding him."

Caro wanted to laugh. *It's a different kind of war here,* she thought.

⁊⁊⁊

A FEW DAYS LATER, Caro stood before General Saxton's office, which was housed in the residence of a planter who had fled the islands. A graceful building, it was two stories tall, adorned with pillars that spanned its height to create a shady porch on both floors. Now it looked a little shabby. The steps had been dirtied by the boots of everyone who came and went on the business of the Sea Islands, military and otherwise.

Caro ran lightly up the steps and rapped on the door, where a white soldier let her in. She could see into the office where General Saxton bent over his papers, his shoulders showing the burden he felt as he signed them. He raised his head and smiled to see her. "Miss Jarvie! Please come in."

When she was seated, he asked, "How are you settled? I hear that you stay at the Oaks."

Gossips, not spies, she thought, since this was a small society where the human telegraph worked as well as it did among the former slaves. "Yes, for the moment, but I may find a place in Beaufort, since it's closer to the camp."

"And you've found a church to welcome you?"

"I will, sir." She had quickly realized that church attendance was the best way to meet the people who would be the grist for her reporter's mill. Male reporters drank with their sources, but she could hardly follow their example.

"How is your cousin?" he asked.

They all knew of the relation, and they didn't mind. It was a relief, but it remained a surprise to Caro that everyone spoke of it as though it were ordinary. "Very well, sir. It's been good to see her again. And Miss Townsend has made me welcome at the Oaks."

"Good, good."

She waited a little, being polite, then said, "Sir, the press pass. I've come about the press pass."

"Of course, Miss Jarvie. I have it ready for you." He looked among his papers—it was too orderly to be called rummaging—and found it. "Here it is."

Such a flimsy bit of paper, and such freedom it promised her! She read it carefully.

Beaufort, South Carolina, Department of the South,
January 6, 1863
Pass: C. Jarvie of the Christian Recorder, behind the
lines under further orders
By Command of General Rufus Saxton. Not
Transferable.

She looked up. "Sir? Why does it say 'behind the lines'? I thought that a reporter would be able to follow the lines of battle."

"We've seen very little battle here since November of 1861, Miss Jarvie. You have free rein in Beaufort, in the camp, and on St. Helena Island. If you wish to travel to Lady's or Parris Island, you'll need a military escort, and I'd prefer you didn't visit Edisto Island at all. The Confederates give us too much trouble there."

She struggled to maintain a polite tone. "Sir, how can I report on the war if I'm restricted in where I can go?"

"Miss Jarvie, my conscience would burden me greatly if I allowed a lady to put herself in danger."

She could hardly say, "But I'm not a lady," when he had gone to so much trouble to treat her with the courtesy he would extend to a social equal. She said, "But I'm also a reporter."

He said, "In Beaufort, in the camp, and on St. Helena, there is plenty to report, Miss Jarvie."

It was like *Hearth and Home* again. News of interest to ladies. "Sir."

He would never look stern, but his smile faded. He said, "Miss Jarvie, I remind you that you are under orders."

She thought, *One battle at a time. Sometimes the gains are very small.* She thought of the armies in Virginia, fighting over the same few acres of ground again and again, and she felt more like a soldier. She rose and extended her hand. "You've been very kind, General Saxton."

She slipped the pass into her pocket and left. She went looking for a drayman willing to take her to the camp. He charged her a dollar.

"You take advantage of me," Caro said.

He grinned, clearly delighted to make a dollar. "How else you get there?" he asked. "I wait, and take you back, too."

"All right."

"Who you visit at Camp Saxton? Maybe I know him."

"Colonel Higginson." She fingered the pass.

"Everyone know him! What business have you got with him?"

"I don't know yet. I'm a reporter. I want to talk to everyone I can."

"Reporter? Like that man from the *New York Tribune*?"

I wish, she thought. "No, with the *Christian Recorder* in Philadelphia. The colored newspaper."

"Never heard of it," he said. He chuckled. "Never saw a colored girl who was a reporter, either."

The man urged his horse toward the camp and stopped before a field filled with small white tents in two neat rows. He said helpfully, "I can find the colonel for you."

A reporter didn't need an escort. "No, it's all right. I'll find him."

Caro made her way down the row of tents. Behind them were tables and chairs, shaded by awnings, where groups of black soldiers sat, talking and joking. As she hesitated, a man called to her, "Who you visiting, sugar?"

One of his companions said, "Show respect, man! She look like a lady."

"Is you a schoolteacher?" the first man asked. He was light of skin and sharp of feature. "You the prettiest schoolteacher I ever saw. Do you have a beau?"

Caro walked to the table and stood before it, unfazed. The second man said to her, "Don't pay him any mind. He from Florida, full of himself." He had the mahogany skin and the accent of the "main," as the locals called the coast of the Low Country.

"I won't," she said. "I'm here to visit Colonel Higginson. Do you know where I can find him?"

The second man rose. He was tall and broad-shouldered, and he was so newly mustered in that his uniform still bore the creases of being folded. "I do," he said. "What business do you have with him?"

She took her press pass from her pocket. "Can you read, soldier?"

He laughed. "No, but I know a pass when I see one."

"Press pass," she said. "I'm a reporter."

"Like Mr. Villard. Man from the *Tribune*."

"Has he talked to you?"

"He talk to all of us." He looked her up and down, taking her measure. "Come with me."

He guided her through the camp. The little white tents were fresh and clean and organized, but the camp was full of bustle, with men eating, drinking coffee, cleaning their boots and sewing on their buttons, singing, and laughing as they talked. Black men, engaged in everything that soldiers did, when they weren't drilling, fighting, or praying.

One of the soldiers called to him, "Sampson! Who you got with you?"

He turned to her, smiling. "Didn't get your name."

"Didn't give it." She held out her hand. "Miss Caroline Jarvie."

She saw a flicker of recognition on his face at the name

"Jarvie." His handclasp was dry and firm. His fingers were long and elegant and scarred with fieldwork. He called out, "This Miss Caroline Jarvie. She a reporter, and you better watch yourself around her!"

The man called back, "She better watch herself around you, too!"

He laughed, and they continued to a tent larger than the others, where an officer sat at a table, papers before him. He looked up. He had the look of a Boston minister: a gleaming white forehead, clear eyes, and a carefully tended beard.

"Colonel Higginson?" her escort asked. "Private Hayward, sir."

"Yes, private?" he said. His accent confirmed that he was a Boston man. "What is it?"

"Brought a young lady who want to see you."

"A young lady? Why?"

Caro stepped forward and introduced herself, proffering her press pass.

The colonel frowned. "You're a reporter?"

"Yes, sir."

Annoyance clouded his features. "Reporters! They're like flies, bothering the men. They haven't left us alone since the regiment formed. This is a military installation, not a spectacle. I don't want you interfering."

Caro glanced at Private Hayward, whose expression was considerably more welcoming than his commander's. She said, "I won't, sir."

He looked at her again, and when he spoke, he softened his tone a little. "What newspaper do you write for?" he asked.

She mentioned the *Christian Recorder*, and he softened further. He said, "I know the editor. A fine man, and a friend to the cause of abolition before the war."

Caro said, "I owe him a good report of your regiments." When Colonel Higginson didn't reply, Caro said politely, "General Saxton would permit it."

Higginson sighed. "Don't bother the men," he repeated. He returned to the paper before him, and Private Hayward saluted and said, "Sir!" before he tugged gently on Caro's sleeve to let her know they were both dismissed.

As she came back through the camp with Private Hayward, she felt even more discouraged than she had in leaving General Saxton. She was forbidden the front lines and constrained in the camp. What would she write about?

"You look a little downcast, Miss Jarvie," he said.

He was cannier than she'd thought. Keen enough to read the mood of a stranger. "So many restrictions," she said. "Don't go there, don't talk to these people, don't get in the way. I'm supposed to be a reporter. What will I report on?"

His eyes gleamed. "Shouldn't be a difficulty for a woman of spirit like yourself," he said.

She laughed. "Now that's just a little bit forward of you, Private Hayward," she said.

"Free man now. Feeling it."

She got a gleam, too. "When did you muster in?" she asked.

"Just after the Proclamation," he said.

"And how do you like being a soldier?"

"Can't wait to get my hands on them secesh," he said.

She glanced at his uniform. "What do you think about the red pants?" she asked.

"Hate 'em!" he said cheerfully. "Miss Jarvie, is there anyone else you want to talk to?"

"I don't know."

"Well, stroll with me. We may find someone."

They returned as they had come, and through the noise, she heard a voice that sounded familiar. She hesitated.

"What is it, Miss Jarvie?"

"I thought I heard someone I knew from Charleston."

"Many a man here come from Charleston," he said.

She shook her head. It was her imagination, sending up another ghost. Her past was like a secesh picket, ambushing her when she least expected it.

But the ghost called to her. "Caro! Caroline Jarvie!"

She turned to see a short, sturdy man dressed in a blue coat and nankeen pants. A man with a seamed, dark face and large, well-shaped hands. When she came close enough, she saw the intelligent eyes in that well-worn face.

He was no ghost. She knew him, very well. She ran to take his hands.

"Sunday! Sunday Desmond!"

He wrapped his arms around her, holding her tightly, saying in his deep voice, "Oh, Caro. Caro. So good to see you, Caro."

She sobbed as he stroked her hair. She asked, "What happened to you? I thought the worst when the letters couldn't go through anymore."

"I'm all right. It's all right." He let her go and gave her a handkerchief, saying tenderly, "Wipe your face."

Her escort waited until it was seemly to speak. He said, "Is you kin?"

Sunday said, "No, but I help her when she come to Charleston, and I shelter her before she leave before the war."

Sampson nodded at the word *shelter*. He touched his cap to her. "Good to meet you, Miss Jarvie," he said, excusing himself. "Hope to see you again."

Sunday grasped her hand and settled her in a rough pine chair. He gazed at her with pride. "Look at you! Dressed like a lady and talk like a Yankee! Did you stay at that college in Oberlin?"

"I did. I got my degree. And I worked at Miss Emily's magazine in Cincinnati." She couldn't talk about the riot. She asked, "Is there news of Sophy?"

Sunday grinned. "She here. In Beaufort."

"Contraband?" Caro asked, letting the word suggest the condition of Sophy's escape.

"Free now. Go visit her; she tell you all about it."

"Oh, I will! What about you? How did you come to be here?"

"Contraband," he said.

"Tell me," she said fiercely, leaning forward. "Tell me how you got yourself free."

"After the war start, my massa take me away from Charleston and set me to building for the secesh in the Low Country. They work me like a dog and don't pay me a dime. All I could think about was getting away."

She nodded.

"One night I run. Weave my way down to the river. I hear pickets in the woods, and I fear for the whole thing. But they ain't secesh. They Yankees, talking the way Yankees do."

"And they let you pass."

"Better than that. They glad to help me. They escort me down to the river. They know there's a Yankee boat on patrol there. They wave and yell that they have someone to take on, and men in blue, they haul me onto their boat and stow me away as contraband."

Caro's eyes gleamed. "Free at last."

"Hallelujah. And it get better, too. One of the officers is a man name Trowbridge, Captain Trowbridge. He in charge of figuring where to put them battlements and ramparts and bridges the army need. When he find out I can build for him, he nearly dance a jig for delight." Sunday grinned. "He tell me that he hire me to work for the army as a carpenter. I ask him, 'Will I get paid?' He say, 'We will gladly hire you and pay you, sir! In good United States specie!' Then I nearly dance a jig for delight."

"So you work for the army?"

"Better than that. I muster into the First South Carolina, and I'm a soldier, too. Most of the time I have a shovel and a saw, but I get a rifle, and I drill along with the rest of them. Glad to be a soldier. Coffee, pay, respect. Everything fine but these fool red pants, and I hear that Colonel Higginson, who have the command over us, hate them as much as we do and get us regular issue pants—blue, like everyone else's."

She laughed.

"What bring you here?" he asked. "Back to South Carolina?"

She thought, *Sometime I'll tell him all of it,* but today she explained only the connection with the *Recorder.* "Don't say anything about colored girl reporters."

"I won't. What you write about?"

"Life on the islands. In the camp." Her eyes gleamed. "I could write about you."

"Me? I ain't important."

"Fugitive and contraband! And now you're a soldier." She pulled her notebook and pencil from her pocket. She held them up, feeling anew the pride that she made a living by writing. "Tools of my trade, Sunday!"

Sunday said, "You write about that man who escort you. Private Hayward. He a hero. Get a dozen people out, women and children." He passed his hand over his eyes, which were wet. "He get Sophy out."

❧❧

As she walked through the camp, Sampson Hayward found her, asking, "Where else can I guide you?"

"Nowhere," she said, reaching for the notebook and pencil she kept in her pocket. "I want to talk to you." She looked up and met his eyes. They were a glowing brown, flecked with copper. "If it isn't interfering with your duties as a soldier."

"No," he said.

"Where are you from?" she asked, pencil poised over the paper.

"Hayward place," he said. "Just up the river from the Jarvie place."

"Mr. Lawrence Jarvie?"

Surprised, he said, "Yes, Massa Lawrence."

"Sunday told me you rescued a lot of people."

A shadow passed over his face. "Thank the Lord," he said.

"I hear that they all owe their thanks to you."

He shook his head. "So hot to get out, I take a big risk," he said. "Bring gals and babies with me." He turned his head, and she saw, with considerable surprise, that his eyes were wet. He took a deep breath to compose himself. "It were touch and go," he said, trying to diminish both the fear and the feat. "But we make it."

She put her hand on his sleeve, and his face brightened a little. She said, "Tell me what happened so I can write about it."

"Don't like to remember it."

"Of course not. If you tell it, and I write it, we help to fight."

He nodded. "All right."

She scribbled frantically to get the words down, and when he stopped talking, she shook out her cramped wrist.

He said, "Didn't think that writing them words down would be hard work."

"Not as hard as chopping cotton or harvesting rice, but in its own way, it is."

"Is I allowed to ask you questions?"

"Of course."

"Where is you from?"

"I was born a slave in the Sea Islands. When my master died, I was taken to Charleston."

"You talk a little like a Yankee."

"I lived in Ohio before the war." She swallowed hard. "I fled north to Ohio."

"You trouble the water, like I did."

"Yes."

"Is you connected with the Jarvies in Colleton County?"

He hadn't forgotten. He'd known all along. "Yes. Lawrence Jarvie, who owns the place now, is my uncle. The man who used to own it was my father."

"Fugitive," he said slowly. "Contraband."

She met his eyes. "Touch and go," she said softly. "I made it, too."

෨ൠ

BACK IN BEAUFORT, SHE knocked on the door of a house that must have belonged to a doctor or a lawyer before the war, since it was too small and too plain for a planter. From the back came the cluck of chickens. Caro smiled. Sophy must be selling eggs again. Whatever had happened to Sophy, she must be doing all right in her freedom.

The door opened, and a plump, round-faced woman, her apron spotless, her kerchief beautifully tied in the Charleston manner, looked at her quizzically and said, "Yes?"

"Does Sophy live here?"

"Who are you?"

"Tell her Caro."

A small figure bustled into the hallway, calling, "Who there, Chloe?"

Chloe stepped aside. Sophy put her hand to her mouth as she took Caro in. Sophy looked wearier than she had in Charleston, her face more lined and worn. Then she pulled Caro inside and hugged her, sobbing.

In the kitchen, which smelled of black-eyed peas and shrimp remoulade, a black-and-white cat twined around her ankles. Sophy held Caro's hand so tightly that it hurt, saying, "I hear you come here. But I can't believe that I see you."

Caro patted the gnarled fingers, and Sophy loosened her grip. Caro asked, "How did you hear? Was it from Emily?"

"No, I don't see Miss Emily, and don't wish to speak

to her, either. But she tell Juno Green, and Juno tell everyone."

"Why don't you talk to Emily? Did you have some disagreement?"

"Hah! Listen to you. Disagreement, like we two ladies having tea. It was what her daddy done, and I don't forgive it."

"Lawrence Jarvie," Caro said. "We know what kind of a man he is. What happened, Sophy?"

"After the war break out, Marse Lawrence worry that Charleston get taken by the Yankees." Sophy made a face. "Did I wish for that. He put all of us on the train, and all his fine things in trunks, and we all go down to Colleton County to get out of the way of the fighting. Once we down there, he put me in the rice field with the rest of my family. I work like a slave again, wade in the water to plant rice, stand in the mud to hoe, bend my back to harvest and thresh."

"Was it for spite? Did he think you helped me?"

"Of course he do. That's how he punish me. Make me a field nigger again. Tell me that's how I see my children, and if I complain, he don't mind selling me."

Chloe looked away.

Sophy said, "So when I hear that Sampson Hayward want to run, I talk to him. He don't like the idea of taking Chloe, who have little ones. But he mad, and he full of himself, and I know he want to stick it in his massa's eye, like I do. So he say he'll take all of us." Sophy closed her eyes, and Chloe reached for her mother's hand.

Caro said, "If it pains you too much to remember, don't tell me, Sophy."

"Oh, it pain me," she said. "But I never forget it." She stilled herself. Took a deep breath. She said, "We run into the woods, all of us. Wait and listen for the patrollers and the dogs." She shuddered. "Them dogs. Tear your throat out. But we don't hear anything. So we inch along. Want to get down to the water."

"Trouble the water," Caro murmured.

"Try to be as quiet as we can. Have babies and little ones with us, and it hard for them to stay quiet." She glanced at Chloe. "Chloe steal laudanum and dose the baby so he don't make a sound."

Chloe's face was impassive.

"We find the river. And then we hear it. Horses. Dogs." She hesitated. "Sampson have a boat ready for us. But it just a bit downriver." It was hard for her to go on, and when she did, it was almost a whisper. "We women, we have a worry the men don't. That when they catch us, they do worse than kill us. They outrage us."

Chloe's face remained impassive.

Sophy said, "Never felt so afraid as I did, creeping through the woods to get to that boat. Thought I'd stop breathing."

Caro reached for Sophy's hand and covered it with her own.

That seemed to strengthen Sophy. "We can hear them dogs barking as we reach the boat. Pile into it, all of us. Start to row away." She passed her hand over her eyes.

"But it ain't over yet. They shoot at us from the riverbank. Dogs slavering mad, barking. Rifles cracking at us, like we animals to shoot at."

"Mama, that's enough," Chloe said. To Caro, she said, "We get away. All of us. No one hurt. No one even let out a sound. Sampson Hayward, he guide us down the river to freedom."

Sophy said to Caro, "You run away, too. You know."

Oh, it pains me. Don't ask me to talk about it. She blinked away her tears. She said, "You're free now, Sophy. You're safe. This house. Chickens in the backyard. So you sell eggs in the market, as you used to in Charleston?"

Sophy nodded. She said, "Sunday promise to build me a new henhouse. He tell me that he build me the finest henhouse I ever saw. That my hens live like queens in it."

Chloe looked less ashen. She said, "Mama crazy about them hens."

Caro sang softly, "Eggs so fresh, eggs so fine..."

Sophy said, "Sell eggs for ten cents each in Beaufort. The war drive the price up."

Chloe laughed weakly.

Sophy asked, "Where do you stay, Miss Caro?"

"I'm at the Oaks with Emily. But I'd like to live in Beaufort because it's closer to everyone I'd want to interview for the newspaper."

"Live here with us." She gave Chloe an admonishing look: *Don't naysay me.*

Chloe pursed her lips. "Just charge her for board."

"Just a little, Miss Caro. To help us out."

"I'd do a lot more than that for you, Sophy," Caro said.

ℰᗡℭℜ

WHEN CARO MOVED INTO Sophy's house, she brought a small object carefully wrapped in brown paper. She cradled it in her pocket to protect it on the ferry and the cart ride from the ferry. When she arrived, she insisted on settling Sophy in the parlor to hand her the package.

"What is it?"

"Open it."

When the wrapping fell away, Sophy was delighted. It was a Dresden shepherdess. Sophy said, "Just like the one I had back in Charleston. Where did you get it?"

Caro said, "Don't ask."

Sophy smiled. "Used to belong to some missus, didn't it? Well, now it belong to me."

ℰᗡℭℜ

NO ONE HAD FORBIDDEN her to approach the women, and it was easy to interview them: the laundry women who worked at Camp Saxton and the freed women, like Sophy, who had settled in Beaufort. Some of them wanted to talk about the way they had escaped, even though they wept and shuddered to remember it. Others were matter-of-fact. One woman said, "Free now. Don't want to recall it." Caro learned to listen to both, to lay a comforting hand on the arm of a weeping woman and to bend her head toward her notebook for a matter-of-fact one.

Without any prompting, they told her about their slavery. How they worked from "can't see to can't see," whether it was for rice harvest or cotton. How they suffered the driver's stick or the overseer's lash. In whispers, they told her how they had been forced by massa or young marse or overseer, the complexions of their children attesting to it. They grieved for everyone sold away and asked her if she knew how to find those who had been sent to Georgia or Mississippi or Texas.

They rejoiced in their freedom, too. More than one woman said wonderingly, "I drink coffee every morning." They went to their labor willingly because the army paid them. Even the most straightforward among them choked up when they told her that their children now learned to read and write. They quoted her the words of the Proclamation. "President Lincoln himself tell me that I'm forever free," the matter-of-fact woman said, savoring the words.

Sophy was the one to ask, "Why don't you visit the people on the plantations?"

She should. But they were likely to remember her, and she wasn't ready to see them, or to remember her father.

One day, when Caro returned from Camp Saxton, she found a stranger in Sophy's kitchen, drinking coffee and eating a biscuit. As soon as Caro stepped into the kitchen, the woman set down her cup and looked at her. "I remember you," she said.

Caro bristled. "Who are you?" she asked.

"Live on Pine Grove. Always have. Ain't you Marse James's girl?"

She said coolly, "James Jarvie was my father."

"Your massa, too."

"My father," she insisted.

"What happen to your mama?"

"My father's brother took all of us to Charleston."

"Where is she now? Still in Charleston?"

Caro said stiffly, "She died just before the war."

"Buried in Charleston, then."

Caro looked away, ashamed for a stranger to see that her eyes brimmed. She reached for her handkerchief.

Sophy said, "Is there something wrong with you? Can't you see how you pain her? None of us like to remember slavery days."

"Some of us should," the woman said. "Some of us awfully high-rumped."

The hand that clutched the handkerchief trembled. Caro said, "You remember in your way, and I'll remember in mine."

Caro had been lying to herself. She didn't care that anyone knew she had been a slave before the war. Every Gideonite, every Union officer, every private in the First South knew. What she dreaded was remembering her father.

He was buried on St. Helena Island, in the graveyard of the White Church. She had never visited his grave. She had never been back to visit the house she grew up in, even though it was close to all the places owned by the

Smiths and the Daltons, houses where she had been a frequent guest since her return.

As much as it pained her, it was time to remember. It was time to visit the Jarvie place where she had grown up.

Not long after, she took the ferry that stopped at Lands End on St. Helena Island, and she walked the rest of the way.

Her father's house on the island had never been a plantation. It was built as a summer retreat, and her father had never grown cotton here. After Lawrence Jarvie inherited it, he sold it, but no one had come to live here, even before the war.

She walked up the driveway, unwilling to get too close, but even from this distance she saw how derelict the place had become. The driveway was overgrown, and the shrubs in the yard had been so long neglected that their branches brushed the windows of the house.

She couldn't come any closer. She couldn't bear the memory of the girl she had been in this house. Pampered. Educated. Beloved. Caro. *Cara.*

It hurt too much to stand here. She turned and ran away.

❧⚬❧

CARO VISITED CAMP SAXTON every day, talking to whoever had the leisure to speak to her. The laundry women always had time for her, but she was careful with the soldiers, waiting until they were released from drill. And she tried the officers. Joshua was curt with her, but Captain

Trowbridge was cordial. Trowbridge had a great liking for Sunday. "In a better army than this one," Trowbridge had told Caro, "Mr. Desmond would be an officer."

Sampson Hayward watched for her and caught up with her as she walked through the camp, her notebook in her hand. "Miss Jarvie!" he said, rising from the camp chair. "Walk with me? Stand in the shade with me?"

The man who sat with him—the fair-skinned, forward man from Florida, whose name was Dennison—snorted. "I won't tell where you go. Or what you do."

"Nothing to tell," Sampson said, feigning innocence. "Give Miss Jarvie some news of the camp, that all."

"Private Dennison, would you like me to interview you, too?" Caro asked, also feigning innocence.

"Will you stand with me in the shade?"

"I'd interview you in the middle of a battlefield, if you'd like," Caro said.

"Hah!" Dennison said. "If we have a battle, be glad to oblige you."

Sampson cleared his throat, and she followed him to "stand in the shade."

"How goes the war, Private Hayward?"

His coppery eyes gleamed. "Call me Sampson," he said.

"Like your sister would."

He laughed. "I'm glad you ain't my sister," he said.

"Are you flirting with me, Private Hayward?"

"And if I was?"

She took out her notebook.

He said, "You don't get round me that easy, Miss Caroline. Trying to interview me again."

She looked up from the paper. "I wouldn't dream of it! But if you've heard or seen anything interesting, tell me."

"Of course I tell you. But all we do is drill and practice our shooting. Even though we itch to meet them secesh."

"Will you? Are there plans for it?"

Sampson said, "Haven't heard. What do Captain Aiken say?"

Joshua had told her to mind her own business so sharply that she pretended to be hurt, saying, "Is that how you treat your cousin?" He had said curtly, "That's how I treat a reporter who wants to pry military information from me." He sounded just like Colonel Higginson.

She told Joshua, "I assure you that anything I'd want to know could be printed in *Hearth and Home.*"

"Then go talk to the ladies," he'd said, dismissing her.

Now she said to Sampson, "Captain Aiken is very close with what he calls *military information.* As Colonel Higginson is."

Sampson put his hand on her arm. She saw afresh the contrast between the long fingers and the scars. "He do his duty. As you do yours."

Why was she surprised that an unlettered man, formerly a slave, could be so astute in his observations?

He faced her. He said, "Why you so cagey with me? Do you have a sweetheart somewhere?"

The question caught her by surprise.

In Charleston, she had loved a man who had promised to marry her and instead abandoned her. He had run with his family to freedom in Philadelphia and had left her in slavery in Charleston. She didn't often think of Danny Pereira. The memory was too painful. But she couldn't shake the recollection of his smile. Of his eyes, which were hazel and changed color with the weather and his mood. She had seen them turn every color save blue. She couldn't recall what color they were when he kissed her. She had closed her own eyes for that.

She tried to blot out the memory of the touch of his lips. The soft caress of his fingers on her cheeks. The feel of his back beneath his fine cotton shirt. The smell of the summer's air in Charleston, thick with the fragrance of gardenia and magnolia, laced with the smell of garbage and rot in the heat.

She took a deep breath of Sea Island air, piney and a little salty, bringing herself back to the present. She fumbled for an answer. "No."

Her hesitation gave her away. He said, "But you carry someone with you."

"What about you?"

He said, "I do, too." He looked away. "But she gone. Sold away."

If she let him, he'd give her more than news of the war. But she didn't want to receive it.

EVEN THOUGH THE WOMEN worked for the army, they were not bound by military duty or military secrecy. As they began to trust Caro, they gossiped freely about the exchange of fire by pickets, the movement of boats up the river, and the rescue of contraband.

Shortly after Sampson flirted with her, she stopped to talk to a group of women who were washing clothes. One of them, who had been matter-of-fact about her escape, leaned on her pole and said, "The work ain't any easier than it was in slavery. But I don't mind it when I get paid for it."

Caro said, "I did wash for money in Charleston, and I know exactly what you mean."

"You? A washwoman?"

"My master let me live out, and he paid me to do the wash." She could still remember the feeling of the five dimes in her palm.

"Hope they pay you more to scribble in that notebook."

Caro laughed. "Is there news?" she asked.

"We hear the men go up the river to St. Mary."

"Why? What's up there?"

The woman leaned close to say in a theatrical whisper, "Supplies."

"Contraband?"

The woman laughed. "No, lumber."

"They're raiding for lumber?"

"Both regiments. First and Second."

Another woman—she had wept to remember her escape—said, "I worry myself sick for my John."

"For lumber? That doesn't sound so dangerous," Caro said.

"They go right by the secesh to get it," the matter-of-fact woman said.

The worried woman wrung her hands. "Don't know where they hide and how they jump out!"

"When do they plan to go?" Caro asked.

The matter-of-fact woman said, "Don't know. Soon. Why don't you ask Captain Aiken? Since he engaged to Miss Emily, who admit to being your cousin."

⁂

JOSHUA WAS UNHAPPY TO see her. "What is it, Miss Jarvie?" In camp, he never called her by her Christian name, even though everyone knew about their connection.

"Captain Aiken, I hear that the First and the Second are going on a mission up the river soon."

He sighed. "Was it the men who told you? Or the women?"

"It's common knowledge in the camp," she said. "I came to ask if I might accompany your regiment. As a reporter."

"I'll have my hands full, commanding the men," he said curtly. "I can't look after you, too."

"I believe I'll go to Colonel Higginson to ask his permission."

"Do you think he'd allow it?"

She lost her temper. "Would he allow Mr. Villard of the *New York Tribune*?"

He glared at her. "I doubt it," he said.

"How can I report on the war if I can't follow the army into battle?"

"God forbid that we need women on the battlefield."

"What about the women who are contrabands? Every one of them risked her life to flee here."

"You aren't a contraband, and you aren't a soldier. Don't waste your breath arguing with Colonel Higginson, Caro."

෨෬

CARO LEFT JOSHUA TO walk stiff-legged back through the row of tents, and Sampson caught up with her near the guardhouse gate.

With a surge of irritation, she said, "How do you know to find me? Do you lurk in wait for me?"

He said mildly, "Whenever you in camp, I know." He tapped her on the wrist. "Do it bother you?"

"What if it did?" she said.

"Then I'd quit it. What you really mad about?"

"I heard a rumor that the First South is going on a mission upriver. I asked Captain Aiken about it."

He said, "And you don't hear anything good from him."

"If you go upriver, I'm not going with you."

"That's what you ask him?"

"War reporter!" she said bitterly. "Report on drill and laundry and find out about the shooting when it's over!"

"Go into battle!" he said, equally upset. "Risk getting shot at! Risk getting captured! Risk getting forced!"

"Well, I won't," she said, sulky. "I'll stay here, and I'll talk to all of you about it when you come back."

They halted at the guardhouse gate. As the guards watched and listened, he said to her, "You stay put and stay safe."

"I reckon I will." She was still sulky.

He dropped his voice. "Will you worry for me while I'm gone?"

The intimacy of the plea bothered her. She said, "I'll worry for all of you."

In the same low tone, he asked, "If I didn't come back, would you grieve for me?"

She was still angry, and she didn't like his insistence. "I'd grieve for any man who didn't come back. But don't say so, Private Hayward. You'll do fine. You'll come back just fine."

He said, very seriously, "Will you pray for me, Miss Caroline?" He bent close to her, hoping for the answer.

Was he trying to kiss her? She was in no mood for it. "If I say yes, will you behave like a gentleman?"

He laughed. "A man go into battle, he want a little sugar to take with him."

Those dark eyes gleamed. He saw through her. He understood her sass and her fear. Danny Pereira, who had been besotted with her, had never known her so well.

She met those perceptive eyes. "Yes, Sampson Hayward, I'll pray for you," she said softly.

ഇ◯ഌ

ONCE THE FIRST AND Second left, Caro lay awake at night, too restless to sleep. She rose to stand at the window, even though the dark was nearly impenetrable, unlit by the moon, obscured by clouds. Both regiments, with Sunday and Sampson Hayward among them, up the river tonight. She felt the worry. Men on the boats were usually safe, but when they went looking for *supplies*, as the army called it, they didn't stay on the boats. They landed, and they were in danger from the secesh pickets. Any exchange of fire could be dangerous. It could be deadly.

She thought, *I wish I was on that boat. I wish I had a rifle and could shoot. I'd like to try my hand at a secesh picket.*

Where had that thought come from? She was a reporter. She fought the war with a notebook and a pen.

But she was like Penelope, fated to wait while Odysseus roamed and fought. She stared into the unforgiving darkness, knowing that she would be unable to sleep, wanting to know, wanting to hear.

Chapter 7: Thirteen Plantations

MATTIE THREW HER GLOVES on the hallway table with such force that they sounded like a slap. Startled, Emily recalled that her stepmother used to express her anger in the same way. She asked Mattie, "Whatever has upset you so?"

"I've just heard the latest about the land sale."

The Department of the Treasury, which was charged with managing the "abandoned lands" of the Sea Islands, had announced that thousands of acres would be offered for sale, and the announcement had sent all the Yankee residents—superintendents, missionaries, and army men—into a frenzy akin to their feelings about the abolition of slavery. Emily sighed. Cotton had always made men crazy in the Sea Islands, and the Yankee invaders, no matter how benevolent their intentions, were not so different from the planters she had known before the war.

Mattie needed no encouragement. "You know how I feel. The land should belong to the people who work it.

Who have worked it, with no recompense. They deserve no less in their freedom."

Emily thought of Rufus Green, who had always made a profit for someone else. She said, "Of course. How would it happen?"

Mattie's voice rose. "The Department of the Treasury should set aside the land for former slaves and sell it at terms they can afford. They should check the speculators who want to buy it for a profit!"

"Speculators?" Emily asked. The term reminded her of the brokers who bought and sold cotton and slaves before the war.

Mattie glared at her. "William Chapman. Look to him and his hope to turn St. Helena Island into something no better than a dark, satanic mill in Lowell, Massachusetts!"

Mr. Chapman had often referred to the workers in Lowell as a model for the freed slaves. "The sons and daughters of New England have learned discipline and thrift, and so will the freed people of South Carolina," Chapman was fond of saying.

"Mr. Chapman hopes to buy land?" Emily asked.

"Of course he does. As though two plantations weren't enough!"

"How many head?" Emily murmured, in the old expression of the Sea Islands.

"What did you say?"

"Mattie, don't bellow at me. Labor. It's the sticking point when you grow cotton. It always has been."

ഇൻയ

LATER THAT DAY, IN the parlor, Mattie, who had not given up her indignation about the land sale, asked Phoebe for her opinion.

Phoebe, who still taught the beginners, had accepted Anna Sterling's offer to tutor her. Anna's curriculum was very dry, but Phoebe was so thirsty that she didn't mind. She always left the tutoring sessions with a broad smile on her face.

It had become a habit to offer Phoebe refreshment after the session. Though she was initially hesitant about taking tea with white ladies, she informally claimed the little settee as her spot. She couldn't yet call a white lady anything but "Miss." Teasing her, Emily insisted on calling her "Miss Phoebe" in return.

Phoebe carefully chewed and swallowed her cookie as she considered Mattie's question. Her eyes slid toward Emily. "My daddy mention it."

"I'm sure he has. What is your opinion?"

Phoebe said, "I haven't studied it, Miss Mattie. Can't say."

Emily sighed. On rare occasions, being a belle who didn't argue about money or politics still came in handy. Sweetly, she asked, "How are you progressing with your studies, Miss Phoebe?"

Phoebe's face relaxed into relief. "I do fine," she said. "Don't I, Miss Anna?"

Anna smiled. "You do wonderfully," she said.

When Phoebe rose to leave, Emily said, "Let me walk you home. I haven't visited your mother for a while."

On the way, Phoebe said, "Why do Miss Mattie care so much about the land sale? Do she want to buy her place?"

Emily laughed. "Now that hadn't occurred to me. I think she has strong feelings about who should buy land on St. Helena Island. She thinks that Mr. Chapman already has his share."

Phoebe said, "My daddy think about buying a place."

"I wish he would," Emily said, suddenly fierce with the hope that Rufus Green could profit for himself.

Phoebe grasped Emily's arm. "Oh, Miss Emily, he would dearly love to," she said. "But he can't see a way to it."

"Money?" Emily asked. Being short of funds had never stopped her father. Like every planter, he had always lived from debt to debt, promissory note to note, crop to crop.

Even though there was no one to hear, Phoebe dropped her voice. "Mr. Chapman," she said.

෨෬

IN OHIO, FEBRUARY HAD still been winter, but in the Sea Islands, it was spring. The magnolia in the driveway had put out its first blooms, and the fragrance was delicate rather than overpowering. In the cotton fields, it was time to plow under last year's cotton plants and to manure the fields for this year's crop.

As Emily and Phoebe neared the kitchen door, they were hailed by a familiar figure in dirt-stained trousers and a flattened, sun-faded hat. "Miss Jarvie," Harry said, as he smiled. "It's been too long since we saw you."

They never saw each other save for a polite moment after church. Mattie disliked William Chapman enough to refuse to invite Harry Phelps to her table. It was easy enough for Emily to oblige Mattie, since Emily really had no reason to visit Ocean Point or talk to Chapman.

How she had missed talking to Harry.

Phoebe, bless her, rescued her. "Miss Emily come to see my mama."

"That's kind of her. I'm sure Maum Juno will be glad of it. Phoebe, will you allow me a little conversation with Miss Jarvie?"

Phoebe gave Emily a quizzical look.

Emily said, "Phoebe, tell your mother I'll be along in a moment."

They watched as Phoebe opened the door to the kitchen and disappeared inside. He said, "Her mother and her father are very proud of her progress as a scholar. They're very grateful to you." He brightened, and she recalled his look in the schoolroom as the children saw the light of learning.

"Phoebe deserves everything good that comes to her," Emily said. "All I do is encourage her."

"I hear that you flourish at the Oaks."

She turned to face him, and the look in his eyes was

a little too eager. "I'm happy there," she said. Embarrassed—as though she had not been happy at Ocean Point—she asked, "How is your sister, now that she's back in Boston?"

"It suits her." He hesitated and stammered a little. "I'm sorry that I haven't seen you. That we haven't spoken."

"I'm more engaged than ever." Oh, that didn't sound right. As though she regretted it.

Harry said, "I haven't made Captain Aiken's acquaintance, but I hope to."

Joshua had never objected to her friendship with another man. He was pleased that she got on so well with her employer at *Hearth and Home*, Asa Reed. But she was the one who felt uneasy at the thought of Joshua Aiken and Harry Phelps taking each other's measure. She would trod safer ground. "How is the crop?"

He laughed. "Always the planter's daughter," he said.

"And you always the planter."

"It's time to plant," he said. "And we're held back by the land sale."

"The people refuse to work?"

"If the land changes hands, they don't know who they'll be working for," he said.

"For themselves?"

"You've heard them speak of it."

"Gossip, nothing more."

"Mr. Chapman hopes to buy more land," he said.

"I've heard that, too."

"If he does, he may elevate me. Give me greater duties." He looked as though the prospect weighed on him. "Allow me a share of the profits."

She met his eyes. She saw the minister and the Gideonite behind the superintendent. "Is that what you want?" she asked softly, as though nothing had ever come between them.

He returned her gaze. His face was clouded with doubt. "I don't know," he replied.

಼಻ಌ

In Beaufort, on St. Helena Island, and anywhere that army men, missionaries, and superintendents had settled, the land sale was a topic of heated discussion. At the Oaks, it competed with homelier subjects, like the prohibitive cost of butter and the fact that the scholars needed shoes more than they needed their letters.

Emily invited Caro to share Sunday dinner, hoping that she might bring them more varied news from Beaufort or Camp Saxton. But at the table, Mattie quickly turned the discussion to her favorite subject these days. Sometimes it was a burden to live with Mattie's conviction that ladies at dinner could, and should, speak freely about politics and war.

Caro daintily ate a shrimp and dabbed her mouth with her napkin. She said, "General Saxton is very fierce in his opposition to speculators."

Mattie said, "Like Mr. Chapman?"

Emily threw Caro a pleading look, and Caro ignored

her. Caro, at her ease at Mattie's table, was glad to oblige her hostess. She smiled and said, "General Saxton is too tactful to say a name. But Mr. Chapman was furious. He's said he'd buy largely, if he chooses."

Mattie asked, "What do the freed people say?"

"The men at Camp Saxton all like the idea of buying land," Caro said. "If they had the cash."

Mattie asked, "What about the people on the plantations?"

Emily blurted out, "You should talk to Rufus Green, who works for Mr. Chapman."

Caro's eyes gleamed. She pulled her notebook from her pocket. "Today?"

Emily asked, "Do you take that everywhere?"

"Of course I do," Caro said. "You never know when you might meet someone who has an interesting tale to tell. Will Mr. Green mind if we interrupt his Sabbath?"

༺ༀༀ༻

THE GREEN FAMILY CABIN had been greatly improved since the arrival of freedom. The Greens had rescued a sturdy pine table and four chairs, refuting the Gideonite claim that the former slaves never ate their dinner together. They had also found an armchair and a rocker. A Turkish carpet, worn in spots but still bright, lay on the floor before the hearth, where pine logs burned, snapped, and gave off the odor of resin. The family dog, a yellow hound, slept before the fire and sighed in his sleep.

Emily introduced Caro, and Juno rearranged all the

chairs so they could fit at the table. Caro pulled out her notebook.

Rufus said, "You came to speak to me?"

"Only if you allow it."

"What tale do you tell the *Christian Recorder* about me?"

Caro smiled to hear that her reputation had preceded her. "It depends on the tale that you tell to me," she said.

He glanced at Emily, too careful to ask outright if he could trust her.

Emily said quietly, "As Miss Caroline's cousin, as Miss Easton's friend, I'm here to listen, not to speak, and whatever you tell the *Christian Recorder* isn't mine to repeat."

Rufus turned his appraising gaze on Caro. He nodded. "There's a tale, all right," Rufus said. "About what's fair and what ain't."

"The sale of the land," Caro said. "We hear what General Saxton says and what Mr. Chapman says. What does a black man say?"

Rufus held himself still. In a big and powerful man, that calm was more worrisome than obvious anger. His voice came out gravelly with feeling. "Miss Caroline, let me tell you something. I was the driver on this place in slavery days. Marse Dalton and young marse after him, they trust me to run this place. I bring in the crop and I make them a profit. When Mr. Chapman come, I teach him how to grow cotton, and I believe he make a profit, too. And now I do the same for Marse Harry."

As Emily had always suspected. It was different to hear Rufus Green say it.

"I know what Mr. Chapman say. That we need to learn how to be like Yankees. To be industrious. To be thrifty." He tapped the surface of the table. "To learn proper manners, like eating dinner together."

Emily heard not only the voice of Mr. Chapman but also of Miss Eliza Phelps.

Rufus's voice surged with his frustration. "He say we need time to learn all that. Maybe some folks do, folks so beaten down by slavery that they don't want to work for their own increase, or are afraid to speak for their own interest. But what I don't learn in slavery, I learn since the Big Shoot."

Caro wrote furiously, wanting to capture every word.

"Don't need to wait any more. Tired of waiting, Miss Caroline. Tired of hoping. Tired of thinking, 'How long, oh Lord, how long.'" Even seated, he seemed to grow taller and broader. Standing, he would tower over Mr. Chapman. "It's time now. I want to buy my own place, and I want to be master of myself."

∞)(∞

OUTSIDE THE GREEN CABIN, Caro shook out her cramped hand. Her eyes gleamed. "Now I need to talk to Mr. Chapman to get his side of the story."

She ran lightly up the front stairs of the big house at Ocean Point. Emily was the one to hesitate. She recalled living in this house, so uneasy with Eliza, so easy with her brother. She reminded herself that they were in pursuit of William Chapman, with whom she was obliged to disagree.

But when the maidservant showed them into the parlor, they found only Harry Phelps, without a cravat and in his shirtsleeves, a Sunday dishabille. A book sat neglected on his lap, and at his elbow was a half-empty cup of coffee. He looked tired and melancholy.

He rose. "Miss Caroline Jarvie, it's good to see you again."

"You've met?" Emily asked.

"Briefly, in Beaufort."

He offered refreshment, but Caro said, "No, thank you. I've come to talk to Mr. Chapman." She was still holding her notebook. "As a reporter."

"I'm afraid you can't."

"Does he take his Sabbath observance so seriously?"

Harry shook his head. "He isn't here. He's in Boston on a matter of business."

Emily saw Caro become alert, like a hunting dog scenting. Caro said, "What's the matter of business? Do you know?"

Harry sighed. "You'll have to ask him when he returns, next week."

"I'll do that," Caro said.

He turned to Emily, and his face brightened a little. "Miss Emily Jarvie," he said, taking advantage of the situation to use her Christian name. "How are you? Are you well?"

"I am. And you?"

"Yes, aside from the fact that a superintendent's work is never done."

Emily let herself remember. She presumed. She smiled. "I expect you to teach them a Sunday school, to improve them after a long week of uplifting labor."

"Don't tease me so. Now it will worry my conscience." He glanced at her, and their eyes briefly met. It warmed her, and she thought, guiltily and fleetingly, of Joshua. "Allow us, all of us, a bit of Sabbath rest."

Caro put a firm hand on her arm. "We'll do that," she said, and they made their excuses and left.

Outside, on the driveway, well out of earshot of the house, Caro turned to her and said, "You have a warm regard for Mr. Phelps."

Emily blushed. "It's all foolishness," she said. "Mr. Phelps was kind to me when I first came here. A friend, like an older brother."

Caro laughed. "Yes, just as Mr. Sampson Hayward of the First South is like a brother to me," she said.

"Just because you flirt, you think that I do, too," Emily said. "You know that I'm loyal to Joshua."

"Because I do flirt," Caro said, "I know it when I see it."

೫೦೧೩

A WEEK LATER, WHEN Emily left the classroom, she found Caro sitting in the parlor, ensconced on the settee that Phoebe liked. The most recent issue of the *Liberator* had been discarded for a copy of *Harper's Weekly*, which was full of news of the war. Caro looked up and smiled, raising the publication. "I'd prefer *Godey's*," she said, meaning the ladies' magazine dedicated to fashion.

Emily laughed. "Not in this house. I think that Mattie would wear a bloomer costume if she dared."

Caro, fashionably dressed in plaid cotton, shook her head. "When the war's over, I'm going to wear silk dresses as often as I dare," she said. "Doesn't it tire you? All this piety. The Gideonites dress as drab as the Quakers do."

"The Friends," Emily corrected her. "Mattie was raised among the Friends."

"They are no friends to fashion, that's for sure."

Emily eased herself into the nearest armchair. "You haven't come here to complain about Mattie's taste in dress."

"The sale's been stopped."

Emily laughed. "I know all about it. It was Mattie's doing."

"Really?"

"Yes, she suggested it to General Saxton, and it was no trouble to persuade General Hunter to use his military authority to stop it."

Caro said, "And of course Mr. Chapman is furious about it." She leaned forward, her eyes bright. "I know why he was in Boston."

"Oh, tell us."

"He was talking to investors. He wants to use their funds to buy as much land as he can."

"That's interesting."

"Yes. Fifteen Boston men of business. With their help, I reckon he can buy hugely."

Emily raised her eyes to her cousin's. Caro was as animated as though she'd been flirting. Emily said, "But that's not right, Caro." Troubled, Emily asked, "Have you spoken to Rufus Green about it? What does he say?"

"Shall we go together to ask him?"

೮)ೞ

When they arrived, a somber Juno sat at the kitchen table. Her face was ashen. Emily went to her and put her arm around Juno's shoulders. Juno shook her head. "No, leave me be, Miss Emily."

Caro said, "Is there something to report on, Mrs. Green?"

Juno glared at Caro's notebook. "Put that away."

Caro obeyed and tucked her notebook into her pocket. More softly, she said, "Can we help you?"

"Don't think so."

Caro sat. Even more softly, she asked, "Is there trouble?"

Juno looked at Caro as though Caro were a fool. She said, "Rufus go to Mr. Chapman about the land sale. Lose his temper. Raise his voice."

"When?"

"Just now. Don't know what will come of it."

Caro rose and Emily did too. Caro said, "Emily, do you mind? I want to talk to him alone."

"I do mind, but I'll let you," Emily said, her face abashed.

Caro found him just beyond the house, staring at his cotton field. "Mr. Green?" Caro said.

He turned. Even though the day wasn't warm, he was sweating. He said, "Go on, Miss Caroline. I ain't fit company right now."

"I didn't come here for company," Caro said, reaching for her notebook. "What did you say to Mr. Chapman, and what did he say to you?"

"A whole life of watching my tongue," he said. "And now I shout at the man I work for, like a man drunk."

"It's time for a free man to express his opinion," Caro said.

"It ain't time for a black man to lose his temper. We ain't that free yet."

Caro said, "I don't mind if you lose your temper. I've seen a black man mad before. What did you talk about with Mr. Chapman?"

It was the news about the investors, he told her. "He boast that he have the money to buy as much land as he please, when the sale set to happen again." He wiped his forehead with his sleeve. "So I go to him and tell him I'm ready to buy some land for myself now. That he might leave me a scrap for myself. And then he tell me to be patient."

"And then?"

"Then I tell him what I tell you. Can't wait. Won't wait. He look at me and tell me that I don't have to worry.

He plan to sell the land at cost. I ask him when. He say when it in our best interest. I ask him what that mean. He tell me that he decide when that is."

Caro nodded as she wrote.

"Then I raise my voice. Too mad to watch myself. Tell him that he don't think of my interest, he think of his own. That he can promise all he like, and I don't trust him to keep his promise. He look at me—he ain't the least bit taken aback or upset—and he remark that he think of me as a man of honor. Remind me that I sign a contract. Believe that I'll keep it. And I'm still mad. I tell him that a man of honor don't make an empty promise he'll never keep."

"What did he say to that?"

"Tell me to go away and cool down, like nothing we say matter very much. I go away still mad. Still feel it."

"What do you plan to do?"

"Right now? Don't know. Still can't think straight." He turned his face away. Despite his passion, he was ashamed that he'd lost control of himself. "Go on, Miss Caroline."

∞⧉

MR. CHAPMAN SAT AT the desk in the study, the planter's spot, his correspondence in a neat pile before him, his open ledger at his elbow. Emily had the uncomfortable memory of standing before her father in his study to beg for clemency for Caro in Charleston before the war. *Stop it*, she thought.

Mr. Chapman, unruffled, looked up to say, "The Misses Jarvie. To what do I owe this honor?"

Caro said, "I'm here as a reporter, sir. I've just spoken to Mr. Rufus Green, and now I wish to speak to you."

Chapman looked from Emily, whom he knew as an ally of Miss Easton, to Caro. He said, "And what did Mr. Rufus Green tell you?"

"That you made him a promise, and he isn't sure you'll fulfill it."

"I see."

"I'd like to hear your side of it, sir," Caro said.

Chapman nodded. "That's only fair."

Emily exclaimed, "Fair!" She gathered her courage. "You owe your position here to Rufus Green. He has made you what you are: the most successful superintendent in the Sea Islands. Because he is industrious and astute. Because he is as much a man of business as you are—more so, in the cotton business. How dare you deny him the chance to profit for himself as he has profited you?"

"Emily!" Caro said, in warning.

"Miss Jarvie?" Chapman asked her, sitting back in his chair. "What should I do, in your opinion?"

The past and the present seemed to blur before her eyes. Emily said, "Tear up his contract and lend him enough money to buy as many acres as he desires."

"That's an extreme position, Miss Jarvie."

"No, it's not. It's a matter of what is fair. In God's eyes, as well as in man's."

Chapman looked at Caro. "Your cousin seems to have mistaken me for a planter."

"I do not," Emily said, fighting the constriction in her

chest. "Because you are a planter." She fled the room and fled the house, standing on the steps bareheaded, too full of feeling to pull on her bonnet. She had defied her father like this, and she had paid dearly for it.

Ⅲ

THE DEPARTMENT OF THE Treasury, which oversaw the "abandoned lands" of St. Helena Island, overruled General Hunter and set the date of the land sale for March 9—exactly a year, to the day, that the first Gideonites arrived. The tax commissioners agreed to set aside acreage for the people of the island.

Mattie was jubilant. "Hallelujah!" she said to Emily. "Rufus Green will have his place yet."

"I'm not so sure," Emily said.

"Why would you doubt? Can't he buy with a note like anyone else?"

Emily said, "Mr. Chapman doesn't think he's prepared yet."

"Prepared for what? The man has been running the Dalton place for years!"

Mattie, who had been in good humor since she learned of the set-aside of lands for former slaves, teased Emily again. "Why, my dear? Are you planning to buy a place?"

She said, "If I bought a plot, I'd sell it to Rufus Green at cost. Right now."

Mattie sobered. "You'd risk Mr. Chapman's ire? For undercutting his designs for uplifting the enslaved?"

"I'd risk Mr. Green's ire. For meddling in his business and obliging him to accept charity."

"How much do you have to spend?"

"Several hundred dollars. Would that be enough?"

All the teasing went out of Mattie's voice. "To vie against Mr. Chapman and his Boston investors? I doubt it."

❧❧

ON THE SUNDAY AFTERNOON before the sale—it had been set for Monday morning—Emily sat listlessly in the parlor at the Oaks. Anna and Mattie had gone for a walk, but Emily had refused their company. The air that flowed through the open windows was scented with a green, fresh fragrance. She wished that she had the liveliness to walk, too.

When Rosa announced Mr. Phelps, she rose from her chair in apprehension. Seeing him, she said, "Mr. Phelps! You shouldn't be here."

He looked disheveled. He adjusted his windblown cravat. "That's quite a welcome, Miss Jarvie."

"Mattie and Anna are out."

"I promise you that I'll behave as though they were here."

"Mattie would send you away. You know how she feels about Mr. Chapman."

He sighed as he sat. "I'm still my own man, last I knew."

"She knows how indebted you are to your employer."

He said, "Not so different from anyone else who works for him."

"He pays you considerably more than he pays Rufus Green," she reminded him sharply.

He rubbed his face. "The people gossip as much as the missionaries do," he said. "Of course that tale has made the rounds."

She didn't reply.

He looked up. There were dark circles under his eyes, and his youthful face seemed aged by fatigue. "I rue the day the tax commissioners decided to sell land on St. Helena Island," he said.

"Mr. Phelps," she said softly, wishing that she could call him by his Christian name. "What torments you so?"

"I know what Mr. Chapman thinks," he said. "That his administration is the best thing for the cotton crop and that the people here will benefit from his oversight. And I've tangled my fate with his by becoming his superintendent." He took a deep breath. "And more than that. He's made me a promise. If he buys more land, he'll give me a free rein at Ocean Point, as much as if I owned it, and he'll also guarantee me a share of the profits." He shook his head. "Do you know what long-staple cotton is bringing in Liverpool, where the blockade drives up the price?"

"I don't follow it."

"Enough to guarantee any planter a fortune," he said. "And half a fortune would be a fortune, too."

She said softly, "The thought of a fortune seduces you. Even as it torments you."

185

He leaned forward and his eyes glistened with emotion. "I didn't come to the Sea Islands for a fortune," he said. "I came for a better reason than that."

She thought of him in the schoolroom. "I know," she said. She leaned forward, too. If she reached out her hands, he could clasp them. "Help them. Help Rufus Green. Help him to buy his own place."

"Oh, Emily," he said, in despair. "What he wants will be the ruin of Ocean Point. I can't do it. I can't even go to Chapman to defend it."

At the intimacy of her name on his lips, she wanted to clasp his hands. To console him. But his loyalty to William Chapman—and her own, to Joshua—held her back. She said, "I don't think I can help you, Mr. Phelps."

He drew back, reminding himself of everything that kept them friends, however precariously, and not more intimate than that. "I know," he said. "Even though I hoped that you might."

❧❧

EMILY DIDN'T ATTEND THE auction, but she soon heard of the results. William Chapman bought eleven plantations, a total of ten thousand acres. The former slaves of St. Helena Island managed to buy two thousand acres, most of it in small plots of a hundred acres or less. Rufus Green remained landless, employed for a wage and a share by Mr. Chapman and superintended by Mr. Phelps.

"Thirteen plantations!" Emily said to Mattie, counting the two that he already owned. "That's more than anyone owned on St. Helena before the war." She shook her head. "And not a single acre to Mr. Green."

Mattie said, "Do you think Mr. Chapman will sell the land at cost?"

"What do you think, Mattie?"

Mattie tried hard to look hopeful. She also tried hard not to snort. "Slavery ended," she said. "There's hope here, too."

Emily felt too weary to jest. Or to argue. Or to say anything at all.

≈

ON THE SUNDAY AFTER the sale, Joshua joined Emily for the service at the White Church. Seeing him, she felt a wave of guilt. When he took her arm to lead her to the pew, she leaned against him, hoping that her nearness would make an apology for her.

After the service, again arm in arm, they made their way into the churchyard. She greeted her friends and introduced Joshua to anyone who had not met him before. And she turned to see Harry Phelps, who stood alone, looking forlorn despite his new coat and bright cravat.

She introduced the two men to one another and saw how they took each other's measure. As she had feared, it made her feel ashamed, as though she had something to be ashamed of. Too sharply, she said to Harry, "How do you feel, now that you've made your devil's bargain?"

Harry said, "Lower your voice, Miss Jarvie, since he stands right behind you."

Joshua looked puzzled. Harry said, "I believe Miss Jarvie refers to Mr. Chapman." To Emily, he said, "That's rather harsh of you."

Emily thought, *Friends don't bicker like this. Intimates do.* Her cheeks flamed. "I think not, Mr. Phelps."

"You'll show me a little kindness?" he entreated her. "Just a little?"

"Emily?" Joshua asked. "Has something slipped by me?"

Her face still flaming, Emily explained, "The land sale, Joshua. We refer to the land sale."

Joshua's eyes shifted from Emily to Harry. He said, "There's been a great deal of passion about the land sale."

Harry flushed. "Yes, there has," he said. "It's good to make your acquaintance, Captain Aiken," and he held out his hand, one gentleman to another.

"Likewise," Joshua said.

ꙮ

JOSHUA REMAINED THE GENTLEMAN during Sunday dinner at the Oaks, politely dodging Mattie's efforts to sermonize about land ownership and returning, again and again, to tales of camp life suitable for the pages of *Hearth and Home*. He made much of the kitten that the First South had rescued. The kitten was called Hark, short for Hercules. It was a joke, since he was small enough to fit in the palm of a hand scarred by picking cotton. "Hark has taken to Private Hayward," Joshua said. "He sleeps curled around Hayward's head at night, like a nightcap, and cries when he's at drill."

Anna said, laughing, "Mattie, the world has turned upside down in the Sea Islands. You relish talk of war, and Captain Aiken's soldiers dote on kittens."

After the meal, Joshua asked Emily to walk with him, and they found shelter under a live oak far enough from the house for privacy. Emily suddenly thought of their first conversation on the Aiken plantation in Sumter County before the war. They had both taken refuge from a crowded ball on a bench under a live oak.

Joshua touched her hand. "Emily, I don't think you've been honest with me."

"About what?" she asked, even though she knew.

"About Mr. Phelps. I've heard all kinds of gossip in Beaufort and in camp. But I've dismissed all of it. Now I wonder."

"We've been friends," she said. "And he's asked my opinion. That much is true. But it's always been on matters of business, Joshua."

"What business?"

"The business of managing a plantation."

He met her eyes, looking bemused. "Which you now call the devil's business."

"I think we agree on that."

"Has Mr. Phelps gone to the devil?"

She was in the wrong, and it made her adamant. "I never met a man less suited to be a superintendent," she said.

"Really?" Joshua slid his hand to her forearm, his touch gentle and insistent. "I'd think the opposite, since he follows Mr. Chapman so closely."

She felt undeserving of that touch. "He disagrees with Mr. Chapman."

"Does he?" Joshua had developed an officer's ability to command, even in a gentle tone. "From where I stand, he looks like Chapman's creature. I'm not pleased to hear you defend him."

"He works for Mr. Chapman. Doesn't he owe his employer a little loyalty? As a military man, you understand that."

"I hardly need a reminder."

She sought his eyes. "Would you deride Mr. Phelps for it?"

He held her gaze. "Loyalty to something dishonorable? To something wrong? We both know where that leads, Emily."

The past that she had fled. The ghost that would not go away. It had pursued her to Ohio, and it had found her in the Sea Islands. The question of her own loyalty, which she could never atone for. Tears rose to her eyes. "Joshua, do you question my loyalty? Do you doubt me?"

"It distresses me to see that you befriend Harry Phelps."

"Do you really doubt me? After what I sacrificed to follow you?"

He let go of her arm. "Emily, I love you. But suddenly I doubt you terribly."

As he walked away, his shoulders sagged in the Union coat. She buried her face in her hands and wept.

Chapter 8: Wade in the Water

As the controversy over the land sale roiled through the Sea Islands, the First and Second South Carolina prepared for their first real military assignment: an expedition to Florida to attempt to free the slaves held along the St. Johns River. Sampson, baptized by fire on the earlier expedition, was full of pride at the thought of engaging in a real battle.

"Who goes with you?" Caro asked him. "Besides the military men?"

"Engineers and their men," Sampson said. "Pilots for the boats. And the surgeon, Dr. Rogers, he come too."

"Any women?"

"I hear we take the washwomen along," he said. "And Mrs. Taylor, who work as a nurse for Dr. Rogers."

"Reporters?" Caro asked.

Sampson groaned. "You ain't going to start with that again!"

Caro said, "I will. And I'll keep at it until I'm satisfied."

She went looking for Colonel Higginson, who thought a little better of her these days since she had confined herself to talking to the women and the soldiers when they were at leisure. He greeted her but didn't invite her to sit. He knew, Caro realized, that people who stood were swifter to transact—and finish—their business. She said, "Sir, it's about the mission to Florida."

"No, you won't accompany us, Miss Jarvie."

"As a reporter—"

"As a civilian, and as a lady, you'll be in our way."

"I hear that Mrs. Taylor is going," she said, sulkily.

"Mrs. Taylor is trained as a nurse and is under the command of our regimental surgeon. She is also an excellent shot."

"If I could shoot, would you allow me?"

"Miss Jarvie, I'm very busy," he said, dismissing her.

Sampson caught up with her when she left Colonel Higginson. He didn't bother to lead her to privacy. They stood in the midst of the camp, the sounds of talk and laughter and singing and fiddle playing all around them. He tapped her on the arm. "Made a plea, didn't you," he said.

She was too irritated to reply.

"And you didn't get your satisfaction."

She shook her head.

"We leave soon," he said, smiling. "Wish me well."

"I do. You know I do."

"Pray for me, too." He said, "It help me last time to think of you praying for me."

She said, "If it helps you, then I'll do it." But she didn't hide her irritation.

"You don't believe?"

"That's my business, not yours." It wasn't fair to snap at him because Colonel Higginson still treated her like a lady, and she knew it.

"Why you so contrary?" he asked, still smiling.

In truth? Because she liked him, and it bothered her. Because he made her recall how she had felt about Danny Pereira. Because he really might fall in battle, and as godless as she was, she would regret it. She said, "I never had a basket name, growing up, but my friend Sophy christened me in Charleston. Would you like to know what she called me?"

"Yes."

"Miss Sass."

The smile deepened. "It suit you," he said. Then he bent close, and to her surprise, gently kissed her on the cheek.

♠♥♣

WHEN THE FIRST AND Second South Carolina regiments returned a month later to a hero's welcome, it was full spring in the Sea Islands, the air full of the promise of summer's heat. The smell of floral bloom, magnolia and gardenia, was strong, even in the camp, which had cut down trees and vegetation to make way for the men's tents and where the smell of the latrines could not be ignored, despite all efforts to treat with lime.

Caro stood with the rest of the women who cheered and waved their handkerchiefs, relieved that their husbands and brothers had returned in one piece. Caro rushed to find Sunday, who hugged her and reassured her that he was unscathed, and told her to interview men who had actually been in battle. Those men talked to her without any prompting, and she listened, nodded, and wrote until her wrist ached.

Sampson found her rubbing her wrist. "You get what you need?"

"For the moment." She flexed her fingers and reached into her pocket.

"No, you save your hand. Had my glory, but I can tell you later."

"But you're all right."

"Shot and shot at, but I am," he said, smiling as though it had been a frolic.

"I heard that the army went to Florida to raid the plantations," she said. "To get the slaves out."

"The massas got too much warning. They fled and took their people with them. The places were deserted." He shook his head. "Colonel Montgomery mighty disappointed. He wanted to free people. Did you know he were in Kansas with John Brown?"

She had known that Montgomery was a fiery abolitionist and a good friend of Colonel Higginson's, but this was news. "No. He must be disappointed indeed. Do you think he'll want to put another expedition together? To try to free people?"

"We just got back. Give him a moment to rest and think about it."

"Oh, I will," Caro said. "I'll talk to the officers later."

Very gently, he touched her sore wrist. "Did you miss me while I was gone, Miss Sass?"

"Yes, I did."

"Think of me before you fall asleep at night?"

She had. "Don't press your luck, Private Hayward."

A stranger, dressed like a recent contraband, approached and called to Sampson. In surprise, he said, "Tobey! When you get here?"

"A week ago."

"You escape?"

The man pushed back his straw hat. He had the look of the Low Country: brown skin, high cheekbones, round face, easy smile. But his pleasant face was troubled as he spoke. "Yes," he said.

Sampson gestured toward the man's civilian clothes. "You don't join the army?"

"Oh, I do," he said. "But I scout, so I dress like this."

"Scout?" Caro asked. "Where?"

"The army mighty interested in hearing about the Hayward place," he said. "And all them places along the Combahee."

"Do you report to Colonel Montgomery?" Caro asked.

"No, never met him," Tobey said. "I take what I know to Mrs. Harriet Tubman."

Astonished, Caro said, "Mrs. Harriet Tubman is in the Sea Islands? General Moses herself?"

"Yes," the man said.

"She rescues people," Caro said. "She leads them out."

"I hear that," Tobey said.

Too eagerly, Caro pressed him. "Is she working with the army? Does the army plan to lead people out?"

Tobey glanced at Sampson. Perplexed, he said, "I don't know."

A reporter should be able to find out.

৶৹ℭ৪

CARO STOPPED TO TALK to the washwomen. Some of them had gone to Florida, and they were as full of stories as the soldiers. Scribbling, Caro thought, *It's a fine thing when a laundress knows more about the battlefield than a reporter.*

She asked them if they had heard anything about Mrs. Harriet Tubman being in the Sea Islands.

"General Moses?" asked a woman who had been in Florida. "General Moses here?"

Caro nodded.

The Florida veteran said, "Don't hear about her. I do hear that Colonel Montgomery think about going up the Combahee. Them planters don't flee like in Florida. They stay put to plant rice."

Caro thought, *Someone must know.*

She sought Joshua, interrupting him as he drank coffee from a tin cup. "Captain Aiken," she greeted him. They were formal with each other in camp.

"Yes, Miss Jarvie?"

She smiled. "I've heard that Colonel Montgomery may be planning another expedition to free people. And that Mrs. Harriet Tubman, who knows him since John Brown's raids in Kansas, is in the Sea Islands."

He was suddenly impassive, the expression leaving his face as he sat more stiffly in his chair. "I can't say."

"I see." She was annoyed and she was tired of politeness. But she wanted this enough to see if she could flatter him into it.

And then, irritated enough to forget his manners. "No, Caro, I mean it. And don't jump to a conclusion because I don't tell you."

"I see," she said.

"I'm beginning to agree with Colonel Higginson about reporters," he said. "Nuisances at best. And at worst, traitors, because they want to publish military information that should remain a secret."

"Is there a plan to free people? Say, upriver, into Colleton County? Is that the secret?"

"Stop it, Caro," he said.

She asked, "May I ask you something you might actually answer?"

"You can try."

"Did you quarrel with Emily?" At his expression, she said, "Surely that's not a military secret."

Stiffly, he said, "I told her I wasn't pleased that she was so friendly with Mr. Harry Phelps."

"Oh, Joshua. He was kind to her when she first came here. You wouldn't begrudge her that."

"It's no secret that I don't care for Mr. Phelps's association with Mr. Chapman."

"Then you should take it up with Mr. Chapman. And make things up with Emily."

Joshua shook his head. "Caro, will you ever learn to mind your own business?"

Not bothering to hide her irritation, Caro said, "I'm a reporter! It's all my business!"

Disappointed, she walked toward the guard gate. If the army thought that reporters were nuisances, she, as a reporter, thought that army officers were human barricades to the truth. She was tired of being admonished because she was a woman, and sometimes a lady, of color.

ಐಓಚ

A FEW DAYS LATER, Caro walked down the path through the row of tents and heard hastened footsteps. "Caro!" Sampson called. "Miss Caroline!"

She sighed and halted as he came alongside her. He said, "I have something for you." Touching the wrist that ached when she scribbled too much. "Might cheer you."

"How do you know I need cheering?"

"Military secret," he said, smiling. "I have a secret for you."

"Yes?" she said, raising her eyes to his. The copper flecks in his eyes seemed to glow in the spring sun.

He bent close to whisper in her ear. "General Moses in Beaufort. No one know where she stay, but she spend her time at the hospital, nursing the men."

She pitched her voice low, too. "How did you find out?"

"I hear things."

"Secrets," she said, so low that he had to bend even closer to hear her.

"Yes." His breath was warm in her ear. "You go to talk to her?"

"I will." She laid her hand on his cheek and felt the scratch of his whiskers under her hand. They were close enough to kiss, if they weren't in full view of the entire First South.

He covered her hand with his own and smiled as he stepped back to look her in the face. "Will you give me a little sugar?"

She laughed. "Depends on what I hear from General Moses," she said.

ഔരു

CARO HAD NEVER BEEN to the field hospital in Beaufort, and she was afraid she would see groaning, wounded, bandaged men. But there had been no shooting lately in the Sea Islands, and the place was empty and hushed. The entryway had been scrubbed spotlessly clean, and the hallway smelled of carbolic soap. The ward she passed was a light-filled room where a man lay resting quietly in bed under white sheets. The place was as peaceful as a church.

She stopped a passing nurse. "I was told that Mrs. Harriet Tubman works here."

The nurse was a slender white woman whose hair escaped her starched cap. "The news travels swiftly," she said, in a New England accent. "She's in the kitchen."

Caro found her stirring a kettle of broth. Mrs. Tubman looked up from her task. She was a small woman—Caro was surprised at how small—dressed in the plainest black dress and a turban, not unlike the headscarf of a Low Country woman. She said, "May I help you?" Her Virginia accent was overlaid with her long residence in the North.

Caro introduced herself, holding out her press pass.

Mrs. Tubman appraised her. "Reporter, are you?"

"Yes, ma'am."

"What bring you here?"

Caro's usual bravado failed her. Despite her unassuming appearance, this woman had led thousands of slaves to freedom. She had shaken the hand of President Lincoln. She had earned the sobriquet of "General Moses." Caro had never worried whether the people she talked to liked her or not. Suddenly she was seized with a powerful desire for Mrs. Harriet Tubman's approval. "Because you are a hero," she said.

Another appraising gaze. "Where do you hail from? I hear Ohio in your voice."

"I graduated from Oberlin College."

"And before that?"

"I grew up on St. Helena Island."

Mrs. Tubman looked her up and down. "Fled north, I presume," she said.

"Before the war," she said.

Mrs. Tubman softened her tone. "I can't talk to a reporter," she said. "But I know a fugitive when I see one. You take care, Miss Jarvie."

෨ඥ

CARO LEFT THE HOSPITAL feeling light-headed. Harriet Tubman had seen through her and sent her on her way. She was used to being dismissed by white people. Harriet Tubman's shrewd appraisal had shaken her badly.

On the road to the camp, a drayman rumbled past her and offered her a ride, but she refused him. It helped to walk, even though the afternoon sun flushed her face and the afternoon heat made her sweat. At the camp gate, she barely heard the guard's friendly greeting. She strode down the path between the tents as though she were marching to a battlefield.

She stopped beneath the tree where Sampson had stroked her wrist. Where he had caressed her cheek. Where his breath had tickled her ear. She leaned against the bark of the live oak, feeling its pleasant, rough surface through her dress. She closed her eyes. The air smelled of magnolia, coffee, quicklime, and latrines. A camp odor. She wished for him as though wishing him could conjure him.

"Caro?"

Her eyes flew open. "Sampson? How did you know I was here?"

"Guard told me. Said you came in looking like you in a daze. You all right?" He reached to touch her forehead, the way a mother checked a child for fever.

She pushed his hand away. She was neither sick, nor a child. "I walked from Beaufort."

"You find Mrs. Tubman?"

"I did."

"General Moses!" he said softly. "What do she tell you?"

Caro said tartly, "She said good day. She wouldn't tell me a thing."

"Couldn't get round her, could you?"

"Couldn't get anywhere near," Caro admitted. "She didn't like me, and she doesn't trust me." The word *fugitive* still smarted.

"She might trust me," Sampson said. "And if you bring me to her, she might like you better."

Caro snorted. "She might be too canny for you, too."

"Next time you meet her, you bring me with you," he said.

Caro thought that Sampson might succeed where she had not.

※

WHEN SHE VISITED THE hospital again, it smelled worse, the broth and liniment overpowered by a sweet, rotten smell. A deep groan, a guttural sound of pain, surged from the ward. The nurse who hurried through the corridor wore a bloodied apron, and she tugged on her cap, which sat askew on her head. Caro caught Sampson by the hand. "This way," she said, pulling him toward the kitchen, where the smell of broth drowned out the smell of gangrene.

In the kitchen, Mrs. Tubman was again stirring a pot of broth, as though she hadn't moved. She said to Caro, "We meet again, Miss Jarvie. Who have you brought with you?"

"This is Sampson Hayward, now a private in the First South Carolina, but before that, he was a slave all his life on the Hayward plantation on the main, up the Combahee River."

Harriet Tubman's eyes flickered. "You know the river? You know the plantations?"

"I do, ma'am."

"I pay the men who bring me information."

Sampson waved the suggestion away. "The army pay me, ma'am."

She put a small, dark hand on Sampson's blue sleeve. "What can you tell me?"

He said, "Have friends and kin still on the Hayward place. Still enslaved. I swear to myself that I get them out. What do you want to know, General?"

Once Mrs. Tubman had heard everything that Sampson had to tell her, she finally spoke to Caro. "You did right, bringing Private Hayward to me," she said. "Thank you."

Caro felt a surge of pleasure at Harriet Tubman's praise. It made her happier than getting an interview would have. "I'm glad to oblige you," she said. She had another bid for General Moses's good opinion. She had two recent fugitives from the Jarvie plantation.

∞CR

AT MIDDAY DINNER, WHEN Caro made her request, Sophy said, "Do she plan to lead people here to freedom?"

Caro said, "She won't say. If it's army business, she has reason to keep it close. But I suspect she does."

"Like they try in Florida?"

"Yes. But up the Combahee this time."

"Where the Jarvie place is."

"And the Hayward place."

Sophy looked away.

Caro laid her hand gently on Sophy's arm. "Do you remember the land around the Jarvie place?"

"Too well."

"Oh, Sophy."

Chloe said sharply, "Don't pester her. You know how she feel about her escape."

"No," Caro said softly. "Not at all. But if you—you too, Chloe—would talk to Mrs. Tubman, you could help everyone on the Jarvie place to escape."

Sophy shuddered and Chloe grasped her hand. "It's all right, Mama," she whispered.

"No, it ain't," Sophy said. She asked Caro, "What do General Moses want to know?"

଼ଔ

WHEN SOPHY OPENED THE door to Mrs. Tubman, Caro
was struck by how alike they looked—small, dark wom-
en, deceptively decorous in their gray dresses and white
headscarves. Mrs. Tubman clasped Sophy's hands in
greeting. She said, "I'm grateful to meet you."

She glanced at the parlor and said to Sophy, "You
have a fine house. You do well for yourself."

"Yes, I do," Sophy said. She invited Mrs. Tubman to sit
in the kitchen. "I have coffee."

Mrs. Tubman smiled. Caro had never seen her smile
before. Chloe joined them as they sat at the pine table,
and Sophy introduced her, saying, "She come out with
me." And her polite veneer splintered. She began to
tremble.

Mrs. Tubman said, "I hear you have a bad time when
you escape."

Sophy closed her eyes. She reached for Chloe's hand
and gripped it tightly.

"Believe me, I know all about that."

Sophy opened her eyes. "Bad dreams?" she said, her
voice barely audible. "Do you have bad dreams?"

Mrs. Tubman didn't say so. Her expression was composed. Caro thought, *She's had decades to put them to rest.*
When she spoke, she said, "The army plans to go up the
Combahee River soon, with the First and Second. They
plan to raid all the places along the river. To get the people out."

Sophy didn't reply. Her body was tensed in the fear that wouldn't leave her.

Chloe said, "Mama, if this is too hard—"

Mrs. Tubman said, "Of course it's hard." Her voice was low and understanding. "If you help us, Miss Sophy, we can get those people out. Many, many people. If you tell us about your old place, the one you escaped from, you can help us save all those people. Lead them all out to freedom."

Sophy drew a long shuddering breath. Her free hand reached for Caro's, and she gripped it as hard as Chloe's. She said, "I do my best, Mrs. Tubman."

Mrs. Tubman smiled again. In a friendly tone, as though she had known Sophy for years and they had coffee together every week, she said, "How far from the landing to the house? Do you recollect?"

Sophy's eyes never left Mrs. Tubman's face. Her grip on Caro's hand never eased. When a dog barked, somewhere down the street, Sophy didn't flinch. She didn't falter. She kept talking.

§§CЗ

CARO FOLLOWED MRS. TUBMAN out the door. On the steps, Mrs. Tubman turned to her. "Thank you," she said. "I can't tell you how much this helps us."

Caro was flooded with feeling. Her voice caught in her throat. "I'll write down what I recall as soon as I can."

"Can you get them to help you draw a map?"

Caro nodded. She was too close to tears, and she

hated the thought that Mrs. Tubman would see her weakness.

Mrs. Tubman's voice was kind. "You had a bad time getting out, didn't you?"

A tear slipped down her cheek and she brushed it away. "The dreams," she said. "When do they stop?"

Mrs. Tubman used the same low, understanding tone she had used with Sophy. General Moses's tone. "When you start to fight," she said.

∞

SHORTLY AFTER MRS. TUBMAN'S visit, Sophy said to Caro, "Come with me."

It wasn't market day, and Caro was confused. "Where are we going?"

Sophy led Caro down the block to the house where the dog barked. As they stopped on the sidewalk, the dog ran toward them, and Sophy froze. The dog barked so loud that the front door opened, and a woman emerged, running into the yard to grab the dog by the collar. "You hush!" she said to the dog. To Sophy, she said, "Do my dog bother you?"

"Don't care much for dogs since I run for freedom."

"This ain't a patroller's dog," the woman said. She rubbed the dog's head. "Just a little spaniel pup, someone's pet. I run too, from Edisto Island, and when I come to Beaufort, I find the dog in the yard, barking and howling. Poor thing, he a runaway, just like the rest of us."

Sophy asked, "Is he friendly?"

"Hold out your hand."

Sophy extended her hand, and the dog licked her fingers. For the first time since her escape, Caro saw the worry on Sophy's face ease. It wasn't happiness, not yet, but Caro could see hope for it.

Sophy straightened. She said to Caro, "We go home, and Chloe and I draw you a map of the Jarvie place. To help General Moses."

⚜

WHEN CARO RETURNED TO the hospital, it was quiet again. Odd that she could know the rhythm of the war by the smell and the sound of the hospital corridor. When she found Mrs. Tubman, she handed her the papers. "The map of the Jarvie place and the notes I made."

Mrs. Tubman's eyes gleamed. "I can't tell you how much this helps us." She rolled up the papers to preserve them and put them in her pocket. "I owe Miss Sophy and Miss Chloe some money for their efforts. You too, Miss Jarvie."

"Oh no. I couldn't take it." She faltered under that intense gaze. "But I wondered if I might ask a favor of you."

"Depends on what it is."

"When Colonel Montgomery takes the regiments up the river, I want to be on the boat."

"Why? No, don't show me your press pass."

Where was Miss Sass? Harriet Tubman incapacitated her. Caro stammered, "I want to free people."

"One of the places up the river is owned by a family named Jarvie. Is there any connection to you?" The dark eyes bored into her.

"My father owned it before he died." She felt Tubman's eyes on her. "After he died, it passed to his brother."

"Like you did." It was a flat statement of fact.

"Yes," she said.

"I need to trust everyone who goes upriver on those boats. Can I trust you?"

"It depends on why you need to trust me, Mrs. Tubman," she said softly.

"To act like a soldier."

"In your army, General Moses, how does a soldier act?"

"Soldiers do what they're told. They don't go running off to do whatever they like. You go on that boat, you stay put, you watch, and you write in that notebook of yours. That's how you fight."

Caro was so relieved that she laughed. "You'll speak to Colonel Montgomery on my behalf?" she asked eagerly.

Mrs. Tubman shook her head. "What you're told to do," she repeated. "Even though it doesn't suit you. Even though you hate it."

"I'll do my damnedest. Isn't that what soldiers say?"

$$\approx\!\infty\!\propto$$

CARO DIDN'T KNOW WHAT Harriet Tubman said to Colonel Montgomery to convince him, and she didn't care. Sampson had no say in it, but she owed him the courtesy of telling him that she was going. She led him through the camp to the relative privacy under the trees to do it. "I'm going on the raid up the Combahee."

"Who allow it?"

"Colonel Montgomery. On General Moses's say-so."

"It ain't a pleasure cruise, Caro!"

"I know that. I'm not going for pleasure. I'm going to report on it."

"Them secesh pickets stand all along the river," he said. "A bullet don't know the difference between a soldier and a reporter. A reporter can get just as dead as a soldier."

"Not if the First and Second are looking after me."

He rubbed his face in distress. "We ain't in so much trouble that we need ladies fighting for us."

"Sampson, stop it. Every black woman is in trouble when she escapes. You know how much trouble."

He looked away.

"I swore to Mrs. Tubman that I wouldn't do anything foolish. I promised her. Sit and observe and write. I won't be fighting. No one will shoot at me."

"I hate it," he said.

"Well, Colonel Montgomery doesn't, so you'll just have to lump it, Private Hayward."

"You're a fool."

"No, I'm not."

He drew close. "If you don't know why I get upset, you are a fool."

"Then tell me."

He said, "If you were shot, if you were hurt, I couldn't bear it."

She had encouraged him to feel that way. She could hardly be angry now. "Oh, Sampson," she said.

He put his arms around her, with considerable urgency. She was aggravated with him, but his embrace was a melting kind of pleasure. He dropped his voice and whispered into her ear, "If any harm came to you, it would break my heart."

"Would it?" she murmured.

He kissed her, with the same urgency of his embrace, and warmth suffused her. She had felt like this back in Charleston, when Danny Pereira had kissed her. She should distrust feeling like this. She should pull away and remind him that they were both soldiers together.

But she did not.

❧❦

WHEN THE *Harriet A. Weed*, a commercial ferry outfitted by the army as a gunboat, went upriver, Caro was on it. Mrs. Tubman had given Caro her orders. Colonel Montgomery, a canny leader, understood that Caro would be best persuaded, and shamed, by General Moses. Mrs. Tubman told her, "You set on the boat and you watch. You observe. You talk to anyone who comes onto the boat, as long as you're not in the soldiers' way. But you stay on the boat. Do you understand me?"

More like an errant daughter than a soldier, she had murmured, "Yes, ma'am."

Now Caro sat quietly as Mrs. Tubman chatted with the pilot. Jack Middleton, recently escaped from the Middleton place, one of the army's upriver targets, was one of Mrs. Tubman's scouts. His master had trusted him to pilot a river steamer, and the ex-slave Middleton knew the Combahee River by heart.

Middleton's realm, the pilot house, served as a lookout; windows extended from floor to ceiling on three sides, affording a panoramic view of the water and the banks. At the very front was the wheel, set into the floor, nearly a man's height. Before it was a stand for the pilot to lean against as he kept his eyes on the watery vista before him.

Caro was prickly with anticipation, but Mrs. Tubman's gaze was on her. She pulled her notebook from her pocket. "Do you mind if I ask you a few questions, Mr. Middleton? While we're waiting?"

"No," he said.

"For a man about to steer us into a raid, you seem very calm, Mr. Middleton."

His face crinkled into a smile. "After making my escape, nothing much bothers me, Miss Jarvie."

Army-issue boots thudded on the stairs, and Sampson put his head into the doorway. This raid belonged to the Second South Carolina, not the First, but Sampson was on loan to them as a scout. When they landed on the Hayward place, he would guide them. He said to Mrs. Tubman, "Just came to see if Miss Caro is all right."

Excitement bubbled up in her. "I'm fine, Sampson."

He looked grave and a little distracted. She said, "Don't worry about me. You go do your duty."

He reached for her hand. In her heightened state, his touch felt electric. "You take care," he said, glancing at Mrs. Tubman. "Don't do anything foolish."

He still thought that her presence on the boat was foolish. She grinned. "I won't do anything you wouldn't," she said, sassing.

∞∞

IT WAS AFTER DUSK by the time the great engine rumbled to life, and Middleton turned the wheel to ease the boat into to St. Helena Sound. She had been on this route—when her father visited his place in Colleton County, they had taken a steamboat up the Combahee—but they had never made the trip at night. Caro gazed into the darkness and failed to orient herself. Both the night and the fog of her memory foiled her.

The boat's lights shone bright, illuminating the water, but the banks were velvety with darkness. "Quarter moon," Middleton said. "Won't rise until near dawn."

"How can you pilot like this?"

He grinned. "Know the river like I know my own hand," he said.

As they left the coast, the smell of seawater gave way to the smell of freshwater marsh, the soggy, weedy soil that rice plants liked to grow in. Trees grew down to the waterline, forming a dense thicket in soggy ground. The sound of the steamboat, the thrumming engines, the rush of the paddlewheel in the water, drowned out any bird or animal sounds. A dark, humped shape raised its head in the water, and as it scrambled to safety, she remembered that alligators liked the river, too.

"Where will we stop?" she asked.

Mrs. Tubman said, "The Nicholls place. How far is it, Mr. Middleton?"

"A ways yet. We get there near dawn. Have our first round in daylight."

Caro asked, "May I go below? Talk to the men?"

"Don't advise it," Middleton said. "You in the way if we meet any secesh pickets."

Caro stared at the close-twined trees, barely distinguishable in the dark. "Are there pickets? Do we know?"

"If they shoot at us, we know," Middleton said.

They moved slowly up the river. Ahead were bluffs. "Field Point," Middleton said. "Just the place for pickets to stand."

Caro strained to see what might be on the riverbank. She had begged for this. She had hoped for battle. But it burdened her nerves to wait for rifle fire.

But none came, and they continued upriver as dawn broke. As the sun rose, mist smoked over the water. The roar of the engines drowned out every other sound. Caro could see the birds among the trees on the bank, but she couldn't hear them. She wondered how the men would be able to hear gunshots.

They continued, and it became full daylight. They approached a break where the forest gave way to rice plants that grew like grasses in the water. Caro asked, "Are we close?"

"Look," Middleton said, and beyond the rice fields sat the plantation house, expanded over the decades as the rice fortune increased. "Nicholls place."

Despite the early hour, slaves worked in the fields, and behind them mounted overseers watched them. At the sight of the boats, the slaves straightened and stared. And to Caro's astonishment, the overseers spurred their horses and rode away. Were they frightened by the sight of the Union's boats? Or were they going to warn of an enemy's approach?

Middleton steered the boat to the landing, and once the boat ground to a halt, the skirmishers began to gather on the landing. The skirmishers would exchange the first shots with the pickets to flush them out and provide cover as the rest of the men advanced into the heart of the plantation to do what they had come to do. She counted about twenty men. She didn't see Sampson's tall frame among them, and she released a breath she hadn't realized she'd been holding.

The skirmishers proceeded carefully. As they moved into the rice field, no overseer or secesh picket raised a rifle. The rest of the company gathered, stepped on the landing, and assembled in formation. Following the skirmishers, they marched crisply from the landing, through the rice field, and past the big house, where they disappeared from view.

Caro rose, hoping to get a better vantage point. She said, "I hate that I can't see what's happening."

"You aren't going anywhere," Mrs. Tubman said, like a chaperone instead of a military commander.

Caro snapped, "I said I wouldn't!"

"You stay calm, Miss Jarvie," Middleton said, his tone soothing.

The smell of smoke began to fill the air. "Fire?" Caro asked Middleton. "What's on fire?"

"Colonel Montgomery give the order to burn the crop." He gestured. "Sheds and mill must be behind the house."

When the outbuildings caught, the rice gave off a pleasant toasted smell, as though it were cooking. But as the fire spread, the smell of rice was soon overpowered by the odor of wood burning to a char.

As the flames leapt into the air, as the air filled with the smell of smoke, a stream of people began to emerge from the slave quarters closer to the house and from the fields abandoned by the overseers. The slaves ran to the *Harriet Weed*, laughing and crying and calling out "God bless!" They carried whatever they could, as though they were going on a long journey. One woman lugged a pot of just-cooked rice, still steaming, and others were loaded down with baskets and bundles. They had brought their livestock, too; one woman had two pigs, one black and one white, and many people carried chickens in their baskets that screamed in indignation at being emancipated from slavery.

The people crowded onto the boat, hundreds of them crushed together, in too much jubilation to care about the crowd or the discomfort. Caro slipped from the pilot house to look at the crush on the deck. The rescued slaves were in a state of exalted excitement, sobbing and laughing and praying. "Free at last!" they said, making a joyful noise of it. "Bless the Lord and God bless the Yankees! Free at last!"

Mrs. Tubman rose and sprinted down the stairs to the deck. Caro followed her.

Mrs. Tubman remained on the deck, pressing hands, offering good wishes, checking for anyone hurt, settling the unsettled. After a moment in the happy chaos, Caro knew that she was in the way. She returned to the pilot house, where Middleton waited, leaning against his stand. He said, "General Moses got them all in order?"

"Give her a few minutes." She stared at the smoke that billowed from the conflagration of the mill and the sheds. The house had also been set afire, and it blazed like a beacon. She said, "That seemed easy enough. I could have gone ashore."

Middleton grinned. "We lucky," he said. "May not be so lucky next time." Then he frowned. "You stay on the boat."

❧❧

IT WAS MIDDAY. As the sun rose higher in the sky, gnats swarmed and swirled over the river's surface, and the birds that fed on them swooped through their clouds. A dark, green odor rose from the river, of leaves and roots soaked in water, and beyond it, a marshy scent drifted from the rice fields. The sun gilded the waxy foliage of the live oaks.

Caro could see the wooden bridge well before the boat approached it. "What is that?" she asked Middleton.

"Pontoon bridge. Used to be a ferry here, but the bridge is faster for men, horses, guns. The secesh throw it together."

"Are there secesh here?"

Middleton didn't turn his head. He said, "The scouts tell us they have pickets. Two, three, five men. Keep an eye out for trouble, send word to the camps at Pocotaligo and Green Pond."

"So they'll send reinforcements once we're there."

Middleton laughed. "If they smart."

Not far from the pontoon bridge, Middleton guided the boat toward the eastern shore, the Colleton County side of the river. He said, "Middleton place just north of the bridge, and Hayward place just south."

On the Middleton place, the shoreline was obscured by trees that grew all the way to the waterline. Caro could not see beyond them. "Where are the buildings?" she asked. "The rice fields?"

"Behind them trees," he said.

On the Hayward place, the rice fields abutted the water's edge, taking advantage of the marshy shore. Intersecting the rice fields was a road wide enough for a carriage or a cart full of barrels of rice. "Why build a road there?" Caro asked.

"Causeway. It run toward the house and the rest of the place."

Caro gazed at the causeway, which bisected two marshy fields where the rice plants grew, lush and green in the summer heat. "It's wide open," she said.

"No place to hide in a rice field," Middleton said. "We see the pickets before they do us any hurt." He laughed. "You think them fine gentlemen of Rutledge's regiment wait for us, stand in mud up to their knees like field hands?"

Caro felt uneasy at the thought of the soldiers of the Second marching across that open space. "I want to be on the deck," she said.

But it was too crowded to do more than crane her neck to look for Sampson. She pushed her way through the crowd a little, and an officer with a lieutenant's stripes told her sternly, "Don't get in the way."

Don't get in the way. Don't get off the boat. She thought, *For all the good I do here, I might as well have stayed in Beaufort.*

❧❧❧

BACK IN THE PILOT house, she watched as the soldiers left the boat, marching onto the causeway toward the Hayward place with as much ease and confidence as if they were on the parade ground at Camp Saxton, a single white officer leading a company of sixty black men. They shared a manner of marching that the white officers couldn't drill them out of. Their gait was loose-jointed, flexible in their hips and their knees, a rhythm of Africa like the lilt of their speech. She couldn't pick out Sampson. There were too many tall men, broad of shoulder, narrow of hip, and proud of carriage. Her heart swelled with admiration, even as she felt itchy with worry.

Wide open to any secesh picket who didn't mind standing up to his knees in mud.

But the fields were empty. Undisturbed, the men continued to advance, their gait jaunty, as though they relished the task ahead of them.

She could see their destination, the Hayward plantation's rice sheds and rice mill, and beyond it, the plantation house, the largest building on the place. And as the men stepped from the causeway to leave the rice fields behind, Caro wondered where the field hands might be. Had the overseers fled here, too?

The sound of a distant shot sent her bolting upright from her chair. She ran to the windows to look for the fight.

Middleton said, "That don't come from the Hayward place. That over at the Middleton place."

"How can you tell? Can't see a thing!"

"I know what's behind them trees."

"A firefight!"

"Must be the mill," he said.

"Secesh fighting at the mill! Sampson might be there!"

He curled his hand about her wrist. Gently. "Set down," he said quietly. "Sixty of us, and all they got are a few pickets."

The sound of the rifles was familiar. Too familiar. She remembered that sound from Cincinnati, when she lay on the floor in the darkness, waiting. Dreading. Raging against her own helplessness and her own fear. She was suddenly like Sophy, transported to her one of her worst moments by memory.

"Miss Jarvie," Middleton said. The warmth of his hand on her wrist brought her back to the present. "Set down and watch, as careful as you can, so you can write in that notebook of yours."

Shaking in the summer heat, she sat. She forced herself to reach for her notebook and her pencil. She put her hand in her pocket and touched the folded paper there. Her copy of the map that she had teased from Sophy. Her map of the Jarvie place.

She righted herself.

Middleton said, "Watch what happen on the Hayward place, since you in the catbird seat for it."

The Hayward place, unlike the Middletons', had no trees along the shore; they had been cleared for the causeway, and she had a full view of the army's activity. Smoke began to billow from the rice shed, and as she watched, flames began to leap from the roof. As before, the air began to smell of toasted rice. A group of soldiers, torches in their hands, moved to the rice mill, carefully lighting the roof, as though they had studied incineration as an art. The roof caught and the flames began to leap. The air now smelled of burned rice, a lazy cook's nightmare, and as the fires fed on themselves, oily smoke rose into the air, adding its own rank odor.

Their first task accomplished, the soldiers surrounded the Hayward plantation house, lit torches in their hands. Caro watched as they set the house on fire with the same exactitude they had used on the mill and the shed. Sampson must be among them. Did he act in his duty as a soldier? Or did vengeance against Marse Hayward sing in his heart as the big house caught fire?

"Miss Jarvie," Middleton said, "I sound the horn. Brace yourself."

Before she could ask him why, the horn blared so loud that she jumped despite his warning. Middleton grinned. "Joshua's trumpet," he said. "They come, now."

"They knew?"

Middleton's grin widened. "When we come to scout, we forewarn them," he said.

And they crowded the grounds of the plantation, approaching the causeway in a wave. Their cries and laughter preceded them.

At the causeway they slowed, arranging themselves two abreast, and in that formation, they flowed on the raised road that cleaved the rice fields as Moses had opened the Red Sea.

Behind them, the Hayward place billowed with dark, oily smoke, and the smell of ruined rice was lost under the stink of burned mill and shed and plantation house.

≈⊙≈

DUSK HAD FALLEN WHEN Sampson finally returned to the pilot house. He smelled of smoke. His cap was askew. His eyes were bloodshot, but they glittered, as with fever. She sprang up, wanting to embrace him. "Are you all right?"

He was too wrought up for affection. "We done what we come for," he said. "We burn the Hayward place to the ground, and we get all the people out." He started to cough, and when he stopped, he looked more feverish than ever. "I took Marse's best horse," he said. He laughed, the sound reedy with nerves. "And his sword, the one he was so proud of, from the Mexican War. Gave it to Colonel Montgomery."

∞

WHEN THE ENGINES FIRED and the great paddlewheel turned, Middleton said to Caro, "Jarvie place coming up next. A few miles downriver." As though they were on an excursion. Caro slipped her hand into her pocket to touch her map.

They moved more slowly now, weighed down with too many passengers and too much cargo. Middleton guided the boat to the landing. In the darkness, nothing looked familiar to her, and nothing sparked her memory.

The soldiers spilled onto the landing, sixty strong, surprisingly disorderly. Caro's memory was faulty, but the image of the map was clear in her mind. Unlike the Hayward place, the Jarvie place had no causeway. The landing gave onto a path instead, and that path led to the driveway.

She ran onto the deck and struggled to inch her way to the door. From the doorway, she watched the soldiers march away. "May not be so lucky this time," she murmured, and she tensed for the sound of rifle fire. It was hard to hear above the sound of the hundreds of the newly free. The laughter, tears, and prayers were accompanied by the din of babies bawling, chickens squawking, and pigs squealing.

She could hardly tell them to hush so that she could listen for a firefight.

The crowd, seething and moving, pushed her onto the landing. To her surprise, no one guarded the landing or the path beyond it. Had they assumed that no one would leave the safety of the boat? She glanced at the chaos behind her and took a few steps toward the path. No one called her back. She slipped onto the path. No rebuke. No hand to grasp her arm. She set foot on the path as though she knew where she was going.

And she went.

She knew this path in daylight, but she had never walked it at night. Her father had planted live oaks on either side, and in the thick, hot air of the coast, the branches had grown together in a natural arch. In the dark, the trees spiked like the cheval-de-frise, the defensive railing on the Jarvie house in Charleston, put up after the Vesey insurrection. Nothing looked familiar to her.

The moonlight shone dim and filtered through the trees. The path threaded its way through trees that grew tall, pines and live oaks. In the low light, she strained to see their trunks. The cypresses were shorter, their branches gnarled and twisted, twined with vines and wreathed with moss.

The path was overgrown with grassy weeds and wet underfoot. The smell of rotting vegetation rose, and the sound of squelched mud underfoot was loud to her ears. The weeds lashed her skirt, and she didn't bend to brush them away.

The night air was not quiet. Crickets sang, a pleasant song, and frogs, who liked the muck under the trees, gave off their calls, bell-like or bellowing. An unseen owl hooted, and the nightjars emitted their odd, low, rasping call. The woods were full of small scurrying sounds. Mice, probably.

She strained to see in the darkness. She strained to hear, too.

She listened for footsteps, horses' hooves in the mud, the snuffle of dogs on the scent, the crack of rifle fire. She expected them, and every moment that passed without them tightened her nerves further. She was acutely alert to every sight and sound, and the fear and the excitement thrummed in her ears and in her chest. The patrollers could shoot her, or capture her for something worse. The dogs could find her and maul her.

She cursed herself for not being able to shoot.

She slowed and tried to breathe normally.

She looked ahead and suddenly got her bearings. She saw the driveway, wide and well-paved enough for carriages, and recalled driving up in Papa's carriage before the war. The coachman had handled a pair of beautiful chestnut horses. The house had been elegant and graceful, like everything that her father owned. She remembered running up the front steps, a little girl with her hand in her father's, as the butler said deferentially, "Welcome, Marse James. Welcome, Miss Caroline." *Oh, Papa.*

But this house was no longer her father's, and it would never be hers. It belonged to Lawrence Jarvie. Lawrence Jarvie, who had treated Caro and her mother as slaves, despite the terms of the will. Who had sent her mother to the workhouse, which had killed her. Who sent the slave catcher after her. Who let the patrollers loose the Negro dogs after Sophy. Anger filled her and propelled her forward.

A rough voice called, "Who the devil are you?"

She whirled around to find a man of the Second South Carolina, a stranger.

A group of soldiers had gathered on the lawn. With them stood several field hands. They were all strangers, too. She blurted out, "I'm with the army."

"The army? You?" the soldier asked.

"I'm a scout. I work for Mrs. Tubman." Her voice rose. "I knew this place before I was free."

"Is you armed?"

Yes, with a map and a faulty memory. In answer, she stretched out her empty hands.

One of the field hands said, "I never see you before."

She caught her breath. She spoke to all of them, soldiers and slaves. "James Jarvie, who used to own this place, was my father. Lawrence Jarvie, who owns it now, was my master."

In surprise, the field hand said, "Kitty's girl?"

Her voice caught in her throat. "Yes."

"Kitty's girl," the man said in surprise, nodding. "Free now." He searched her face. "What happen to your mama?"

"Gone," she said.

"God bless."

A soldier said impatiently, "We have a task here. Army business."

She saw the pile of kindling in their midst.

"Set fire to the house," the field hand said, a slow grin spreading over his face.

The soldier added sternly, "Colonel Montgomery's orders."

Anger surged in her, as bright and hot as a bonfire. She reached out her hand. "Let me help you," she said. "Hand me one of those sticks."

⅋℧

WHEN THE HOUSE WAS alight, people began to pour onto the lawn. Caro slipped into the midst of the crowd and let it swallow her up. It bore her along without any effort on her part, a torrent seeking the river. She was part of a tide too powerful to stop, and they swept her onto the landing and onto the boat.

As Caro stood, squeezed tight by the crowd, she was greeted with a scream of recognition. "Caro, is that you?"

Dulcie had been a house servant to Caro's father in

Charleston, a fixture of her childhood in her father's house. After her father's death, Dulcie and her family had been slaves to her father's brother Lawrence, and when he mistreated her, Dulcie had done her best to help.

"Dulcie?"

A pair of strong arms encircled her and hugged her so tight that she gasped for breath. "How do you come to be here?"

"It doesn't matter. Are you all right? Where is your family?"

"Right here." Dulcie tugged on her husband's hand. "Henry right here. And my children, too."

Caro let a tear escape and put her head on Dulcie's shoulder. Dulcie, now that she was safe, permitted herself a sob. Her voice thick, she said, "Happy day. Don't know why I cry."

Dulcie drew a deep breath, let Caro go, and wiped her eyes with her apron. "Have to get myself together," she said, but her daughter Peggy, now grown, and her son Hank, nearly old enough to join the army, clustered around her and supported her.

Henry said, "House, barn, stores, mill, all on fire. The soldiers flood the fields, too. The place a wreck."

"Where were the overseers?"

"They run away. Off with the secesh."

"Was anyone hurt?"

"Didn't see it when we ran. But don't know about everyone." He wiped his face, suddenly overcome. He said, "I need to set down," his voice reedy.

She turned and saw someone else familiar.

Bel.

Bel, who had been her mother's servant once. Who had hated her. Who had tormented her when Lawrence Jarvie dragged her back into slavery. Who had delighted in betraying her when she ran away after her mother's death.

Bel was thinner and toil-worn, but her sullen, angry expression hadn't changed. Caro burst into a gale of laughter. "You! I came here and rescued *you*!"

As they steamed downriver, the boats heavy in the water with their cargo, the heavens opened and a storm poured down. They slowly returned to Beaufort accompanied by the dazzle of lightning, the crack of thunder, and the sluice that was a Low Country tropical rain.

As the storm raged, the newly free sang. For themselves, they sang "Jehovah, Hallelujah." And for those still in chains, those still left behind, they sang "Wade in the Water."

Chapter 9: Flag of Truce

As MATTIE AND EMILY sat in the parlor after midday dinner, fanning themselves in the summer heat, Rosa announced that a visitor had arrived at the side door. "Says she knows Miss Emily but won't give her name."

Mattie reminded Rosa, "Visitors don't come in at the side door. Show her into the parlor, whoever she is."

And Rosa returned with the visitor in tow. Someone with a very familiar face. "Dulcie!" Emily exclaimed. Her father's slave, who had been in Charleston when Emily fled. Where had she gone since?

"Miss Emily," Dulcie said, glancing around the parlor, unable to hide her uneasiness.

"I'm surprised to see you," Emily said, as uncomfortable as Dulcie.

Dulcie hesitated, and Mattie said, "Emily, where are your manners? Miss Dulcie, please sit. Can we offer you anything?"

Dulcie stared at the proffered armchair. She sat as though the seat were upholstered in briars, saying, "Thank you, ma'am."

Mattie smiled. "That's better."

Emily asked, "What brings you to the Sea Islands? I thought you were in Charleston."

Dulcie shifted in her chair. "Left Charleston when the war break out. I was at your daddy's place in Colleton County."

"How long have you been here?" Emily asked, and suddenly realized that Dulcie was here because she had fled. She was a contraband.

"Since the raid, Miss Emily."

Mattie said, "Was there an expedition we didn't hear about?"

Emily thought, *If Joshua still visited us, we'd have heard.* Not for the first time, she regretted that they had quarreled.

"You really don't hear, Miss Emily? I thought everyone knew."

Emily shook her head. Mattie said, "Please tell us."

"The army go up the Combahee a few weeks ago. Colonel Montgomery, who command the Second South Carolina, he ask Mrs. Harriet Tubman to help him. They get hundreds of people out."

Astonished, Emily said, "Harriet Tubman? Hundreds of people rescued?"

"I thought Miss Caroline would tell you."

"No," Emily said. In the past few months, since the land sale, Caro hadn't visited the Oaks, either. Emily told herself that Caro was busy with reporting. Or with Sampson Hayward. "Why would she know about it?"

Dulcie said, "Because she on the boat that get us out."

Emily sat back in her chair. So Caro had finally persuaded someone in command to let her follow a regiment into battle. "Caro went on an army expedition?"

"Yes, she help Mrs. Tubman. Tell her about the Jarvie place so they can rescue us. She help to free us, all of us."

Why did she feel so hurt? Military expeditions were kept secret until they were accomplished. If Joshua were still calling, he wouldn't have told her, either. "Your family?" she asked Dulcie, awkwardly. "Are they with you?"

Dulcie nodded. "We all came out together, Henry and Peggy and Hank and me."

"Where are you staying?" Emily asked. The question sounded foolish, as though they had arrived in an ordinary way.

"At the camp for now," Dulcie said. "Henry and Hank both join the Second South Carolina. Peggy and I, we think about settling in Beaufort."

Emily asked, "Did everyone on the place come away?"

"Yes, Miss Emily," Dulcie said softly. "We was all rescued by the army."

No one left to open and close the sluices or to tend the crop. Had the overseer gone, too? "What happened to the place? With no one to work it?"

Dulcie dropped her gaze. It clearly pained her to speak. "Oh, Miss Emily, I hate to tell you," she said.

Emily forced herself to keep her voice gentle. "What happened, Dulcie? Please tell us."

"The army leave it a ruin, Miss Emily. Burn the big

house to the ground. Burn down the mill and the stores. Take all the livestock away and burn the barns. As they go, they open all the sluice gates. Flood the fields. Make a ruin of the crop, too."

Shock nearly rendered her speechless. "The army destroyed it?" Emily said slowly.

"All gone, Miss Emily. The army don't leave a thing."

"Utterly destroyed," Emily said, letting it sink in.

"Afraid so, Miss Emily."

Emily said, "Gone. Ruined."

Dulcie turned and left the room.

Emily ran from the parlor. She ran down the front steps. It was too hot for such a pace. Panting, she halted under the big sycamore tree in the side yard, where the mosquitoes whined in her ears and tried to settle on her face. She brushed them away and blinked against the tears.

Mattie's step, brisk and resolute, gave her away. Mattie touched her shoulder. "Oh, Emily," she said.

"Leave me alone," Emily said.

"I won't."

Emily reached for her handkerchief and crumpled it in her hand. "I'm glad that my father's slaves are free," she said. "And I know why the army ruined the crop and burned the rice mill. That's a tactic of war." She was too close to tears. She swallowed hard. "But to burn the house!" She dabbed her face, pretending that she felt too warm. "That place in Colleton County was my home. I lived there until I was twelve, until my mother died. All my memories of her were there. Now it's gone, burned to the ground, and it's as though I lost her all over again."

Mattie put her arm around Emily's shoulders and hugged her close. She said, "Are you surprised that you grieve?"

"I should rejoice," Emily said, her voice muffled by Mattie's embrace. "Sound the loud timbrel."

"Your father's people are free. But your home is gone. You can rejoice in one and grieve for the other."

Emily raised her head. "Am I a traitor again?"

"To mourn for the memory of your mother? I think not."

"Ruined," Emily whispered. "Destroyed. How would you feel, Mattie, if your home in Pennsylvania were destroyed?"

Mattie hugged Emily, and Emily could feel how she shivered. "The Confederate army approaches Pennsylvania," she said. "I hope I will never know."

&)(&

THREE WEEKS AFTER THE battle of Gettysburg, Rosa told Emily that she had a visitor and showed him in. He looked weary as well as travel-worn. Every journey these days was shadowed by the added travail of war. But his expression was familiar: grave, reserved, and kind. He had always been dignified. But something new had added to his gravitas.

Still, she knew him. She rose, her hands outstretched. "Ambrose!"

Her father's servant, who had been so helpful to her as she befriended Caro and fell in love with Joshua.

"Miss Emily," he said, inclining his head.

"Excuse me," she said. "Do you go by a new name, now that you're free?"

"Strangers call me Mr. Hutchinson. But you ain't a stranger, Miss Emily."

His bearing prompted her manners in a way Dulcie's had not. "Please, sit down. Let me ask Rosa to bring you something."

"That's kind of you, Miss Emily." He sat.

It didn't seem peculiar for the former mistress to offer the former slave refreshment and to watch as he partook of it. For all his politeness, Ambrose was hungry and thirsty.

When he was sated, Emily asked, "How did you come here? How did you find me?"

"It's a long story, Miss Emily."

"Tell me," she said, as hungry for his news as he had been for her coffee and biscuit.

He settled himself and licked his lips, as the slave storytellers always did. "When your daddy went off to war—he volunteer right away, just after Fort Sumter—he take me with him, as his servant. I weren't keen to go, but at that time I didn't have a say-so. I go along; I take care of him. For a while it weren't too bad. We stay in the Low Country, at the camp at Pocotaligo. Don't see battle, and most of the officers game and drink a lot instead of getting ready to fight. So it weren't too different from being back in Charleston."

He picked up another biscuit and bit into it. "These are fine," he said. "Praise the cook, whoever she is." He sighed. "Things change at the beginning of the year. Marse Lawrence's regiment don't stay at Pocotaligo to game and drink. They get their orders to go to Virginia."

"Where General Lee fights a real war."

"Yes, Miss Emily. They fight at Fredericksburg—it don't go well, the men ain't used to soldiering. We servants, we stay behind the lines, but it ain't the same. We feel it. We in the thick of it, too." He sighed. "We go into Pennsylvania near the end of June."

"Gettysburg," she said slowly. "The First fought at Gettysburg." It was odd, she thought, that her father's regiment and Joshua's were both called the First South Carolina.

"Yes, Miss Emily."

"It's bad news, isn't it?"

Ambrose nodded. "Your daddy fell at the battle of Gettysburg. I have the last letter he write the night before. For Miss Susan."

Emily shivered. She had seen letters like those, anticipating the worst. She had lived in dread of opening one from Joshua. *If I die tomorrow...*

The man who had hated her kindness to Caro and who had threatened her with the madhouse unless she broke with Joshua was gone. The man who had wanted to send Caro back into slavery and deliver Emily herself to the hangman's noose was dead. She had never expected to make things right with him. But now she never would.

He handed her the letter. She couldn't look at it. "Ambrose, how did you find me?"

"After the battle, everything in confusion. I tuck away the letter and I find my way to the Union lines. Contraband. They take me in, and I start to ask after you. I find some Ohio men, and they don't know you, but they know Mr. Joshua Aiken. They tell me he go back to South Carolina to Camp Saxton. Now that's quite a thing, Miss Emily, an Aiken man a captain to a regiment of black men."

Her eyes stung. "He's a fine officer. And he tells me he commands the best men in the Union army."

Ambrose nodded and permitted himself a small smile. "So I make my way to Port Royal. Keep asking after you. And in Beaufort I meet Sophy and I find Caro, too. They tell me all about you, how you do such a fine thing yourself, teaching the little children that used to be slaves."

She wasn't sure whether he believed it or was praising her from the long habit of slavery.

She said, "Such a long journey, Ambrose. And a dangerous one." She didn't ask why he hadn't tried to mail the letter. No Confederate letter could go through the United States mail.

"I felt duty-bound to find you to tell you," he said. "And I wanted to see Port Royal. Black men free here. Now that the best thing I ever saw." He paused, and she could see the fatigue beneath his powerful sense of duty.

She looked down at the letter. The envelope was creased from its long journey.

"Will you read it, Miss Emily?"

She held the travel-worn paper between her fingers. She said, "I reckon it's for my stepmother to read. I'll leave it sealed."

"You'll take it to her?"

Emily realized that she had just promised to do so. It was odd to think that she had made a binding promise to Ambrose. "I wouldn't want you to try. You'd have to go through the Confederate lines, and they won't respect your freedom."

"Thank you, Miss Emily."

The letter seemed to burn in her fingers, as though it were covered with a residue of gunpowder. "I'll find a way," she said, wondering how. This letter couldn't cross the Confederate lines, and neither could she.

"Miss Emily?" Ambrose said. "I know there was bitterness between you and your daddy. But I'm sorry that he's gone, and I grieve for you because of it."

𝕾𝕺𝕮𝕽

A DUTIFUL DAUGHTER WOULD have dyed all her dresses black, but Emily couldn't bring herself to do it. She asked Mattie for her opinion. Mattie said, "We are all in mourning, with a war on." Emily shook her head. But from that day forward, she wore a plain gray dress and put away her only ornament, the cameo brooch she wore at her throat.

Before the week was out, a black-bordered note came from Joshua, in words as brief as a battlefield report, asking if he could call on her. She sent her own curt note back, telling him that he could. Sunday afternoon would be best.

As soon as he saw her, even before he sat down, he said, "You aren't in mourning!"

"Oh, my dress," she said. "Under the circumstances…"

"Your father," he said, taken aback.

"Joshua," she said, "you know why, better than anyone."

It was as though she had said, "At ease." He relaxed inside his officer's coat. "Yes, I do. But I'm sorry. Not the least sorry for him. But I'm very sorry for you, Emily."

"Thank you," she said.

Awkwardly, he said, "It was wrong to argue with you."

She hoped he would mention Mr. Phelps, to make the apology deeper, but he didn't. She said, "It doesn't matter now."

He stammered. "I came here because I hoped that there was something I might do for you."

"Yes," she said. She pulled the travel-worn letter from her pocket. "My father's last letter to my stepmother." She explained how Ambrose brought it. "I want to make sure that it goes to her."

He was awkward again. He said, "It's a very simple matter. Put it on the next packet and they'll take it to the military mail exchange in Virginia."

"She'll never get it that way. I want to get it into her hands."

"You know that can't happen."

"Of course not. I can't cross the lines, no more than

Ambrose can. But there must be a way to get it to some-one who has reason to visit Sumter County."

He rose. "Put it on the mail packet," he said. "That's more than enough."

She rose, too. "If you fell in battle, don't you think that your family would want to know?"

"As far as they're concerned, I'm already dead," he said.

༄༅

ON A WARM, BRIGHT afternoon, the Monday after Josh-ua's visit, Emily smoothed the skirt of her gray dress, put on her plainest bonnet, and took the ferry to Beaufort so that she could call on General Saxton.

Saxton still looked kindly, but he was wearier than ever behind his desk in his Beaufort office. "Miss Jarvie!" he said, his face brightening. "I hear great things of your school."

"We have more scholars than ever, sir. All eager to learn."

"I'm glad of it." He sobered. "I heard of your father's death in battle. You have my condolences, Miss Jarvie."

She slipped her hand into her pocket, where the letter sat. "Thank you, sir. I've called on you because of it."

"What is the matter?" he asked.

She drew out the letter. "My father's servant found me here. Mr. Ambrose Hutchinson had come to the Union lines after the battle of Gettysburg to look for me and to claim his freedom. He journeyed from Pennsylvania in considerable peril. Mr. Hutchinson is a fine man, sir, very brave, very steadfast."

"And he brought you the news."

"Yes. And he brought me this letter, which my father wrote on the eve of the battle. It's for his wife. My stepmother."

Saxton hesitated. He said, "Your father was a Confederate man."

"Yes, sir, of the First Regiment, South Carolina Infantry of the Confederacy. He was an officer." Now she hesitated. "I'm sure you've heard the story of my escape before the war. My father and I were very badly estranged."

"Nonetheless, he was your father. I'm sure that you grieve for him, and I'm sorry for your loss."

"Thank you, sir."

"This war has torn many families asunder," he said.

"Yes, sir, it has."

"It's a simple matter to deliver a military man's letter across the Confederate lines," he said.

"I know, sir. But I feel obliged to make sure that my stepmother receives it, and as soon as possible."

"And she lives in South Carolina."

"Yes, sir, behind the Confederate lines in Sumter County."

"We can make sure that a letter reaches her, Miss Jarvie. We send Confederate letters in the mail to City Point in Virginia."

"That's good to know, sir. But I don't want to mail the letter. I want to make sure it gets into her hands."

"You'd like someone to carry it to her."

"Yes, sir."

He gave her a saddened look. "Certainly you aren't obliged to do so, Miss Jarvie."

"I feel that I am. It's my duty to my stepmother and my father."

"Even though you were estranged."

"War gives us odd obligations, General Saxton."

"Yes, it does," he said, his gaze suddenly far away. Emily knew from Joshua that the general and his underlings had written many letters of condolence after the recent battle of Fort Wagner, when the Fifty-Fourth Massachusetts—the third black regiment to fight in South Carolina—had been so badly wounded in the fighting.

"Something else occurs to me," he said. "When we exchange prisoners—their pickets that we've captured, for ours—we travel under flag of truce. We could take your letter with us and find someone to take it to Sumter County."

"Sir, might I travel with the prisoners under a flag of truce? To hand over the letter myself?"

He sighed. He couldn't refuse her, his earnest, loyal, troubled teacher, part soldier and part daughter to him. "Yes, you could travel to the camp at Pocotaligo under a flag of truce the next time we exchange prisoners." He shook his head. "It won't be pleasant for you. They don't like us much since Colonel Montgomery's raid up the river."

"I know," she said, thinking of the emancipation of her father's slaves and the ruin of her father's house.

He sighed again. "But a prisoner exchange, and a flag of truce, are part of the rules of war. They're our enemies, but they want their men back. They may manage to be decent to you. Let me make the arrangements."

☙◗◖

WHEN SHE LEFT GENERAL Saxton, she went looking for Caro, whom she hadn't seen for weeks. She had been too absorbed in the dilemma of her father's letter to dwell on Caro's silence. Now, as she walked down the path between the white canvas tents, she recalled that Caro had always absented herself when something bothered her.

Caro wasn't in camp; one of the soldiers directed Emily to Beaufort. She had time before the ferry left, and she found herself at Sophy's front door.

Caro opened the door to her knock. She looked distracted, and behind her, on the dining room table, was a scatter of paper and an inkwell.

"I've disturbed you," Emily said.

"No, it's all right. Come in."

The house was quiet. "Is Sophy here?"

"She and Chloe are out."

They sat in the parlor, the silence thickening and becoming awkward. Caro was restless in her chair. She was upset. Emily wondered what troubled her. But when she spoke, Emily blurted out her own unease. "I came because we haven't spoken since I learned of my father's death."

Caro was equally blunt. "Did you really expect me to

pay you a condolence call? You hated him as much as I did."

Emily pulled the letter from her pocket. Every time she hefted it, it seemed heavier in her hand. "He left me something. Ambrose entrusted it to me."

"That? I offered to take it. Ambrose wouldn't give it to me." Caro's eyes glittered. "He knew I would burn it."

Bitterly, Emily said, "Have you become a firebug? Like the Union army?"

"I was on the raid," Caro said, her tone equally bitter.

"Yes, I know." Why was it so easy to be angry at Caro? "Dulcie told me. She thinks you rescued her."

Caro said, "Put that miserable thing in the mail and be done with it."

"I can't. I'm going to Pocotaligo with the next prisoner exchange. I'll find someone to take it up to Sumter County. And then I'll be done with it."

Caro blanched—her fair skin showed it—and she didn't reply.

"Do you think that makes me a traitor?" Emily said, angrier than ever at her cousin.

"No," Caro said. The unspoken words hung in the air. *He hated me enough to re-enslave me. But he hated you enough to wish you dead.* "I think that it makes you a fool."

৯৩৫৪

SEVERAL WEEKS LATER, IN the heat of early August, she waited by the boat that would go up the river, its United

States flag replaced by a white flag of truce, large enough to be seen for miles. The officer who helped her board was a lieutenant in the Second South Carolina, whom she had never met. He said, "Let me escort you to the pilot house." When she hesitated, he said, "The prisoners are on the deck. I'm sure you'd rather be elsewhere."

"Are they surly?"

He was young, with a shock of wheat-colored hair and an accent that belonged to the Ohio Valley. "They can be as surly as they like," he said. "They're in shackles and handcuffs, and they aren't going anywhere. Follow me."

On the boat, he preceded her to the stairs to the pilot house. She got a good look at the prisoners as she mounted the steps. They were surly indeed. Their guards were tall, unsmiling private soldiers from the Second South Carolina Colored Troops.

She laughed.

The pilot was a black man, too. The officer introduced him. "Jack Middleton. He piloted the *Harriet Weed* on the raid up the Combahee last month."

She settled into the proffered chair and gazed out the windows. "It's quite a view," she said.

Middleton grinned. "Pilot needs a good view," he said.

The breeze that wafted from the sea was humid and salty. As they left the sound and turned into the river, the sun danced on the water. If not for the prisoners below, it would have seemed a pleasure cruise.

She asked the officer, "Why such a big boat for so few men? Do you take cargo, too? Here, or back?"

He laughed. "No, this isn't a raid, Miss Jarvie. We have a cart below and two horses to draw it. Once we're upriver, we'll go inland, and we don't expect a lady to march to Pocotaligo."

She thought, *Too bad. It would serve those Charleston Dragoons right to trudge back to their camp shackled like slaves.*

The lieutenant excused himself to join his men on the deck.

Even though it had been years since she traveled up the Combahee, she recognized the landmarks. "The bluffs," she said.

"Field Point," the pilot said. "You know the river?"

With a pang, she said, "My father owns... owned..." She faltered. "When I was a girl, I used to visit," she said.

"On the river?"

"The Jarvie place," she said.

"We go past it."

She gazed out the windows, and the path of the raid was soon apparent. Where the rice fields abutted the riverbank, the plants had been drowned where the army had opened the sluice gates. "The crop is ruined," she said.

"Colonel Montgomery's orders," the pilot said cheerfully. "Jarvie place coming up."

She stared at the eastern bank, the Colleton County side, and said, "I don't see it."

"Right here," the pilot said.

Opening the sluice gates had submerged the landing and the path that led toward the house. The trees that had shaded the path were halfway up their trunks in water, which must have spared them, because beyond them, fire had ravaged the house. The windows were gone. The pretty white exterior was charred beyond recognition. The columns had burned through, and the second-floor piazza had collapsed onto the steps. The smell of char still lingered.

Emily said, "The army did this?"

"Yes, miss," the pilot said, still cheerful. "Saw them do it."

Emily stared at the ruins. She struggled to speak. "Did you think it was right?"

"Is this your family house?" he asked.

"It was."

He turned his attention to the river. "Colonel Montgomery's orders," he said.

When the boat docked upriver, the pilot said, "Hayward place." The pilot pointed. "See that causeway? Turns into a road past the house. Take it to Pocotaligo."

"How far?"

"Not far. Five mile, maybe."

Five miles in a horse-drawn wagon, in the company of four shackled men, past a ruined plantation. She had asked for this. Pleaded for it. She slipped her hand into her pocket to touch the letter that Ambrose had brought her. Her father's last words, a Confederate's words of love and courage for her stepmother.

She should have put the letter on the mail packet bound for a military post office. She was as foolhardy as any man in the Charleston Dragoons. As she seesawed between Union sympathy and family loyalty, she was in pursuit of a cause she could never win.

She glanced at the prisoners as the lieutenant boosted her onto the seat next to the wagon driver, a Second South Carolina private of such dignity that she was sure he had been a coachman before the war.

ℰᏩᏣᏒ

In contrast with Camp Saxton, orderly and well-maintained despite its sprawling nature, the Confederate camp at Pocotaligo seemed makeshift. The tents were stained and tattered. The men were ill-clad and ill-shod. The smell of coffee, omnipresent at Saxton, was absent. Outside every tent, no matter how ragged, sat black men, sewing on buttons, polishing boots, brushing dusty coats. Valets and body servants, like Ambrose. Still slaves.

Each man stared at the black soldiers in their blue coats. The white men glared at them with loathing. The black men hooded their eyes, as slaves did when they wanted to disguise their fascination.

The men of the Second South Carolina waited as their lieutenant explained Emily and her errand to the provost marshal. She was grateful that the provost marshal was a stranger to her. He stared at her in pure astonishment and wordlessly took her to see Major Emanuel.

Major Emanuel, whose dilapidated tent was twice

as big as an enlisted man's, hid his expression behind a luxuriant dark beard. The provost marshal stood back as the major settled her at the table that served as his office. By the tent, sitting cross-legged on the ground, was the major's valet, who sewed a button on his master's shirt.

The major let her explain, and he said, "Lawrence Jarvie? Your father was Lawrence Jarvie?"

"Yes," she said.

He said, "Your father and I were cadets together at the Citadel."

The world she had left behind was very small. She braced herself for words of judgment.

And they came. "I've heard about you," he said. "How you shamed and betrayed your family. Why should I oblige you in any way?"

She could feel two pairs of eyes on her: the provost marshal's and the slave's.

"It's not for me, sir," she said. She laid the letter on the table, letting him see the dirt and the creases that revealed its journey. "It's for my father, a Confederate officer, and his wife, who deserves to know that he's gone. Surely you can understand that."

The silence was fraught. Painful. The major clearly had divided loyalties, too. He hated the messenger, but he remembered the writer of the message as a comrade and friend.

The major's valet spoke, in a soft, conciliatory voice. "Major, sir," he said, slurring it as slaves did: *suh*. "Do you recall that lady from Georgia, that nurse who stop with us when the railway under fire? She bound for home, and she hail from Sumter County."

"How do you know?" The major's tone was crotchety and affectionate at once.

"I help her with a sick man the other day. Suh, she might agree to take that letter with her."

Emily cast a sidelong glance at the valet and was met by a similar sidelong glance. The trusted servant was her ally.

Major Emanuel's thoughts followed the path that his valet had illuminated for him. He said, "Well, it would be out of my hands."

"I find her, suh. Bring her to you."

"You do that, Pompey." He rose and addressed the provost marshal. "Keep an eye on her," he said, gesturing to Emily, and he left them.

As Emily waited, she wondered who the nurse might be. She ransacked her memory for a Sumter County family that would allow a young lady to leave home to serve as a nurse for the Confederacy.

Pompey returned with a woman in a plain white cap and an even plainer brown dress. But nothing could disguise her honey-colored curls or her pretty face, and the voice that cried out, "Emily Jarvie! What are you doing here?"

It was Camilla Aiken.

Camilla, who had been the most lustrous belle of prewar Sumter County, daughter of the richest planter in a princely South Carolina family. Camilla, whose dressmaker bills had sent her father into a rage and who had once beaten her maidservant with a hairbrush because her hair hadn't been curled properly. Camilla, who had thrown her together with Joshua and had protected the secret of their affection.

Emily gasped, and under the gaze of a Confederate provost marshal at Pocotaligo, her presence tolerated by a flag of truce, she replied, "Camilla Aiken, I might ask the same of you!"

Camilla seated herself at the table, arranging her skirt as though she still wore hoops. She threw the provost marshal a flirtatious glance. He blushed. She said to Emily, "I thought they told you that I'm a nurse for the Confederate army."

"I didn't know it would be you. How did you become a nurse?"

"I was going mad at home, knitting socks for the soldiers. I wanted to do something useful. I met a woman who nursed in a field hospital in Georgia, and she had such tales to tell! So I signed up."

"I'm surprised your family would allow it."

"They didn't want to. But I insisted. I told them that I'd go whether they allowed it or not." She laughed. "You set quite an example."

Emily ignored this. She asked, "How long have you been in Georgia?"

"Since the beginning of the year. They made me go home for a while. The doctors are afraid the nurses will break down." She said defiantly, "Not me! I'm a little tired, but my spirits were fine. No nerves for me!" She stuck out her chin in defiance. "And after I visit home, I'm bound for Richmond. In the thick of it. Where the worst cases go."

"So it suits you."

"It does. It maddens me when there's little we can do. So many are too badly wounded for help. Sometimes the only thing left is to read the Bible or to write the last letter home." She brightened. "I'm glad when nursing does some good. Rest. Food. Clean bandages. I can provide that to the ones who have a chance to recover."

Emily tried to think of flighty Camilla changing a bandage or assisting a surgeon. "Does any of it disgust you?"

Camilla laughed, a sound to chase away the smell of the grave. "No, none of it. I've learned I have a strong stomach."

Emily stared at the girl whose considerable energy had always been engrossed in finding a rich man to marry. She asked, "You don't regret not getting married?"

"I get a proposal a week from a grateful soldier. Some of them are officers, and very handsome, too."

"And you refuse them?"

"I don't want to marry a man to be his nurse," she said. "I like working as a nurse. It makes me feel useful. When the war ends—if it ever ends—the world will still need nurses. I may want to continue as a nurse, even though it will give my mother worse conniptions than when I first went to Georgia."

"I never dreamed I'd meet you like this."

"War makes for strange connections. And stranger circumstances. What in the name of the Lord are you doing here?"

Of course Camilla would ask. And she needed an explanation, if she were going to do Emily a favor. She explained about her father's fall at Gettysburg. About the roundabout journey the letter had taken. About her sense of obligation to see it into her stepmother's hands.

Camilla said impatiently, "No, how is it that you're here under a Union flag of truce, escorted by a troop of niggers?"

The word was like a match held to her skin. "A Negro troop," she corrected. "Soldiers—and fine ones, too."

Camilla laughed, her prewar peal. "Still the renegade," she said. "Where do you stay? Is it in Ohio?"

"No," she said. She wanted say something that would embarrass Camilla. Or shame her. "I went south to the Sea Islands. I teach at a school on St. Helena Island."

"Teach the little runaways?"

"The children of the freedmen and freedwomen."

"What can they possibly learn?"

"To read, and to write, and to do sums. They're very eager to learn."

Camilla laughed. "You, a schoolmarm to a roomful of little pickaninnies who should be in the fields!"

Emily thought, *And you a glorified servant, tending to men who should have been left to die on the battlefield.* There was no shaming Camilla.

Camilla asked, "And what of Cousin Joshua? I bet he joined the blue-bellies."

"He mustered into an Ohio regiment when the war broke out," Emily said. "Now he's an officer with the First Regiment South Carolina Volunteer Infantry. A Negro regiment."

Camilla laughed again. "What a tale to carry to Sumter County," she said. "You and Joshua. The nigger officer and the nigger teacher."

Emily was suddenly very angry. She said, "You can't even be civil to me. Why should I trust you to carry my letter up to Sumter County?"

"You can hardly take it there yourself." Camilla leaned forward as though she wanted to share a confidence. "They're still baying for your blood in Sumter County."

A red haze swam before Emily's eyes. The slave catcher. The hangman's noose. She blinked to allow her eyes to focus. "I'd rather let the letter go to the dead letter office. I'd rather burn it!"

Camilla shook her head. "Don't be a fool." She reached out her hand for the letter. "I'll put it into your stepmother's hand, I swear it."

Emily picked up the soiled envelope. She glanced at Pompey, who pretended to be engrossed in his mending. He had been listening intently all the time. Emily thought, *Pompey, run to us. We'll make you a free man and a soldier.* She handed the envelope to Camilla.

Camilla slipped the envelope into her pocket. Still cheerful, she said, "You and Joshua are traitors, but you're still family."

Chapter 10: Teach Me to Fight

AFTER THE JUBILATION OF the raid wore off, throughout the summer, Caro slept poorly. She dreamed of the slave catcher again. She woke with a pounding heart and forced herself to take long, deep breaths. In the warm, scented darkness, she thought of the dark path on the Jarvie place. She remembered her fear, and it fueled her conviction that she had been a fool to go on a raid unarmed. She pushed away the thought that she had aided the Union army on the Combahee River raid with a match. *Firebug*, Emily had said, and her teasing was not kind.

She thought of the heft of a gun in her hands. If she wanted to be a soldier, she needed to issue herself a rifle. She knew plenty of soldiers. One of them was likely to oblige her.

That morning, at Camp Saxton, she stood with Sampson in the relative privacy of the live oaks, the shade dappling their faces, a relief in the August heat. She smiled at him. "Sampson, would you help me?"

"Depends on what you ask for." He smiled back.

"Would you teach me how to shoot?"

"Quite a thing to ask!" he said, trying to tease.

She pushed away the fear and summoned the prewar belle. "Don't fox me. I want to be able to handle myself if I ever go on another expedition."

He moved close. "You got off the boat."

"Hah! How would you know?"

"I saw you getting back on. What were you doing?"

He couldn't possibly have seen her on the front lawn. "Helping the army," she said.

"On the Jarvie place? To do what?"

She dodged the question. "I saw you when you came back from the Hayward place. You told me you stole your master's horse!"

"That horse was spoil of war."

"And his sword. That was spite."

He rested his hand on her arm. "And what did you do for spite, Miss Caroline Jarvie? On the Jarvie place?"

She repeated what the soldiers had said. "Colonel Montgomery's orders."

He laughed, a rich, low rumble in his throat. "You set a fire," he said. "Was it the house? Did you burn down your massa's house?"

He knew. And he knew the answer to a question that had come to her in the middle of the night to disturb her sleep, when it wasn't rent by nightmare. "When is it war, Sampson, and when is it vengeance?"

He didn't cosset her. He gave her the answer that any officer would give him. "If I meet my massa in an alley in Charleston and shoot him, that's vengeance. If I meet him on the battlefield and shoot him, that's war."

She didn't need to pretend to be troubled. Her part in the raid fueled her fear and her anger—and her determination. She raised her eyes to his. "I got off the boat. I was in danger when I did. Why shouldn't I be able to take care of myself?"

"Take care of yourself, that's one thing. Put yourself in danger, that's another."

"I want to fight."

"You do. Like a reporter."

"No," she said. "Like a soldier." She felt queasy with fear but she tried to look beguiling.

He was gentle but insistent. "Caro, you know that you wasting your breath even to ask. Can't use an army-issue rifle and bullets to teach you. And can't take the time from my duty as a soldier, either."

She laid her hand on his cheek. He had shaved close this morning, and his skin was bumpy from the razor. "What if I asked you to show me how to scout?"

"Why? Don't tell me you hoping to go on another raid!"

She smiled. "If I did, wouldn't it help if I knew how to scout?"

He shook his head, but he put his hand over hers. "You trying to get round me."

"Of course I am. Would you do anything for me if I went straightaway?"

"For a little sugar, I might," he said.

He had made it easy for her. This teasing was a kind of scouting, too. She laughed very low in her throat. "If we go into the woods, where it's quiet, and where there's no one to know…"

He leaned close enough to kiss her, but he knew they were in full view of anyone who passed by on the street, and he didn't. He pitched his voice low, like a scout or a lover. He said, "I could show you. Still don't know what good it would do you."

She curled her fingers around his. "It would help me," she said.

He sighed. "All right. I show you. When you come back, wear an old dress and good boots."

℘℘℘

LATER, SHE APPEARED AT Camp Saxton in a plain dress— no crinoline beneath—and her stoutest boots. Sampson looked at her with approval. "You did good. No petticoat to rustle."

She said tartly, "I've been on a raid, don't you recall? It isn't the occasion to wear hoops."

"Nothing to make a noise," he said. "Come with me."

They walked through the camp. Past the trees where they usually stood to talk. Into a deeper wood.

"Where are we going?" she asked.

"It ain't where we go. It's how we go."

She followed him deeper into the woods. He stepped so lightly that nothing made a sound underfoot. She watched as he searched the path ahead and turned his gaze into the grove. "What are you doing?" she whispered.

"Look at all this like a scout."

"How is that?"

"I survey it. Take it in. Is the land flat or hilly? Anything to walk on? Do I see trees or foliage? Anything to hide behind?"

She thought, *In this peaceful place, he thinks of danger.* She nodded.

"I listen, too." He fell silent, and they both listened to the drowsy silence of afternoon in the Sea Islands. The birds slept at this hour, and even the crickets diminished their song to a hum rather than a chirp.

He said, "Even though it quiet here, I listen. Listen for the smallest sound. Could be a bird or other harmless critter, or it could be a snake. Or it could be the enemy, trying to watch and listen like I do."

She was silent too, imagining sure-footed secesh scouts in the woods.

It was cooler in this glade than it had been in the camp, and the sunlight came green and shadowy through the foliage of the cypresses and live oaks, which grew tall and stately in the undisturbed woods. To Caro, who moved daily through the camp, the nearby woods were unfamiliar. Through Sampson's eyes, she saw and heard them as strange. She could imagine danger here, the secesh hiding behind the great tree trunks, waiting for a hapless Union soldier to blunder into their sights. She felt the fear of a runaway slave, tracked by the secesh as well as the patrollers and their dogs, and she let the fear heighten all her senses.

She watched him, every sense heightened by the possibility of threat, and she remembered, all too well, the very moment of peril in her life. Her first escape, when she fled Lawrence Jarvie to take refuge in Charleston Neck. Her second, when she and Emily hid in plain sight on the steamship north. And her third, when she lay helpless on the floor of the Baker house in Cincinnati, waiting out the riot.

She felt too dizzy to stand. She said, "Sampson, can we stop? I need to rest." She put her hand to her chest, trying to breathe more deeply.

"You ain't all right," he said. He offered her his arm and led her into a little clearing. She leaned her hand against the nearest tree to steady herself.

He kept his hand on her shoulder to support her. "What bother you?" he asked, his voice low in sympathy.

"When I escaped—" The tears came, and she couldn't stop them.

His hand rested on her, as heavy as a comforter. "What happen?"

She shook her head. She struggled against the tears. "I'm so afraid," she said. "I was then, and I am now. I hate it. I can't forget it, and I can't make it go away. It makes me so angry, Sampson."

He moved close. "I know," he said. He enfolded her in his arms, a whole comforter's worth. He stroked her hair.

Her words came out muffled against his chest. "I want to fight. I'd feel better if I could fight. And I can't."

"It's all right," he said, his words muffled by her hair.

She pulled back to look him in the eye. The gaze of his copper-flecked eyes was very soft. "Oh, Caro," he said, speaking her name like a sigh. Like a caress. He kissed her cheek, the softest brush of his lips, and she turned her head toward him, seeking a greater comfort.

He bent to kiss her, carefully at first, and with more passion. She felt warmth suffuse through her, and she remembered the last time she had felt this way, with Danny Pereira. The memory disintegrated and drifted away. She rose to the kiss, returning it, and she relished the feel of his hands on her back, caressing her. His hands, big and capable, were as gentle with her as with his little cat. He murmured, "Oh, Caro. Sugar."

She was giddy again, with a barely-remembered pleasure. She had felt this way in Danny Pereira's arms, too. She distrusted the memory and the pleasure. It had been as fraught, and as dangerous, as her run for freedom.

She broke away and turned. She pulled her handkerchief from her pocket and wiped her face. And when she turned back to face Sampson Hayward, she was safe again. She was Miss Sass, who kept fear and peril away with a sharp tongue. "And I thought you were a man of honor," she said.

He sighed. He recognized Miss Sass, and he knew what to say to her. "I am. You know I am." Gently, he said, "Won't kiss you again if you don't like it. Promise you that."

She was in a corner, and she knew it.

"But you do like it," he said, smiling.

In the guise of Miss Sass, she pretended to be indignant. "I meant your honor as a soldier. Walk in the woods! I thought you were going to teach me how to scout."

"Will that help you?"

"Help me?" She was startled that he would ask.

"Help you put the fear aside. Help you fight."

It was a greater gift than the kiss, and he knew it. "Yes," she said, putting her handkerchief away and standing up straight.

"Come with me," he said. "I school you."

෩൦ൟ

SOPHY WAS STILL GRAVE, but her mood had lightened. Shortly after Caro's scouting expedition, Sophy set her down in the parlor and made an announcement. "Sunday ask me to marry him," she said.

Caro thought, *I should be happier for her. But I'm not.*

Doubt flitted over Sophy's face. "I weren't sure. Tell him I still remember my escape. Haven't set it right for myself. Tell him I fear I won't be a good wife to him, fear over me like a shadow." She took a deep breath. "But he say he trust me. Even though the fear stay with me, even if it shadow me forever. He insist we have to take the chance to be happy now. The chance to look to the future, too. Take whatever happiness we can." She smiled, a look of pure sunniness. "So I say yes."

She said, "That's good news, Sophy. When will it happen?"

"Soon," Sophy said.

Caro nodded.

Sophy said, "Something bother you, and it ain't that I get married."

Many things bother me, Caro thought. She said, "I'm glad for you. Don't worry about me."

Sophy continued to veer between happiness and worry, and it grated on Caro's nerves. As in apology, she was now overly attentive. Shortly after the scouting session, when Caro returned from Camp Saxton, Sophy said to her, "You all flushed."

"I walked in the heat," Caro said.

"You see Sampson?"

"I usually do."

"You know he think the world of you."

"That's no surprise, Sophy."

"You don't have a mama to pay attention to you, and I been remiss, but even I know that Sampson Hayward sweet on you. Whenever you come back from Camp Saxton, you bothered. Is it about him?"

"Please, Sophy. Don't press me."

Sophy said, "I know he ain't a free man of color from Charleston." Danny's ghost hovered in the air.

She thought of Danny's fair skin and his cultivated

speech. And she thought of Sampson, dark-skinned, rough-spoken, tender-hearted.

Sophy said, "You could do a lot worse in life than Sampson Hayward."

"Don't fox with me, Sophy," Caro said, her nerves strained. "Just say it straightaway."

Sophy had a lifetime of foxing people, black as well as white. She laid a hand on Caro's sleeve. "I worry about you," she said. "Want to see you settled in life."

Caro blushed, and the way her face betrayed her made her angry. She yanked her arm away. "I don't want to be settled," she said.

Sophy's eyes were too knowing, as they always had been. "May not always feel that way," she said. "May change your mind someday."

"Not now! Leave me be," she snapped.

Sophy smiled, as though she had asked Caro a question, and Caro had answered her.

ഇറ

THE NEXT MORNING, CARO awakened to the smell of baking: white bread and peach pie. From the kitchen came the sound of voices, Chloe's and Sophy's. Caro saw Sophy setting the table in the dining room. Sophy had found real china and crystal glasses in the ruin of Beaufort, and she surveyed her table with satisfaction.

Sophy told Caro that she had invited Sunday Desmond for dinner after church.

A little too acidly, Caro said to Sophy, "A lot of trouble for Mr. Desmond."

Sophy smiled. "Why not? We celebrate."

And at church, Caro knew why Sophy looked so sly. Sergeant Sunday Desmond had left Camp Saxton to attend the service in Beaufort, and with him was Private Sampson Hayward, his blue Union coat brushed to a parade cleanliness.

Furious, Caro thought, *Settled! We'll settle this, all right.* But with the eyes of black and white Beaufort upon her, she smiled her best belle's smile and politely extended her hand to the man that Sophy thought should be her suitor.

She got through dinner, smiling and nodding as Sunday regaled Sophy with stories of camp life, making her laugh. Sampson was quiet. He ate with exaggerated politeness—clearly, camp life had taught him more genteel table manners than slavery had—but he made little conversation. His gaze slid to her, and he risked a small, apologetic smile.

It was a shame that the peach pie stuck in her throat.

After the meal, when they rose, Sampson asked Caro, "Would you care to promenade with me, Miss Caroline?" He glanced at Sophy. "If you allow it, Miss Sophy."

Caro thought, *As though I'm a parcel to be handed from one to the other!* She said, "Mr. Hayward, I believe I'm able to decide for myself." She held out her arm. "Shall we?"

He nodded and took her arm. Looking like a courting couple, they left the house to stroll down the street. The midday heat was wet and oppressive, and the air had the smell of a Low Country town, the fragrance of blooming shrubs fighting with garbage and manure.

He guided her to the waterfront, where the air also smelled of salt. They halted to gaze over the water of the sound. Caro was suddenly assailed by the memory of standing on the Battery in Charleston before the war with Danny Pereira. He had stood close, as Sampson was too polite to do, and had roused in her the desire to kiss him in public.

She said, "Sophy didn't tell me she'd invited you."

"I knew they up to something."

"Is that all right with you?"

"I can tell it don't sit right with you."

"No, it doesn't."

"I thought we got on fine when we went scouting," he said.

"Scouting," she said. "Not more than that."

He chuckled. "Miss Caroline, don't lead me on," he said.

She drew away. "I wouldn't."

He regarded her with affection. "I won't press you," he said. "But if there's anything I can do to oblige you, I will."

She looked him in the face. "If you do care for me, there is something."

"What is it?"

"You can teach me how to shoot," she said.

His face crinkled into a smile. "It's a fool notion," he said.

She pulled away. "It isn't."

He reached out to touch her cheek, and she shook her head. "You said you wouldn't press me," she said.

"Just a little. Tell me what you so mad about."

She shook her head again. It was too painful to recall, let alone to talk about. Her feverish love for Danny Pereira. The disapproval—and the fury—that a girl who was a slave would dare to fall in love with a free man of color. And when they had figured out how to marry—if her uncle Thomas could buy her as a slave—the bitterness of Lawrence Jarvie's asking price. It had been too high to pay, even for a free man of color. Danny Pereira had abandoned her to flee north with his family.

Before the war, she had been a slave forbidden to marry a free man of color. Now, a free woman, she was too much enmeshed in her past to think of marrying a man who had once been a slave.

Sophy's meddling had been bad enough. Sampson's affection was worse.

As evenly as she could, she said, "Let's go back." She held out her arm.

Sampson's face fell. But he took her arm and said, "I oblige you."

After Sampson left, she sat in her room. She was sick of subterfuge. She wanted to heft a rifle in her hands and carry it to protect her from everything that frightened her. Everything that angered her. Anything that broke her heart.

She still needed someone to teach her how to shoot.

She thought of the most independent woman she knew, who hated slavery and yearned to wear a bloomer costume and felt adamant that a woman should be a doctor rather than a doctress. If anyone might take her seriously—if anyone might advise her without prejudice—it would be Mattie Easton.

She could manage just a little subterfuge. She wrote to Emily, asking if she might call. She had been cautious with Emily since the raid. But Emily wrote back apologizing for the unkind words she'd said before she went to Pocotaligo, asking Caro to visit to set things right. She wrote, *We may disagree, but we're still family.*

₧℃

AT THE DINNER TABLE at the Oaks, Emily was quiet, and Caro could see something still bothered her. She decided to try to divert. Over a dish of roasted chicken, she asked brightly, "Miss Easton, do you think that a woman should know how to shoot?"

Mattie asked, "My goodness, Miss Caroline, what happened to you on that raid?"

"No one shot at me," Caro said, which was the truth. "But it made me think that I should be able to take care of myself." She looked from Emily's saddened face to Anna's startled one to Mattie's. "Did you know that Mrs. Tubman can handle a rifle?"

Mattie said, "Very little about Mrs. Tubman surprises me. It's not a bad idea, is it, Anna?"

Anna, who looked as though it would pain her to wring the neck of a chicken for dinner, looked askance.

"Well, Miss Caro, if you want to learn how to shoot, you're in the right spot at Camp Saxton," Mattie said.

"I'm having trouble finding anyone to teach me. Private Hayward says he can't, and he swears that Captain Aiken won't." She glanced at Emily.

Emily said, "Don't ask me to speak to him, because I won't, either."

Anna sighed. "He hasn't called for weeks," she said to Caro.

Joshua hadn't called? Emily hadn't said a thing. But Emily's unhappy look—and Mattie's warning expression—silenced her on the subject. She addressed herself to Mattie. "So I'm at a loss. I don't know who to appeal to."

Mattie said, "I could teach you."

Anna said, "Mattie! I thought you hated to harm anything living!"

"I've never shot for pleasure. But I used to go hunting with my brothers when I was a girl. I know how to handle a gun."

"Do you have a rifle?" Caro asked eagerly.

"No, but I can buy one in Beaufort, and I can show you how to shoot." She looked fierce and pleased at once. "We can be Amazons, both of us."

Caro was so delighted that she couldn't resist a little sass. "Didn't the Amazons arm themselves with bows and arrows?"

Mattie laughed. "Modern Amazons would arm themselves with rifles," she said.

Caro grinned. "I like that!"

∽◑◠

MATTIE KEPT HER WORD. She bought a good Springfield rifle and boxes of bullets in Beaufort. She gave Caro lessons in handling the gun—using the safety, loading the bullets, and holding it properly to reduce the kick. When it came time to learn to shoot, she asked one of her tenants to build stands, and she made targets out of paper. "We won't shoot at a tree for practice," she said. "Because it's a living thing." She guided Caro and watched her until she was satisfied that Caro could shoot at the target without wounding anything else. "You can practice all you like," Mattie said. "Let me know if you run low on bullets."

Caro had been practicing her shooting for several weeks when Mattie stopped to check on her progress. Emily trailed after her. They both watched. Caro showed off. She crisply raised the rifle to her shoulder, squinted as she sighted, and shot. Emily stared at her. "I don't know what's come over you," she said, and she left to make her way to the schoolroom.

Caro stopped showing off. She lowered the rifle. "What's gotten into her, Miss Mattie? We're at war. What does she think that Cousin Joshua does in battle?"

"She fights with the slate and the speller. It troubles her that you want to fight with a rifle."

Caro bit her lip. She said defiantly, "How better to fight?"

Mattie put a kindly hand on her shoulder. "Something happened on the raid," she said softly.

Oh, yes, Caro thought, remembering how Emily had accused her of being a firebug. "I saw the light, Miss Mattie. It's easier to fight a battle with a rifle than with a speller."

Mattie sighed. "You have a good eye," she said. "You'll be a good shot." She patted Caro's shoulder. "Use that rifle carefully."

"I plan to," Caro said.

₞ℓ₠

EMILY NEVER CAME TO watch Caro at her shooting practice again, but Mattie did, and one day, when Caro had put away her rifle, Mattie called her into the study instead of the parlor.

"Is it a matter of business, Miss Mattie?"

"It isn't a matter for the parlor, that's for certain."

Mattie opened the desk drawer and curled her hand around something. She opened her hand to show Caro the object that lay in her broad palm.

"It's a pistol!" Caro said, surprised.

"A ladies' pistol. Small enough to fit in a dress pocket."

Caro took it. The barrel was very short, and the wooden handle curved pleasantly around her fingers. "It's so pretty," she said, as though it were a piece of jewelry. "I could carry this with me."

"It's still a firearm. Be careful with it."

"Oh, thank you, Mattie!"

Mattie regarded her across the desk with a rueful expression. "I hate fighting as much as Emily does, and I think you're mad. But I'd do anything to help a woman take care of herself."

☎☙

KNOWING HOW TO SHOOT gave Caro a new confidence. She walked through the camp, watching the men clean their rifles, and thought with pride of the gleaming barrel of her Springfield and the pretty curve of her pistol.

She passed Joshua as he sat with his men over the remains of midday dinner. She wanted to talk to him, partly to boast and partly to pry. "Captain Aiken, may I have a word with you?"

"Is it military business?"

"No," she said, and dared to add, "Cousin Joshua, it's personal business."

He brought her back to his tent, and they sat at the little table, thankfully in the shade, where he conducted business. "I feel disquiet whenever you want me for anything, Caro."

She sighed theatrically. "What you think of me," she said. "No, it's all right. I wanted to let you know that Miss Easton has been giving me shooting lessons. Not that I feel any danger," she reassured him. "But we agree, she and I, that it's not a bad thing for a woman to know. She gave me a pistol that I can carry in my pocket."

"Do you have it now?"

"Of course not."

He regarded her with an older brother's rue. "After you asked Private Hayward to teach you how to shoot, he told me he'd refused you. Asked me if he'd done right."

"Why would he?"

Joshua laughed. "I told him that as a soldier, he'd done just right. But as a man courting, he might want to make it up to you."

Now Captain Aiken was meddling, too. She didn't need a spat with him. She put on the belle's mask. "Oh, la, Captain Aiken. Why do you think we're courting?"

"Whenever you want to speak with him, he takes you behind the biggest tree in camp for privacy," Joshua said. "And he comes back to his tent with a big grin on his face."

If she had a fan in her hand, she'd use it. "Courting!" she said, forcing herself to smile. "All I do is interview him." She went on the offensive. "How are you and Emily? Mattie tells me that you haven't come to call for quite a while."

Beneath his soldier's tan, beneath his beard, he blushed. "My duties keep me in camp," he said.

She met his eyes with a younger sister's sass. "I see," she said, in a teasing tone, letting him know how much she believed him.

⁊◌འ

ON SOPHY AND SUNDAY'S wedding day, the churchyard
was full. Around Sunday clustered his fellow soldiers in
the First and Second South Carolina, who were engaged
in ribald jokes about his wedding night, even though he,
like his bride, was of mature years. Captain Trowbridge,
his commanding officer, stood nearby, a smile on his face.
As Caro greeted him, he said, "I can't think of a man who
deserves more to be happily married. Don't you agree,
Captain Aiken?"

Sophy's friends—all the freedwomen of Camp Saxton and Beaufort, by the looks—clustered around her,
exclaiming at the beauty of her black silk dress and pressing her hands as they wished her happiness. Sophy looked
tired but happy, too. Caro knew what it felt like to fight
fear with excitement. She had summoned all the courtesy
she had ever learned and wished Sophy happiness early
this morning as she helped Sophy into her dress.

Emily stood at the edge of the crowd, flanked by Mattie and Anna. Caro thought, *So she hasn't mended things
with Sophy. Or with Joshua, either.*

Sampson detached himself from the crowd around
Sunday and greeted her. He said, "I happy for them."

"So am I."

"Will you set with me in the church?"

Today she wore her best silk dress, which required
a crinoline and full hoops. He wouldn't get close to her,
even if he wanted to. "Yes."

The church was full, and the smell of old incense—a relic of its Episcopal days—mingled with the fragrance of flowers. The crowd, from the highest-ranking officer to the newest contraband, smelled of soap, starch, and just a little of sweat.

Colonel Higginson, who had been ordained as a minister before he received his military commission, conducted the service, dressed in his Union coat and insignia. The married couple stood before him, composed and straight-backed in their wedding clothes. Sunday gripped Sophy's hand tightly. At the words, "Until death do you part," the freedmen and freedwomen raised their voices as though they were at a ring shout. They all remembered the vow, "Until death or distance part us."

Caro felt Sampson sit taller beside her. She felt too hot. She tried to think of the future ahead of the newlyweds, tinted rosy with happiness, instead of the fear that dogged everyone who had been in slavery.

When the groom kissed the bride, the newly free clapped their hands. And when Sampson, who joined in, finished applauding, he put his hand gently on her arm. It would be churlish to shake it off. She let it rest there for a moment. Then she moved her arm and smiled at him, the public mask of the flirt and the belle.

At the wedding celebration—General Saxton himself had offered his house for Sunday and Sophy—Caro stood with Sampson at the dining room table laden with food. Sunday had never made his preference for cake known, so Sophy and Chloe had made a white cake and a lemon cake, as well as fruit pies of all kinds. Music from the yard floated through the open windows, played by Sunday's fellow soldiers, a group of fiddlers who could turn their hands to any kind of music for dancing. Colonel Higginson had provided a regimental brass band, as well.

Sampson ate his cake with surprising daintiness. When he finished, he said, "Miss Caroline, would you dance with me?"

Out of politeness, yes.

They danced a reel together, and when the brass band took over for the fiddlers, one of Sampson's friends reached for her hand, and she danced the polka, too. When the fiddlers resumed, Sampson Hayward held out his hand to her for the cotillion, a statelier dance where only the hands were joined together. But his eyes were alight.

When the music stopped, he said softly, "Stand in the shade with me."

"Will you press me?"

"Hear me out."

In this yard, as at Camp Saxton, he had found a tree to give them privacy.

He said, "We dance well together, Miss Caroline."

"That we do."

"Then you won't mind what I say to you."

"It depends on what it is."

"I'd be happy if you'd dance with me, the two of us, all our lives." He smiled. "Even though we'll lead each other quite a dance?"

Oh no. She thought of the words a lady was supposed

to use in a situation like this one. "You do me an honor…
But I must refuse…"

Very gently, he cupped her chin, a gesture that was
tender and possessive at the same time. "I love you. Hope
you might love me, too."

She was silent.

"Thought there wasn't anyone else. Not even a memory of someone else."

Of course there was a memory. Danny Pereira. She
thought of Charleston, where all the love in the world
counted for nothing because she wasn't free. Sampson's
kindness prompted the sadness as well as the anger. As
the tears caught in her throat, she thought, *We are all free
now.* And she didn't fight the tears.

He touched the salt droplet that trickled down her
cheek. "Someone disappoint you?"

"A long time ago."

"Someone break a promise to you?"

Tears webbed her lashes. "Yes," she said.

"And the pain of it linger."

She thought of Sophy, assuring Sunday that she
would try to vanquish the past. Sampson would swear to
help her, if she made the same pledge. "Yes."

"Will you ponder it? You take all the time you need."

"Yes," she said. "That I can promise."

ഇരുജ

THE NEXT TIME THAT she visited St. Helena Island, she
didn't go directly to the Oaks. Instead, she walked from

the ferry to the White Church. It was August, high summer. Fever weather. Five years ago this month, her father had died of yellow fever.

Since returning to the Sea Islands, she had attended the White Church with Emily, Mattie, and Anna whenever she visited the Oaks. But she had never made a visit to the place that her feet now took her.

She had never visited her father's grave.

The graveyard was neat and well-tended, the grass trimmed around the gravestones that bore the names of Daltons and Smiths. The former slaves respected the dead, even the slave-owning dead. As much as the past pained her, she was glad to see that the cemetery remained intact.

She had to wander the graveyard to find what she sought. At her father's funeral, she had been denied the service at the graveside. She had been a servant then, a slave and not a member of the family.

She found the stone, and she knelt before it. A good stone, made of marble, but no statuary. Emily's stepmother, deeply ashamed of James Jarvie's slave family, had buried him swiftly and without ostentation.

She had never seen the inscription. His name. His dates, a life too short. The stone read, "Beloved son and beloved brother." She was acutely aware of what it did not say: "Beloved husband and beloved father."

She reached to caress the marble, cold even in the Sea Island heat, and bent her head to hide the tears that slid down her cheeks, the tears she had never wept after he died, not in Charleston, not in Ohio, not in Beaufort. "Oh, Papa," she whispered.

Chapter 11: Hallowed Ground

EMILY HAD DELIVERED HER father's letter, but discharging her duty had given her no peace. A few days after her return from Pocotaligo, Mattie asked her, "What did you expect? These are people who were glad to tell you that they are still baying for your blood."

"What do the freed people say? That they have laid their burden down? I thought I would feel like that." She sighed. "And I still carry it."

"It's not a load of wash. It's a guilty conscience. You've done everything you can to ease it." Mattie gestured toward the live oak visible through the open window, where Emily and Anna held the school in the summer's heat.

"Not enough, evidently," Emily said.

Mattie grabbed her arms. "I want to shake you," she said. "What will let you know that he's really gone?"

Emily raised her eyes to Mattie's, surprised at her rough touch. "I want to stand over his grave."

"In Pennsylvania?"

"Yes, at Gettysburg."

Mattie let go of her arms in apology. "I don't understand you, Emily. You won't wear mourning because he hated you, and you hated him. And you want to travel to the battlefield where he fell so that you can pay your respects to him."

Emily rubbed her arms because it would bother Mattie to think that she had caused pain. She said, "I never said I wanted to pay my respects. I said that I wanted to see his grave."

₞⃣

THAT DAY, EMILY TRAVELED to Camp Saxton to speak with Joshua. The guard at the gate questioned her and made her wait for an escort. A private from the First, a short, light-skinned man who was a stranger to her, marched through the camp at such a brisk pace that she had trouble keeping up with him. He delivered her to Joshua's tent, saluting smartly and saying, "Captain Aiken, sir, I bring your visitor!"

Joshua shaded his eyes as he regarded her.

She said, "You aren't pleased to see me."

"I'm surprised to see you. Don't stand like that in the sun. Please, sit down. I can't offer much in the way of refreshment, unless you want a cup of water."

"No, I don't need it." She sat. It was a relief to be out of the afternoon sun.

"What brings you here, Emily? Is there some business? If it were private, you would have invited me to the Oaks."

"I'm keeping it from Mattie."

He looked at her with a sneaking smile, a ghost of his old humor with her. "Don't tell me you've quarreled with her, too!"

"I'm in a quarrelsome mood these days. Caro and I aren't speaking much, either."

"It's not like you."

It was good to hear him tease her. She said, "All the more reason to regret how I've quarreled with you. It weighs on me, more than ever."

He looked away. When he replied, his voice was pitched low. "Yes, on me as well."

She laid her gloved hand on the table. "Would you help me?"

"It depends on what you ask of me."

"I want to go to Gettysburg. Where my father fell."

"Don't tell me you've taken on the duty of bringing him home to bury him!"

"No," she said. "Just to see where he fell."

"If you need a pass, you should apply to General Saxton," he said. "It's not up to me."

"Don't call me a fool, Joshua," she flared.

He flushed. "I haven't, and I won't. But I'm curious about your reason for going."

"I don't go to mourn him," she said, gesturing at her gray dress. "I go to remind myself that he's dead."

"He is dead. His ghost has quite a grip on you still, Emily."

"I hope to let it go," she said, her tone stubborn, her

eyes misting. "I want to see for myself. The battlefield and the grave."

He sighed. "You seem bound and determined to cause yourself pain," he said, reaching for her hand.

She didn't clasp it. She was too angry. "What is war?" she asked, looking around the camp. "It is all pain."

ℰᴑℭᴙ

She left Joshua to visit General Saxton to tell him that she wanted to find her father's grave at Gettysburg. She asked him if she needed a pass. He said, "You'll need one to board a steamer to New York, but after that, there's no need for a pass. You can take the train to Pennsylvania without any help from the Union army."

"Is Gettysburg open to anyone?"

"Yes, to the regret of the army and the Sanitary Commission, which oversees the aftermath of the battle."

She regarded the kindly, weary face. "General Saxton, do you disapprove of my errand?"

"Not at all, Miss Jarvie. But I've heard of your reception from the Confederates at Pocotaligo. A very cold reception."

"I won't be easy in my mind, or in my heart, until I undertake this, sir. We've mentioned before that war gives us peculiar obligations."

He nodded, remembering. He said gently, "I'll talk to the provost marshal about the steamer pass. You have my best wishes, Miss Jarvie."

ॐ৩ॐ

A FEW DAYS LATER, Emily leaned back in her seat, as much as the hard, wooden bench of the train to Gettysburg allowed her to lean. Before she left, she put on a black dress and a black bonnet. She told Mattie, "It will be easier in Gettysburg if I play the role of a bereaved daughter."

Opposite her sat two women, sisters from their looks, their faces stricken with grief. They wore the veils of deepest mourning. They clasped each other's hands and said nothing. When Emily addressed them, they nodded without speaking.

The car was full of men dressed for business, in every manner from elegant to rough. They wore wool suits and beaver hats; they wore nankeen trousers and worn caps. Emily wondered what brought men of business to an abandoned battlefield. Besides the grieving and the enterprising, the crowd included people garbed for an excursion. A woman in a striped dress said to her male companion, her voice high with excitement, "I hear the battlefields are quite the sight!" The thought of sightseeing at a battlefield turned Emily's stomach. She wished she could rebuke them into respecting the dead.

When she alit from the train, the crowd at the depot—fellow passengers and previous arrivals—jostled her. As she tried to get her bearings, someone apologized for brushing against her. It was a young woman in the black dress of widowhood, her accent firmly Yankee. She was accompanied by an older woman, also dressed for bereavement, her face lined with sorrow as well as age. "Excuse me," the younger woman said. "Are you here to seek someone?"

"Yes," Emily said. "My father. And you?"

Her face darkened under her black bonnet. "You're a Southerner."

Wearily—it was too much to explain to a stranger— Emily said, "I was born in South Carolina, but I moved to Ohio before the war."

The stranger's expression opened a little. "I've come to find my husband," she said. "My mother-in-law is with me. I'm Mrs. Sallie Garvey, and this is Mrs. Eleanor Garvey."

Emily introduced herself.

"We came from Minnesota," Sallie Garvey said. "We live in Hennepin County, across the Mississippi River from St. Paul—do you know of it?"

"I'm afraid I don't," Emily said.

Sallie Garvey said, "I know my husband fell here in battle, but I have no idea how to find him."

Emily said, "Where are the battlefields? Are they in walking distance?"

"A mile or two," said Mrs. Eleanor Garvey. "Don't you recall, Sallie? We heard so, on the train."

"I don't remember hearing." Sallie pressed her hand to her forehead. "I'm not myself, Mother."

The older woman took the younger's free hand. "I know, my dearest," she said.

Emily said, "Let me ask for directions." She turned to look for someone who might be a Gettysburg native and hailed a woman with a basket over her arm. When she asked the best way to find the battlefields, the woman's expression became harassed, and she said, "If you follow the Emmitsburg Road, you'll come to them." She added, "You won't be alone on the road."

Emily expected that her trip to Gettysburg would be a solitary pilgrimage, but the Emmitsburg Road, like the village itself, was crowded. Carriages and wagons vied for space, and both were slowed by people on foot. The conveyances, like the train, carried both the saddened, clad in black, and the sightseers, got up for an afternoon of pleasure. On one of the wagons sat a woman, her face in her hands, her head hidden by her bonnet's mourning crape. Next to her sat a pretty girl who chattered in her excitement: "Oh, Charley, look! Such a horrid sight!"

The road had been cleared, but on either side the detritus of battle littered the ground. Pistols, rifles, swords, caps, boots, fragments of uniforms—Emily shuddered at the sight of a sleeve until she realized that it was empty. Men walked into the battlefields and picked up the weapons where they lay, a grotesque gleaning. As they strode across the ruined earth to collect their booty, their boots crunched over a carpet of minie balls.

The air, which had a foul undertone in the village itself, began to smell worse and worse, a stench of rot that overpowered the lingering odor of cordite and smoke. Emily saw the decomposing skeletons of horses, and their half-fleshed skulls gave her a start. Many horses died here, too. Joshua, who had lost more than one horse he treasured, had told her how the horses screamed when they were hit.

The earth mounded where it had been disturbed. Emily tugged gently on Sallie Garvey's sleeve. "I believe these are burials," Emily said.

They walked onto the field together. The minie balls felt like tiny cobbles under Emily's feet, an unsteady covering. All of them looked downward, watching their step as they searched. The dirt had been disturbed everywhere. It was impossible to tell whether it was the aftermath of battle or a hasty burial.

Sallie was the one to see it. She knelt. "Look, Mother," she said. "A marker. A name and a regiment." She touched the crude wooden marker gently, respecting the stranger buried here.

"Minnesota?" Eleanor asked eagerly.

"No, Pennsylvania. But there may be other graves marked."

They walked slowly, their eyes alert for markers. Pennsylvania. Ohio. Michigan. Where were the Confederates? Emily wondered. Were they here? Who buried them, if they were buried at all?

They walked and walked until their legs ached and their eyes burned and their noses and mouths were foul with the smell of rotting flesh. Discouraged, Sallie said, "We could look for days and not find him, Mother."

"Where on the field did his regiment fight?" Emily asked. "Someone must know." She said, "Didn't the army remain to run a hospital? They might be able to advise us."

They trudged back to the town, which was as thronged as before. Emily stopped a blue-coated soldier with his arm in a sling. She asked, "Is there an army hospital here?"

He said, "You're a Southerner."

"By birth. I left. My family remained. My father fell in battle here."

He regarded her with a curious look. "So you're some of both. North and South."

"I believe I am," she said wearily. "The hospital. Where is it?"

"Camp Letterman, just east of town. Ask the Sanitary Commission. They have a setup near the depot. They can direct you."

They joined another pilgrimage to the camp gates. These people, brothers and sisters and mothers and fathers, were not dressed in mourning. They spoke words of hope in Yankee accents. Emily recognized the sound of New England, as at Port Royal, and of the Midwest, like the Garveys. "Thank the Lord," a man was saying. "He's wounded, but he lives." Beside him a woman wept, tears of relief and joy.

Sallie Garvey asked, "Is he a Minnesota man, by any chance?"

Surprised, the man said, "A Wisconsin regiment."

"Do you know if there are Confederate soldiers at the hospital?" Emily asked.

"No," the man said. "I thought they had all gone in the retreat."

At the gates of Camp Letterman, the guards answered the same question over: Where can I find him? They replied, over and over, "Ask at the Sanitary Commission."

At the Sanitary Commission's tent, a nurse greeted them, a cool-headed, competent woman who reminded Emily of Camilla Aiken. Sallie Garvey explained her quest. The nurse said, "On the wards there's no distinction as to regiment, but I can make some inquiries among the men who are convalescing."

Emily said, "I'm looking for a Confederate man who might know what happened to the First South Carolina."

The nurse said, "The Confederate men are separate, and they are fewer. I can direct you to their section, and let you inquire there."

The Garveys were successful. The nurse was able to direct them toward a tent where they might find a Minnesota man. "I'll come with you," Emily said. She was dreading her own errand, and it would hearten her to see the Garveys find what they sought.

It was much easier to walk past the hospital tents than it was to traverse the battlefield. Despite the difficult task here, all was order: spotless tents, neat beds inside, men skillfully bandaged, men carefully nursed. One of the nurses said, "Minnesota? Yes, we have a man from Minnesota here. He's healing well."

He was well enough to establish that they didn't know each other, since he hailed from Red Wing, far from Hennepin County, but that the regiment fought in the wheat field, and the men who fell were buried there by their remaining comrades. "We put up markers when we could," he said.

The Garvey women both clasped his hands in thanks and wept. They would walk the battlefield to seek the marker.

ℰᏏᏏᏏ

THE CONFEDERATE SECTION OF the hospital was no different from the Union, equally tidy, equally orderly. The wounded Confederates received the same treatment as the Union men. It surprised and pleased Emily to know that they had extended this decency to their enemies.

Emily put her head inside the first tent she found and asked the nurse about the South Carolina regiments. The word went around the ten beds inside. They were all Virginia men.

Emily went from tent to tent and kept asking. After half a dozen inquiries, she was discouraged. Outside the seventh tent sat a man recuperating from a shoulder wound. He said, "Miss, what brings you here?" He had a gentlemanly accent.

She explained her errand.

He said, "I never thought to see a Confederate lady here."

She had to tell him part of the truth. "I left South

Carolina for Ohio before the war. My family remained."
She added, "My father joined the Confederate army."

He smiled. "South Carolina? Which regiment?"

"The First."

His smile faded and he hesitated.

"I need to know where they fought," Emily said impatiently. "So I know where he might have fallen."

He said, "I know a man from the First South Carolina." He gestured. "He's a tentmate of mine."

She blinked. She said to her brother and enemy, "Thank you, sir," as she entered the tent to find a man from her father's regiment.

The nurse wasn't pleased at her intrusion, but she allowed it. "Don't press the patient," she said. "He isn't strong."

The First South Carolina man, his eye bandaged, his face wounded, had a bad pallor and could not sit up. He was from Kershaw County, and she was relieved that she had never met him. When she asked where he had fought, he said, "The peach orchard." He leaned back on his pillow, closing his good eye. "Cut us to pieces there. Not much to find. We never went back to take care of the dead."

"Who did?"

He opened his eye. "The Federals hired a bunch of niggers to bury the dead."

Fatigue detail. In the early months of the war, the men of the First and Second South Carolina colored troops had fought with a spade, digging breastworks and latrines instead of drilling and learning how to shoot.

"Are they still here? The gravediggers?"

"The hospital has a cemetery. Ask there."

He closed his good eye again, and he was so waxen that Emily knew what he would look like in death.

The head of the gravediggers for the hospital cemetery, a tired-looking black man with a seamed face, said, "You want Joe. He work on the gravedigging detail just after the battle. Ask him."

"Did he bury Confederate soldiers?"

"He bury Union men, he bury Confederates, he bury horses, too. Ask him."

Joe was a dignified black man who introduced himself to her as Joseph Derrick. She greeted him as "Mr. Derrick." In surprise, he said, "Never thought to hear a Southerner call me 'Mister.'" She explained herself, and he looked at her with a thoughtful expression. "The peach orchard?" he said. "I buried many a man there. I can take you there to show you."

He would be her guide over the River Styx into the land of death.

As they walked, she asked about him. He was Virginia-born; he became a contraband as soon as the Union army came to Virginia, escaping from slavery with his family by running to the Union lines. He had been working for the Union army since. "Mostly with a shovel in my hands," he said. "Dig ditches, latrines, and now graves."

He knew where to go. They walked past the many shallow graves and saw again the detritus of battle, the minie balls underfoot, the pistols and swords dropped and never taken up, the ground an odd color, a mixture of gunpowder and dried blood. She breathed in the smell, an awful miasma, like a penance.

He led her to a bigger grave, the dirt mounded and bumpy. He said, "Didn't have time to do it right. Bury nearly fifty men in there, in such bad condition they was hard to bury. Don't know if your daddy was among them, but he could be."

She said, "This is the likeliest place."

He said, "Yes, miss."

They stood beside the grave, and Christian charity failed her. She thought, *He is dead, he may be buried here, and I can't bring myself to pray for him.*

Joseph Derrick, who watched her stand with her head bowed, lightly touched her arm, a familiarity no Southern slave would permit himself. "I'm sorry for your loss, miss."

And she told him the truth, that her father disowned her for hating slavery, and that she fled the South before the war.

He said softly, "Bad blood. But he still your daddy. Still a loss to you."

She drew a deep breath. To this stranger, she said, "I came to make sure he was really dead."

Joseph Derrick waited. Then he confessed to her, too. "I felt that way about my old massa," he said.

She nodded. It would be slight to tell this man, formerly a slave, how well she understood him.

He followed her gaze, which rested on the disturbed

dirt. "Been fighting this war with a shovel since it began," he said. "Hope and pray for the day when a black man can fight for freedom with a rifle."

"Black men are soldiers in South Carolina," she said. "I've seen it, with my own eyes. My affianced is a captain in their company."

"They really soldiers? They been in battle?"

"Yes, at Fort Wagner, where the Fifty-Fourth Massachusetts also fought and where Colonel Shaw fell." She gestured toward the grave. "A mass grave, where he is buried with his men."

"Miss, I tried to do my best by those Confederate soldiers. Meant no disrespect."

"I know." She turned to face him. "Keep hoping and keep praying, Mr. Derrick. For a war in which black men fight as soldiers."

"I will," he said, smiling despite the gravity of their task. As she had many times at Port Royal, she saw the mask of slavery fall away, and she saw a man like any other. No, a man better than most, who had compassion for his bitterest enemies. "God bless you, miss," Joseph Derrick said.

She held out her hand, and he clasped it.

She turned to go. Her father was dead and buried, and for the moment, his ghost was quiet. It was time for her to return to South Carolina, where she still had her own war to fight.

PART 3

Soldiers of Light and Love

1864

Chapter 12: Into the Wilderness

SAMPSON HAYWARD'S OFFER BOTHERED Caro all the time—when she regarded her unwashed face in the mirror in the morning, when she sat at her writing desk in the parlor of Sophy's house, and worst of all, when she slept. The steamer and the slave catcher no longer troubled her dreams. Instead, she dreamed that she was on the threshold of a church, getting ready to bind herself to a man who would promise to love and cherish her forever.

She woke in a sweat despite the chill in the room. She sat up, holding the cover to her chin, letting her eyes adjust to the dark. She was lucky to have a room to herself in Sophy's house. If she threw off the covers to rise, even if she lit a candle, she would bother no one.

She strode to the window and lifted the curtain. The street outside was plunged into winter darkness. She listened, but nothing disturbed the night. Beaufort, full of Gideonites, retired early and slept deeply; if the soldiers drank, they did so in the confines of Camp Saxton.

She felt hot, as if she had fever. She wiped her forehead with her sleeve. If she stayed in this room, if she went back to bed, she felt that she would go mad.

She threw on an old dress and a shawl over her night-clothes. She took her walking boots in her hand, to slip down the stairs in silence, and she opened the drawer of her dressing table—carefully, softly—to reach for the pistol hidden beneath sheets of writing paper. She let the derringer rest in her hand, the wood cool against her palm, and put it in her pocket, where she could feel it nestling against her leg.

She opened her bedroom door as quietly as she could, wincing at the faint whine of the hinge, and made her way softly to the stairs. She felt carefully for the tread, guarding against any sound, and she was halfway down the stairs when Sophy's door flew open and a disheveled, puffy-eyed Sophy, in too much of a hurry to put on a dressing gown, ran down the stairs after her. "What you doing?" she demanded.

Since the wedding, Sophy had been calmer. But something had disturbed her tonight. Caro decided that the truth was no worse than any fib. She said, "I couldn't sleep. I thought I would go out for a walk."

"At this hour? Is you crazy?"

Caro, whose own dread had wakened her, was tired of Sophy's. "I'll be all right. I have this." She pulled out the pistol.

Sophy's eyes went wide. "Who give you that?"

"Miss Easton. She taught me how to use it."

"You put that away and put on your nightdress and get back into bed."

A sleepy voice came from Chloe's room. "Mama, something the matter?"

Caro called, "It's nothing, Chloe."

Sophy was shaking. "If you can't sleep, you take a draught. You don't wander about to get into trouble."

Chloe's youngest woke and began to cry.

"Now we all need one," Caro said.

"Back to bed," Sophy insisted, as though she were a wayward child, and she grasped Caro's arm for good measure.

℘)℘

BUT IN THE MORNING—WHEN everyone in the house was a little heavy-eyed from being awakened in the middle of the night—Sophy asked Caro to linger at the breakfast table. The morning light, unusually brilliant for winter, made last night seem like a bad dream. The big wood-burning stove filled the kitchen with a caressing warmth. "Does you want any more coffee?" Sophy asked Caro.

"Yes, thank you." Sophy poured coffee as the kitchen cat sat at Caro's feet. She bent down to pet the hard little head. "You'll have your milk later," she told the cat.

Sophy watched as Caro sipped the coffee and put down the cup. Her eyes were shadowed from her own broken sleep. She said, "Didn't mean to be so sharp with you last night."

"I know." Caro reached for Sophy's hand. "You worry about me."

"I do. Not just because I worry more than I used to. Something weigh on you, even though you don't tell me what."

Caro thought of all the secrets she had kept from her mother before the war. Now she was treating Sophy with the same disrespect. She said, "It's not really a secret. But it's something that I don't like to talk about."

"Is it about Sampson Hayward?"

Caro nodded.

"If he wrong you or if he hurt you—"

"Oh, Sophy, no. Nothing like that. He asked me to marry him."

"What do you tell him?"

"I promised to consider it."

A familiar gleam of understanding lit Sophy's face. "Ah, that the thing that bother you," she said.

"I reckon so."

"You ain't still pining for Danny Pereira?"

"Of course not," she said, as though protesting it would make it true. She rose. "I should get to work," she said. "I need a new subject. There's not much news from the camp these days."

"Come to the market with me?" Sophy asked. "Maybe the market women have some news."

"Maybe," she said, remembering her first excursion to the Charleston market with Sophy and the first coin she ever earned.

"Or maybe go visit your cousin. See if they have any news."

Sophy still couldn't say "Miss Emily." The hurt and anger over Lawrence Jarvie was still too great.

"She isn't so fond of me either these days," Caro said.

"Miss Mattie be glad to see you." Sophy's eyes gleamed. "You take that pistol away and leave it with her."

Caro thought, *On St. Helena Island I could roam at night.* "I'll take the ferry over today," she said. "And if they'll have me, I'll stay for a while."

ဆါၣ

MATTIE WAS GLAD TO oblige her. "Stay as long as you like," she said. "Send for your things. I don't know if we have any news, but you're free to talk to anyone at the Oaks."

"Or Ocean Point?" Caro asked, sassing making her feel a little better.

"We don't have much to do with them, but you're free to roam there, too. And they're free to talk to you, or not."

At the midday dinner table, Emily was in a better humor than Caro had seen in her since she received news of her father's death. She still wasn't wearing mourning dress, a scandal to anyone who thought a dutiful daughter owed her father a year of unrelieved black.

Caro asked about Emily's expedition to Gettysburg. Emily told her about the mourners, the scavengers, and the sightseers. "All of them looking for something," she said.

Caro asked, "Did you find him?"

"As much as I could."

"Did you bury him?"

"The Union army buried him," Emily said, as matter-of-factly as if she'd said, "Yes, I'll pass you the butter."

"Did you put him to rest?"

"Caro," Mattie said.

Emily said, "Mattie, we talk about war all the time at this table. We talk about death, too. Yes, Caro, as much as I could. I stood at his grave, such as it was, and now I really know that he's dead."

After the meal, Emily said to Caro, "Put on your shawl. I want to talk on the porch."

"Why don't we walk a little?"

"Even better."

As they walked, shawled and gloved and bonneted against the cool air, Caro said, "I shouldn't have needled you about your father."

"I've said worse to you."

Firebug. "Why are we fighting, Emily?"

Emily curled her hand around Caro's. "It's become a bad habit," she said. "I've quarreled with Joshua, too. It's better than it was, but I haven't mended it properly."

Caro said, "I thought so, when I saw you at Sophy and Sunday's wedding with Mattie and not with him."

Emily squeezed Caro's hand. "I saw you," she said. "Sitting in the pew with Sampson Hayward." She smiled. "Will that be our next wedding?"

Caro caught herself before she retorted. She said, "Careful how you step, Emily."

Emily didn't release Caro's hand. "Ah, we're not properly mended yet, either," she said.

"Not yet."

ΩΟΩ

ONCE AGAIN, CARO COULDN'T sleep. The walls of her pleasant room seemed to press too close. She had come here to run away from the things that most troubled her. She threw off the covers, shivering in the chill. She quickly buttoned her dress, pocketed her pistol, and took her shoes in her hand. She slipped down the stairs and out the side door without incident.

Behind her, the house was dark, and before her, the yard was dark. The air was chilly and damp. She wished that she had brought a lantern. Or a candle. She thought of Sampson and nearly laughed aloud. A scout with a candle! She would move slowly, letting her eyes adjust, letting her feet find the way. She put on her boots and laced them up. She rose. Still thinking of Sampson, she walked with care.

On the driveway, she could feel the gravel beneath her feet. The sounds in the trees were faint, the sounds of little claws and little wings. Reassuring sounds. She could remember waking up as a child to hear the call of an owl outside her window. It was too distant a memory to be painful.

She came to the end of the driveway where it let onto

the road. The trees were thicker here, and the path was deeply shrouded in darkness. The overcast sky was little help here.

What did her direction matter? She had no destination. She could go either way.

She tried to recall Sampson's brief lesson in scouting, and she had to admit that she was as inept at scouting in the woods as Sampson would be in taking tea in a Charleston drawing room.

As though he'd spoken to her, her thoughts turned to his question. *Yes, I'll ponder it.* She stood in the darkness, unable to decide which way to go, her thoughts tangled like the branches of live oaks grown together.

You could do worse, Sophy whispered. *Will yours be the next wedding?* Emily asked, smiling.

La, courting? she told Joshua.

And Sampson himself echoed in her ears: *Someone break a promise to you?*

Yes.

The two men who had loved her best. One of them was buried on this island and the other was lost to her as though he were dead.

She had been a fool to think that wandering in the darkness would make her feel any less pain. She was a woman lost in the dark. She could feel just as bad in her room at the Oaks, and she would be considerably warmer, too.

Then she heard a voice. "Do you hear something?"

It was a Charleston accent. An educated man's accent. Was there a secesh picket on St. Helena Island?

Where would she go for cover? The voice came from somewhere in the trees. She froze. She breathed shallowly, trying not to make any sound. For all she knew, they were as acutely vigilant as Sampson.

Another voice said, "Another night on picket duty. Nothing to scare up but a bird or a bunny rabbit." A Yankee voice.

And another voice, this one a Sea Islander's, with a deep chuckle. "Be glad of it."

She went limp with relief. They were Union pickets. And they were no scouts, if they made that much noise.

She waited for them to pass by, and when she was sure that they had, she retraced her steps back to the Oaks in the dark.

ⅎ⅏

WHEN SHE RETURNED, A candle burned in the study. Mattie met her as she closed the door. She wore her dressing gown, and her hair, a plait as thick as rope, tumbled over her shoulder. She said, "I couldn't sleep. I came downstairs to read." Mattie looked her up and down and asked, "Have you been out?"

Caro thrust her hands into her pockets to hide that they trembled. "I couldn't sleep, either."

Mattie shook her head. "You were," she said. "It's not wise."

"I took this." She showed Mattie the pistol.

"Even with that."

"Has there been trouble here with the secesh?"

"Why do you ask?"

"I passed by a group of pickets. I overheard them talking. Ours."

"They're always here," Mattie said. "They spend more time looking for runaways than secesh."

"One of them was black," Caro said. "Does the First South patrol here? Or the Second?"

"They might. I don't know. They don't call on us."

Later, upstairs, in the comfort of her room, Caro wondered about the Charleston-sounding voice. She had met all the men of the First South, and most of the men in the Second, and there were no Charleston men among them.

ⅎ⅏

CARO DRIFTED THROUGH THE day, too heavy-lidded to visit the classroom or talk to the people on the place or even to sit down to contemplate what she might write about. After midday dinner, she excused herself for her room, where she took off her shoes, her dress, and her corset, and lay down under the coverlet.

But sleep wouldn't come. In its stead, she remembered how afraid she had felt the night before. She tried to push it away, but it only increased. It brought more fear in its wake. She thought of every moment in her life when she had felt afraid and helpless, waiting for the slave catcher's step, listening to the gunshots of the riot. The fear swelled in her like a sickness, and she sat up, pressing her hands to her belly against it.

With shame, she thought, *Soldiers don't feel like this.* She felt no better.

She breathed deeply and told herself that she would go out again, and again, and again, into the fear and the darkness, until she could muster a soldier's courage.

ം)ൽ

WHEN SHE WOKE IN the middle of the night, she rose to look out the window. The sky was clear, an inky color, and moonlight spilled over the yard, a cool yellow beacon. She dressed and picked up her pistol, its smooth handle reassuring in her hand, and slipped from the house.

Tonight, she had her bearings, and she easily found her way down the driveway and onto the road, where the moonlight continued to guide her. She knew exactly where she was. She turned toward the direction of the ferry at Lands End. Toward her father's old place.

The cold air felt good on her skin, and now that she could see, the night's quiet was pleasant. She felt the tension in her body ease. She remembered Sampson's scouting walk, measured and purposeful. She moved that way and thought, *This is all right. I don't feel afraid.*

She also remembered Sampson's alertness. She wasn't taking a promenade on a Sunday afternoon. She needed to pay attention.

But there was nothing to rouse her attention. Even the woodland creatures seemed to be asleep tonight. And there were no voices in the trees, neither Yankee nor Low Country, neither white nor black.

She wished that Sampson could see how well she handled herself.

The thought of Sampson, the memory of the desire in his eyes when he asked her to dance all her life long, stopped her on the path as though he'd called to her.

She had prepared herself against fear. She hadn't been prepared to be ambushed by affection. Or regret. Or confusion.

She stood unmoving in the moonlight, remembering the kindness on Sampson's face when asked her, "Will you ponder it?" In the darkness of St. Helena Island, a haven a stone's throw from the war, she was far away.

The owl's call brought her back. She raised her eyes to the sky to follow the swooping flight. She forced herself back into a scout's bearing. Wherever she went, no matter how she tried to run from it, she would carry Sampson with her. As she pondered his offer, his lessons in scouting lingered with her to protect her.

That knowledge was as bad as the fear, and as debilitating. She tried to reach for a soldier's anger. For a soldier's courage. But all she could find was her own weakness.

§⧉CR

CARO REMEMBERED THE RESOLVE she had felt when she first learned how to shoot. She kept her rifle in her room at the Oaks. After her second foray into the woods, she picked up the rifle and slung it over her shoulder. She stood before the dressing table mirror and regarded herself. She thought of her beautiful mother, who had spent so much time at her dressing table, who had so often turned to her daughter to ask, "How do I look, Caro?"

How do I look, Mama? she asked her mother's ghost. *Do I look like a soldier?*

As though her mother had raised her to be a soldier.

She turned to get a better look at the way the rifle rested against her back. Mattie, a better guide these days than Caro's own mother, had told her that she was a good shot. She held the rifle in her hands, feeling the silkiness of the stock and the smoothness of the barrel, newly surprised that a gun could be a thing of beauty. She glimpsed her reflection again. Today, a rifle suited her better than a new bonnet or a pretty shawl.

She would go out properly armed next time.

Still looking in the mirror, she thought, *If I dressed like a boy, no one would wonder why I carried a rifle.*

She had disguised her face and voice to become a fugitive when she escaped from Charleston, and she had been successful enough to pass to freedom. She would put her ability to deceive to good use once again.

She knew where to find a boy's clothes. The American Missionary Association, still worried about keeping the newly free warm in winter, had just sent a bundle of clothes to the Oaks. The box sat in the back parlor, where Anna did her sewing. Caro went to find it.

She was in luck. Anna had already sorted through the box, putting the clothes in order according to sex and size. Caro found a shirt and a pair of trousers that looked as though they'd fit, and to her delight, she even found a cap. She didn't dare search for shoes, even though her stoutest boots were a girl's, not a boy's. In the dark, they'd pass.

She took her prizes to her room. They were wrinkled and a little worn, but that suited her purpose. She dressed. The shirt was too big and the pants were too short, but that helped, too.

She checked her reflection in the dressing table mirror and was pleased with what she saw. She'd have to bind her chest. She'd find a rag.

She twisted her hair into a knot and stuffed it into the cap. She was adjusting the cap on her head to hide more of her hair when Mattie's voice floated from the hallway, startling her.

Mattie asked, "What are you doing?"

Trying not to sound cross, Caro said, "Can't a person have a little privacy in this house?"

Mattie glanced at the rifle that rested against her bedroom wall. She said, "What are you up to?"

Caro pulled the cap down and stared at her reflection in the mirror. She still didn't look right. She asked Mattie, who dressed and conducted herself without any nonsense, "Didn't you ever want to dress like a boy?"

Mattie said, "Over my mother's dead body. Caro, what are you doing?"

"This way, when I go out at night, no one will bother me."

"You're awfully pretty for a boy," Mattie said.

"You can blame my mama for it. She was a beauty."

Mattie looked from the rifle to Caro. "Be careful, Caro."

She had an inspiration. In her best Low Country accent, she said, "Call me Jim."

೫ಌ

CARO DIDN'T WAIT LONG to test her disguise. On the next moonlit night, she dressed herself—binding her chest was worse than she expected—and readied herself to leave the house. She lifted the rifle to her shoulder and caught a glimpse of herself in the mirror in the low light. She stood straight and still. She wondered if Sampson would be proud of her. Or whether he'd castigate her for acting the fool.

Probably call her a fool. She picked up her boots and hurried down the stairs, putting them on as she sat on the side steps. She rose. Having a rifle over her shoulder was different from hiding a pistol in her pocket. She felt braver.

She left the grounds and followed the road that led to Lands End. She felt jittery and excited. She adjusted the rifle on her shoulder, fiercely glad of its weight against her side.

The air was a little warmer tonight, and the woods were noisier. Her nerves sharpened her hearing. She heard the rustling and scrabbling sounds of small animals, likely squirrels, and the soft calls of nightjars. Nothing to fear. But it was as though Sampson accompanied her. She could hear him whisper: *Stay wary.*

Then she heard steps. Not an animal's feet. The feet of men in boots, men who made no effort to be quiet. This time she knew to slip into the trees on the other side of the road, to watch.

And she heard the voice again. The Yankee voice. "Did you hear that?"

"Heard something," someone else said. A black man's voice.

The Union pickets she had heard on her first night out.

The soldiers stepped from the woods onto the road, their rifles drawn. The Yankee voice said, "There's something in the trees." The voice was a Yankee's, but the face was a black man's.

"Who goes there?" he repeated, his rifle drawn.

He was a handsome man, not dark, with features that betrayed white ancestry. He was slight and no taller than she was. A black Yankee, and she had never seen him before.

She showed herself, and he stared at her. He asked, "Are you contraband?"

The words came in a rush, the Low Country accent as sure as if she was born to it. "Oh no, sir. Live around here on the island. Just out for hunting."

"It's a damn poor night for hunting," the soldier said.

She rejoiced at the oath. He thought she was a boy.

"My name Jim," she said. "From the Oaks place. Work for Miss Mattie Easton." Mattie would permit that fib.

"Does your employer know you roam at night?"

"She allow it." Which was true.

The soldier shook his head. "Edwards," he said, "what do you think we've got here?"

Edwards was older and darker than his companion. His accent reminded Caro of the older men she'd known in Ohio. He said, "I think we got a restless boy that used to be a slave." He addressed Caro. "Son, you belong at home, tucked up in bed."

Caro thought exultantly, *He thinks I'm a boy! I'm getting away with it!* She spoke to both of them. "Union men," she said, working on sounding naïve. "Where is you from?"

Edwards chuckled. He said, "We're both with the Twenty-Sixth Regiment New York Infantry, Colored Troops."

She had never heard of the Twenty-Sixth New York. They must have just arrived at Camp Saxton. She said, "Maybe I can be a help to you." She threw Edwards a glance. "I grow up on this island. Know it well. I scout for you, guide you."

Edwards said to his companion, "Why not, Archer?"

"Who is he?"

"He used to be a slave. Do you really think he's a secesh spy?"

Caro risked a glance at Archer. She said, "No love for the secesh, sir. Believe me."

"It would be a help to us," Edwards said.

Archer looked at her with such penetration that she was afraid he would guess her secret. But he said, "All right."

Caro asked, "Who is you?"

Archer stood up very straight. He said, "Private David Archer of the Twenty-Sixth Regiment New York Infantry, Colored Troops."

She got on famously with the pickets of the Twenty-Sixth New York, and they never cottoned to her disguise. She went home near dawn, shaking with excitement. She was too wrought up to be quiet on the staircase to the second floor. As she stepped onto the landing, Emily's door opened. Emily had tugged herself from sleep. Her nightdress was wrinkled, her hair was loose, and her face was marked from the wrinkles on her pillow. Fuzzy with sleep, she stared at Caro as though she were an intruder.

Caro whispered, "Don't you recognize me, Emily?"

Emily woke enough to take in the boy's clothes and the rifle. She stared at Caro again. Without speaking, she shut her door.

෨෬

EMILY WAITED TO TAKE Caro aside. That afternoon, she waylaid Caro outside her bedroom door. She said, "Come into my room, Caro. I want to talk to you in private."

Emily's bedroom, like the rest of the house, had been patched together from bits and pieces salvaged from the big house after the Big Shoot. It was austere compared to the kind of room she had slept in before the war. She had a narrow bed with a white coverlet, a wooden wash stand with a plain white slop jar, a small desk covered by a plain blotter, and a rocking chair. Her dresses hung from a coat tree in the corner.

She said, "What are you doing, Caro?"

"Helping the army," Caro said.

"Have they asked for your help?"

"I feel obliged, whether they have or not."

Emily said, "Now I know you've gone crazy."

"For going out at night?"

"For exposing yourself to danger."

"There's not much danger," Caro said. "I met the Union pickets who guard the island. They're bored stupid. They ambushed a bunny rabbit last night. That's how much danger we're in."

"Why are you doing this, Caro?"

"Doing what?"

"This business of playing at soldiers."

Caro's anger flared. "If I were a man, I would have mustered into the First South Carolina long ago."

"Is this about Sampson Hayward?"

She knows better, Caro thought. She said. "No. Not this."

ഇൽ

THE MEN OF THE Twenty-Sixth were on picket duty overlooking the Harbor River, located on a small hill behind some trees. It gave them a good vantage point to watch for boats that might land on the spit of sand below. They sat, talking quietly, listening for the sound of oars in the water or footsteps.

They were used to "Jim" and nonplussed that he carried a rifle. Archer was on duty again. "Good to see you, suh," Caro said.

Archer said irritably, "I draw picket duty too often. And we're short a man tonight. Matthews took sick."

Caro sat and the men fell silent. They shifted their attention toward the river.

The sound of footsteps had them on their feet. As the footsteps came closer, the man called out the sign. "Don't shoot," he said.

A South Carolina accent, a surprise. He said, "I've come in Matthews's place." He glanced at Caro, whose face was in shadow, and said, "Who's that?"

Archer said, "Jim. He's a local boy. He scouts a little for us, brings us news."

The new man saw the rifle more easily than he saw her face, for which she was grateful. Forgetting himself, he said, in his Charleston accent, "Does your master know you roam at night and carry a rifle?"

Before Caro could defend herself, Archer said, "There are no masters here. His employer is Miss Easton, the doctor, who permits it."

They sat again, on the ground, the new man joining them. Caro made sure to keep her face in shadow. They fell silent again, listening to the sounds of the night, alert for anything unusual.

Caro was the one to say, "Do you hear that?" It was the sound of oars splashing in the water, with little attempt to muffle the sound.

Were they fellow soldiers? Contraband, so desperate they didn't care if they made a noise? Or secesh?

In the quiet, voices floated toward the shore. "I hear the pickets are niggers," said a voice, in the accent of well-to-do Charleston. Someone laughed in response.

"We'll pick them off like crows," said another voice, in the rougher accent of the backcountry.

The men were instantly on their feet, shooting in the direction of the boat to prevent it from landing. The incline prevented them from descending to the shoreline, but it gave them the advantage, Caro realized. It was easier to shoot down the hill than up.

She rose to her feet and pointed her rifle toward the sound of the boat beaching on the sand. Archer was by her side, saying, "No! Don't! Get back!"

As the men disembarked and looked for shelter in the brush on the hill, the pickets continued to fire. The men ran into the shrubbery, and the pickets fired at the disturbance between the branches.

From their cover, the secesh returned the fire.

Caro watched from her step backward. Her gaze swept from Archer, who was shooting, to the Carolina man at her side.

He was frozen. He held the rifle as though it was too heavy for him. He lifted it but let it fall again. Even though bullets flew in his direction, he couldn't aim. He couldn't pull the trigger.

Caro couldn't stand it. She whispered fiercely, "Shoot! Fire back!" But he didn't move. She pushed him aside, raised her rifle, and fired at the sound of fire from below.

Someone cried, "Damn, I'm hit!" and the footsteps in the brush halted. The fire from below halted, too. One of the secesh said, "We won't take them. They have the high ground." Someone else said, "Nigger pickets!" and made a sound as though he were spitting.

The first voice said, "Let's go," and they scrambled down the hill back to their boat, pursued by the sound of shooting.

As the men retreated onto the river, Archer said, "We missed a chance. We didn't get any of them." He said to the South Carolina man, "Are you all right?"

Dazed, he said, "I thought I heard the voice of a girl I knew in Charleston before the war."

Archer said curtly, "It wasn't enough of a battle to get that upset." He turned to Caro and scolded her. "I told you not to get yourself in the line of fire!"

Caro couldn't fade into the darkness fast enough, and the man with the Charleston accent got a good look at her. "Caro?" he asked. Caro didn't move or reply. "Caro?" he said again, and pulled the cap from her head. Her hair tumbled down her back. "Caro," he said, still stunned.

Archer asked, "You know this—person?"

319

Still stunned, he said, "Caro! What in God's name are you doing here?"

It was a very familiar voice. It belonged to Charleston, and her past. She said, "Danny Pereira, I might ask the same of you."

Chapter 13: Preempted Land

IN JANUARY, PHOEBE ASKED to call on Miss Anna and Miss Emily. Mattie, the busybody, joined them when Phoebe arrived. Phoebe perched on the settee and politely accepted a cup of tea. Before she could state her business, Emily said, "How goes the school, Miss Phoebe?"

"We have over a hundred scholars now."

"Is there anyone to help?" Emily asked.

"I'm the only teacher. It wear me out."

"Wears me out," Anna corrected.

Phoebe struggled to control her exasperation. "I know, Miss Anna," she said. "Harder to talk proper when you tired."

"No wonder you're worn out," Emily said. "You can't manage a hundred children by yourself."

Phoebe sighed. "I know it won't last," she said. "Marse Harry write to the Missionary Association to ask for another teacher at Ocean Point. They tell him they look for someone. But it can't happen overnight."

Emily thought, *She's learned from her father. How to ask without seeming to.* She said, "Might I help you?" She was free to beseech, and she did. "Miss Sterling, can you spare me?"

"Emily, do you really want to return to Ocean Point?" Anna asked. Soft-voiced Anna was masterful at phrasing a command as a question.

Emily knew very well what Anna suggested. "Oh, I can't stay there," she said. "Now that Miss Phelps has gone back to Boston. But if you could spare me, Anna, I could go for the day to help Phoebe until the new teacher arrives."

Anna made a disparaging noise, and Mattie said, "Anna, don't fox with her. Of course you can spare her, and she's hardly likely to have the time to flirt with Mr. Phelps if she's busy with a hundred scholars in the classroom."

Emily laughed. "I'd like to help Phoebe," she said, warmed by the smile that brightened Phoebe's face. "And I promise not to encourage Mr. Phelps to propose marriage to me."

The atmosphere in the room lightened, and Phoebe took a drink of her tea. As she reached for a cookie, Mattie asked her, "What do you think of the latest news about this year's land sale?"

Emily wanted to groan. "Mattie, please. Wasn't the last sale bad enough?" Rufus Green had been bitterly disappointed last year, when William Chapman prevented his employees from buying land and himself became the biggest landowner on St. Helena Island.

Mattie said, "About the preemption plan."

That was General Saxton's doing. He had insisted that the newly free should be allowed to "preempt" plots of their choosing, the price per acre the same as the homesteaded lands out west, a dollar and a quarter. Any man who worked for wages on a cotton plantation could have saved enough to buy forty acres.

Phoebe set down her cup and said carefully, "We hear all about it."

Now she was treading lightly. When Rufus Green lost his chance last year, the whole Green family had shared in the disappointment. Phoebe was much too tactful to remind them, even though she knew they sympathized with her father.

Mattie, whose conviction overrode her discretion, remarked, "We hear the soldiers are quite enthusiastic. They'll be allowed to buy land with a deposit of two-fifths of the value of the plot. Even a private could save enough to buy forty acres." She looked brightly at Phoebe. "What does your father say?"

"Goodness, Mattie," Emily murmured.

But Phoebe met Mattie's enthusiasm with a reply as measured as her father's. "Well, he remember last year, and he try not to hope too much. But if what General Saxton say is true, and it come to pass, he might want to put his name to a preemption slip." She rose and said politely, "Miss Emily, when do we see you at Ocean Point?"

∞CR

EMILY ARRIVED AT OCEAN Point to the familiar well-tended yard. The neatened house. She met Phoebe on the front steps. "Are you still in the ballroom?" she asked.

"Yes. We squeeze in."

She hooked her arm through Phoebe's, and they ran up the grand staircase together. The ballroom was now crowded with wooden benches, and primers and spellers, neatly piled, covered the wooden table. "Do you still give them biscuit?" Emily asked.

Phoebe sighed. "I believe we have a rebellion if we don't," she said. "They eat like a plague of locusts, all of them."

The sound of feet scuffling on the stairs was familiar, as was the clamor while they settled. Phoebe hadn't exaggerated. The room was steamy with the heat of so many small bodies.

Teaching had become easy now, and after Phoebe introduced her, they kept order together and set the scholars to their task, whether they were just beginning their acquaintance with the cat and the mat, or whether they had become fluent enough to help the beginners.

After the children left, as they tidied the room together, Emily said to Phoebe, "You've become a good teacher."

Phoebe laughed. "You good at keeping them in order now," she said, and they left as they had arrived, arm in arm, as they swept down the stairs.

At the foot of the stairs stood Harry Phelps.

"Miss Jarvie," he said, removing the battered hat he wore into the fields. "I wanted to thank you for coming to our aid." He looked very tired, but the blue eyes still sparkled.

"I'm glad to be able to help Phoebe."

"We've missed you here." The bright smile hadn't dimmed, either.

She should go. But she was irritated at Mattie for the way she'd poked at Phoebe. She thought of how much she had always liked Harry Phelps, and how much Joshua disliked him.

As she lingered, Mr. Chapman emerged from the study. He said, "Miss Jarvie! I hear that you've returned to us to help Phoebe in the classroom."

"The school flourishes, but a hundred children! It's too much for one teacher. She'll be glad when the Missionary Association sends another."

"We want to thank you. Please, dine with us."

"Mr. Chapman, I really must go—"

His eyes twinkled. "Certainly Miss Easton doesn't keep you in thrall," he said. He seemed pleased and prosperous, his coat well-brushed, his trousers creased, his shoes shining. He looked like a man who never walked in the fields.

"Of course not," she said, glancing at Harry.

Which was how she came to dine again at Ocean Point, at the table with its mismatched chairs and mismatched china, where she had suffered under the gaze of Eliza Phelps.

Mr. Chapman asked politely after the school at the Oaks. After Captain Aiken and his success in camp. After Caro and her health, as though Caro were fragile and had the vapors. In a moment he would ask her what she had been reading. It was as though he were at home in Boston.

Harry Phelps ate in silence as Mr. Chapman talked.

She thought of Mattie's table, where all the news of the day was considered proper conversation. She asked, "What do you hear about the land sale, Mr. Chapman?"

He said, "Oh, I'm not in the market for land this year."

She thought, *I would hope not.*

"But we hear of it." He looked at Harry, who was eating his soup with studied politeness. "I've encouraged Harry to buy his own place. To become an entrepreneur himself."

"Really, Mr. Phelps? Are you considering it?"

"I have been," Harry said.

Emily said, "Would Mr. Chapman consider selling you part of Ocean Point?"

Mr. Chapman laughed. Harry put down his spoon. "I have my eye on the Pine Grove place," he said. "Three hundred and twenty acres."

Mr. Chapman said, "It won't go cheap this time. There are too many speculators interested this year. But he has nothing to worry about. I'll back him, whatever it costs me."

⁐⁐⁐

EMILY REMEMBERED RUFUS GREEN'S disappointment over the previous land sale so vividly that she hesitated to ask Phoebe if her father had filled out his preemption slip yet. It was odd to think that losing a plot of land could break a man's heart.

But Rufus Green himself told her when she trailed after Phoebe into the kitchen the next day. Juno was at the stove, but Rufus sat at the table, warming his hands around a cup of coffee, a good-humored smile on his face. "I hear you do well with the school," he said to Emily.

"I'm glad to help."

Juno turned to ask. "You want coffee, Miss Emily?"

"Yes, thank you." She recalled when getting a cup of coffee from Juno was a surprise, and a gift. She joined Rufus Green at the table. "You're in a good humor, Mr. Green."

"Phoebe don't tell you?"

She glanced at Phoebe. "About what?"

"About the preemption."

"You've decided to preempt?"

He grinned. "Better than that," he said. "I go up to Pine Grove, Dalton place, and I pick out my hundred acres. Best hundred acres. And then I go to Beaufort and file my preemption paper."

"A hundred acres," Juno said, her face soft. She allowed herself to dream.

Rufus said, "Forty planted in cotton, twenty for corn, and room for a big garden for Miss Juno. Room for a house, too. I build, once I get it." He looked at Phoebe with affection. "Phoebe save all her money from teaching, and she insist we use it for this. Have enough for land, horses, plows, and seed, too." He laughed. "Forty acres planted in cotton, Miss Emily! And long-staple cotton at over two dollars a pound in England!"

"You aren't worried that someone else wants it?"

His eyes gleamed. "I know who want it. Mr. Chapman hope to buy it for Mr. Phelps. But the whole place preempted. Mr. Chapman can't have it, and neither can Mr. Phelps. Mr. Chapman won't be in my way this time."

℘℘℘

LATER THAT DAY, AT the Oaks, she waylaid Mattie, who asked how the day had gone.

Emily thought of Harry Phelps and Rufus Green, two men who wanted the same plot of land, and she replied lightly, "Swimmingly. Tell Anna that Mr. Phelps asked me to elope, but I refused him."

"Do they talk about the land sale?"

"Yes, as everyone does."

Mattie grinned. "I've heard that his people are planning to preempt their own land. Mr. Phelps would be free to return to Boston to finish his studies in divinity."

"I don't think that would satisfy him," Emily said, recalling Harry's bright smile as she thought of his hope for the Pine Grove plantation.

"It would do my heart good to see Rufus Green with his own place."

"Mine as well," Emily said. She thought of the joy on Rufus Green's face at the thought of foiling his employer. The conflict was not hers to gossip about. She would fox

Mattie into believing that she cared more about Harry Phelps's friendship than Rufus Green's hopes. "But it's cruel to dash anyone's hopes. Even a superintendent with the best of intentions."

"The road to hell, Emily."

"I know better than anyone, Mattie."

Emily had been relieved to learn that Rufus Green planned to preempt the plot that Harry Phelps hoped to buy. The matter was in the hands of the tax commission, and no concern of hers. Harry Phelps could find another plot of land to buy, if he wanted to go into debt to grow cotton. And as much as she worried for Rufus Green, he had decades of practice in handling the powerful white men he worked for. She didn't like to think that he also had decades of practice in tamping down his own hopes.

❧❧

THE NEWS OF THE changed preemption plan tore through the Sea Islands like a bout of yellow fever. It flew from Beaufort, where it originated; to Camp Saxton, where it set the place abuzz; to St. Helena, where the superintendents and teachers, as much as the former slaves, passed the fever to everyone in the Sea Islands.

The newly free would not be allowed to preempt the land they wished for, the land they knew, the land they had worked for generations in slavery. Instead, the tax commission would set aside sixteen thousand acres for preemption—lands abandoned by prewar planters, now owned by the federal government and unoccupied by superintendent or former slave. Sixteen thousand acres was too little for everyone who wanted to buy a plot. The tax commission would allot the privilege of preemption to men they deemed "worthy."

Just after the news broke, Phoebe arrived at the schoolroom late. Her face was closed and grim, and she couldn't meet Emily's eyes.

"Is it the preemption plan?" Emily asked.

"What do you think, Miss Emily?"

"How is your father?"

Phoebe came as close as she could to defiance. "You ask him."

Emily said, "I'll be right back," and she flew from the house, hoping that Rufus Green was still at breakfast. He was. In his cabin, he sat at the pine table he was so proud of, one of the several emblems of his freedom, and stared at a tin cup as though coffee disgusted him.

She said, "Mr. Green, I heard about the new preemption plan, and I am very sorry."

"You ain't the tax commission."

"Is there any hope that you can preempt a plot?"

"Not on the Pine Grove place. That go to anyone who have the money. Mr. Chapman. Mr. Phelps. Or some speculator, like General Saxton rail against."

Emily recalled, with some pain, that before the war, "speculator" had been another way to say "slave dealer."

"The tax commission, they decide to set aside some other land for us. Ain't decided what or where. All I know is that they throw away my preemption paper for the land

I grow up on. The land I work all my life. The land that's my home." He shook his head. "Sixteen thousand acres! Ain't enough. Not near enough."

"I know," Emily said.

"The tax commission, they know what's best for men like me. Men who used to be slaves. They decide who gets to preempt. Get to decide who they think is worthy. Now where do I hear that before?"

Emily remembered. It had been Mr. Chapman's refrain last year, when he bought his ten thousand acres for nearly nothing.

"I think I make a visit to Mr. Brisbane." William Brisbane was one of the Department of the Treasury's three tax commissioners for Port Royal. "Let him know how worthy I am." His voice was heavy with disgust.

"Mr. Brisbane has slavery on his conscience," Emily said. "As I do. When you go to Beaufort, take me with you."

MR. BRISBANE, THE TAX commissioner, was a South Carolinian who had repented of slavery and had become an abolitionist before the war. He was a tall, slender, courtly man who still spoke with the planter accent of his youth. Emily knew better—Brisbane had broken painfully with South Carolina over the subject of slavery, going so far as to free his own slaves when he moved to Ohio—but he was eerily like her father in appearance. She reminded herself not to judge him, as she had been so often and so unfairly judged.

In a soft voice, Brisbane asked his black manservant to bring coffee.

Rufus sat on the edge of his chair, too wrought up for refreshment.

Brisbane said, "Miss Jarvie, even though we haven't met, your tale precedes you. Your conversion, and your escape."

Emily sat on the edge of her chair, too. She said, "Mr. Brisbane, you understand better than anyone how weary I am of talking about my own past." She gestured toward Rufus Green. "I haven't come here on my business today. I've accompanied Mr. Green on his, in the hope of helping him."

Brisbane nodded. "Yes, the matter of preemption."

"Has there been any decision about the charitable set-aside? Or the men who might be eligible for it?"

Brisbane sighed. Before he could begin his speech, Rufus Green spoke. "Came here to persuade you how worthy I am." He was too angry to be polite; his tone was as acerbic as it had been in his own house. "I been a good worker for Mr. Phelps, who superintend me now, and for Mr. Chapman, who precede him, and for Marse Dalton for many a year before that, even though I never see the profit of that. I save every penny I can. I go to church every Sunday, Brick Church on St. Helena Island. We get the minister to attest to it, if you like. And my family set at the table to eat our dinner every night. But not until we say grace over it."

Mr. Brisbane sighed. He looked at Emily rather than at Rufus Green. "It's not my decision to make."

Emily felt her face flush with anger. "Mr. Brisbane, do you make an assessment of the worthiness of every white man who comes to bid at a land auction? Or do you only look at the color of his money?"

"Miss Jarvie, it's not a matter of my personal opinion. I wish it were. It's up to the commission as a whole, and the Department of the Treasury will have a say as well."

"Besides yourself, the tax commission consists of Mr. Smith, who is a sot, and Mr. Wording, who has no opinion that you haven't had first. And surely you have sway with the Department of the Treasury."

Brisbane cleared his throat, a dismissive sound. "I'll use it, as we await their decision," he said.

Anger surged through her like whiskey. She rose and asked him the question that she herself had been asked, over and over. "Do you truly care about the plight of those who used to be enslaved? Or are you still a South Carolina planter deep in your heart?"

ನಿಲ್ಲ

AFTER THE VISIT TO Beaufort, Emily vacillated between resignation and hope that there might really be a list of worthy freed men allowed to preempt their land. She regretted that Rufus Green would be unable to wrest Pine Grove, or part of it, from the hands of Harry Phelps and William Chapman.

She returned from the school one Tuesday to find Mattie in the parlor, still wearing her doctoring dress, which was odd. Mattie didn't mind wearing something worn and soiled in the parlor, but Anna hated for her to sit on the red velvet sofa unless she'd put on something more presentable. Emily said, "If Anna sees you, she'll have a conniption."

"This is no time to care about my dress and the sofa," Mattie said. "Haven't you heard? Weren't they abuzz at Ocean Point?"

"No. What is it?"

"The tax commissioners have decided to rescind the preemption plan."

Emily dropped onto the settee. "Whatever do you mean?"

"To ignore it."

"What about the set-aside? The charitable lands for worthy men? I thought the commission was still considering it."

"Nothing," she said.

"How will men like Rufus Green buy land?"

Mattie snorted. "They'll have to bid for it like anyone else," she said, in a deeply sarcastic tone.

"But they'll be competing with speculators! Men who can drive the price up, way beyond a dollar and a quarter an acre!"

Mattie said fiercely, "That's fairness in the Sea Islands! That's justice, as dispensed by the Department of the Treasury!"

Without excusing herself, Emily rose and ran from the room. Ran from the house. Ran down the driveway and hastened back to Ocean Point.

She found Rufus Green sitting on the steps of his cabin, idle in the middle of the working day. He didn't rise as she approached. "Catch your breath," he said. "Don't waste it like you did at the tax commission."

"What will you do?"

He turned his face away. In a low voice, he said, "Miss Emily, can't say."

She reached for his arm, but he moved before she could touch even his sleeve. She said, "You mean you're too angry to say."

He was hoarse with the effort of controlling himself. "I go to auction. I bid, just like anyone else."

"But there will be speculators there. Men with backers, like Mr. Chapman last year! How can you bid against them?"

The low, slow voice was worse than a roar of rage would have been. He said, "If God help me, I get the plot I have my eye on, and I put my thumb in Mr. Harry Phelps's eye to do it."

And as she hastened back to the big house, she met the last person she wanted to talk to. Harry Phelps greeted her, saying, "Miss Jarvie, what brings you back here this afternoon?"

"The land sale," she cried out. "No preemption! Every lot to the highest bidder."

He reached for her arm. "That's the tax commission's decision, not mine," he said.

She pulled away. "So it wasn't enough to make the devil's bargain last year."

"What do you mean?"

Her anger at Mr. Chapman and her affection for the Greens made her sharper. "Do you know the story of the tarbaby?"

"Yes, I've heard it from the people here."

"It wasn't enough to put one hand in. Now you've added the other."

"Don't speak of Mr. Chapman like that."

"Mr. Chapman is a speculator, and so are you."

He winced. "I heard that you sought your father's grave at Gettysburg."

"What does that have to do with it?"

"Nothing. But it has to do with you."

She stared at him. "Does that matter to you?"

His voice softened, and she heard the tone of the minister in it. "Yes."

She took a deep breath. "It's true. I went to Gettysburg."

"Why? If you were estranged and had no love for him?"

She thought of the bitter things she could say. "To know for sure that he was dead," she said finally. "That he could no longer find me or hurt me."

"Did it help you?"

"When he was alive, he sent a slave catcher after me." She did not care how bitter she sounded. "And now that he's dead, there's still a price on my head in South Carolina. They would try me and hang me, if they could."

"Miss Jarvie, that kind of bitterness is a devil's bargain, too."

Infuriated, she said, "Would you tell me to forgive him?"

He shook his head. "It's not so simple."

"If you become a planter, it will corrupt your soul."

He met her eyes. "With all our flaws, we Boston men are not planters. You must remember that."

☙◊❧

The day of the auction dawned sunny but chilly, and it didn't deter the crowd that gathered at the Rhett place, which served as an impromptu auction house. There were many men whom Emily didn't know, most of them Yankees, judging by their accents. Like the speculators of her youth, they were dressed like gentlemen, in presentable frock coats and top hats. Harry Phelps was there too, in his Sunday coat. When she tried to catch his eye, he looked away. He was pale and drawn as he turned to talk to William Chapman, who had come to watch.

Emily thought of the service at the White Church yesterday, preached by the incendiary Reverend Dysart. He spoke of preemption as though the Archangel Gabriel would deliver it and urged the former slaves in the crowd to defend their plots with hoe handles. For would-be insurrectionists, the freed people were remarkably restrained. They sang a hymn with a pointed message—"Jehovah Hallelujah," which referred to the homes of the wild creatures, while human beings were left homeless. The Green family had been in attendance, and they sang in agreement. After the service, a wagonload of former slaves, including the Green family, passed Mattie's carriage on the road, reprising "Jehovah Hallelujah."

Today, Emily searched for women in this crowd, but the only representative of her sex was Caro, who talked to a stranger in a top hat and scribbled in her notebook as he spoke. Caro looked up and flashed her a smile.

As though the proceedings might cheer somebody.

Emily found Rufus waiting to register to bid. She had to elbow her way to join him in line. An indignant Yankee voice said, "Hey!"

She turned and gave him a scornful look. "I'm helping this man," she said.

The Yankee stared at Rufus Green, and Emily stared at the Yankee.

When they reached the head of the line, the clerk addressed Emily. "Here to bid?"

Rufus Green said, "I am, sir."

In a dismissive tone, the clerk said, "We aren't selling preempted lands today."

"I know. Want to bid fair and square. Write me down and give me that paper with the lots listed on it."

The clerk's eyes flickered, but he wrote down Rufus's name. In the tone he'd use for a child, he said to Rufus, "Remember, when you want to bid, hold your hand up high."

He said curtly, "I been to an auction before. I seen it done." He took the listing of the lots and strode away.

Emily had to hurry to follow him. She asked, "When were you at an auction?" and immediately regretted it. Had he seen anyone sold away?

He said, "Used to help Marse Dalton buy horses." He bent to scan the listing. "I go into Beaufort to see the auction listing. Want to know when my parcel on Pine Grove come up. Mr. Brisbane tell me they don't print the list yet. They have it the day of the auction." He paged through it, looking for the plot he intended to bid on. And went ashen.

"What is it, Mr. Green?" Emily asked.

"Thought they'd sell it in forty-acre parcels," he said. "Like they surveyed it." He looked as though he'd been punched in the gut. "But they don't. They sell it entire. All three hundred and twenty acres."

"Let me see." He gave it to her, and she read the listing, sick to realize that he wasn't mistaken.

He said, "I can't even lift up my hand for three hundred and twenty acres."

"If it went for a dollar an acre—"

"It won't, and even if it did, I don't have the money."

"Won't they take a note?"

"Not here. Not today." He gestured toward Harry Phelps. "Mr. Chapman lend him the money on a note, but Mr. Phelps bring all that money today. At an auction, you pay cash down." He said, "I been a damn fool."

"Mr. Green—"

He turned toward the black men in blue coats. "I stand with them," he said.

They stood quietly, their posture straight, as though

they had learned it in the army. At their head, like a commanding officer, was Prince Rivers. He was very tall and very dark of skin, and he had been a man of consequence among whites as well as blacks when he was a slave. He had been known for his education and his eloquence even in slavery. Now he had risen to be a sergeant in the First South, and he relished his prominence.

Rivers detached himself from the troop to ask the auctioneer, "May I speak?"

"If you're brief," said the auctioneer, a local man friendly to the Union army.

One of the waiting bidders protested, "This is no time or place for a speech."

"Let the man talk," the auctioneer said.

Rivers raised his arms, as though he were a minister bestowing a benediction, and began to speak. He spoke against the decision to rescind the original plan for preemption. He reminded the crowd of the promise and the way it had been broken. He told them that it was unjust, and no way to treat those newly free, many of whom had been willing to risk their lives on behalf of the United States of America.

Emily bowed her head, too upset to watch for Rufus Green's reaction.

Rivers thanked the auctioneer for giving him a chance to speak, then returned to his phalanx, which stood as quietly as before, their expressions grim, their eyes dark with banked anger.

The auctioneer began, and as he disposed of the early lots, the bidding was brisk and competitive. William Chapman had been right; the bids quickly rose to more than ten dollars an acre.

When the Pine Grove parcel came up for auction, Emily watched Harry. The bidding began at two dollars an acre, but someone else wanted the place. Emily couldn't see who. The number climbed in excruciating increments of fifty cents, to five dollars an acre, then seven, then ten. Throughout the bidding, Emily kept her eyes on Harry, who looked troubled and very pale, as though the act of bidding caused him pain.

The gavel fell at eleven dollars an acre. Emily drew in her breath. Over thirty-five hundred dollars, not counting whatever horses, plows, and seed might cost. Harry Phelps would be well over five thousand dollars in debt before he broke ground.

She supposed that William Chapman would be good for it.

§⋑⋐℞

WHEN EMILY CAME TO teach on the day after the auction, Phoebe hadn't arrived, which was unlike her. Uneasy, she waited, but none of the children came, either.

The land sale, she thought. She watched out the window.

And as she watched, all the people on the place filed

into the yard—men, women, and the truant children, too. They were orderly and they were quiet.

Rufus Green led them, Juno and Phoebe just behind him.

They stopped before the front door and waited as Rufus Green walked deliberately up the front steps and knocked on the door, the sound emphatic and heavy in the cold winter air.

Harry opened the door and stood on the landing, surveying the crowd, which remained silent.

Emily flew down the stairs and out the door. On the front steps, she hesitated. "Mr. Phelps!"

Harry turned. "Emily—"

Emily ran down the steps.

"Miss Emily," Rufus said. "You stay out of this."

"I'm already in it," she said. She joined Phoebe, who made room for her without losing her somber expression.

Rufus Green said to Harry, "Mr. Phelps. We preempt that land on Pine Grove."

Harry swallowed hard. "There were no preemptions," he said. "The tax commission voided them."

"That were our land. When you buy it, steal it from us." The crowd remained silent.

"No," Harry said. "It was offered for sale, fair and square. I bought it, fair and square."

"If you expect us to work for you, you wrong."

"I need you to work for me." Rufus didn't reply and the crowd didn't respond. Harry looked ashen. "I'll draw up a fair contract."

"No," Rufus said, in a quiet voice that was more frightening than a heated rage. The restraint of the crowd was frightening, too. "Won't work for you. Won't sign a contract." He said, "None of us sign a contract. None of us work for you."

Not with their hoe handles, Emily thought, as she walked back to the Oaks. But with the best way they knew to avenge themselves on a white man, be he superintendent or master.

A planter without a labor force, slave or free, was a man in a world of hurt.

Emily supposed that she should be ashamed of her satisfaction over Harry's plight. But he had wanted so badly to master these people and to profit by it, and now he reaped what he had sown.

Phoebe eventually sent word that she wouldn't be appearing at the school, and Emily sent word back. She stayed away the next day and the day after that. That afternoon, their maid Rosa came into the parlor to announce that a gentleman was here to see her. Emily sighed. "Who is it, Rosa?"

"Marse Harry," she said.

What would she say to Harry Phelps? How could she turn him away?

Emily said, "Send him in, Rosa."

Harry rushed into the parlor. His hair was disheveled, his cravat was untied, and his eyes were ringed with fatigue. "Don't throw me out," he said.

"Say your piece," Emily said.

"May I sit?"

"All right."

He slumped into the nearest chair. "Emily, I'm in a very bad way," he said.

She said sharply, "Have you been drinking?"

"That's the least of my troubles."

"It's about Mr. Green, isn't it?"

"It started there. But it's about more than Mr. Green now."

"The work stoppage?"

"Not a one of them will sign a contract. Not a one will agree to work for me."

Emily said, "The same trouble as any planter."

"Emily, please. I'm up to my eyes in debt to William Chapman. If I can't bring in a crop this season, I'll go bankrupt."

"You've made the devil's bargain. You can't be surprised."

"Stop it!" he cried, startling her. She had never heard him angry like that.

"Don't raise your voice to me," she said. "If you have something to say to me, say it like a gentleman."

He reached out his hands. "Rufus Green listens to you. He takes your advice. Will you speak to him? Use your ability to sway him?"

"Should I?"

He grasped her hands like a drowning man. "Help me, Emily." He tightened his grip. "Please, Emily."

Footsteps sounded in the hallway, and before Rosa could announce anyone, Joshua stood in the doorway.

Emily cried, "Whatever brings you here?" Joshua hadn't visited in weeks.

"I heard there was trouble at Ocean Point," he said. "I came to make sure you weren't in danger." He took in the scene, Harry sitting much too close to Emily, Emily's hands tightly enfolded in Harry's, and said stiffly, "I see you aren't, and I believe I intrude."

Emily yanked her hands away. "We were talking about the auction."

"I see it's aroused a great deal of passion here."

Collecting himself, Harry said, "Miss Jarvie doesn't misspeak. We were talking about the auction. I forgot myself."

"You certainly did," Joshua said, with ice in his voice.

Harry rose. "You'll excuse me, both of you."

Joshua watched as Harry left and waited until the front door closed behind him. "Good God, Emily, what is going on here?"

Emily redirected her anger toward Joshua. "Rufus Green has refused to sign a contract. Mr. Phelps is very distraught. He came to plead with me to intercede with Mr. Green."

"He has an unusual way of conducting business," Joshua said acidly. "Pressing his knees to yours. Taking your hands in his."

Emily shouted, "It was for Mr. Green! I only thought to help Mr. Green!"

"I wish I could believe you." Joshua turned to go.

"Try harder!" Emily yelled, loud enough to make her mother turn over in her grave, as Joshua left the house.

Chapter 14:
Bicker and Snipe, Attorneys at Law

CARO WAITED IN THE hallway outside General Saxton's office. It was unseasonably hot for late winter, and she was sweating in the most unladylike way. She shifted on the hard wooden chair that the General's aide-de-camp left for visitors—to discourage them, no doubt. She dabbed at her face with her lavender-scented handkerchief. Was he truly busy, or was he giving her time to repent of her sins?

He would take away her press pass, she was sure, and he would probably send her away. General Sherman had court-martialed a reporter, but that reporter was a man, and General Sherman had been condemned as short-tempered and dismissive of freedom of the press.

If General Saxton sent her away, where would she go? She twisted her handkerchief until it was a damp rag between her fingers as she thought of the circumstances that had led her here.

ഌ

THAT NIGHT, PRIVATE DAVID Archer of the Twenty-Sixth New York had looked from Caro, whose hair tumbled over her shoulders, to Private Daniel Pereira, who had unmasked her. He demanded of Pereira, "How do you know this woman?"

He said, "She's my cousin. We knew each other in Charleston before the war."

"Charleston!" Archer said, glaring at Caro. "You told us you were from St. Helena Island!"

"I grew up on St. Helena Island," Caro said, trying not to sulk. "When my father died, my new master brought me to Charleston."

"And why are you on St. Helena now?"

"I came here last year as a reporter for the *Christian Recorder* in Philadelphia. General Saxton gave me a press pass. I don't have it with me."

"How do we know you aren't a spy?"

She fixed Archer with a withering gaze. "I was a slave. Do you think I'd spy for the secesh?"

Archer said, "We don't know who you are, or why you're here. All we know is that you're willing to disguise yourself and lie about it." He grabbed her arm. "We'll take you to the provost marshal, and he'll take care of you."

"You'll have to let Colonel Silliman know," Pereira said.

"We'll wake him for this," Archer said, shaking his head. He tightened his grip on Caro's arm. "Give up your rifle, and come with us."

At their encampment, they turned her over to the provost marshal. He was a tough-looking black man, older than most recruits, who informed her that he had been a bodyguard in New York before the war.

"I won't give you any trouble," she said.

"Empty your pockets," he said.

"They're empty."

"Show me."

She turned out her pockets. "When will I get my rifle back?"

"Maybe you will and maybe you won't. Depends on what you tell Colonel Silliman."

"What will he do with me?"

"That's up to him."

He brought her to an empty tent, and he set two soldiers to guard her. "We found her wandering around the countryside, unable to give an account of herself. Don't let her charm you."

When the provost marshal left, she said to no one in particular, "That's the thanks I get for scouting for the Twenty-Sixth and helping them out in a skirmish."

The elder of the two said to her, "We aren't in need of reckless young ladies to fight for us."

"Are you going to shackle me?" she said, feeling angry and defiant.

The older man laughed. "Why would we? Private Highgate, perhaps we should offer the young lady some coffee."

"I don't want any coffee," Caro said, still sulking a little, but reassured.

He said, "We need you to sit down where we can watch you."

She sat on the ground outside the tent, and they sat cross-legged beside her, their rifles resting on their laps. Their stance told her that they considered her no threat, and she had no thought of snatching up a rifle or running away. As soon as Colonel Silliman sent an inquiry to General Saxton, this would all be a misunderstanding. It would be an amusing story to tell Emily.

She broke the silence like any lady making conversation. She asked the elder man when he had mustered in and where he was from. Despite the provost marshal's caution, he answered, clearly pleased to guard a young lady who was not only pretty but well-spoken too.

He was from New York City, where he owned a bakery, which his wife and children ran while he soldiered. His companion, a baby-faced young man, told her he was from Syracuse, where his entire family embraced abolitionism. He told her of Syracuse's annual celebration of a slave's escape, the Jerry rescue. She asked him if he had acquaintances at Oberlin College. He did.

She asked, "What is Colonel Silliman like?"

The older man said, "He's fair-minded, but he has a temper."

"How bad a temper?"

The older man laughed. "You'll find out soon enough," he said.

The provost marshal reappeared. He said to the two

soldiers, "I told you not to let her charm you." To Caro, he said curtly, "Come with me."

"Am I going to see Colonel Silliman?"

"I reckon so," he said.

"Is he in a temper?"

The provost marshal grinned. "He's always in a temper."

This encampment was small, a cluster of tents for the men, a cookpot or two under an awning, and a slightly bigger tent, two small tents sewn together, for the colonel. Like every commanding officer she had ever interviewed, the colonel sat at a rickety pine table.

He had woken and dressed in a hurry. His hair was disheveled, and the collar of his nightshirt showed beneath his army coat. He glared at her and didn't invite her to sit.

The provost marshal, whose grip on her arm had not loosened, addressed the colonel. "I've brought the prisoner, sir."

"I see." He looked Caro up and down. It was different from a slave dealer's appraisal. He was taking her measure, trying to decide if she was a military risk or just a silly girl. "Private Archer says you're a spy, and Private Pereira says you're his cousin from Charleston. What account can you give of yourself?"

She explained, or tried to.

"What in God's name did you think you were doing?"

"I only meant to help your men, sir," she said. "I offered to scout for them, since I know the island."

"With a rifle? In disguise?"

She took a deep breath. She reminded herself that a few words from General Saxton would easily set this right. "Sir, with all respect, I thought it would be safer to go out at night dressed as a boy. The reason for the rifle, too."

"Do you think this is some kind of amateur theatrical?" Silliman said.

"Of course not, sir. I wish I could fight. I wish I could muster in."

Colonel Silliman rose. He was clearly furious, but he was too disciplined a soldier to raise his voice to her. His icy tone was worse than a bellow. "If you were one of my men, I'd court-martial you." He stepped back. "You'll stay here tonight under guard. No more flirting with the guards! Tomorrow morning, I'll release you into the care of General Saxton. I'll let him handle you."

℘℃

Now, IN THE DAMP heat of General Saxton's hallway, his aide-de-camp said brusquely, "Miss Jarvie? General Saxton will see you."

She entered his office with a slow step, still clutching her sodden handkerchief.

He looked up. His face bore its usual expression, kindly and weary. He smiled. "Miss Jarvie! Please, have a seat."

Sugar first. Then the punishment.

He leaned forward and said, "Colonel Silliman has written to me about your indiscretion."

Indiscretion? As though she had forgotten the proper table service at dinner. She stammered, "Colonel Silliman seemed to think it was much worse than that. He threatened to court-martial me."

"We don't court-martial civilians," General Saxton said. "Miss Jarvie, what you did was very foolish."

She dropped her eyes. "I know, sir." And raised them. "But I want so much to fight, sir. The subterfuge was the only way I could think of."

"We like a fighting spirit," he said. "But in wartime, we need people to obey orders, too."

"I was wrong, sir."

He nodded. "I've given a great deal of thought to using your fighting spirit," he said, "without getting you into trouble with my fellow officers."

"So you won't take away my press pass? Or send me away?"

"No, I have something else in mind for you."

Relief swept through her. She sagged back into her chair.

"Are you aware of the way that people on the island are tried for crimes?"

Puzzled, she said, "I know the superintendents see to it. They hear the details, and they decide the punishment."

"The local people don't think that's fair, and some of the superintendents are troubled by it, too. I've been thinking of finding an advocate for the local people in their dealings with the commissions, the informal courts on the plantations, for some time." He paused. "I've just learned that one of Silliman's men is a lawyer, called to the bar in New York. Who better to plead the case for the freedmen than a lawyer of color?"

"Yes, sir." She wondered which one of Silliman's men had been a lawyer.

He asked, "You were well educated at Oberlin College, were you not? You are fluent in Latin?"

"Yes," she said. "Also Greek."

"Do you write a fair hand?"

"A good hand, sir."

"A lawyer needs a law clerk. Someone who knows Latin and writes a good hand would be an ideal choice," he said.

"Certainly, sir."

He leaned far forward, his eyes bright. "I would like you to assist this man, this legal agent, in his work. As a clerk would."

"General Saxton, sir. Who is he? What is his name?"

He looked at her with twinkling eyes. "I believe there's a connection," he said. "His name is Daniel Pereira."

It took all her ability to dissemble—as a belle and a scout—to not shriek and fall off her chair, but to say instead, with a smile, "General Saxton, sir, how could I say no?"

∞

EVEN THOUGH CARO HAD been in General Saxton's office many times, she had never been invited to his home to sit in the parlor or join him and his wife at the dinner table. To that, she owed her elevation as Mr. Pereira's clerk. As she readied for the dinner, she hesitated at the door, fumbling with her bonnet strings.

Sophy watched her. "You riled up."

She tugged on the strings. "I am not."

Sophy sighed. "It's about young Mr. Pereira, ain't it?"

"No, it isn't," Caro retorted.

Sophy said, "You find the courage to run to freedom. I reckon you can manage to set at the table with your cousin from Charleston."

Caro shook her head. "Maybe I should take my pistol for courage," she said. She fastened her bonnet with an untidy bow.

"Don't think so," Sophy said. She patted Caro's shoulder. "You act the lady, like you good at."

Caro fumed at Sophy's good intentions as she walked the short distance from Sophy's house to General Saxton's. Pigs and dogs still plagued the streets of Beaufort, and she glared at a sow and growled at a dog too lazy to move out of her way.

General Saxton himself greeted her as soon as she entered the house, a genial smile on his face. Even for an informal dinner, he wore his Union coat. He held out his hands to her. "Miss Jarvie," he said. "You do me an honor."

Despite her ill temper, it was a pleasure to receive his courtesy. She rarely thought of her mother, dead before the war, but now it gave her a twinge to think how delighted she would be to see her daughter treated this way.

The Saxton house, like every building in Beaufort, still bore the scars of the Big Shoot. The sofas, the tables, and the chairs in the parlor were all handsome mahogany pieces in the Sheraton style, but the wood was scuffed and the upholstery worn through in places.

On a battered wing chair sat Daniel Pereira, who rose at the sight of her.

Lately a private in the Union army, he was a gentleman again, dressed in a civilian's black frock coat. In this light, she could see the man he had become. He was more substantial than he had been in Charleston. His face was fuller and graver. When he greeted her, she heard the North in his voice, too; like her, he had learned to adapt his South Carolina accent. "Miss Jarvie," he said, a gentleman meeting a lady, with no hint of the past between them.

She reached for the hand he extended to her. "Well, Mr. Pereira," she said, tamping down her irritation, speaking as easily as any actress. "So we meet again!"

He turned to Mrs. Saxton. "A pleasanter encounter than our latest," he said. "We met while I was on picket duty."

Mrs. Saxton said, "Miss Jarvie, please join us. We were just getting acquainted with Mr. Pereira." She smiled. "He has told us that he is a South Carolinian, like yourself, but Charleston born and raised."

"Yes," Pereira said. "My family was free before the war."

"How did you come to muster into the Twenty-Sixth New York?" Mrs. Saxton asked.

Yes, Caro thought, *how did you?*

"Just before the war, my family left Charleston for the North. We settled in Ohio—in Cincinnati—where my family intended to make a living at the tailoring business."

Caro remembered her uncle Thomas's words in Cincinnati: "He's safe. He's well." But her cousin had not been in Cincinnati then.

"Did you establish yourself there?" Mrs. Saxton asked.

"It was difficult." He smiled, as though he were recounting a pleasantry. "The good people of Cincinnati were loath to patronize a tailor of color. One of our few customers—a good abolitionist, God bless him—recognized my ambitions for an education and told me about Kenyon College."

In surprise, Caro said, "I didn't think that Kenyon College would admit a man of color."

"They admitted me." A shadow passed over his face. "The only student of color."

She understood. "I attended Oberlin College. Not so far away."

His face softened.

Caro realized he knew how much she had yearned

357

for Oberlin. It had been the first secret she had ever told him.

Here, now, he only said, "That's quite an achievement, Miss Jarvie."

She couldn't resist letting Miss Sass have her say. "Yes, it helped considerably with the Latin and the good handwriting."

Mrs. Saxton intervened. "And after Kenyon College, Mr. Pereira?"

"I decided that I wanted to take up the law, and a good friend to Kenyon College, a lawyer in New York, agreed to take me on as a clerk. I was in his office when the Twenty-Sixth USCT was raised in New York City. I mustered in as soon as I could. And I was delighted to learn that I would fight on my home soil."

General Saxton said, "We're very glad of it, Mr. Pereira. Of all the happy accidents that have brought you to us."

Pereira asked politely, "Miss Jarvie, what brought you to the Sea Islands?"

General Saxton looked at her fondly. "I know Miss Jarvie well. She came to us as a reporter. She is intelligent and steadfast and very dedicated to the cause of the Union." He chuckled. "Very dedicated indeed."

"Let Miss Jarvie speak for herself," Mrs. Saxton chided her husband.

Caro met the eyes of the man she had known in Charleston before the war. Her first love. The man she had hoped to marry. She would even have dispensed with marriage, if his family hadn't fled in the terrible months before the war, when free people of color were arrested and sent to the Work House to await auction as slaves. It was too dangerous to take her along. She knew, as she would never have admitted in this parlor, that he was the man who had broken her heart.

Caro was glad for a moment to collect her thoughts. "It was safer than Ohio" was clearly the wrong answer. She said to Pereira, "I came to fight, just like you. Glad to do it on my home soil, just like you."

But by the end of the first course, her bravado deserted her. She excused herself and escaped into the passageway to the kitchen, which was dark and close and smelled powerfully of the beeswax that the maid used to polish the furniture. She leaned against the wall, exhausted with the effort of pretending that Daniel Pereira meant nothing to her. She remained there long enough for someone to join her.

Pereira stepped into the hallway. "Caro?"

"Leave me alone," she said, not hiding her annoyance.

He came close and dropped his voice to an angry whisper. "Did you put him up to this?"

"What? Inviting us to dinner?"

His whisper grew angrier. "This appointment! This situation!"

"Of course not!" She let all her hurt and anger spill into her voice. "Do you think I like it any better than you do?"

"After Charleston…"

"Don't speak of Charleston."

"Have you forgotten?'

"No," she said. "I haven't forgotten a thing. Have you?"

ഇൻ

ON THEIR FIRST DAY in business, Caro sat with Pereira in the parlor of the pleasant house that General Saxton had rented for the law office. It was a four-up-and-down furnished with contraband from the army's warehouses and had very nearly been restored to its former comfort. It had likely belonged to a lawyer before the war.

Perched on the settee, Caro remembered her first day at *Hearth and Home*, where Asa Reed had welcomed her and set her to work, relying on the good handwriting she was so proud of. She said brightly to Daniel Pereira, "How should we get on?"

He sat opposite her in a red velvet wing chair, its seat well-worn by some white gentleman before the war. He was unable to get comfortable in it. "We'll see." He tugged on his cravat as though it bothered him. "Give it some time for the word to get out. Once they know about us, they'll find us."

"Might we encourage them? Visit the plantations or the churches?"

He shook his head. "Lawyers don't chase after business," he said irritably. "They wait for business to come to them."

She shouldn't say it, but the memory of efficient,

kindly Asa Reed goaded her. "You haven't an idea of how to proceed," she said, equally irritable.

"I was a clerk for nearly two years. I was called to the bar. I know the law."

"That I don't doubt. But it didn't occur to you to put an advertisement in the *Free South*?" That was the weekly Beaufort paper, the voice of the Gideonites. "Or better yet, ask the editor to call on us and write about us."

"Drum up business!" he said derisively.

The sound of the doorknocker startled them both. Caro sprang up. "I hope that it's a client."

It was Emily, who stood on the porch, smiling at her. Caro put aside her feelings. "Come in, come in," she said.

Emily followed Caro into the parlor and looked around. "It's very pleasant."

Pereira rose. "Miss Jarvie," he said. "It's been a long time since we met in Charleston."

Emily pulled off her gloves. "I'd just as soon put Charleston behind me."

Pereira asked, "Caro, would you bring our visitor some refreshment?"

Caro said, with a tinge of resentment, "Do law clerks see to refreshment?"

"Yes, they do," Pereira said. "Ask Dinah."

"I know where the kitchen is. And where Dinah is." As she left the room to speak to Pereira's cook, Dinah, she stuck out her tongue. Pereira couldn't see it, but Emily could, and despite her serious air, she smothered a giggle.

In the kitchen, Dinah said, "Coffee? Now?" Dinah

wasn't sure of either of them, light-skinned Charlestonians turned abolitionists.

"Hurry." Pereira would start without her, she knew it. When she returned with coffee and cookies, she asked, "What did I miss?"

Pereira said irritably, "Miss Jarvie asked me if my comfort had been provided for in my move to Beaufort. I assured her that I am quite comfortable."

Caro set down the tray, and Emily took a cookie out of politeness but didn't eat it. Pereira asked, "Miss Jarvie, how can we assist you?"

Caro thought spitefully, *He sounds just like he did in Uncle Thomas's shop.*

"Oh, I don't have any legal trouble, thank goodness," Emily said. "This is a social call. To wish you well in your new endeavor." She glanced from Pereira to Caro and back. "Both of you."

"You haven't brought us any business?" Caro said.

"No. Although it was right of General Saxton to appoint you both to your task."

Pereira said, "There are no thefts you know of? No assaults? No contracts gone awry?"

Emily raised her eyes to Pereira's. "Do you attend to contracts, too?"

"We can, if we're asked to," he said.

"Well, it's not mine to bring to you," she said, "but there's quite a fuss on the place Mr. Harry Phelps bought last month at the auction."

"What's happened?" Pereira asked, and out of habit, Caro reached for the notebook that she always carried in her pocket.

"The people on the place have refused to work for him. None of them will sign a contract. Mr. Phelps is frantic about getting the crop in."

Pereira asked, "Why? What happened?"

Emily and Caro explained the circumstances of the land sale. Emily said, "Rufus Green is heartbroken, but they're all furious."

Pereira's eyes gleamed. "I hadn't heard. That's very interesting."

"Don't sharpen your teeth for a fight," Caro reminded Pereira. "None of them have come to us to ask for our help."

"So you don't have any business yet," Emily said pleasantly.

Pereira said, "We're getting on very well."

Caro shook her head in exasperation.

Emily looked at Pereira, then at Caro. "And the two of you? How are you getting on?"

Before Pereira could speak, Caro said, "Bicker and Snipe, attorneys at law, at your service."

Emily laughed. "You haven't changed a bit since Charleston, either of you," she said.

Pereira gathered his dignity. "Miss Jarvie, we'd be glad to assist you, or anyone, if you have a legal question for us."

Emily said, "I'll spread the word." She smiled. "I can't help you with each other." She laughed outright. "Justice is served, for both of you! Justice is indeed served!"

ℰℭ

EMILY'S NEWS OF RUFUS Green raised Caro's hackles as a reporter. The next morning, as soon as she shut the door to their office, she told Pereira, "I'm going to St. Helena Island today."

"Not to drum up business," he said.

She laughed, her coquette's weapon. "Of course not. I'm going to see if I can drum up a story for the *Christian Recorder*."

When she arrived at the Greens' cabin, she found all three of them—Phoebe and Juno as well as Rufus—working in Juno's kitchen garden. Rufus Green wiped his face and leaned on his hoe. "Juno, sugar," he said, "I rest for a bit, if you don't mind, to talk to Miss Caroline."

Juno rose from the bed she weeded, and so did Phoebe. "We all take a rest and talk to Miss Caroline," she said.

Inside the house, over coffee and biscuit, they all talked without prompting. Rufus said, "I don't work for Mr. Phelps anymore, and Phoebe and Juno stop work for Mr. Chapman, in sympathy. And no one sign a contract with Mr. Phelps, either."

Caro wondered how long the Greens would be able to afford coffee. "What happened between you and Mr. Phelps?"

"Didn't Miss Emily tell you when she call on you yesterday?"

Caro took out her notebook. "I want to hear it from you," she said. "All of you."

They spoke and she scribbled, tamping down her anger. She asked, "Has anyone else decided not to sign a contract?"

Rufus said, "The men who work for Mr. Chapman, they so mad that they write up a petition. They say he don't pay them fair wages and that he prevent them from preempting the land after he promise he would. They send that petition to President Lincoln in Washington."

"Have they heard anything yet?"

"Not yet."

Caro said, "Have you heard about General Saxton's appointment of the legal agent for the freedmen and freedwomen?"

"Oh, we hear about it," Rufus said. "That he a free man of color from Charleston and that he learn to lawyer in New York."

Phoebe said, "I hear that he was your sweetheart before the war."

"Is that what Miss Emily told you?" Caro said. "How people talk!" She spoke to Rufus and Juno. "He's charged with representing black people in any legal proceeding with the superintendents. Perhaps he'd look into this matter of your contract with Mr. Phelps." It gave her pleasure to defy Daniel Pereira.

"I keep it in mind," Rufus said.

"Please do," Caro said, thinking that Pereira would be furious if he knew that she was drumming up business.

ഇൽ

WHEN SHE RETURNED TO the office in Beaufort, Pereira asked her, "Did you find something to write about?"

"I believe I did," she said, taking off her bonnet.

There was a sharp rap on the door, and Caro called, "Dinah, I'll get it."

She opened the door to Sampson Hayward, who said, "Had army business at General Saxton's office. Just down the street."

She knew perfectly well that he had finagled this errand to visit her. And he had probably dawdled down the street until he saw her at the door.

He added, "I hear that you been appointed to assist the legal agent for the freed people. Wanted to see how you do."

"I do very well," Caro said.

Pereira came to the door. "Caro? Who is this?"

The two men stared at each other, dispensing with army honor and the politeness of South Carolina before the war.

Sampson asked, "Who is he to call you Caro?"

Caro flushed. "Private Sampson Hayward, this is Daniel Pereira, of the Twenty-Sixth New York and now General Saxton's legal agent. He is also my cousin. We've known each other since we were children."

"I see," said Sampson.

Pereira asked Sampson, "What is your regiment?"

"Used to be the First South Carolina. Called the Thirty-Third US Colored Infantry Regiment now. Commissioned in 1863. That's when I muster in. When did you muster in?"

"When the Twenty-Sixth was raised. Early this year."

"What you do before you muster in?" It wasn't a polite inquiry.

Pereira flushed. "I was a lawyer in New York City."

"I was a soldier."

"And before that, Private Hayward?"

The needling did its job. Sampson was annoyed. "I was a slave, and I ain't ashamed of it."

Caro turned to Pereira and said fiercely, "Don't! Don't boast to him that you were never a slave! It's beneath you!"

"I see indeed," Sampson said. "And I see enough. Excuse me. I have to get back to the camp."

She followed Sampson onto the porch and onto the muddy sidewalk. She said fiercely, "Why did you do that?"

"To get his measure. Now I have it."

"You should have left it alone," Caro hissed.

Sampson put his hand on her arm. He looked saddened and weary. "Is he the memory, Caro? Is he the one who break the promise?"

She was so startled that tears rose to her eyes. "It's none of your business!"

When Caro ran back inside, Pereira grasped her arm. "Who is he?"

"I introduced you."

"Who is he to you?"

Caro shook off Pereira's hand. "A friend," she said, rubbing her arm, which didn't really hurt.

Unabashed, Pereira said, "Quite a good friend, by the looks of it."

"He's asked me to marry him." Caro glared at him.

Pereira scoffed. "A man who used to be a slave?"

She had thought the same thing. But at Pereira's words she spat out her reply. "I'm going to see General Saxton. I'm going to tell him that he's made a mistake. I don't care to stay here to be insulted. You can right the wrongs of the former slaves *all by yourself.*"

"Yes. It's a fine thing to abandon our venture before it's begun." His tone was sarcastic. "How will you explain it to General Saxton?"

"Why do you care?" She rushed into the topic that really bothered him. "Do you have a sweetheart back in New York? I bet you do. Some ivory-skinned abolitionist who has hair so straight she has to curl it. Why are you hectoring me?"

He glared at her. "There's no one in New York. Not that it's any of your business."

"Hah!" she said.

His voice rose. "Why are you grinning? Does it please you that I'm angry?"

"Absolutely." She began to laugh. "Bicker and Snipe, at your service!"

"That's not the least bit amusing. No one wants to hire two cousins who squabble like children. They'll want to hire a lawyer and a clerk who know what they're doing!"

"As though we do!" she said, still laughing, even though she knew it was mean to make fun of him.

He reached for her wrist. "Can't you act with gravity, even for a moment?"

"Can't you act with levity, even for a moment?"

He was still angry, and she knew it wasn't about their work together. "General Saxton has entrusted us with a higher purpose. We have to put our feelings aside. We owe it to him."

"Higher purpose!"

He tapped her wrist, a gesture that might be mistaken for affection. "Freedom and justice, in case you forgot."

She met the hazel eyes that changed color according to the light and his mood. "No, I didn't forget."

"Now I recall. You're the one who hasn't forgotten a thing."

Annoyance and warmth warred within her. "Don't remind me," she said. "And let go my wrist." She thought of Rufus Green. Of his trouble. Of his right to legal recourse. Pereira was right, as much as she was loath to admit it.

He clasped her wrist before he let her go. His eyes gleamed. "A higher purpose," he reminded her.

ஐஹ

BUT NO ONE CAME to test their resolve, and within days, they were bored and snappish again. He said to her, "I'll be the one to go to General Saxton to tell him that our services aren't needed. Since no one wants to consult us."

But not an hour later, Dinah put her head into the room. "A lady come to see you. Miss Easton, from the Oaks. Should I bring coffee, Miss Caroline?"

"Yes, Dinah." To Pereira, she said, "Mattie is a good friend of Emily's."

"If it's another social call, I'll spit," Pereira said.

"Would you really spit?" Caro asked. Even as a boy, he'd been much too refined. "I'd like to see that."

They settled in the parlor, Mattie on the sofa, Pereira and Caro opposite her. Mattie looked unusually subdued and worried. Caro felt a stab of fear. Was there trouble at the Oaks?

Pereira said, "Miss Easton, how may we be of assistance to you?"

Mattie knotted her hands in her lap. "Two men came to blows on our place," she said.

"Was anyone hurt?" Pereira asked.

"One of the men suffered a black eye," Mattie replied. "We're all rattled. The people at the Oaks have always been peaceable. We've never seen anything like this."

Caro thought that Mattie's employees must be good at hiding their differences if she had never known them to argue or fight.

"Who was involved in the fight?" Pereira asked.

"The man who was injured is someone I know well," she said. "Jefferson Smith. He's our yardman. The other man is a stranger to all of us."

"When did you first see him, Miss Easton?"

Caro thought, *It's a different kind of questioning than I do. I let them tell the story. He wants to hear the facts, one by one.*

Mattie said, "He arrived a few days ago. He told me he'd been a slave on the island before the war, and he'd come back now that he was free. He asked me for work, and I told him that his chances were better at Camp Saxton, but he was welcome to stay for a few days. We found him a place to sleep with one of the families who works for me."

"When did the fight happen?"

"Last Saturday night. On Saturday nights, the people on our place rest from their labors. Those who are musical will play, and they dance a little. It's always been friendly and companionable. I often sit on the porch to listen to the music."

"And last Saturday?"

"They were dancing. Jefferson danced with his wife, Rosa, whom I know well. She works for me in the house." She took a deep breath. "The stranger tore into the crowd. He grabbed Jefferson by the shirtfront and began to punch him in the face. There was screaming and shouting, and some of the men had the presence of mind to pull them apart."

"And then what did you do?"

"We decided to lock the stranger into the old slave jail. I hated to use it, but it's the only building on the place that we can lock up and watch easily. And I went to talk to him. But he refused to say a word to me. I thought of you. I thought he might speak with you, as he won't speak to me."

"He might," Pereira said. His face took on the gravity that he had insisted on with Caro. "Yes, I'd be glad to help. Miss Jarvie, would you assist me?"

On its face, it was a brawl. Caro would lay money it was about a woman's affections. But it was legal business, part of their higher purpose. "I certainly will, Mr. Pereira," she said, in a tone to match his.

∽◯∾

AT THE OAKS, MATTIE showed them to the study, where three armchairs had been arranged before the desk. Pereira took his place at the desk to sit in a wing chair that elevated him. Caro said, "Do you remember how your uncle Benjamin used to sit in his office? Just like that."

He smiled. "The judge's bench is always elevated above the counsel and the witnesses," he said. He gestured to a side chair. "Bring that close to the desk. That's for you."

"Ah, that's the fate of clerks. To be reminded that they are low."

Mattie ushered in the man who had been assaulted.

He was short and sturdy, with the round face of so many of the Sea Islanders. His eye was puffy and purpled. "My name Jefferson Smith," he told them. As he spoke, he touched his cheekbone, emphasizing that he was the injured party in every way.

"Mr. Smith, tell us what happened," Pereira said.

"I were dancing with Rosa at our Saturday frolic, and the man rush at me and start to hit me. Pummel me in the back and punch me in the face."

"Did he say anything?"

"No, not a word."

"Do you have any idea why he'd be angry with you? Why he'd strike you?"

"I never see the man before." He touched his cheekbone again.

Caro asked, "Did Miss Rosa say anything to you?"

"No. She get all upset, and she don't say a thing. Ain't like her. We husband and wife; we don't keep secrets."

Pereira glanced at Caro, who smiled. "Mr. Smith, everyone has secrets," she said.

"Please, Miss Jarvie."

Gravity, she thought.

After he left, Pereira said to Caro, "Now we'll hear from the assailant."

"His secret."

Exasperated, Pereira said, "His side of the story."

The assailant's arrival took a while, since he needed to be released from the jail. Two men from the place brought him in, their faces somber with their duty.

He was tall and broad-shouldered, like many of the men in the First South. His skin was a deep brown, and despite the wear of age and slavery, he was still a handsome man. He looked at Pereira with defiant eyes and said, "Now I have a black man to pass judgment on me and decide how to punish me."

Pereira said mildly, "That's not why we're here. We'd like to find out what happened, according to you." He gestured to the chair that Jefferson Smith had just vacated. "Please, sit."

"Who are you?" he asked, looking askance at both of them.

Pereira introduced himself and Caro. Caro added, "I grew up on St. Helena Island before the war. On the Jarvie place."

He didn't respond. He was still angry.

Pereira steepled his hands, just as his uncle Benjamin used to do, and said, "Let us begin. Please, sir, tell us your name."

"Tobias Baldwin," he said, as though he hated giving it up. "Was called Toby back in slavery."

"And where are you from?"

He looked surprised. "Here. Born here. Grew up here. Lived here until I was sold away before the war. That's why I come back. Because of Rosa."

Pereira's eyebrows rose. "What relation is Rosa to you?"

Tobias Baldwin stared at Pereira with renewed bitterness. "She my wife."

෨෫

As they waited for Rosa, Caro said to Pereira, "I thought it might be like that."

"We don't know what it's like," he said, his voice surprisingly neutral. "We haven't heard the whole story yet."

Rosa entered the room, and Caro shut the door behind her. Rosa's expression was full of distress. She clasped her hands tightly in her lap and said, "Never thought it would happen like this. Never thought it would come to this."

"Miss Rosa," Pereira said. "Why don't you tell us, whatever you can, about your connection with these two men."

"I don't meant to keep it a secret, but it become one," she said.

Caro threw Pereira a glance, but he ignored her.

Pereira said, "Tell us what you can, and we'll do our best to help you." His voice was more than courteous. It held sympathy. Caro was startled. She remembered listening to his uncle Benjamin Pereira, who had been her father's friend as well as his lawyer. Benjamin Pereira had spoken to her in just that tone of kindly understanding.

Rosa covered her face with her hands and wept. When her tears abated, Pereira offered her a handkerchief, his own. "What is it, Miss Rosa?"

Caro thought, *I'd be glad to tell him a secret, if he talked to me in that tone.*

Rosa clutched the handkerchief as she spoke. "I were married to Toby before the war. We work on the place together, but we love each other, and massa bring in the white preacher to say the service. I know we ain't truly married, because we can't be, but we felt married, and we act like it. We have a little one together." She lifted her head to meet Pereira's eyes, which were soft with sympathy. "And then massa go into debt, and he sell my husband Toby away."

Pereira nodded to encourage her.

"It break my heart, and I grieve for a long time. But finally I tell myself that he never come back. I think about myself, and about my boy. And when Jefferson start to court me, I allow it. I like him, and he act good to my son. When he ask me to marry him, I say yes, and this time we have a black preacher read the service, and I get married again."

"When was this?" Pereira asked.

"Was after the Big Shoot, but before we get free."

"1862," Pereira said.

"Like before, we feel married, and we act married. We have a baby, a little girl, not a year old yet. I still think about the husband sold away, because my boy resemble him. But he gone, and I never expect to see him again." She drew in a deep, ragged breath. "And then he come back, and it all come out."

"There's no shame in it, Miss Rosa," Pereira said. "For what happened in slavery." He glanced at Caro. "But there is a dilemma."

Caro had too many memories at once. She heard the

voice of Benjamin Pereira in Charleston, as she and Danny sat in his office, reminding them that no slave could contract a marriage. And she thought of Sampson Hayward, a free man, asking her as a free woman if she would dance with him all their lives long, until death parted them.

Rosa said, "Now that I can marry proper, can't be married to two men at once." She looked to Caro, hoping for a woman's perspective. "To be married, have to choose one."

"That isn't a matter for the law, Miss Rosa," Pereira said gently.

Caro answered her, too. "It's a matter of the heart." She felt a twinge, saying it. "Now that you're free to consider it."

Rosa made an odd sound, halfway between a laugh and a snort.

Caro said, "Freedom's an odd thing, isn't it, Miss Rosa? Not just the freedom to come and go. To choose when and where to work, and how much to get paid. But the freedom to figure out what your heart desires and to choose it."

So this was the higher purpose, and it was too close to her own circumstance. If it didn't hurt so much, it would make her laugh that Rosa would ask advice from a young woman torn between two men. She thought, *Listen to yourself*, and when Pereira met her eyes, Caro looked away.

ဆာ

WHEN THE TWO MEN returned to the room, they eyed each other with suspicion and settled uneasily next to each other. Pereira said to Jefferson, "Now I understand why Mr. Baldwin struck you. He was married to Miss Rosa before the war."

Jefferson stared at Rosa. He said to Pereira, "That explain it. It don't excuse it."

Pereira said, "You could charge him with assault. He'd be punished for that."

"He already spend a night in the slave jail," Jefferson Smith said. "What more? Whup him?"

Caro said, "I doubt Miss Easton would agree to that."

Jefferson considered this. "I want him to say that he sorry." He glared at Tobias. "And to mean it."

Tobias Baldwin said, "So eager to see Rosa again that I forget myself. Don't intend to hurt you."

Jefferson spoke very stiffly. "Whatever you intend, you make a mess of my face. Why you so mad at me?"

"Not at you," Tobias said. "Anyone you love ever sold away?"

Jefferson stared at Tobias. "Yes, I know about sold away." As though it hurt him to speak, he said to Pereira, "He been punish enough for hitting me."

"Miss Rosa, are you satisfied with that?"

Rosa said, "The part the law can fix, that's all right. But I still got two husbands and two families and a dilemma, like you say, Mr. Pereira, and trouble in my heart, like you say, Miss Caroline. Can't fix that, not yet."

Pereira let his gaze rest on one face after another, to let them know that he spoke to all of them. His voice was intimate, befitting his words. He said, "You're right, Miss Rosa. The matter of marriage isn't a legal dilemma. We can't make a legal decision here. As Miss Jarvie has so eloquently said, it's a matter of the heart."

Rosa regarded first one husband, then the other.

Pereira said, "For this, you'll have to consult your own minds and your own hearts. You're free, all of you, to choose, even in this most private of matters."

Did he really have such a depth of feeling? Or did lawyers learn to speak with feeling as a matter of professional performance? Despite herself, Caro was impressed by his eloquence.

He paused to regard each one of them again. He said, "I entrust this decision to you. I leave it in your hands."

All of them looked grave. Rosa asked both men, "Can we do that? For ourselves and for our children?"

As though he swore an oath, Jefferson said, "I reckon so."

And Tobias said, "I do my best."

∾∽

ON THE FERRY BACK to Beaufort, both Caro and Pereira were too restless to sit. They leaned against the railing to look over the water, as they once had leaned on the

Battery to gaze at Fort Sumter. Caro tapped Pereira gently on the arm. She said, "You're very like your uncle Benjamin."

He turned to meet her eyes. His own were a soft brown in this light. "I hope that's a compliment," he said.

"It is," she replied. "I thought it would be like that."

"Like what?" His voice was soft and even more intimate than when he offered his judgment.

"A dilemma," she said, her voice equally soft.

He smiled. "Let's hope that the next one is a simple, uncomplicated contractual dispute that's easy to resolve."

She laughed. "Something tells me that nothing we'll see will be simple, uncomplicated, or easy to resolve," she said.

When they returned to Beaufort, it was dusk. He asked, "Would you come back to the office with me?"

"At this hour? Why?"

He grinned. "Because there's brandy in the house, and I don't want to drink by myself."

"Good brandy?"

"French brandy. From before the war."

She grinned, too. "Yes," she said.

When they entered the house, Dinah called out, "Mr. Pereira? Do you need anything?"

Pereira called back, "No, Dinah, I'm fine. Miss Jarvie is here. We're working on something."

"Hah!" Caro said, as he ushered her into the study. "A glass of French brandy."

She fell into a chair as he poured her a glass. He sat

and they both drank. She said, "You did very well today. Solon and Solomon at once."

"Thank you," he said. "So did you."

"Not all problems are legal."

He drank some more. "I know."

She hadn't eaten since this morning, and the brandy went right to her head. "Oh, this is good," she said. She took another swallow, enjoying the feeling of being lightheaded.

"Do you think they'll figure it out?" he asked her.

"One way or another."

"Who do you think she'll choose?"

Caro felt as though she were floating. "I can't guess."

He moved his chair closer so that his knees touched hers. She didn't mind. He said, "What about you? Who are you going to choose?"

"I wasn't aware I was making a judgment," she said.

He leaned forward. "I was the first."

"Two kittens in love. Nothing serious."

He put down his glass. "Not at all. I recall that it was serious indeed."

"I'm not sure you remember right."

He reached for her hands. "Then let me remind you."

He pulled her upright. She was only giddy, not drunk, and she came willingly. She asked, "What do you remember, Danny?"

He cupped her face in his hands, and she knew what he intended. He leaned forward and kissed her, a gentle brush of lips on lips, and she was full of shame as well as desire because she remembered those Charleston kisses all too well. But she didn't pull away.

He kissed her with greater heat and pulled her closer. They were belly to belly and thigh to thigh. She thought, *This is so badly wrong*, even as she filled with heat.

He whispered, "You once told me that you would be my wife."

Yes, in a moment of madness, thinking that if she gave herself to him, he would be obliged to take her away from slavery in Charleston. She whispered back, "You're wicked to remind me. And unfair."

He twined his hands in her hair. "Am I?" He kissed her again. She slid her arms around him, and they pressed together. Cleaved together through layers of wool and cotton, of frock coat and corset, making her ache at the thought of his flesh underneath.

She couldn't reply. She was overcome. In a moment she would fall and not care that she would never be able to get up again.

She turned her head, and he kissed her cheekbone. He kissed her temple. He stopped kissing and pressed his cheek against her hair. He sighed. "Such a dilemma. And such an easy resolution for it."

She looked into his eyes. She couldn't tell what color they were. If the devil had hazel eyes, they would be that color. "What?"

"Promise to marry me."

She drew back. "You aren't serious."

He touched her cheek with the softest of fingers. "I believe I am."

She put her hand over his, not sure whether she wanted to caress it or pull it away. "And if I said yes? Would you be serious then?"

"Ponder it," he said softly.

She thought of Rosa. She thought of Sampson. And she thought of Charleston, when he had refused her. She wrenched herself from his embrace and pushed him away. "I have to go," she said, and she fled without bothering to put on her bonnet.

ಬಾಡ

SHE RAN. How MANY times had she run away? From the real danger that threatened to enslave her or kill her and from the imagined danger of her memories and her unbearable feelings? Now she ran home—to Sophy's house, her home in Beaufort. She threw open the door and slammed it behind her.

Sophy ran into the parlor. "Oh, it's you," she said, clearly relieved. She sniffed. "You been drinking!"

"Just a sip of brandy," Caro said, having difficulty with her voice.

"Who give you brandy?"

She forced the words out. "Mr. Pereira and I took a little. Our first case went well."

Sophy took her arm. "More than a little. What go on?"

Caro put her hands to her face and began to sob. She couldn't stop.

Sophy tightened her grip and said, "What did he do to you?"

She took a deep breath, ragged with tears, and said, "He asked me to marry him."

"Oh dear Lord," Sophy said, in the tone of affection and exasperation familiar from Charleston. "Come into the kitchen. I give you coffee and a talking-to."

They settled at the kitchen table, and Sophy said, "Do you speak yet to Mr. Sampson Hayward, who also ask you?"

Caro shook her head.

"Well, I tell you what I think. Danny Pereira always been in love with himself, and he don't have much for anyone else. He leave you once before, he break your heart, and I don't think he any different now. Sampson Hayward ain't a gentleman. We all know that. But he a good, kind man who love you and cherish you. If you have a grain of sense, you marry him. And you let Danny Pereira find another woman to torment."

Caro felt the tears rise again. She shook her head. Without speaking, without excusing herself, she fled upstairs. In her room, she collapsed on the bed, and she wept until she fell asleep.

෨൯

IN THE MORNING, HER face stiff with salt and her ribs sore from sleeping in her corset, Caro washed her face and exchanged her wrinkled dress for one that was clean and pressed. She didn't need to look alluring, not for this errand, but she hated the thought of looking hollow-eyed.

She hired a carriage to take her to the gates of Camp Saxton, and before she greeted the guard at the gate, she straightened her skirt and her spine. She needed every shred of resolve she could summon.

She was early enough to interrupt Sampson at his morning coffee, before drill and other duties of the day. She said, "May we speak privately?"

Concern shadowed his face. He could tell that something wasn't right. He rose and extended his hand. "Come with me."

In the privacy of the trees, he touched her face. She took his hand away. Kindness would undo her. "I can't marry you."

Sampson said, "I know I used to be a slave. Ain't educated. Won't ever be a gentleman. I know all that."

"We won't suit," Caro said, "but that isn't why."

"Then tell me why."

"Because your life has made you kind. And mine has made me mean. I can't make you happy. I can't even make myself happy. You deserve better than that."

He grasped her wrist with some urgency. "That ain't it all at. You afraid to be happy. Afraid you can't be. Daddy dead, Mama dead, sweetheart left you and broke your heart. That's what you so afraid of. That I hurt you, too."

She looked up. She hated that he was right.

He looked into her eyes, even though he knew how it bothered her. He didn't ease on his grasp, either. He wanted her full attention. "When you feel afraid, you pick up a rifle to feel brave. No rifle for this. No running away for this. You have to stand still for this."

Her voice came out sounding choked. "And what happens if I marry you? I have to give up reporting. Writing. I lose myself, if I become your wife."

"I see how much joy it give you to be a reporter. That's how you fight. Wouldn't dream of taking that away from you. It make you happy, and I want your happiness as much as my own."

She had to look away because her eyes had begun to brim with tears.

"Caro, sugar, look at me."

When she shook her head, he released her wrist and touched her cheek instead. That bothered her even more. He said, "I think about what I want to do when I muster out. Do you think I want to plow twenty acres of cotton for some white man's increase?" He spread his arms as though they were wings. "The war make the world wider than that. Freedom make it wider than that. We go into it together, and we see what we can find there. Something bigger. Something better."

"Let it go. Let me go."

"I won't. You ponder all of that. And I wait to hear what your heart tell you."

Consult your mind and your heart, she recalled. *I put this in your hands.*

She turned away. She could feel his eyes as he lingered in the trees, watching her.

≈

OBLIVIOUS TO EVERYTHING AROUND her, she returned to Beaufort, getting off the wagon at the law office. She walked up the stairs and pulled open the door. In the parlor sat someone very familiar. It was Rufus Green, who had slung his hat over his knee as he faced Pereira, who had the vantage point in the wing chair. Before she could sit—before she could take off her bonnet—he addressed them both. He said, "I been wronged. I hear that you can help me."

Chapter 15: Common Ground

AFTER RUFUS GREEN LEFT the Beaufort office, after Pereira had learned the history of the land sales and their broken promises, Pereira slumped in his chair. He said, "Mr. Green has been wronged, that's certain. But I can't see how it's a legal matter."

Through the open window, a spring breeze wafted, bringing in the Beaufort odor, floral fragrance and horse manure and the faintest hint of the sea.

"Why not?" Caro asked.

"The sale was legal, little as Mr. Green liked the way it was managed."

"What about the terms of the sale?"

"What the Department of the Treasury and the tax commission did was mean-spirited and unfair, but it wasn't illegal," Pereira said.

Caro said, "You're taking too narrow a view."

He stared at her. "Did General Saxton appoint me to defy the law? I thought he asked me to advise and represent the former slaves in legal matters."

"It's like the other circumstance. A moral question."

"That was a private trouble."

"So is this."

"No, it isn't. It's a matter of public policy. Public opinion. And public scrutiny." He took a deep breath. "If South Carolina had a state legislature, this would be its biggest task. To assure that former slaves can become cotton farmers on their own land." He shook his head. "No one can force a man to sell a hundred acres, which he legally owns, because it's morally right."

"Perhaps we can't change the law regarding a sale. But we might consider changing the mind of the man who owns that hundred acres. Might a lawyer help with that?"

He said slowly, "Lawyers do that all the time. We do it through negotiation. We sit people down to negotiate until they can agree."

"It's another kind of dilemma," she said. She couldn't help giving him an arch look.

"Not that kind of dilemma," he said.

"Might we try that?"

He sighed. "I can draft a contract. I can broker a negotiation, if two people are agreeable. I can't perform a miracle."

"Why don't we talk to Mr. Phelps?" He didn't reply, and she touched his sleeve. "At least we'll know where he stands."

"We already have an idea," Pereira said, and the burden of Rufus Green's trouble weighed down his shoulders and shadowed his face.

⊱⊰

MR. PHELPS INVITED THEM to a meeting at Ocean Point. "That's odd," Pereira said. "Doesn't he live on the Pine Grove plantation?"

"He does," Caro replied. "Ocean Point is Mr. Chapman's place."

"What is Mr. Chapman's interest in this?"

"You'll soon find out."

On the way to Ocean Point, Caro asked the coachman to drive past Pine Grove. He said, "It ain't on the way, Miss Caro."

"I know. I want to show Mr. Pereira what it looks like."

The Pine Grove place had the look of a plantation no longer tended by black hands. The cotton fields were still thick with last year's trash; no one had cleared or plowed. The gravel of the driveway hadn't been smoothed, and it showed the ruts of carriage wheels. In the front yard, weeds grew in the flower beds.

"All of his employees have stopped working," Caro said.

Pereira said, "As Mr. Green told us."

"You see the neglect."

The coachman said, "You see what you came for, Miss Caro?"

"Yes, thank you."

Mr. Chapman's front yard was in better condition that Harry Phelps's because Chapman still managed to employ some of his house servants. The shrubs had been trimmed and the grass cut. The servant who answered the door was a very young girl whose apron was too big for her. They followed her into the study, where William Chapman sat before the hearth, unlit in the springlike warmth of March, and Harry Phelps rose to welcome them. He looked distraught, but someone had seen to brush his coat and to straighten his cravat. Caro wondered if Mr. Chapman had lent out his valet.

Pereira said, "I haven't had the pleasure to meet either of you."

"You reputation precedes you," Chapman said. "You're a New York man?"

"Called to the bar in New York, sir. But I was born and raised in South Carolina."

"A free man, I hear," Chapman said. "From a distinguished family of color in Charleston."

Caro thought, *He can flatter, too.* She noticed that neither of their hosts bothered to flatter her. They knew her too well.

They all sat in the chairs before the hearth as though this were a social call.

Harry sighed. "What has Rufus Green told you?"

Pereira spoke carefully. "He feels wronged in the matter of buying a parcel of land on the Pine Grove plantation. And he's reluctant to sign a labor contract with you until the matter can be addressed."

"That's a very tactful way to put it," Chapman said.

Pereira allowed himself a smile. "I hope we can start that way, Mr. Chapman."

Harry said, "I know the people on St. Helena all feel wronged by the way the tax commission handled the preemption of lands here. But when I bought the Pine Grove plantation, I acted in accordance with the procedures they laid out, and now I own it in accordance with the law."

"I've looked at the title transfer, Mr. Phelps, and I know that's the case," Pereira said. "That's not at issue here."

"Then what is?" Harry asked.

"Mr. Green doesn't want to sign the labor contract you've offered him. He would like to change the terms."

Harry said, "No, Mr. Pereira. That's not what I've heard. He refuses to sign the contract unless I promise to sell him the land he wants on the Pine Grove place. And as much as I regret the tax commission's decision, I can't do that."

Caro said, "Mr. Phelps, certainly you're free to dispose of your land however you wish."

Chapman leaned forward in his chair. "Of course he is. But I'd advise him not to."

"In what capacity, Mr. Chapman?"

"I hope that Mr. Phelps considers me a friend. But I also have a financial interest."

Harry flushed. "Mr. Chapman invested in my enterprise, as his backers in Boston invested in his enterprise last year."

Pereira nodded. Caro had told him about the eleven plantations, purchased with the money of investors from Boston, Chapman's cronies. "A common practice among cotton cultivators," he said.

Chapman said, "Of course, I want to see a return on my investment. But I'm not as worried about the debt as I am about setting an example. The former slaves have just begun to work for wages and develop the habits of free labor. They aren't ready to run their own enterprises. Selling Rufus Green a plot of land would undermine everything that I've tried to do since I came to the Sea Islands."

Harry Phelps clenched his hands and unclenched them. He said, "I wish I could do differently."

"You might. But you should not," Chapman said softly.

Pereira asked Harry, "Would you meet with Rufus Green?"

"I doubt it would do any good," Chapman said.

Pereira gave Chapman a level gaze. "In the early stages of a negotiation, it's often helpful to bring the parties face to face, even if all that it proves is that they are very far apart."

Caro felt a surge of pride.

Harry said, "Will, how can things get any worse? I'd allow it."

"I don't advise it," Chapman said. "But it's up to you."

৪০৪

Harry Phelps had agreed to hold the meeting with Rufus Green at Pine Grove. On the ferry to St. Helena Island, Pereira said, "I thought of inviting them to Beaufort, where they'd be on neutral ground. But it's enough trouble to make them sit down together. I didn't want to press it."

As the carriage made its way up the driveway, as it approached the house, Caro said, "I see why Mr. Phelps wanted to meet on his place."

"To be out of Mr. Chapman's sight?"

"That too. See how ragged the yard looks? He's poor-mouthing himself."

Pereira shook his head. "It may matter, and it may not."

Harry himself ushered them inside. Pereira asked, "Is there a table where we might all sit?"

As Caro walked into the dining room, she was assailed by the memory of Benjamin Pereira at the table with her aunt Maria and uncle Thomas in Charleston, pleading the case for allowing Caro and Danny to marry. That had been a private matter, too, and it could have been resolved with the right contract. A bill of sale, she recalled, not a marriage license.

Let it go. To hide her emotion, she said lightly to Pereira, "It's a shame that his servants refuse to work. I wish there could be refreshment."

The doorknocker sounded. Caro said, "Let me get it."

Rufus Green stood outside, looking impassive, as though he had willed himself not to get angry. At the sight of Caro, he asked, "Is Mr. Chapman here?"

"No. Just Mr. Pereira and me."

He entered the house with a self-possessed step. In the dining room, he took a seat opposite Harry Phelps, and the two men appraised each other across the expanse of dusty mahogany.

Pereira rose and said, "Mr. Green, Mr. Phelps, thank you for meeting here today."

Both men nodded.

"I know that you aren't in agreement," Pereira said. "But I want you to hear from each other, nothing more. We can't find common ground unless we start with that."

"I know what he wants," Harry said.

Pereira said, "Let Mr. Green tell you."

"Don't lawyer me, young man," Rufus said, his voice hoarse and weary. "Everyone know what I want. I want to buy the hundred acres Mr. Phelps deny me, and until he agree to sell, I don't work for him, and no one else on the place work for him, either."

Harry's voice was also hoarse with weariness. "I want you to sign a contract, a fair contract, and to go back to work as my employee. I want you and everyone else to get the crop in." He had no energy to command. It sounded like a plea.

Rufus said, "You say you own that land free and clear. Well, you can sell it to me free and clear."

Harry said, "I can't do that. You know I can't. Not with the best will in the world."

"Ain't a matter of will. It's a matter of fairness, and you know it as much as I do."

"The terms of the contract are fair."

"No, they ain't. I get forty cents an hour, and you get two dollar a pound. When the crop come in, two hundred dollar for me and twenty thousand dollar for you. That don't sound fair to me."

It's not, Caro thought.

Harry said, "Mr. Green, you're an intelligent man. I believe you know the difference between an owner and an employee."

Rufus rose. "Yes, I do. Like I know the difference between a master and a slave."

"You are not a slave. And I am not your master."

"Then act like it," Rufus said.

Harry said, "A contract, that's all I can offer you."

"A hundred acres, that's what you owe me," he said.

"Get out," Harry growled.

Rufus turned his back on Harry, a whipping offense before the war, and left the room with a heavy tread.

§∞Ↄ

ON THE WAY BACK to Beaufort, Pereira was silent. On the sidewalk outside the office, he said, "Caro, you're free to go today. I don't need you."

She faced him. "I know it didn't go well. But it wasn't as bad as that."

He didn't reply. He turned to open the front door without replying to her. She followed him inside and said, "If you want to talk about this in private, we'll sit in the study and shut the door."

She followed him there as well. He sat at the desk, trying to bolster himself, but he slumped in his chair and said, "They're very far apart."

"We thought they would be," she said.

"I don't see how we'll bring them closer together." He spread his hands on the blotter and stared at them. The confidence of the lawyer cracked, and beneath it Caro saw the boy with whom she had fallen in love when she was a slave. She felt pity for those two young people, rather than pain. She pulled her chair closer to his. She said, "This situation is more like the other than we first thought."

He shook his head. "What do you mean?"

"Two hearts and two souls that have fixated on a hundred acres," she said. "What do they really want? That's not a matter of the law. Just like the other, it's a matter of the heart."

He snorted. "Which could be resolved with a contract, if they would agree to one."

She reached for his hands. "Marriage is a legal contract, isn't it? But it's a matter of the heart first."

In despair, he said, "No, Caro. Not that. Not now."

"Listen to me," she said. "Look at me." He raised his head. "Do you recall how Benjamin Pereira handled the matter of our wanting to marry in Charleston?"

"Too well."

"How he appealed to your mother and to your Uncle Thomas?" She tightened her clasp. "Not a word about the law. He talked of our happiness and of the strength of family feeling. Made it a matter of the heart."

"I'm sure you recall how well it ended up."

"With Lawrence Jarvie? It didn't work with him. He was always a heartless man." She thought of Emily, who still carried the price her father had put on her head. "But it persuaded your mother, who had set her heart against me from the beginning."

"Why remind me?" he asked.

"Because that's how we fight, here and now." She was surprised to hear her own words. She had none of the anger and the bravado of the reporter, the scout, or the would-be soldier. She thought with detachment of the pretty little pistol in her dresser drawer. Daniel Pereira had shown her the way to a more powerful weapon.

"I still don't see it," he said.

"We start with Rufus Green."

He met her eyes, and it hurt to see the feeling she had stirred in him. He said, "You should be the one to talk to him."

"Both of us," she insisted.

"No. You know the circumstances here, as I never will. He'll listen to you. He'll trust you." He drew a deep breath and steadied himself, not as the confident free man of color, not as the clever lawyer, but as a man uneasy with matters of the heart. "I trust you."

For a moment she allowed herself to dream of a life with this man, seeing him capable of generosity and capable of kindness. She blinked the dream away. They had a higher purpose, and she was now entrusted with it.

❧❧

SHE FOUND RUFUS GREEN behind his cabin, currying a horse with a chestnut coat, carefully grooming the heavy neck. "My new horse," he said. "Bought it at the second auction, where they sell livestock and equipment. Used to belong on the Pine Grove place." Chuckled. "Bought from under Mr. Phelps." He patted the straw-colored mane. "I pay a lot for this horse to call me massa," he said.

"You paid a lot for spite," she said, and was immediately ashamed of herself. She had done worse, much worse, for spite.

"Did you bring that high-rumped Charleston lawyer with you?"

"No."

"Do he send you to soften me?"

"No."

"You won't talk me out of my hundred acres," he said.

"I don't intend to."

"Say your piece," he said, impatient.

"Mr. Green, I was a slave on this island. Kitty's girl. James Jarvie's daughter. Lawrence Jarvie's property. I came out of slavery in a fury. For a long time after that, everything I did was fueled by my anger."

"You come by it honestly," he said.

"No doubt," she replied. "But I've had time to consider how well it serves me in a life of freedom."

"It serves me to fight for what's due me."

"The war is about ending slavery. But on the Sea Islands, it's about freedom. What does freedom look like? What does it feel like? It's more than the absence of slavery. It's something better than that. What do you want in your freedom, Mr. Green? What does that hundred acres mean, in your heart and in your soul?"

"You should know that."

"Tell me outright."

"Dignity," he said.

"Do you think Mr. Phelps doesn't know that?"

"Don't act like it."

"Under the planter, he's still a man of God," she said. "And he's very troubled in his soul about the wrong done to you."

Rufus said, "I coddle and beguile a white man all my life. I'm done with that."

"One cotton farmer to another. One free man to another," Caro said. "Might there be common ground?"

Rufus looked beyond her like a man surveying a cotton field. He didn't reply, and she knew better than to press him further. She had troubled the water, as Emily put it, and she would let Rufus Green's conscience rise to the surface to do battle with his anger.

ℴℴ

THE DISPUTE BETWEEN RUFUS Green and Harry Phelps had upset Emily badly, and she woke in the middle of the night, sick in her soul, and rose to think. She had learned not to misuse her prayers. Demanding an answer of God was selfish. God had given her the intelligence and the fortitude to demand the answer of herself.

She knew the answer. After a particularly bad sleepless night she traversed the path that led her to Rufus Green's cabin. In the cool mist of early morning, she found him sitting on his front steps, alone, lost in thought. Perhaps he hoped to hear from God, too.

He rose and greeted her, and she insisted that he sit. She sat beside him, tucking her skirt beneath her. When he protested, she said, "I can see that Miss Juno sweeps them very clean."

He shook his head and asked, "Did Miss Caroline send you?"

Puzzled, Emily said, "No. Why would she?"

"Thought she might. Because of her association with Mr. Pereira."

Caro must have talked to Rufus Green, too. "No, it has nothing to do with him. It's something that's been troubling me, mind and heart."

"Not sure I want to know, Miss Emily."

She put her hand on his arm. "Please, Mr. Green. Let me help you in this matter with Mr. Phelps."

He pulled away gently. "Miss Emily, it ain't your fight."

"Let me make it my fight."

"No, Miss Emily. I stand up for myself."

"Of course you do. But it's not a fair fight. I'd hope I could offer you an advantage in it."

"I'm a free man," he said. "Not a slave. Don't need a missus to speak for me."

She sighed. "Not you too, Mr. Green. Questioning my loyalty to the cause of freedom." She looked into his eyes. It was still strange to meet a black man's eyes. "My father was a planter. But I'm free of him, too."

"Leave it be, Miss Emily."

"I've paid a very high price for my feelings about freedom," she said. "I'm entitled to them, as much as you're entitled to yours."

"You sure you don't talk to Miss Caro about this?" He met her eyes with an unblinking gaze.

She rose. "Now I have reason to," she said.

ℰℬⅭℛ

EMILY MADE SURE TO find Caro at home, not at her office. She had an instinct that Mr. Pereira would think she was meddling. Rufus Green's admonition had been painful enough. She hoped to avoid a rebuke from a man as articulate as Daniel Pereira. And she was startled to realize that Danny Pereira, the shy tailor's apprentice from prewar Charleston, had become a man whose authority she respected and whose reproach she feared.

When Emily arrived, Sophy and Chloe were at the market, attending to business, and the house was quiet in the spring afternoon's heat. Down the street, a dog barked. Caro said, "That dog used to bother Sophy something terrible."

"And not now?"

"Now she knows he's a little lapdog. She treats him like a pet. Can I offer you anything? There's coffee."

"No, I'm all right."

"Shall we sit in the parlor, like ladies? Or at the kitchen table?"

"Where do you want to sit?"

Caro laughed. "Freedom, even in the smallest things. In the parlor. I'll let you have the most comfortable chair, which isn't the same as the best."

Emily glanced around the room. "Is that Dresden shepherdess yours?"

"Goodness, no. It's Sophy's. She likes china figurines. She has some Staffordshire, too."

"I'll remember that, if I want to give her a present. She still doesn't like me, does she?"

"Not yet." Caro stretched out her legs far enough to expose the toes of her shoes, which were pointed and elegant, as far removed from a slave's shoes as she could own and still walk in. She teased, "Have you forgiven me for being a firebug?"

"You and the Second South Carolina. That was war, Caro. Nothing to forgive."

"What is it then, Emily? Why have you come to see me?"

"I've talked to Mr. Green. He asked me if you'd sent me. I wondered why he'd ask me that."

"Mr. Pereira and I are looking into his dispute."

"Have you made any progress?"

"No."

Emily leaned forward. "I want to help Mr. Green. I've come to ask for your advice."

Caro raised her eyes to her cousin's. "Mr. Phelps," she said softly. "Is he still a friend of yours?"

"I hope so."

"Can you speak to him? Heart to heart?"

"I can try." She sighed. "It's a very odd way to fight."

"For you? A soldier of light and love?"

Emily shook her head. Caro laid her hand on her cousin's arm. "You can hardly approach him with a Springfield rifle."

Emily glanced at her in surprise. "That's not like you."

"I've learned the hard way. I've had a change of heart."

Emily looked down at her hands. She spread them in a kind of supplication and sighed. "I told Mr. Green I'd do my best to give him an advantage."

"Don't fail him," Caro said.

❧❧

When Emily rapped on the door of Pine Grove, Harry himself answered. He had never looked so weary. His coat hadn't been brushed, and his shirt was wrinkled.

She said, "I see that your servants haven't come back to work, either."

He searched her face as though he were trying to gauge whether she, too, might desert him. He said, "They are all solidly in agreement with Rufus Green." He sighed. "Come in, even though I can't offer you much."

The house felt empty. She had never realized that servants, however quiet, made a presence in a house. She was truly alone in this house with Harry, as she had never been with anyone, and she suddenly heard a disapproving voice whisper inside her head to remind her that a lady didn't sit alone with a gentleman.

Even if she was here on a matter of business, and not a social one, it was still true.

They sat awkwardly in the parlor, which was unpleasant with a film of dust. The usual household smell of beeswax polish had faded in this room. It smelled of ash from the hearth and the wet, green odor of the untended foliage outside.

"It's good to see you," he said. "I've been very lonely here."

"Certainly Mr. Chapman hasn't deserted you."

There was no gleam of mischief, or of happiness, in his eyes today. They were gray with sadness. He said bitterly, "He laughs and tells me to be firm with these people."

She said, "I know that's not in your nature."

He raised his eyes to hers. In the quiet, she dropped her voice. "I know how kind you are."

"Oh, Emily," he said, a liberty that both of them knew he shouldn't take. "It does my heart good to hear the sweetness in your voice."

She should declare her business. She should bring up the matter of Rufus Green. But hearing him speak her name beguiled her.

He said, "I should have spoken to you a long time ago." He leaned forward. "I should have told you how much I care for you."

"As a friend?" Her voice came out hushed. Sweet.

"More than a friend."

Yes, she knew. And she knew what he wanted to say to her. But she hadn't come for that. As a belle, she had been schooled in tactful refusal. But she was not here as a lady. She was here as an emissary.

She held her breath as she chose her words. Then she spoke. "Mr. Phelps." She corrected herself. She owed him more kindness than that. "Harry. I understand you. But don't speak of it."

He sighed.

She said softly, "I will always love you as a friend. As a sister loves a brother. But you know that my loyalties lie elsewhere. Not only with Captain Aiken, but with Rufus Green and the justice that's owed him."

"If the world were arranged differently—"

She met his eyes. She was a soldier of light and love, and she let her purpose show in her gaze. She said, "The world is arranged differently, since the war." She didn't pull away. She dropped her voice. "As a friend, a good friend, there's something you can do for me."

They were still eye to eye, like a promise. But promises came in all forms, from vows of love to legal contracts. People swore to both. He asked, "What is it?"

"You can listen to your conscience."

ഇറ

CARO TOLD PEREIRA TO write to both parties to get them back at the negotiating table. He said, "Do you know something I don't?"

She said, "It's in God's hands now."

"That's quite a statement from a godless woman."

"Isn't that the last resort?"

When they arrived at Pine Grove, they found a crowd outside, friends and neighbors of the Greens. Inside, the two opponents, Rufus Green and Harry Phelps, sat at the big dining room table, and they had brought supporters with them. Rufus was accompanied by his family, Juno and Phoebe, who showed the burden of the dispute in their shadowed eyes and solemn expressions. And next to them, at Phoebe's elbow, sat Emily. Beside Harry Phelps, his hands resting on the table, sat William Chapman.

Pereira whispered to Caro, "I didn't expect an audience."

"We can hardly throw them out."

They had left the seat at the head of the table for Pereira and the seat at the foot for her.

Outside, the crowd chatted and laughed, sounding as they did in the churchyard before the service. Caro was surprised at their cheer. Perhaps they knew something she didn't. Of course, they were on much better terms with the Almighty than she was.

Pereira rose, and everyone at the table gazed at him expectantly. He spoke, but not with the sonorous public tone of a lawyer. His voice was quiet and intimate, as though he spoke to a group of friends.

"The last time we met, you were far apart, Mr. Green and Mr. Phelps. I was sorry to hear how angry you were. I doubted that you'd want to talk again, let alone to try to find common ground. But here we are, at this table." He rested his eyes on each face, including Caro's, and she remembered thinking that she'd open her heart to a man who looked at her like that. "But today I have hope. We may not come to a resolution today. As a soldier, I learned that we fight one battle at a time. But I'm confident in our progress. We may yet win the war."

Caro thought, *He frightens me. He sounds as though he means it.* She glanced at Emily, but Emily was gripped by Pereira's words.

Rufus Green leaned forward. He was roiling with something, and he was impatient to let it out. "Mr. Pereira, may I speak?"

"Mr. Green, I'll insist on a courteous tone. Mr. Phelps, I ask the same of you."

Both men nodded. Pereira said, "Go ahead, Mr. Green."

Rufus Green sat up straight, taking strength from the presence of his wife, his daughter, and his ally, Emily Jarvie. He said, "As a free man, I want to better myself. Want to come up in the world. Want to see the advantage of my labor. Want an increase. Want a profit." He let his eyes rest on Harry Phelps's face. "What every man in business want."

Harry Phelps allowed himself a small, startled smile.

"But better mean more than that. How to live by my better nature. How to be a better man. Ask God for a little help with that, because it ain't easy. Mr. Phelps, you a man of God, you know that, too."

"Yes, I do," Harry murmured.

"Want to do what's right, Mr. Phelps. Do right by the crop. Do right by the place. Do right by my own mind and heart." He paused, and Harry Phelps seemed to be listening to the silence. Rufus continued, "I want to help you, Mr. Phelps. But I need you to help me."

Harry nodded. He was still listening.

Rufus Green pressed his palms on the table. He said, "When you come here, Mr. Phelps, Mr. Chapman help you. He make you a superintendent, and he give you the dignity of the title and the fifty dollars that go with it. He offer you half the profit of the crop in the land you superintend. And then he help you buy your own place." His eyes never left Harry's face, and Harry listened.

"Deal with me as Mr. Chapman deal with you," Green said.

Chapman said, "I can't—"

But Harry stopped him. "Will, let him finish."

Rufus pressed his hands harder into the mahogany tabletop. Caro saw a lifetime of restrained anger in that gesture. He said, "Grant me a hundred acres to superintend. Call me a superintendent and pay me like one, too. Assure me half the profit on the crop I raise. And after the crop picked and baled, on January first of next year, we have a private land sale, between the two of us. You sell me that hundred acres at the government rate. I ask that because I know I can pay it." He took a deep breath. "You do that, and we bring in the crop together."

The room was silent, and outside, the crowd had hushed, dropping to a murmur.

Chapman said, "Harry."

Harry laid his hand on his investor's arm. "It's all

right, Will." He said, "Mr. Green, I've had reason to search my soul, too." His voice was soft, but it carried with the weight of a sermon. "I've never appealed to God for help in business before," he said. "But His word was very clear."

Rufus reached for Juno's hand and for Phoebe's, and his knuckles strained with the force of his grip.

"A fair contract," Harry said. "And enough land to live a decent life in freedom." He turned to Pereira. "Can we draft a labor contract with the terms Mr. Green describes? The superintendent's title and pay?"

Pereira allowed himself a look of relief. "Of course."

"And a contract for the sale of the land, to be effective on the first of next year?"

"Yes," Pereira said, and he smiled in a joy that a lawyer must rarely allow himself.

Chapman shook his head. "God help you, Harry," he said, letting the irony echo.

Harry looked at Emily. The worry slipped from his face, and in its place was the most serene smile. He extended his hand across the table to Rufus—he had to stand upright and to reach—and despite the awkwardness, the two men shook hands with the warmth of partners.

෨෮෨

THE GREENS LEFT THE house in triumph, and as soon as the waiting crowd heard the result, they roared and cheered. In their emotion, as on the boat after the Combahee River raid, they sang. The strains of "Jehovah

Hallelujah" rose to the spring sky, no longer bitter, but hopeful.

Caro stood on the porch with Pereira, watching as the Greens were overwhelmed by embraces and good wishes. The air was thick with the fragrance of spring. She sniffed the odor of magnolia and thought of a new crop. A new start. A new life. Tears rose to her eyes, and she blinked them away.

Pereira said softly, "Happy day, Caro."

She summoned Miss Sass. She said, "Now he'll have to catch up. Since he got a late start."

Emily joined them. She laughed. "I heard that," she said, smiling. "He'll be all right. I have full confidence in Rufus Green."

Pereira looked a little dazed. He said, "Not just the contract. But the miracle, too." He looked at Emily, then at Caro. "What did you two say? What did you do?"

"I reckon we found a new way to fight. Haven't we, Caro?"

Caro smiled. "Who needs a Springfield rifle?"

They stood shoulder to shoulder, smiling in their triumph, united in their purpose, soldiers of light and love together.

Chapter 16: A Wider World

A FEW WEEKS AFTER Harry Phelps and Rufus Green made their agreement, after the fields had been plowed and the cotton seeds planted, Rosa announced to Mattie and Emily, who sat in the parlor reading letters, that Harry came to call at the Oaks. Mattie, whose estimation of Harry had warmed, told Rosa to show him in. He entered the parlor with a jaunty step. The bright smile had returned to his face.

Mattie asked, "How do things go at Pine Grove?"

"Better than I could have imagined." It was good to see him sunny again. "Mr. Green has become my greatest ally. At every stroke of the hoe, he thinks of profit. He inspires all of us."

Mattie laughed. "What does Mr. Chapman think?"

"He's not happy. He tells me that they'll all want to buy land next year." His eyes gleamed. "If they do, I'll be glad to sell it."

"And put yourself out of business, Mr. Phelps?" Mattie asked. "What will you do?"

He looked at Emily. "After we see the crop in, I'll

return to Boston. There's plenty of work to do, even from afar."

Emily felt a pang, but she let Mattie say, "We'll miss you, Mr. Phelps."

He laughed. "I'll be here for a while. There's no reason to say goodbye yet."

He sat at his ease, asking Mattie about the progress of the school and the health of all the islanders she saw to. Emily watched as Mattie softened toward the man she had dismissed as Chapman's creature. Emily was pleased at this new accord. But she was unsettled too, knowing what had passed between herself and Harry Phelps.

When he had drunk his cup of coffee and sent his compliments to Rosa for the cookies, he asked Mattie, "May I take Miss Jarvie for a walk in your garden?"

As though he were asking her mother for permission to propose to her. Mattie allowed herself a little surprise. She said, "Miss Jarvie is her own woman, Mr. Phelps. You can ask her yourself."

Emily said, "Of course I'll walk in the garden with you, Mr. Phelps."

They left the house together, but he made no effort to guide her toward the side garden, where the great trees would shelter them from Mattie's sight. She breathed a little easier.

"I owe you a debt of gratitude," he said. "I also owe you an apology."

"For what?"

"For the words you wouldn't let me say."

"They're forgotten," she said, feeling a rush of relief.

"It weighs on me. Are you certain?"

"Mr. Phelps," she said, insisting on the distance of the formal address. "You know why I came to you. It was for justice, and for freedom."

His face was grave, but his eyes twinkled a little. "We've come full circle, Miss Jarvie. I'm a planter, and you're a Gideonite."

"I wish you every success with the crop, Mr. Phelps," she said.

He said, "I'm afraid I've caused you a great deal of trouble with Captain Aiken."

"No, you haven't. It's his trouble, and mine. I'm the one who has caused the trouble."

"I have every hope you can mend it," he said gently. "The two of you belong together. There is so much common ground between you."

☙ℭ

THAT SUNDAY, JOSHUA ANSWERED her summons to the Oaks, appearing uneasy and uncertain despite the dignity of his Union coat. Mattie left them alone in the parlor, where he sat on the edge of his chair, picking up his teacup and setting it down again.

She thought, *He's come to break it off with me.*

"We've all heard about the agreement between Mr. Green and Mr. Phelps," he said. "The camp is abuzz with it."

"The men must be glad," she said.

"They are. It gives them all hope for themselves."

"Forty acres and a mule."

He put down the fussy little cup and said, "Mr. Phelps had quite a change of heart."

"I know. I was at the negotiating table."

"More than that," he said, his voice low.

"Joshua," she said impatiently, "whatever it is, just tell me."

"Did you have a hand in it? Was it you, who persuaded Mr. Phelps?"

Anger began to bubble up in her. "And if I did?"

"How did it happen, Emily? Did you take his hands and look into his eyes?"

"So that's what you think of me. That he changed his mind because I flirted with him."

"Am I wrong?"

A lady didn't lose her temper, but a soldier might, even a soldier of light and love. "Yes, you are. You are so badly wrong that I wonder how you can imagine such a thing of me."

"I know what I've seen."

"Do you know what's in my heart?"

"No," he said. "I fear that even more."

"You've told me you doubt me. You've told me you wonder about my loyalty."

"I don't deny it," he said.

She rose. She wanted the advantage of height as well as fury. "Loyalty! I came to the Sea Islands to prove my loyalty to freedom. I've struggled to prove it, every day that I've been here. I embroiled myself in Rufus Green's dispute because of it. And I went to Harry Phelps because of it." She threw him a fiery look. "And I saw justice because of it."

He said, "I may be foolish. And selfish. But I want to know about your loyalty to me."

"Why did we come together, you and I? Why did we fall in love? Why did we risk our lives? It was for freedom. Have you forgotten that?"

He said, "A Union man doesn't forget that."

She wasn't ready to be softened. "What about you? Are you loyal to me?"

He stood. "I've asked the wrong question."

Her anger began to recede. In its place was a stab of fear. "Then ask the right one."

"I will." The soldier's posture relaxed, and she could see the man she knew inside the army coat. "Do you love me?"

She stared at him in surprise.

"Not just for the past. Or for the ideal we share. Do you love me, here and now?"

He had ambushed her. She said, "Is it possible to be in a rage with you and love you at the same time?"

"I believe so," he said. "Because I feel the same way." He held out his hands to her. "Can you forgive me?"

She took his hands, strong and warm, the skin coarsened by his life as a soldier. It was hard to speak. "Yes. Can you forgive me?"

He met her eyes. In a voice hoarse with emotion, he

said, "Dearest Emily, I can do better than that. I'll marry you, if we still suit."

"If we're in agreement?"

"Yes," he said. "Where should we start, Emily? To find the common ground that will bind us together for the rest of our lives? Tell me what you want. For yourself, and for us."

She thought of Rufus Green calmly advocating for himself. "I want us to be friends. Companions. Equals. To go through life side by side. Loyal to each other and to the highest purpose we share." She took a deep breath. "I never want to do that in the shadows again. I want to do it for the world to see."

He smiled, and she saw all their past in it, and all the hope for their future.

She insisted, as she had for Rufus Green. But now it was for herself. "Can you agree to that? A marriage like that?"

He searched her face. Then he smiled and turned his head to kiss her palm. In the soldier's oath, he said, "I'll do my damnedest."

She smiled in return. "So will I."

They drew close, and she cradled his face in her hands. They kissed with a heat that was a promise of its own, and in that embrace, there was nothing to divide them.

§∞Q

AFTER THE RESOLUTION OF the Sea Islands' most contentious dispute, Pereira was a hero, and even Caro found herself warmed by the fire of adulation for his cleverness and tact. She was surprised by how little it bothered her. She knew, as Emily knew, how the agreement had truly been made.

Pereira was in a better mood than she had ever seen him. He was volatile, as Sampson Hayward was not. She found herself making the comparison all the time. That bothered her.

They had a rush of business now, people on the Pine Grove place who wanted Pereira to assist them with their labor contracts. He spent his time reviewing the contracts, and after he emended them, Caro spent her time writing them out in a fair hand. Her wrist ached as it had at *Hearth and Home* back in Cincinnati.

They were taking a few minutes from their labors, drinking a midmorning cup of coffee in the parlor, when Pereira looked up and said, "There's still one more dilemma to resolve."

"Another contract?" she asked. Her mind was far away, intent on making sure that a former slave named Pompey was assured fifty cents an hour for his work.

"No." His eyes shone with too much emotion for a legal problem. "Ours."

She was startled from her clerk's thoughts. "Not that!"

"Why not?"

"I thought you were drunk when you proposed it." She immediately regretted the word *proposed*.

"I was, a little. But I meant it."

"You don't know what you mean."

418

He reached for her hands. "I love you. Do you love me?"

She let her hands rest in his. "God help me, I do. But that's not enough for a life together."

Hurt, he took his hands away. "What is?"

She shook her head. "I have to go."

"Where?"

As though she would never have a reason to be elsewhere than here.

"To St. Helena Island," she said. "To call on Emily." It was only half a fib. She would go there, afterward.

She wanted to visit her father's grave again.

And once there, too many things echoed in her head at once. Pereira's words. Sampson's words. Her father's.

What had her father wanted for her? Her happiness, even though he had done nothing to assure it.

She would never bury the past. She would always carry it with her. But Sampson was right. The world was now wider, with room for happiness as well as pain.

She thought of the oddity of asking her father's ghost for permission to live a life that was hers to choose.

She bent to touch his gravestone with its lies of omission, her mother and herself, and let the tears rise to her eyes. He was her father, but he had failed her. But she was now free to lay him to rest.

When the war ended, when she could walk the streets of Charleston as a free woman, she would visit her mother's grave, too.

∞CR

Caro invited Sampson Hayward to Sophy's for Sunday dinner. He brought Sunday Desmond with him. Sunday had found a bottle of hock. He said, "You can buy anything you like from the sutler in camp, if you have the money."

The wine made them convivial. They gossiped about Emily and Joshua. Even Sophy, who was still unhappy with Emily, was pleased that she had patched things up with Captain Aiken. Sophy gave Caro a sidelong glance as she said, "I hear we have a wedding soon."

They celebrated Rufus Green's contract and drank another round to him. Sophy said, "I see Juno in the market, and she tell me that Miss Phoebe take a page from her father's book. She go to Mr. Chapman and tell him that she a teacher. Should be called one, and paid as one, too. And he say yes to her." Sophy looked pleased. "Just before the new teacher get here. Caro, do you hear about that? The Missionary Association send a young woman of color to teach here. She from Ohio. You might be acquainted with her."

Caro laughed. "Oh, I am. She's written to me to tell me. She was my classmate at Oberlin College. Miss Frankie Williamson." She raised her glass. "A toast to her, too."

And after dinner, Sampson asked Sophy and Sunday, as the parents they were, if he could speak privately with Caro in the parlor. They nodded and smiled as they went into the backyard, hand in hand.

In the parlor, Sampson joined Caro on the settee, letting it squeeze them together.

She said, "I reckon you know why I asked you here today."

He turned to look at her, his copper-flecked eyes very soft. "I do."

She sat very still as she waited for him to speak.

He enfolded her inkstained fingers within his warm, calloused palms. "I love you," he said. "I want to spend the rest of my life with you. Miss Caroline Jarvie, will you marry me?"

She thought of her own advice to Rosa, that she was free to choose in the most intimate of matters. Free to fall in love. Free to marry for love. Free to live entwined by law and love, and to be parted only in death.

For once, Miss Sass had nothing to say. Instead, Caroline Jarvie replied from her own unguarded heart. "Yes, I will," she said.

Historical Note

Whenever I read a work of historical fiction, I like to know how much of it is historical fact. I'm glad to satisfy a similar curiosity here.

The major events described in this book—the two land sales, which generated so much controversy, and the Combahee River raid—were taken straight from the historical record. Harriet Tubman's presence in Beaufort and her role as organizer and spy for the Union army was a happy accident for this story. She sat in the pilot house of the steamboat *Harriet Weed* and welcomed the freed slaves as they streamed from the Hayward and Middleton plantations.

The military men in this story were real historical figures. General Rufus Saxton was the military governor of the Department of the South during the time encompassed by this story, in charge of the black regiments raised in the Sea Islands—the First and the Second South Carolina Volunteer Infantry Regiments, Colored. They were later renamed the Thirty-Third and Thirty-Fourth South Carolina Infantry, United States Colored Troops (or USCT.) He was a Massachusetts man and a staunch abolitionist, and according to contemporary accounts, he was both kindly and prone to bouts of despair about the progress of freedom in the Sea Islands.

Colonel Thomas Higginson, who had an illustrious career as a minister and author before the war, was the commander of the First South Carolina Volunteers. Colonel Charles Trowbridge, the Brooklyn-born engineer, was his counterpart for the Second South Carolina. Colonel William Silliman was the commander of the real regiment that Daniel Pereira slipped into—the Twenty-Sixth New

York Infantry, USCT, raised in Manhattan and comprised of free men from all over New York State. I did take a liberty with his temper—although I suspect that any military man would be angry to be roused from sleep to handle a prankster.

Several of the main characters in this book were based on real people, Northern-born abolitionists who came south to serve as teachers and superintendents after the capture of the Sea Islands in November of 1861. Mattie Easton was inspired by Philadelphia-born Laura Towne, who worked as a teacher and doctor on St. Helena Island throughout the war. She and her companion, Ellen Murray, established the Penn School, the first and most significant educational institution for former slaves on the island. She remained on the island after the war, making it her home until her death in 1901.

William Chapman was based on the entrepreneur Edward Philbrick, a Boston abolitionist who fervently believed that wage labor would uplift former slaves to freedom. In 1863, Philbrick became the biggest landowner on St. Helena Island, with thirteen plantations under his supervision. His employees were so angry after the second land sale in 1864 that they sent a petition outlining their grievances to President Lincoln. In response, the Department of the Treasury dispatched an agent, Austin Smith, to investigate the situation. Sadly, Philbrick never agreed to sell them land, although he did raise their wages.

The inspiration for Harry Phelps was William Channing Gannett, nephew of the redoubtable abolitionist Boston minister William Ellery Channing. He went south as a teacher, but after Philbrick befriended him, he became a superintendent and eventually a landowner. He had a guilty conscience about the way he profited from

Philbrick's assistance—and the red-hot cotton market—in 1863. He capped his 1864 earnings to several thousand dollars and went back to Boston before the war ended.

The rest of the story is fiction.

Further Reading

Willie Lee Rose, *Rehearsal for Reconstruction: The Port Royal Experiment* (University of Georgia Press, 1999). The best book on the Sea Islands during the Civil War, with a comprehensive discussion of the abolitionist vision for freedom through education and labor, and how the "Port Royal Experiment" planted the seeds for both the high hopes—and the soul-crushing failure—of post-war Reconstruction.

Laura M. Towne, *Letters and Diary of Laura M. Towne: Written from the Sea Islands of South Carolina, 1862–1884* (Kessinger Books, 2010). The bulk of the letters cover her Civil War experience. The everyday detail is wonderful, as is her antipathy to Edward Philbrick.

Elizabeth Ware Pearson, *Letters from Port Royal Written at the Time of the Civil War (1862-1868)* (W. B. Clarke Company, 1906). Pearson's brother, Charles Ware, was a friend and an employee of Edward Philbrick. Philbrick's entrepreneurial point of view is well represented in these letters.

Thomas Higginson, *Army Life in a Black Regiment* (Riverside Press, 1900). Higginson's portrayal of the campaigns and the camp life of the First South Carolina is a vivid portrait, filtered through a white abolitionist's position of privilege with the best of moral intentions.

For insight into the life of the black people of the Low Country, free and enslaved, see the website Lowcountry Africana (https://low-countryafricana.com/). It includes a wealth of information about slaves and their owners, free black workers and their employers, and soldiers in South Carolina's black regiments.

If You Enjoyed This Book…

Discover the Novels

I've written a number of books that share a theme: stories of white and black, slave and free, often connected by kinship, in the decades on either side of the Civil War. Visit my website for more information about my other books at https://www.sabrawaldfogel.com/books/.

The Low Country Series

The first book in the series: *Charleston's Daughter*. A Charleston belle with slavery on her conscience. A slave with rebellion in her heart. In South Carolina in 1858, no friendship could be more dangerous. As South Carolina hurtles toward secession, will their bond destroy their lives—or set them both free? Find out at mybook.to/CharlestonsDaughter.

The second book in the series: *Union's Daughter*. A renegade planter's daughter who abhors her past. A fugitive slave who fights for freedom. Will their battle for emancipation leave them casualties of war? Find out at https://www.sabrawaldfogel.com/books/unions-daughter.

The Georgia Series

The first book in the series: *Sister of Mine*. Slavery made them kin. Can the Civil War make them sisters? Find out at http://mybook.to/SisterofMine.

The second book in the series: *Let Me Fly*. The Civil War is over, but it isn't. For two women, one black, one white, a new fight is just beginning. Find out at mybook.to/LetMeFly.

Join the Inner Circle of Readers

Want to stay in touch? Get the first look at new books: covers, back stories, and prepublication sneak peeks. And as a thank-you, I'll send you a copy of my story, *Yemaya*. When a slaving ship meets an avenging African mermaid…what happens? Find out at https://www.sabrawaldfogel.com/sign-up/!

Leave a Review

Please let other readers know about this book by leaving a brief review at Amazon, Amazon UK, or Goodreads. Just a few lines will help other readers find the book and make an informed decision about it. It's the electronic version of telling your friends or your book club (although that's great too). Thank you so much!

Author Biography

 Sabra Waldfogel grew up far from the South in Minneapolis, Minnesota. She studied history at Harvard University and got a PhD in American history from the University of Minnesota. Since then, she has been fascinated by the drama of slavery and freedom in the decades before and after the Civil War.

Her first novel, *Sister of Mine*, published by Lake Union, was named the winner of the 2017 Audio Publishers Association Audie Award for fiction. The sequel, *Let Me Fly*, was published in 2018.